EVELESS EDEN

By the same author

BABE
WENT SOUTH
SEPARATE CHECKS
HERSELF IN LOVE
JOHN DOLLAR
BET THEY'LL MISS US WHEN WE'RE GONE

MARIANNE WIGGINS

EVELESS EDEN

HarperCollins*Publishers*

Grateful acknowledgement is made for permission to reprint lines from "Paradise," part three of "The Garden of Earthly Delights" from *The Collected Poems 1931–1987.* © by Czeslaw Milosz Royalties, Inc. First published by The Ecco Press in 1988.

This book was originally published in Great Britain in 1995 by Flamingo, an imprint of HarperCollins Publishers.

FIRST U.S. EDITION

ISBN 0-06-016951-6

95 96 97 98 99 GB/HC 10 9 8 7 6 5 4 3 2 1

for Joseph Brodsky;

and for Deborah Amos
and Karen DeYoung.

I am these two, twofold. I ate from the Tree
Of Knowledge. I was expelled by the archangel's sword.
At night I sensed her pulse. Her mortality.
And we have searched for the real place ever since.

—CZESLAW MILOSZ
from the poem "Paradise"

ACKNOWLEDGEMENTS

I owe a debt of gratitude to the journalists in whose company I have been allowed to be both vigilant and delighted: Deborah Amos, Henry Champ, Rick Davis,
Karen DeYoung, Alma Guillermoprieto, Michael Herr,
John Hockenberry, John Kifner, Jane Kramer, Howell Raines,
Alan Riding, Martin Walker.

Everything I know about Cameroon I learned from *National Geographic Magazine* and the *Central Africa Travel Survival Kit* published by Lonely Planet.

For reviving my courage to write I am forever grateful to Leon Wieseltier and Lloyd Cutler.

Ellen Levine gave me generous and unstinting support through the early pages of this novel.

...and I would never have gone to Romania if it weren't for my beloved daughter, Lara.

1991

NEW YORK, NEW YORK

the butterfly

IT STARTED—for the sake of starting somewhere—with the butterfly on Fifth. It was a butterfly, a white one. You may wonder how I know the difference between butterflies and moths but you'll have to take it on good faith that I was once a Boy Scout in Virginia where the two proliferate, and I've been to Africa enough to have a walking knowledge of the perils found in fauna when one cannot identify the motherfucking bugs. So it was a butterfly and not a moth—a white butterfly, spanning almost three full inches—that came careering out of Central Park into my face on Fifth in front of Frick's house. It was high noon of one of those rare days New York serves up every summer as appeasement for the shit it regularly dishes out—a grassy July day, the kind of day on which the sight of fritillaries frolicking among the spurges would not be so exceptional but who the hell expects a bat-sized butterfly to whip across Fifth Avenue and hit him in the face?

Not me. My first reaction was disgust originating in the fear that butterflies, like Tinker Bell, transmit a fairy dust which is decidedly non-macho. So I bobbed and swatted at her (all butterflies are female, in my view) and she flew off to fulfill her destiny, living out the rest of her brief life in some faubourg of New York, leaving me fucked up for the seven millionth time with thoughts about the loss of love. As the sign once warned us: CAUTION. ONE TRAIN MAY HIDE ANOTHER. She and I were stranded at some godforsaken border station in Cameroon, I think, on I can't remember which of all the many stories. We were stranded there because the airline folded or the Jeep broke down or there was yet another hijacking stroke coup stroke revolution—waiting for a train—and there beside the track was this hand-lettered sign which read CAUTION. ONE TRAIN MAY HIDE ANOTHER, and I made her take a picture of it while I stood behind it because right then I thought that sign in all its wisdom was just the deuce of all discovered truths, another of God's random tablets falling on some shit-laden seldom-travelled place on earth, reinforcing my belief that God, that joker, makes a healthy sideline in revealing truths, those fey mirages, in places like the Sinai or the Great Salt Lake where thirst for everlasting meaning is the secondary, therefore lesser, thirst. *One train may hide another*, one thirst might hide, one word might hide, one dream, one man, one Love, one thought might hide, and almost always does, another.

So there I was on my way to meet a stranger in New York when slam a butterfly bangs into me, and I'm overcome by longlost love and all the freight of shit that it hauls with it. Women. I blame my mother for prohibiting me at an early age from learning to generalize about her sex but oh man if I could. There are times I'd like to launch a riot of foul destinies against that sex, pay the whole lot back for damage done to me by one of them, but I'm getting by, despite the fact, thank you. I'm getting by. The hands are shot the wrists are made of glass, the fingers are discrepant but the liver's holding up and I've managed to retain my hair. But things are not, well, what they used to be. The architect of heartache in my case is the daughter of a Butterfly—a Sorrow by the name of Lil (better known as Lilith.) Lilith's not to blame, though, for things other than my ego and my heart that fell apart around the time she left me. For the destruction of my hands she is entirely blameless. For the destruction of my hands and of my manual dexterity, for the onset of the hellshrike that sets the nervous system back a decade every time I try to lift a knife and fork, or button up my fly, or continue in the irritating lifetime habit which is the wont of every journalist of sitting down and actually FUCKING TYPING I can safely say, folks, that it isn't Lilith's fault and lay the sorry case to rest at the doorstep of the nation's leading paper in whose noble sweatshop I have plied my meagre wage all these many years until a thing called carpal tunnel syndrome woke up in its coffin to stalk the fastest and most frequent typists in the field. First I lost my girl and then I lost the way to do my job. But before that happened there was one fine golden year, a year unlike any other in the history of eyewitness correspondents. That year was 1989. In 1989 Communism fell in Europe. In 1989 the Berlin Wall was breached by freedom. In 1989 Prague liberated itself. In 1989 the Ceauşescus were brought down. People will talk about 1989 for centuries to come, its cipher will hang from history's balance side by side with other heavyweights—not a date; a *year*—like 1492 or 1848, suggesting not just one event but many, a small series of events with grand effect pursuing one another across a stage designed by time. Within a span of months that year I went from Teheran to Islamabad to Srinigar to Beijing to Shanghai to Leipzig along the Trabant Trail from Austria through Czechoslovakia into Hungary and Bavaria, to West

Berlin, back to Leipzig, to Prague, back to Berlin those first and second weeks in November, back to Prague, to Timişoara in December, then to Bucharest. Entire social systems were disintegrating—for a print journalist it was the equivalent of having been an actor on the Globe's stage while Shakespeare was alive or having taken down, as witness, a chapter at the time of Christ. But the Gulf War came and changed the way people in my line of work fulfill their jobs. Maybe it was not the Gulf War alone, exactly, that brought an end to the way news was gathered and reported. Maybe the end had been cumulative. Maybe (as those die-hards down at City Hall complain) the end to dignity in print journalism started when department stores began to advertise in dailies. Pleasing Mr. Macy's may have marked the end to certain kinds of writing, I won't argue. Or maybe news began to die off bit by bit way back on Grenada under Reagan, who knows. For me its final collapse occurred during the brief incursion earlier this year known as Desert Storm—but maybe that's my own Judeo-Christian gene chain producing endorphins which favour showy climaxes in a desert setting. A lot of people left the business after Desert Storm, a little march of print merchants, a little exodus of journalists into the promised land of television—but I'm getting ahead of myself. Back in 1989 TV magazines had not significantly displaced persons from my field—it is only in the last year or so that it seems that people in the United States have come to believe that, like the pursuit of happiness, an appearance on a television talk show or a TV magazine is an individual's right, a condition guaranteed by the Declaration and the Bill. Eventually—one day—you, too, will have your chance to have your say or (better yet) to be a witness at the scene of something mediocre yet real and, therefore, essential to all television. But back in 1989 the incidental Zapruder-type of citizen would never have considered him-or-herself an actual *reporter*. But all that has changed. Not only do Joe and Josie Citizen believe they stand a chance of one day seeing themselves on national TV, they've come to trust in what they see there more than they trust in what they read. And the reason for this relatively new phenomenon seems to reside in the national belief that the camera never lies, but language does. I'm thinking of the Gulf War and those horrifying on-the-spots of the vid kid fighter pilot killing *real* and killing *live* not just to keep his fingers busy and improve his score, but to fulfill his right to make good television while at the same time fighting for his nation. The end of news is in its repetition. And "hard-bitten" is an adjective most commonly associated with criminals and newspaper reporters, both of whom disguise their lovability with cynicism. One guise might hide another, one rôle may —be careful where you step. The accidental tourist might become an accident statistic these days anywhere on any street in any city in the world, an accidental Frau Karenina beneath a rushing train (a Russian train?): here's what I was thinking on that sunny day the butterfly began it all while I was making my way north on Fifth: I was thinking about Faust, I was thinking about selling out. Doesn't everybody think about it, I mean, don't you? Even Mom Teresa must indulge a secret thought or two from time to time about the streets of heaven being paved with gold, so why not me? Why not? Heart's been broken, hands are shot, plate tectonics of my craft are shifty as all shit so why the hell not come on down, as Monty Hall and Beelzebub would say, and make a deal. One curtain might disguise another, not that everyone's a Natural (in the Malamud-sense of the word) for television. Despite the fact that home videos prove that anyone can do TV, everybody has a geezer aspect, that side of the innate performance artist which proves to be dysfunctional, that moron sitting on a high stool in the corner of us all, inarticulate and spittle-laden, incapable of any action more complex than squeezing the air nuggets in the bubble paper—but I *had* been asked (not once; six times) to meet with this producer and, besides, I couldn't do my old job anymore because my hands are shot and, furthermore, I couldn't do my old job anyway because there are only about a thousand people left on this planet who do the kind of work I used to do, a thousand people, the numerical equivalent of a village, a thousand bite-the-bullet yahoos like myself, grunts whose by-lines are our bivouacs in a minefield full of photo opps and sound bites, and (fuck it) who wants to be the holdout of a dying breed when the kind of money this TV network is offering promises a rich tomorrow?

So I was tooting along on a train of thought that was trying to link big bucks to principles—and Faust, a fellow passenger was in a Pullman car ahead of me—when wham the butterfly and I smacked into one another. At that moment my thought process proceeded kind of thus:

—Faust is an archetype of evil.

—*Doctor Faustus* is the name of the play on the subject by Chrisopher Marlowe.

—*Doctor Faustus* is the name of the novel on the subject by Thomas Mann.

—*Faust* is the name of the drama on the subject by Goethe.

—*Faust* is the name of the opera on the subject by Gounod.

[incoming butterfly . . .]
[butterfly strikes!]
[butterfly flies away . . .]

—A butterfly plays an important role in Thomas Mann's novel *Doctor Faustus*.

—Like *Faust*, *Madama Butterfly* is an opera.

—Lilith's father produced *Madama Butterfly* in Paris.

—Lilith's mother sang the role of Butterfly in *Madama Butterfly*.

—Lilith played Butterfly's child Sorrow in *Madama Butterfly*.

—The world is full of Sorrows.

—Lilith broke my heart.

—ONE TRAIN MAY HIDE ANOTHER.

—The man she left me for is called Adam.

—Adam is man's archetype.

—The man she left me for is an archetype of evil, like Faust.

So there it is—how the butterfly began it all. After that, what happened next was only the inevitable.

The TV producer lived in one of those luxe buildings on Fifth Avenue which overlook the park where each apartment occupies a whole floor. On the street outside the building there was a doorman in a dark green military-looking uniform from some Ruritanian fantasy who asked me what my business in the building was before he let me cross the threshold. Inside there was a desk like a hotel desk behind which sat two more gents in dark green uniforms. I gave them my name and I told them I was there to see Mr. TV-so-and-so and one of them picked up a phone and said A Mr. John is here. Then he put the phone down and told me to go up, "Elevator's at the rear. Just press P for Penthouse." The kind of alphabet which designates P for Penthouse must begin with A for Arbitrage, but when I reached the elevator the needle of the dial above the door was stuck on B for Butterfly. I pressed the button labeled UP (definitely my direction). There ensued a disconcerting wait during which the phone rang at the desk and a dog, outside, was heard to bark. Then I heard a gear engage, the needle jumped from B to L (from Butterfly to Lepidoptera) the door slid open and there stood the largest butterfly anyone has ever seen, I mean this thing was huge, man-sized, wearing pants and a nifty pair of elegant Italian shoes.

Okay—it wasn't a butterfly.

It was a man holding an open newspaper in front of him, his arms raised high like he was wrapped up reading something really tiny at the bottom of the page or like he was bent on taking up every cubic inch of space there was inside the elevator.

Skiuze-me, I said and wedged myself inside as the door was closing which meant that he and I were standing so up close my nose was breathing in his newsprint like air.

I reached around behind me and punched the P for Penthouse. I could see the button for the twelfth floor was already lit, two buttons below the P. I tried to move but the man behind the paper wasn't giving me an inch.

Then something on the front page caught my eye and I must have let out an involuntary *oooh* or *ah* because there in the lower left-hand column beneath the fold was my by-line on a piece I'd filed two weeks before, what we call "a reader", a unit of relatively vital but largely boring information not likely to change in the near future. This one was on cab drivers in London.

Right; stop the presses.

Someone in the elevator gave a moan just then and marveled, "—I *wrote* that?" and I'm pretty sure the person in the elevator who said that was me because the next thing that happened was the guy behind the newspaper began to lower it column inch by column inch until first his cap and then his forehead and then his eyebrows then his eyes came into view over the top of the news until our faces were no more than six inches from each other with the newspaper between us like a flimsy backyard fence over which we caught each other spying.

Oh holy shit, I said. "It's *you*."

There are times—I've been through them too often—when even the most highly-trained observer either can't believe his fucking luck or can't believe his goddamned eyes, and it may have started with the butterfly and ended shortly after with the death announcement but for the moment I was caught entirely off my guard and utterly dumbstruck and speechless to discover I was standing face to face in an elevator in New York with the most sought after and notorious author of the later part of this war-sodden century. I would have recognized him anywhere—anyone who watches television would—but he and I had actually met, so I side-stepped away from him a little (now that he had put the paper down there was room) and said, "Noah John. We've met," and extended my right hand for (what would have been for me a painful) handshake which he left begging. "We were on the news," I said. "In London. You and I. A couple of times. Together." I should have had a question ready—or a word—or a quip—or some expression readily at hand (less demanding types can always fall back on WHAT DOES IT FEEL LIKE TO BE YOU?) and I felt a sort of meter's-running panic as I saw the light go out behind the button on the elevator panel that read "12" and I felt the elevator slowing and my chance—the chance every journalist dreams will come his way during all those stupefying speeches about potato production in the newly-formed ex-Soviet republics—was slipping by me. I should have had a question ready if for no other reason than I had played the game so many times on flights from Beijing to Warsaw, from Tel Aviv to Athens:

Let's say you run into [choose one:]
—Arafat
—Amelia Earhart
—Hoffa

In the [choose one:]
—men's room
—desert
—elevator

—What's the ONE BIG QUESTION *you will ask?*

But just as I was going to say, "Listen—if you don't mind —there's one big question that I'd like to ask you . . ." my beeper went off—not a very loud noise, but an alarming one in the benign sense of the word—and I saw a look of terror grip him, a look of such palpable fright that I felt a sudden need to comfort him or reassure him as I would some kid but as I fumbled for the beeper in my pocket to display it to him the elevator bounced a little, stopped, and then the door slid back and he stepped off into a muted rush of warm applause and the hum of a good party.

Then I made the brief and solitary ride on up to P for Penthouse, where I was greeted by a friendly woman in her twenties who said Mr. John? He'll be with you shortly? Can I offer you a cappuccino? Mineral water?

"I need a phone," I said and pointed to my beeper in a way designed to leave no doubt that I was a heart surgeon being summoned for a life-saving procedure.

The part of the apartment that the elevator opened onto had been furnished to serve as a reception area-cum-office technologically equipped, or so it looked, for a moon flight on a moment's notice. If the place were ever robbed the thieves could rake in a fortune worth of sound and video equipment without leaving the elevator. A wall of shelves divided this area from the "living" area, apparently, and in front of the shelves there was a desk the size of two double beds on which there were three different kinds of phones, a laptop computer and a TV set. The TV set was on—tuned in to the Court Channel with the sound down low. On the street-side wall there were windows, waist to ceiling, with a view of Central Park and The Dakota on the far side.

"Nice," I said.

"Isn't it?" She handed me a cordless phone. "Sometimes I stand here?" she said, while I called my office, "and I can see Woody and Mia with their kids walking in the park? Don't you think they're just the cutest family?"

Before I had a chance to answer, she turned a quarter turn away from me to give me privacy while I made my call.

"Hi," I said into the phone. "You beeped."

"Boot wants to speak to you—I'll have to page him . . ."

While Boot was being paged I turned to the woman and said, "What's in the basement?"

"What basement?"

"Where you go when you press B inside the elevator—is

there any way someone can get down there without going through the lobby of the building?"

"Oh, that's not really B? That should be G? For cars?"

"'Garage'?"

"Yes?"

"How do you get into it?"

"From over there?" She pointed to the north-side street beyond the wall of shelves behind her.

"You wouldn't happen to know who lives on the twelfth floor, would you?"

She smiled at me and said she'd only worked here for a month and didn't I agree that people in New York never notice who their neighbors are unless their neighbors are celebrities?

Boot came on the line and I turned again to look out on the park.

"Noah—?"

"Boot."

"Where are you?"

I remember—such clichés!—watching children running in the park, a woman with a pram; two lovers.

"Are you near a wire?"

"Maybe."

"Get to one."

"Cut to the chase, Boot—"

"Adam's dead."

The children running in the park did not slow down, but the rhythm of their movement, of the movement of the traffic in the street, became accentuated by a kind of visual acuity, a sudden crispness to both my sense of sight and sound.

"—when?" I said.

"This morning."

"—how?"

"Scotland Yard ain't sayin'—"

"Book me on the red-eye—"

"This ain't your baby, baby, this belongs to London—"

'Don't start to tell me what's the London desk's, what's *not* the London desk's, I *am* the London desk—"

"Not anymore, if I may be so bold as to remind you, my good friend, I only thought you ought to know because of—"

"Make the goddamn reservation, Boot. I'm going."

I gave the woman back her phone and headed for the elevator. I pressed the button and the door slid open right away. Backing in, I asked the woman to apologize for me. "Tell your boss I had to go," I said. "I'm sorry—"

"What is it?" she said, coming toward me. "Is something wrong? What's happened?" She looked back toward her desk at the TV. "Is it something we should know about? Is it something big?"

"Yes," I told her.

The door closed.

Adam was dead.

The Third Man

"I had paid my last farewell to Harry a week ago, when his coffin was lowered into the frozen February ground, so that it was with incredulity that I saw him pass by, without a sign of recognition, among the host of strangers in the Strand."

—that's not me, that's Graham Greene, scribbling down on the back of an envelope what would become the idea for the story and screenplay called *The Third Man*, a movie much on my mind from the moment Boot had told me, "Adam's dead."

Does that ever happen to you? Everyone hears songs, sure, or phrases of songs, involuntarily—everyone hears advertising jingles, that's the point of advertising jingles. I see scenes from films—only scenes from certain films—but I see them regularly, doubly exposed over my life. When this happens there is usually no dialogue—or if there is, there's a line or two, only, like, "We'll always have Paris"—and I've come to realize that the scenes that I call up for mental replay are really scenes where no one's speaking: that image of Omar Sharif on horseback emerging from a band of watery light above the desert in *Lawrence of Arabia*, for example, or that crane shot of Coop in *High Noon*—you get the picture. And for these kinds of images, *The Third Man* is an undisputed beaut. The first time I saw it I had never been to Europe and I think I made my mind up there and then I had to go. I was always finding evidence of shot and shards of the Confederacy on the land around our place and I had walked the grassy rounded earthworks between Richmond and Petersburg, Virginia, where I grew up so I understood where history was, where it was buried, how it surfaced now and then as a reminder, but seeing those images in *The Third Man* of Vienna half in rubble from the war, its gingerbread in crumbs, only to discover through that image of the kiosk in the square that underneath the city there was another man-made world intact, made me an on-the-spot convert to the hackneyed view that there had been a lot of living done by man, a lot of history had passed underfoot (no kidding), on that distant continent and I was going to get there, somehow, to see it for myself. For a while, when I was young, I had thought the Underground Railroad, part of which had reportedly run through our yard, had been a track below ground, and I was pissed off to learn otherwise. Then, too, I was more than a little disappointed, on a visit with my dad, to discover Americans had not actually built and inhabited Luray Cavern, while in almost every European city there were catacombs and sewer systems dating back to the Romans and in Spain and France there were even caves with paintings in them signed with the handprints of pre-historic artists. Europe is a bloody place, as violent in its ongoing landgrab-at-any-cost on its own turf as those enterprising Europeans were, grabbing the Americas. But it continues to seduce me—which is the damndest thing to have to try to explain to myself and others who ask why I went there in the first place and why I've been away from "home" so long and if I miss the South (only Southerners ask that) and if I ever think of coming back. I always think of coming back. When Lilith and I were talking about living out our lives together, living out our final years in one place, that place was always in Virginia, in my mind. Maybe it was always in the south of France in her mind, but when we talked about a house with a darkroom that was hers—a house where I might put a book together, keep a dog, do a little farming and learn to play the harpsichord—I was always playing Thomas Jefferson at Monticello, I guess, to her George Sand wherever the hell it was George Sand had her house in France. Lilith in Virginia made about as much sense as Maria Callas keeping house on some volcanic outpost in the wine-dark sea—but I thought about it anyway. People think about such things when they're in love. We were always either at her place in Paris or at my place in London or together on the road or meeting up some place between assignments where neither of us lived—but we never had a home that either of us called "ours", except that home we talked about, that Eden we'd inhabit, someday, and for me that Eden was back home in Virginia. That's why *The Third Man* had come into my mind the moment Boot had told me, "Adam's dead." I started seeing the last scene of it while Boot and I were still talking, while I was watching children playing in the park and traffic crawling southbound on Fifth Avenue —I started seeing that long walk the character called Anna makes down that broad deserted avenue between the trees toward Joseph Cotten leaning on that graveyard wagon. The first time I saw that movie I had just begun to notice girls and the ending shocked me. Every movie I had seen until that one had had a happy ending. The week before I saw *The Third Man* I had seen an Elvis Presley movie where he gets Ann-Margret and that seemed to set the standard I expected when it came to boy meets girl in films. I hadn't yet seen *Casablanca* (a good thing, too, or else I might have wound up in the Foreign Legion instead of winding up a foreign correspondent), but between *Casablanca* and *The Third Man* I fell in love with foreign places and women in fedoras and I got used to seeing women in fedoras walk away from men who love them. If you've never seen *The Third Man* then I need to tell you that the scene that came to mind when Boot told me, "Adam's dead," is a long one, for a scene where virtually nothing happens. It's a waiting scene. The character named Anna walks and walks and walks toward Joseph Cotten from the distance until she walks right past him without looking at him, then she walks past *us*, right off the screen —and it's a waiting scene that's even longer than the scene in *Lawrence of Arabia* when we're waiting to find out what the hell is riding toward us out of that mirage: But what makes the waiting scene in *The Third Man* doubly evocative is the zither music. I've had people say to me the zither music *makes* that scene which is easy to disprove some night when you are home between assignments or in a hotel room in Athens when the movie comes on late: Turn off the sound. (Of course in Athens the effect is spoiled somewhat by Greek sub-titles, but you get the point.) It is a great classic movie written by a great man and you need to know two more things to understand why it, in particular, came to mind when I heard Adam was dead. The first thing you need to know is that the character played by Joseph Cotten in the film (a character called Holly Martins) has fallen in love with his dead friend's girlfriend except the dead friend (Harry Lime, played to-a-fucking-T by Orson Welles) isn't really dead until Holly shoots him in the sewer. Once Harry is really dead, Holly hopes to stand a chance with Anna (the old girlfriend in the fedora), just as I (subconsciously, or not) hoped that once Adam was dead Lilith would come back to me. That's the first thing—although we need to stop here to consider the actual probability of any woman ever falling for a guy who looks like Joseph Cotten after having been in love with and having been loved *by* Orson Welles: Help me out here, if you can. I mean, the only problem with *The Third Man* is *sexy*

the way that Joseph Cotten looks—and I should know, because I grew up in the Virginia town where he was legendary, where signed studio photographs of Joseph Cotten were on sale at the local five & dime, where I delivered papers, my first job, to Joseph Cotten's family manse overlooking the Appomattox River. The reason that I bring this up is that I was told I looked like the young Joseph Cotten when I was growing up—a statement which was meant to be a compliment coming as it did from Joe's hometown, but which, outside Virginia, was a sort of worthless sexual currency. Now that I'm nearing forty-five I find to my surprise that women find me sexier than they ever did before (when I really needed it) and only women over fifty tell me that I look like Joseph Cotten. Younger women tell me I remind them of Gene Hackman. In other words—I'm not conventionally sexy. In other words—I'm sexy 'cause I'm *getting older*.

Adam, on the other hand, was a ladykiller. I don't mean to lead you into thinking he was handsome—he was not. He was tall—taller than I am (I'm six feet tall)—with a large head, a high forehead and a bob of white hair in a page boy the way that Liszt and Wagner wore theirs in their dotage. His hair was prematurely white. His features were, in my opinion, gross—along the lines of Aristotle Onassis's (another ugly guy whose sex appeal was legendary.) Like Qaddafi (and like Wagner, too), Adam liked to *dress*. He was not a fop, he didn't play the popinjay like Tom Wolfe or Oscar Wilde—he used clothes theatrically, as props, to heighten a particular effect. In London, for example, his style guru was Armani, but in Bucharest he wore peasant garb, richly hand embroidered. I watched him more carefully, of course, than other journalists did. I made the error of investigating him in an attempt to find his flaws so I could expose him to his lover. I mean—for christsake—does that tactic *ever* work? It didn't work for Joseph Cotten in *The Third Man* and it sure as hell did not work out for me in real life. Why do we do it? Why do we do it when we know damn well all the really brainy, hot and headstrong women are going to attract their own disasters anyway? Do we think we're saving them from something? If so—from what? From the men they love instead of us? Jesus, did I really think that when I massed a dossier of evidence against Adam the scales were going to fall from Lilith's eyes, that she was going to fall down on her knees and kiss the hem of my so-holy cassock, renounce him and pledge to stay with me forever out of gratitude? Hell no. Take my advice, if you ever find yourself in this position—get out and get out good. Go quietly, go fast and go for good before you shoot your foot. That's what I did the first time. Hated myself afterwards for behaving in a way I came to think was cowardly, but I was too shell-shocked and humiliated at the time to put up a fight for someone who clearly didn't want me as the center of her sexual life anymore. To be honest, the reason I got out of Dodge so fast after I discovered them together was I was afraid of what I felt like doing to her. That was in January 1989—we'd been together since the night before the cry-die back in Cameroon in '86, not even two and a half years. That's not long, not long at all. Couples have un-coupled after much longer times—lifetimes together, decades. What's a measly two and half a years? Nothing. A proverbial drop in the ocean. I thought maybe her affair with Adam might turn out to be a passing thing, I really did. The odds were overwhelmingly against it lasting—she was on the road, even more than I was—and his government would never let him bring her to Romania to live, despite his personal importance to Ceauşescu, or because of it. So I walked away—and went to Pakistan. Then I went to Srinigar—then China. I thought for certain I'd meet up with her in China—but she never came. It was the first frontline human rights story Lilith had failed to cover in two decades, she had dropped out of sight and off the map. On my way to Leipzig from Shanghai I went to look for her in Paris, but the shutters on her windows were bolted and she'd changed the lock. Madame Rossini, the concierge, had been confined by gout and her replacement, Monsieur Habib, had never heard of me, had never seen me, didn't trust me (even when I showed him my old key wrapped inside five hundred francs) had no information and kept referring to Lilith (wrongly) as *la juive*. She didn't come to Leipzig, either, nor to the border when it opened and all my messages to her remained unanswered. There was about a week in there, somewhere, where I just lost it. Okay—hell—not a week; a month. Don't tell me that you haven't had one of them, a night, a week, a month like that. When she left, she left me nothing. There was nothing left of her, no trace, no clue, except—much to my surprise—her American passport, tucked inside my spare shaving kit along with notarized copies of both our travel documents and drivers' licenses. The fact that she had left it was a stupid oversight, and even I'd forgotten we'd put it there for safekeeping. Her American passport was not the one she usually used, and she rarely even took it with her as a spare except in places where it was still marginally the best doc in the world for getting out of jams. It was relatively new—it still had seven years on it—she had just renewed it before going off to Cameroon and she had used it only once more since then, when we had gone to Delhi together in August '87 to cover India's fortieth anniversary as an independent state. That's how it had ended up in my shaving kit—a lot of countries don't allow unmarried couples to room together in hotels so, following the universal deskclerk logic every journalist acquires, we had taken her American passport with us as a spare to prove we were the same nationality in case our co-habitation was challenged during registration. (It's more tolerable to the desk clerks of this world if two unmarried Americans want to sleep with each other than if an American wants to sleep with a French national in a foreign country. Don't even try to wonder how or why this works—it does.)

Then, I saw her again. After ten months, I saw her in Berlin. If you weren't there when the Wall came down, I need to tell you two things—first, it was freezing fucking cold that week, Berlin gets colder than you think any city could when you're sitting in your livingroom in New York or Chicago watching Germany on TV. The wind that bites Berlin is meaner than a North American wind and there's no nationalistic sentiment in that assessment, merely an opinion formed from miserable experience: stay away from places hit by Baltic wind in winter. The second thing you need to know about that week in Berlin that started on November 9th is that through the day that followed there was a party going on, a saturnalia, part love-in, part happening, part tourist event, part media-generated frenzy, part genuine atmospheric stupefaction arising from each and every Herr Ordinary and Frau Average, East or West. West Berlin was—in its half-life—a hip seductive city suddenly confronted not with its twin or with its cousin or its ghost but with itself, a self shaped differently by time. People-watching was the major news event that week—watching people meeting people, watching people watching people, seeing people baldly childlike in their joy—it was one of those rare times when even *I* could come away with great and moving pictures from my point-and-shoot: it was a field day for professional photographers, and I should have known no power from heaven or on earth—not even Love—could have kept Lilith away.

It tells you something about the power of events that week when I admit that, for once, the thought of running into her was the last thing on my mind. Or maybe it was simply that by the time I ended up in Berlin, I had ceded hope, and supplanted it with quiet rage directed—who knows?—toward myself or toward humanity in general toward the fleeting gift of Love, toward men with larger penises than mine toward women with great tits toward women with tight asses toward the cold, toward women. In short, I found myself despairing in Berlin. Maybe I was having what used to be called a nervous breakdown but which—since Dan Rather's "Kenneth" question was raised in our profession—is now just passed off as another common occurrence in a nation of daily psychotic events. Maybe, too, the reason I was feeling weird was that everyone was there—people I hadn't seen for years, men and women who were usually posted to Asia or South America, Stateside-based people, it was as if the world's news-gathering forces were having a homecoming week—and, of course, people who hadn't seen me for a long time asked me about Lilith as if she and I were still a couple. You'd think in a business so driven by gossip and talk, my friends (my acquaintances) might have heard we'd split up, but the fact that they hadn't illustrates a sad truth of my trade. Newspeople rarely talk about lives of newspeople because newspeople rarely have lives beyond work. Marriages, lasting ones, are few and those made within the last decade tend to be profession-specific: newshounds marry newshounds—and why not? We are the only people we meet —everyone else is The Public.

By Saturday morning, November 11th, The Public (*Die Allgemeinheit*) in Berlin was abuzz with the rumor, that a hole in the Wall was about to be made at the Brandenburg Gate (they were wrong: the big break came at Potsdamer

Platz the next day)—and the concentration of news crews with their trucks and their satellite dishes at the Gate grew intense. The Gate became live TV's permanent backdrop, so by Saturday night I decided to look for stories anywhere, everywhere else but there. It was around seven o'clock, a good time of day, the east coast back home was just digesting its lunch with yesterday's news and before me there was a whole night and a morning to find a new story. So I started to walk. I decided to walk the Wall from the Gate down to Potsdamer Platz, then pick up a cab into town to check out the street celebration. Away from the glare of the lights near the Gate there were still thousands of people milling around in the darkness, re-inventing the Wall, touching it, going at it like sculptors with chisels and hammers and spikes they had on them, god knows, for no other reason than to be artists, making small fires from trash and dried leaves to light their creation. Sparks and the chinks from the chisels were the sights and sounds defining that darkness: the cold played a role, it was the cold of Berlin, Berlin cold, a cold war, that sang in the metal that night. Friction of metal on stone in the cold set off sparks you could see down the length of the wall like phosphorescence in surf or tiny beacons signalling from cities off in the distance. People were singing to the rhythm of cold metal's carillon, slow reverent tunes, many accents, one language: the Beatles'. Occasionally, too, there was an isolated white light, like a ghost roaming the wall, of somebody's flash camera. I came upon a group of six young people squatting on the ground around a fire of dried branches by the Wall, working, by turns, a hammer and a chisel, singing with German accents, ". . . in times of trouble, Mother Mary comes to me, speaking words of wisdom, 'Let it be'," so I stopped. Another person had stopped there, too, coming from the opposite direction and as I watched she dropped to the ground, crept near them, raised her camera and photographed their faces lit by sparks and the white ghost of her flash. For an instant, I thought she was Lilith—I wished it. Be careful what you wish, some people were saying that week in Berlin —meaning, of course, you might get what you wish for, but at a terrible price. A day later, I finally found her. At least once a week, since then, no matter where I've been for nearly two years, I dream about that morning in Berlin, I dream that I'm again transported on that rage, and then I wake with an erection, sometimes ejaculating, sometimes my aching hands gripping myself with the ferocity with which I gripped her—but never, 'til that day in New York City when Boot told me, "Adam's dead," did I have that dream awake, a waking dream, that sudden uncontrollable excitement—on my way to read the wires for myself, in the back seat of a taxi, for christsake.

DEAD IN ENGLAND

I never really liked Boot but he seemed to think I did and I guess the reason that he thought that is that, over the years, I'd been very decent toward him, while everybody else he works with responds to him in a manner which befits the way he acts, which is like an asshole. It's always hard to say, in life, whether the job defines the man or whether people find themselves in nerdy jobs because they're basic nerds from the beginning, but in Boot's case I'd hazard the informed guess that his personality was radically deformed during its tadpole stage which guaranteed he'd grow up to be the perfect desk man. If Boot were ever drafted into field work he'd be swallowed whole by us more rapacious types. But as it is, where he is, he gets to prey on us.

When I came into the office he handed me a print out of the Reuter's wire which ran:

> FORMER CEAUŞESCU AIDE FOUND DEAD IN ENGLAND
>
> (London) Adam Pentrú, former Romanian Minister of Trade under Nicolai Ceauşescu, was found dead yesterday, Scotland Yard reported.
>
> It is not known why Mr. Pentrú was in England at the time of his death.

I looked at Boot. "That's it—?" I said.

"That's it," Boot echoed. "Apparently, Goodchild's been plastering your bulletin board with urgent messages all day—"

"Oh, that'll make me popular at GCHQ . . ."

I reached for a phone to place a call to Goodchild in London and asked Boot, "You book me on a flight tonight?"

Boot seemed distracted.

"I wonder if he was murdered," he said in his nerdily curious way.

"Guess who I saw in an elevator earlier—*hello*? Noah John for Simon Goodchild. Noah. John. *John* . . . which part can't you spell—?"

"Who? Who did you see—?"

"—I don't have a 'Christian' name, sweetheart. I have a *first* name. You want me to spell my *first* name? My first name is Noah, like the captain of the Ark. The Ark. Well, I have a problem with *your* accent, too . . ."

"—not Ivana Trump, I hope. Ivana's seen by everyone—"

"—a message? Me? What gives you that idea? *Of course* I want to leave a message—"

"—shame to waste a Reuter's wire on some dildo Romanian—"

"—*yes*: tell him Noah John called. From New York. I'm coming over on the—what flight, Boot?"

"Red-eye."

"—on the red-eye. I'll phone him from the plane—"

I put the phone down and started to call the wires up on Boot's computer.

"You know . . ." Boot said. "I'd just like to hazard one thing . . ."

". . . has the Beeb reported this?"

". . . no."

He may not be dead.

"—World Service?"

"No."

"Only Reuters?"

". . . listen. The thing is this. Did you ever read those English novels? Try this on for size: He may not be dead." He watched me move the cursor. "A fake death—you know what I mean? Jesus, you type like a fucking fish—"

". . . can't type—"

"—like what's his name, Orson Welles."

"Not Orson Welles—"

"Yes, Orson Welles—"

"*Harry Lime*—yeah, I read those English novels."

"—here, let me do that—you're slower than the second coming—how do you ever work?"

"I'll need to take an EVE with me."

"Like hell—Kifner called me up today. They've got an IBM system they're trying to put into place over at his shop. Their wine correspondent came down with it—what the hell is that guy's name? So he comes into *The Times* with like a truckload of these 'wine sleeves', Kifner tells me—yeah. These 'wine sleeves', you know, you put around chilled wine bottles to keep them cool on picnics, they're like padded gloves only filled with foam or something, *The Times* people are wearing them on their wrists up to their armpits to try to help them to come back on the system, Kifner says, so maybe you should try them, maybe they would help . . ."

"—'wine sleeves'."

"Wine sleeves. For carpal tunnel. Kifner says it works."

"Do you ever listen to the shit you say, Boot, or do you just say it?"

"—nothing here . . . crime this guy has to be some fuckhead from Romania of all the places, why couldn't it have been—"

"Oh so like I started to tell you—guess who I get into an elevator with today?"

"Arafat?"

"I'm waiting to go see this TV producer and—"

"Oh yeah—how was that? I hear they're interviewing everybody. Don't tell me—Hoffa."

"—and the door comes open and—"

'What'd you ask him?"

"—there's this . . . *person* . . . standing there, you'll never guess . . ."

"I would have asked him why he wears that tea towel on his head."

"You would have asked him—"

"—why he wears that tea towel on his head."

"—Hoffa?"

"Arafat. I probably would have asked him about the chauffeur, you know, the Israeli one. You know—like what did he do, advertise? 'Driver wanted. Must have license and a Mossad card' . . ."

"I'm not going to share my story with you, Boot. My story is too good for you."

"So are you going to take the TV job, or what?"

"No."

"Oh, so they didn't make an offer."

"Can I have a travel EVE, or not?"

"Probably . . . *not.*"

"Why not?"

"Because a) There is no story. Look for yourself—no one's picking this one up, there's nothing to pick up, the Brits have jammed it in a coffin, even AP isn't breaking out with updates —b) I wouldn't want you on this story, even if there was one, c) You can't write from the field no more, and d) There are only four travel EVEs. And you ain't getting one."

"London isn't 'from the field', Boot."

"That's right, it's not. We've got a nice big office there in London, filled with nice bright people who could do this story, if it is a story. I don't mind you going back there—I can't stop you, hell, it's where you live. But once you're back, you'd have to work for Ivy. And if memory serves me, I think I can recall why Ivy doesn't like you. Don't try to convince me that you're going back there for the paper—you're going back for *you*. Like some kind of renegade. I can't commit a piece of expensive company equipment to a person I suspect of acting like a renegade, now can I, Noah?"

"—fuck you, too, Boot."

"—especially since I just had to commandeer the last available EVE from D.C. to have it sent to Kennedy so it will be sitting in Air Cargo for Moran to pick up when he flies in from Chicago late tonight on his way to wherever the hell it is Moran is going . . . Moscow."

"Is she already programmed for Moran's voice?"

"Yeah—but she'll accept a copy of your hard disc from the mother unit. I already checked."

"You're a prince among us, Boot."

"Yeah, well, Moran will have your ass, that's not my problem . . . so who was it? In the elevator."

"Amelia Earhart."

"No, come on."

"Lord Lucan."

"Who the hell's Lord Lucan?"

"English guy. Tried to kill his wife but killed the nanny by mistake, then disappeared and faked his death."

"That must be some kind of really *European* thing to do . . ."

"—a European thing?"

"—Harry Lime, Lord Lucan . . . Ceauşescu . . . Christ."

"What are you talking about—?"

"—faking your own death. Boy, I hope they faked this—it would make a better story. Like a John le Carré. Man, I really dig those English writers. They have such a way with words. And Noah?"

"What?"

"I hope this means . . ."

He seemed to try to find a way to say her name.

I tried to find a way to say I understood.

So expressive, two such assholes. Such a way with words.

10:15 PM
WEDNESDAY 17 JULY 1991
BRITISH AIRWAYS FLIGHT 176

FROM JFK
TO LONDON HEATHROW

NOW IS THE TIME FOR ALL GOOD MEN TO COME TO THE AID OF THEIR PARTY, remember that? Remember THE QUICK BROWN FOX JUMPED OVER THE what-the-fuck? Nonsense stuff we had to learn to learn to type. EVERY DOGDAY HAS ITS EVE and this is mine.

My EVE, that is. The gal who's just my type.

I talk; she stores.

I talk while she converts.

I command, she prints.

I say, "Someday my prints will come," and lo she gets it right (she gets it write), she's faster than the speed of light and smarter than a steno. She works something like the thing that Stephen Hawking uses to express his voice, but in reverse, and she's manufactured by the Japanese, who seem to own the corner on amazingly small gizmos. Her name—EVE—stands for Electronic Voice Epigone. Or maybe it stands for Every Vegetarian Eats, who knows, everyone should choose his or her own nominal anagram. EVERY MAN SHOULD HAVE AN ANAGRAM and mine should be Not On Any Hitlist. Adam's? All Devils Are Mutants. All Draculas Are Murderers.

From the beginning, from Cain and Abel, the second and the third man, respectively, the story of man's kind has been murder and mutation—murder and betrayal.

Betrayal first, then murder.

The first son born of man was a murderer. No woman was involved in that act of betrayal, that first murder. The only woman in that story was the only woman, period—Eve—which reminds me of that old classic problem for the scrupulously well-mannered:

> Q: What is the proper form of condolence to a woman whose one son has killed her other son?
>
> A: "I'm sorry you didn't have daughters."

Why am I thinking so much about murder?

Because if Adam had been blotted from existence by a quick clot to the brain, the announcement of his death would have included that small detail.

You need to learn to listen for what *isn't* said.

I called Goodchild from the airport and he thinks either Adam's been deported to some hellhole of a place (like back to Romania), or he's been murdered. Goodchild doesn't think the Brits are smart enough to fake his death, but that's because he's an innocent, a true believer in the Labour Party, a grown man with a soft spot for border collies and aging members of the monarchy, so his sympathy for loopy dogs and pale-eyed Windsors blocks his comprehension of the natural coloration of long-standing governments to cloak their evils. Good men are almost never turned by power to do evil, but when they are the result is of one of the more tragic wrinkles in our human fabric. Goodchild wouldn't recognize the guise of evil if it slithered down his tree of knowledge and offered him its cut-rate low-cal pommy diet to his face. Some people can spot rotten apples, while other people think all men are taffy on a stick, go figure. Some people believe in the innate wellness of the human spirit while others think we all climbed, Harry Lime Lites, from thick slime that clings to us our lifetimes and with which our souls are clotted. Goodchild is of the wellness camp, a prelapsarian jolly who believes bad things befall good folk because of diet not because of some strain in the species, as in Rottweilers and lions, for blood violence.

But I am of that latter camp.

After years of witnessing the fall of man in all its many forms I have to say, despite the eddies and occasional displacements upwards on the wings of angels, the spiral that connects us all is winding downward. War threatens again in Europe, a sexually transmitted plague is decimating Africa and Southeast Asia, the very canopy of heaven is a thin disintegrating parchment and any planetary age of innocence is well and far behind us.

What a pity that the whole thing depends upon reciprocal destruction, Freud is reported to have said that while contemplating the infinite expanse of heaven one particularly bright and starry night. And although he was referring to the universe, he might as well have been referring to man's history . . . or (the cynics would propose) to Love.

But I'm not a cynic—a cynic has no eye for freshness except for looking for fresh hells; and I am frankly sick to death of hells on earth and I am frankly in great longing right now for a freshening of Love.

So there, I've said it.

That despite this end-of-century hurtling towards a reciprocal destruction I still hope for solace in the healing property of human Love.

In fact it is my only hope.

In fact it always peels me to the core when I discover traces of it, grace of it, among my fellows.

Certainly betrayal of a love—a kindred love, familial love, or love between two lovers—is one form of villainy; but are villains fundamentally desensitized to love? I don't think so —perhaps they are incapable of a sustained, sustaining love, but they are surely capable, from evidence, of feeling all the pangs and thralls and transports carried on in love's name. What makes them truly evil is not the fact that they *cannot* love, but that they can.

I am thinking, now, of murder and of villainy—of fake death and betrayal—because I'm thinking long and hard about the life of Adam (which is appropriate, given the announcement of his death) and about the kind of man he was.

Long, extremely long, airplane voyages lend themselves to this type of meditation, and even though this voyage is not nearly long enough, by the time I land in London (with the aid of a replenishing Club Class liquor license) I hope I will have sorted out (or merely reinforced) my emotional confusion.

Do I hate him or despise him, do I loathe him? And if he's dead *did* I hate him and despise him? If he's dead, does that make it all the worse because I'll never have the chance to tell him that I hated and loathed him? I'll never have the chance to see if I could murder him myself.

Maybe I am drunk already, or maybe it's the cozy weirdness of whispering to EVE (who, after all, is a machine) and experiencing the time delay before she exhales words like air bubbles onto the screen propped on my knees, but I'm feeling grandiose and whoozy, as if I've just survived a rollercoaster ride. I'm feeling philosophical—triumphant, too (HE'S DEAD!)—imbued with not a little godlike whimsy.

God was more to the first man, the first Adam (the original) than just the Arbiter of Taste—God was more to Adam than merely the Big Prig of all nutrition (you can eat this, but you can't eat that), El Señor Ix-nay with the fruit loot . . . God was Adam's agent of procurement, *God was Adam's way of getting laid*, provider of the woman, just as I was instrumental in providing Adam II with the accidental chance of meeting Lilith.

Don't think I never wonder what might have been if they had never met: I think about it every day—and although it would have made my life much happier and saved me from a *personal* response to him, their not having met wouldn't change the text of history and the fact that Adam was a villain.

Now you should ask—or, better, we should *all* ask—is there such a thing as villainy and is there such a person as The Villain?

Yes.

[Although his opposite—The Hero—is a harder thing to prove.]

Not all showmen are villains but *every villain is a showman*: just think about it: you may think the villain lives in darkness, but the villain needs the light, every shadow does, *Der Schatten*, everybody knows the shadow, everybody's felt a shadow fall across her heart, The Shadow knows no natterjacking, shadow loves the light because The Shadow is the shade that shapes humanity, its *edge*, the line between the halo and all heaven.

What Adam did is still beyond my means to write about in any way that can sound orderly, dispassionate, so I select distorting language: overheated: air balloons.

During the 1970s and 80s in Nicolai Ceauşescu's Romania, every female between the ages of 18 and 30 was required to give birth five times, to bear five children. Birth control was outlawed. Many of the children born were the result of rapes, rapes in the work place or on streets, in public places. Children of these rapes were given over to the State, prospective members of the workforce. But until they reached a working age in early adolescence their maintenance was costly to the State, and there were tens of thousands of them in the orphanages.

Adam was the Romanian Minister of Trade.

In Europe—even in the Cold War—humans were not sold, whole, outright, as commodities, unless as babies, for adoption, not as slaves. Romania, exporting everything it had, including its own population's food to maintain a balance of trade, could not afford to sell its future workforce, even if there'd been a market, somewhere, for its children. So it started trading liquid assets, started trading its liquidity.

When I saw Lilith for the last time in Berlin almost two years ago, I didn't know then what I know now about Adam—and even now I can't prove much, the threadbare fabric that I've woven out of rumours gathered here and there is made of skeins that don't connect. What bothers me is whether everything he did—his trade in blood and human organs—was done with or without the knowledge of the British (if, in fact, he was funded by them, which he might have been—otherwise what's his elegant corpse doing laid out somewhere on that Scept'red Isle?) I didn't know two years ago that the blood that he was trading in, the children's blood and various blood products, plasma from those orphan donors (if you can call conscripted children "donors")—the plasma wasn't treated, heated, before being offered up for sale—none of it was screened for HIV. Two years ago I didn't know how HIV had entered there, into Romania, and that the incidence of AIDS was greater there in children than in the neighbouring countries, in Hungary and Bulgaria. Two years ago I didn't know, in fact, that six weeks after I would see her for the last time in Berlin, she and Adam would disappear off the map, smuggled from Romania, presumably by British agents as "payment" for Adam's role in bringing down Ceauşescu.

Or maybe none of this is true.

—but if not, then why the death announcement? Why not let him sink from view, forgotten, like some old mummer about whom one person in a million might remark, "Well he's either dead, or he's living somewhere in Bermuda."

I learned an interviewing trick from observing the old Shah (the final Shah) of Iran back in the 70s (actually, *two* tricks:)

Get the subject to reveal his secret vanity.

Ask the subject what he fears.

Some men think they'll never die, they think their light will shine eternally, like a vampire's, that they are utterly unanswerable for their actions by any standards other than their own. They are their own best standard bearers in a parade of one: every act the villain makes is motivated by his ego only, the way his cigarette is lighted, the way he stands, the *where* he stands, the way he condescends to view his people and their future.

The vanities reveal themselves, eventually, if you watch closely enough—and the advantages to the interviewer of discovering a person's secret vanity are plentiful, because once you compliment a person on his secret vanity (in the Shah's case, his belief that he was Voltaire to his father's Napoleon), he'll tell you things he never meant to tell you.

Discovering a person's fear is a much more delicate endeavor, because it begs real intimacy. Maybe that's why a villain always fears surveillance, though he hungers for an audience. Villains are afraid of never being noticed. When their times for action come, they're afraid a hiccup in the universe might occur during which the cosmic audience will blink, the audience will have its eyes closed at the villain's Moment, so (wild as it seems) Adam, himself, would have wanted his own death announcement to appear, even though he would be turning in his grave a couple of times because it hadn't made the front page news.

. . . but what if Adam *isn't* dead?

Maybe some attempt (to kill? to capture? kidnap?) was made on Adam (by what are called "armed terrorists" as if "unarmed" terrorists could do the trick)—some armed terrorists made an attempt—which *failed*—and the Brits are trying to send the standard disinforming message down the pipeline.

Or maybe he *is* dead and there was one or more inconvenient chatty and possibly informing witness(es) on hand whose impending tabloid story has to have official cover.

And where was Lilith?

Where *is* Lilith?

Who is Lilith?

Don't think it hasn't occurred to me to make up some fantastic plot to rationalize her betrayal—there, I've said it: Her Betrayal.

Because all this crap about Adam, this obsession that I have with him, is really a secondary symptom of my primary obsession with *her*, I know that. I wouldn't give a flying fuck about him if it weren't for her—he'd be just another villain in a long line of villains that I've witnessed from the Horn of Africa to Watts to Kabul to The Hague, trading liberties, trading in lies and trading lives. If it weren't for Lilith I might not have even noticed him among the others—especially that year, 1989, when so much else was going on—if it weren't for her he might have been just another story missed, another bad guy gone unnoticed by the Western press because of one of all the many reasons stories get not told—because the car and driver don't show up, because the car breaks down, because the translator prevaricates, because the translator is on the take, because the desk man doesn't think the two day trip to Transylvania will produce a story that's as riveting as who(m) or what a certain Trump card or a Mr. Milken are screwing . . . or your djinn, your vest-pocket piece of luck, your lephrechaun, spends all day in the local gin mill and you end up in the wrong place at the wrong time, dry. Such is journalism, baby, but the fact is she betrayed me; and she betrayed me with *him*—and if, as in the book of Genesis, the ol' Biblical two-step runs Betrayal first, then murder, it follows that I tried to kill her by trying to supplant the joy I knew with her with something else, with anger and distrust—I tried to slant her beauty, thrust her, with some rage-fueled booster rocket, onto a distorted plain. Such was my insanity about a year ago that I tried to make myself believe that she had never loved me, that everything we'd done together was a lie. I tried to make myself believe that she deceived me from the start, that her heart was a deceiver. When that didn't work, I tried to convince myself that she hadn't betrayed me at all, that she'd gone off with him because she was a spy—hell! in my mind I made them both spies! Why not? Make us *all* spies, make the whole world a conspiracy, a global Romania! and why *not*? Under Ceauşescu everybody spied, the pathology of the spy State, enforced by the Securitate, proved women will spy on their husbands for a head of cabbage and a father will spy on his son for an egg and a student will spy on his teacher for nothing, for meat, or the hope of a job in the future.

the beginning

Why did she leave me for him?

Was it for sex?

. . . for some fucked-up reason from childhood?

Why?

Christ, if she had left me for Peter Jennings, that's one thing —or for a scion from the house of Fiat or for a Doric sponge fisherman—but she left me for Adam and to understand *why*, I must understand *him*.

And to understand *him*, I must understand *her*.

And to understand *her*—

(one train may hide another)

—I must go back, to the beginning.

The first time I ever saw her was in Cameroon.

1986

EAST AND WEST CAMEROON

The first time I saw Lilith

WE WENT to the cry-die.

. . . but first, we met.

And let me tell you, we did not meet cute (as they say in Hollywood), unlike the way she and Adam met, which—if not cute—was certainly dramatic.

The first time I saw Lilith I was standing at the bar in Chez Josette in Yaoundé, Cameroon, with Dick-the-spokesperson from Our Embassy, taking notes about the gas cloud which had erupted from a lake and killed two-to-five thousand people while they slept a few nights before in several villages to the northwest, near Wum.

This was in August, 1986—and the explosion from the lake was on the night of August 21st, to be exact. On that night an enormous lethal submarine gas mass composed of carbon dioxide and hydrogen sulphide had erupted from the depths of Lake Nyos into the atmosphere and rolled, like an invisible lava, down the surrounding foothills, killing in its wake at least two thousand people and twice that many cattle and domestic animals. It had killed the insects, too—including flies—but it had not killed plants, in fact the plants had flourished in its wake, because flora feast on carbon dioxide.

"You mean it was a sort of killer belch?" I asked Dick-the-spokesperson from Our Embassy, trying to get a technical handle on the chemical process.

"More like a fart," Dick answered.

I put down my pen.

This was my first time in Cameroon, and to tell the truth, I was sorry to be there. But when a lake explodes (farts/belches) and kills thousands of people and your paper wants you to be there, you go.

As it happened, I was in Geneva on another story and I flew from Geneva direct to Yaoundé on Swissair—a bit of the ol' magic djinn at its best, weaving the journalist's luck, because to have flown from anywhere else in Europe that week would have been a hellride into the seacoast capital, Douala where it was raining god's cats and dogs. Yaoundé was dry.

Africa was never my beat.

It was pure chance that I was in Geneva in a week when everyone else who had more experience to cover an African story was taking home leave or was gripped by the shits or was tired or lost or stranded in Chad. So I went.

Maybe I should tell you what it's like to land, solo, in a place you've never been, to get a story. It's hell; but it's a known hell, after you've done it most your life.

The first thing that you need to do is to find someone other than yourself who speaks your language, who can describe this new hell to you in terms that you can almost understand.

You never know who this "someone" will be—but, most likely, this first time, this "someone" will be the first camel driver you meet who speaks your language, or the "Information" official at the airport who inspects your papers, or the Press Officer from the local government or the Press Officer from *your own* government, or an unemployed university student, or a pimp, or a desk clerk, or a concierge, or a money changer or a thief, or a drop-dead-dramatic lady with a heartbreaking come-on, or a cop. If you're lucky, you'll stop with the camel driver.

In Yaoundé I was lucky, because that part of Cameroon had wrested independence from the French, and I spoke a little French. Also, it was the official capital of the formerly un-unified Cameroons, so the relatively savvy Ewondo and Fulani and Bamoun and Bamiléké at the airport sized me up and looked me over and herded me, like collies on an errant ewe, into the One Car That Was Meant For Me, driven (of course) by a man called Ahmadou, namesake-for-democracy-in *tout*-Cameroon.

One long taxi ride to my hotel on Mont-Fébé and sixteen phonecalls later, I was standing at the bar, surrealistically acclimatized, in Chez Josette near the U.S. Embassy in the Place de l'Indépendance, having not yet taken any measure of the city or the country, smelled its alleys, seen its mists and dawns—I was standing at the bar in Chez Josette with Dick-the-spokesperson from Our Embassy, interrogating him about The Event for history, mom, and all the eager readers hanging on my every word Back Home.

"Jog?" (I thought he said.)

"—sorry?" (I think I answered.)

". . . you-*jog*?" he said.

"Ah, no," I answered.

"That's good you won't get shot."

"I won't get—?"

"—shot. Kid last year—nice kid, from California—got up in the morning and went jogging. Normal. Five o'clock, so what? Still dark. Jogged around the Presidential Palace. Boom."

". . . um, could you tell me a bit more about the explosion on the lake—"

"So I wouldn't go jogging around the Presidential Palace if I were you."

". . . I won't."

". . . the police here don't really want to shoot you, they're just looking for some extra money. False arrest for bribes—that's the pattern—false arrest and bribes—it's quite a business. You'd be surprised how many times we're called just because most of our nationals don't know how to spring themselves from jail . . ."

I began to look around the bar, thinking I would like to spring myself from Dick if I could find another source for information. Chez Josette was not a place designed along the classic lines of Rick's American in *Casablanca* with its pale walls and airy spaces—Chez Josette felt *squeezed*, somehow, close and cramped despite the ubiquitous ceiling fans, even though the crowd dribbling in from Embassy Row was still thin. Then it dawned on me the bar had been constructed at the wrong height. The bar was at waist level. Next to it, I must have looked like a giant. Dick looked like a giant too.

"—most of them were sleeping," Dick was saying. "Went to sleep and never woke. Imagine that. Asphyxiated in your sleep. But a lot were still awake—it was a market day. A lot of people wait for night—the coolness—to make the journey home from market. And they say . . . I mean, the reports are, those people just fell down. Dropped in their tracks. Smelled the smell of rotten eggs—that would have been the sulphide—smelled the smell of rotten eggs, felt a warm sensation and passed out. Around nine thirty. Suffocated, just like that. Never knew what hit them.'

". . . a '*warm* sensation'?"

"—warm."

"—what is that?"

"—you don't know what a 'warm' sensation is?" Dick asked.

"—*why* the 'warm' sensation?" I amended.

". . . apparently a symptom of that kind of suffocation. You'll have to ask somebody from the WHO . . ."

"The WHO are here?"

"Crawling with the WHO. Crawling with all kinds of *médecins*. Lots of French. And lots of Catholics."

"Any present danger?"

"No one knows for sure."

"Was WHO the first relief team in?"

"—no, the Swiss were. Missionaries. Crawling with Swiss missionaries. Saw it from their helicopter . . . *Hélimission*."

"Survivors?"

"Not very many. Town was packed, because of market day. People in from Lower Nyos . . . Subum . . . Cha. Those were the villages worst hit. And Fang. Crawling with Save The Children people there, too. Scavenging for orphans. You ought to do a piece on them. That's the piece you ought to do. On NGOs —a piece on all the non-governmental organizations doing business here. CARE. Someone ought to do a piece on CARE's influence on this continent—talk about cultural intervention! That's the piece I'm waiting for someone to do."

I had stopped taking notes the instant Dick had started sounding like Captain Kirk aboard The Enterprise. You get these civil servants talking and the next thing that you know they've told you most of their frustrations and their fantasies. Their frustrations are usually along the line of too little or too much "cultural intervention", and their fantasy is to tell you how to do your job.

"I thought Cameroon was actually one African nation feeding itself, producing enough food—free from CARE, in other words,' I humbly submitted.

"Oh you *have* done your homework," Dick assessed. "I suppose I don't have to tell you, then, how Cameroon got its name . . ."

I signalled the bar man for another (what else?) Coke for Dick and switched, myself, from Primus (brewed by Heineken in Zaïre) to the much lauded Gala brew from Chad. My antennae told me my djinn had let me down, Dick was not going to develop into the perfect source (the perfect source would have asked me to his home tonight, cooked me a great meal, revealed state secrets and introduced me to El Presidente's wife . . .)

"*Camarões*," Dick was saying, "*camarões* means 'shrimp'. When the Portuguese came here they called this country *cameroon* for all the shrimp they found . . ."

Whereas the English would have had the sodden sense to name the country after one of Us, a familiar voice boomed behind me. "And while we're on the subject—can anyone explain this *ripping stench*?"

I turned around, and there was Duff.

He was, as always, at the center of his own mess, but there in Chez Josette he looked particularly disgraceful—tie, well, *burned*, actually, shirt, as usual, two-thirds out of his pants, a jacket that was probably white linen beneath its encrustation, florid face and tousled hair, dusted, this time, by a substance much like cornmeal. And of course, as ever, drunk.

He had with him a similarly drunk white male whom I determined to be Duff's imperfect source from Their Embassy.

"I told you," Duff's imperfect source was detailing, "it's fecal. Flying. Dust."

I am a journalist.

"That's right," Dick said. "Flying *fecal* dust, actually. Deadly new. It's a sort of space age cholera."

"It gets in your lungs," Duff's person said. "Where—oddly—you can't smell it . . ."

"But when it starts to rain," Dick said, "which it does every evening here this time of year for about an hour—then you can really smell it—it *is* fecal, after all—and it stinks up everyone and everything it falls on—"

"Including crops?" I asked.

"Fuck the crops," Duff roared, "what I want to know is is it going to *kill* me? Because if it's going to kill me I'm not going down alone . . . If it's going to kill me I demand that it kills Noah, too, in the spirit of true non-lateral the fuck agreement . . . Hallo, Noah. Good ol' Noah. Why the fuck are *you* here?"

Because *it's happening, baby*, I said.

"Fucking fart lake, is it?" Duff focused, falling somewhat toward the bar, where he demanded, "What the hell is this, something out of Munchkinland?" and ordered up a double gin. He clapped a swollen pink hand, like a mullet, on my shoulder and looked at me slyly from the corner of his eye. "What you and I should do," he stage-whispered, "is lose these flat-earth people, halve the cost of some local muleteer for the morrow and hie ourselves to Wum for a co-national inspection."

Absolutely, I agreed, that's what we should do, Duff, I said, trying not to have to prop him up.

"Now tell me more about this fecal flying matter," he announced to everyone in general while attempting to ignite a sodden match to light his cigarette. "I ought to warn you, though," he broadcasted, inhaling god-knows-what, and then exhaling eerie ochre stuff, ". . . *I am a journalist.*"

Which was true, technically, though by then Duff had

become a shadow of his former self, a caricature of what he had once been. He did not 'report', as such—he wielded language as a weapon. He was deadly clever and the slick sheets paid him large for dishing British royals and Brit expats around the pools in Hollywood. He looked the part of Richard Burton in the movie *The Night of the Iguana*—always sporting that sad linen jacket that wouldn't button over an open-throated beef-fat-cum-*pistou*-stained collegiate shirt missing several buttons two-thirds tucked into a waistband over which a roll of alcoholic-calories-made-flesh pushed a moraine of bodyfat ever downward toward his center of the universe. His diction, rolling like a thunder over plummy wastes of some lost dialect, commanded everyone's attention, but I had known him long enough to know that if you hitched your towline to his dizzy elocutions he would drag you back and forth across a single latitude on stale wind. It was always better to avoid him on assignment in the larger world beyond saloons—but in saloons he was great company, although I had to wonder why he'd come to Cameroon, why he'd landed in, as Bogey says about Rick's place in *Casablanca*, "a saloon like this". No one was gambling much of anything in Chez Josette—not a single *laissez-passer* was for sale, it was the fag end of a (fecal) dusty August day in Africa, about to rain, there was no Claude Rains in sight and I was standing at a midget bar with one drunk Brit and several shitheads from as many embassies on the rue du Cercle Municipal in a former French colonial backwater where the hotels are all called Indépendance, de la Paix, Impérial or Terminus, where, across the street, I could get a sheepmilk-and-goatmeat Croque O'Burger or a korma-and-teriaki at one of the many Indian-&-Nip joints, and I was there to get the angle and the motive and the background into focus to transmit my so-wise and essential tidbits of What's Happening to London and thence to New York to land at your front door tomorrow morning—when, of all the gin joints in all the towns in all the world, she walks into mine.

Duff was having a go at some Frenchman who had caught his bloodshot eye at a nearby table, "Feel free," he was saying, "to speak in French when you can't think of the English thing to say, but answer this before you do, please, because I am a journalist: Is there *any* nation on this earth whose citizens consume as many frogs as yours?" when in she came.

She swept in, really, like a gust of weather, her entrance stage-managed to perfection like (to fuck this metaphor completely) a Puccini heroine, like Mimi or like Butterfly, whose melody is heard off-stage before we see her face. There was a high-pitched commotion at the door of Chez Josette behind a set of weather curtains, then an adjunct (one of Ours), scurried towards Dick and Duff *et moi* and stopped in front of Dick and said, "I'm sorry, sir. The Africans insist. There's been a mix-up, sir. Two of their policemen. And a child."

"'A child'?" Dick said.

"A girl, sir," came the answer, "*one of ours.*"

With that, all heads at the bar at Chez Josette turned toward the entrance as the curtains broke and in swept two of Yaoundé's Finest hustling between them a slim something, soaking wet and cursing, stinking of fecal dust, dressed in nothing but a yellow plastic poncho to the middle of her thighs, and a pair of rubber thongs.

It was the get-up, studiously devised, that made her look, at first glance, like a child—that, and the size of her head, which was small with small features (except her eyes), and the way she wore her hair (short and sleeked back.)

Her eyes were (and are) lighthouse-lamp-size.

Her legs were (and are) *fantastic.*

They seemed to start at her armpits.

They were long, long from hip-to-knee-to-anklebone, and smooth, with not a bubble on them—and as she was hustled in, between *les flics*, she appeared to grow so that by the time she reached Dick and *moi* and Duff and several Frenchmen who had stood up from their table, she no longer seemed a girl. This is Lilith's gift—she is the mistress of a million guises. Or, to put it as a bad cliché—she can assume the form of any woman, any time, for anyone. Or so I thought. But I'm the last person you should trust to tell you about Lilith because I was—from the beginning—utterly in thrall to her.

Timing, as we say in the scoop business, is everything.

Maybe I was ready to fall hard for any woman who showed up at that hour—or maybe, as Isak Dinesen would have it —it was *Africa*. But I fell facedown into the alphabet soup, the c-d/e-f—*coup de foudre*.

Level-headed Southern boys shouldn't handle lightning bolts, they shouldn't play with *coups de foudre*—not before their suppers—because their preachers and their playwrights teach them *coups de foudre* lead straightaway to broken hearts and crimes of passion. Level-headed Southern boys, like stately plump buck mulligans, should stay sober, marry wisely and invest their money in legumes. They should not —repeat, should *not*—look for love in foreign places where the lakes explode.

She was perfect for me.

I was a dead man.

The last woman to throw the switch on me that way was Pretty Ass Patty Ann, prettiest nurse in the corps, fatally perfect, six years earlier in Beirut (but don't get me started on *that*.)

And there had been flings and submissions (christ knows!) through my life (and even a marriage—and a divorce).

But when Lilith struck, she struck without warning—not

like a train (which you can hear coming), not like a tornado (which gets its wind up) or like cyclones and hurricanes (ditto and ditto)—but like something that falls from the sky, which proves the existence of myths, and dead gods.

The two policemen set her down in front of Dick who indicated, with a nod of his head, that they should *un-hand* the lady, and then he asked, in his best Embassy-speak What Was (as if he couldn't guess) *happening*.

Officially, Dick couldn't cough up the necessary bribe in front of everyone, but Duff had already reached into his pocket for his billfold and was laying out with an impressive flourish paper money from all sorts of sovereign nations as if dealing tarot cards across a gaming table.

I, on the other hand, couldn't move because I couldn't take my eyes off Lilith.

In Cameroon (then, as now) it was illegal to carry a camera without A Permit—and it was illegal to photograph anything which might embarrass the government.

One never knew what, exactly, might embarrass the government, but it was understood that walking around with a camera was more or less an invitation to at least a bribe or at most a confiscation of your camera and your film.

Presuming you had triumphed over the *douanier*'s insistence at immigration that *he* owned your camera and your lenses and your film, and that—in addition—you had secured A Permit, it was okay to photograph obeche trees and buffaloes and elephants and hippopotami and antelopes and kundus, monkeys, baboons, lions and giraffes and birds. But it was not okay to photograph any of these animals or the obeche trees if there was someone sitting near them *begging*.

Photographs in Cameroon of people begging were *verboten*.

Likewise, photographs of buildings, airports, bridges,

railway stations, railroad tracks and ethnic and religious practices.

In other words, you were free to take a lot of photos, as long as those photos didn't have a trace of humankind in them.

And not only was Lilith suspected by the policemen who accompanied her of photographing illegal and embarrassing subjects (in her case, child prostitutes in Yaoundé), but she didn't have A Permit, nor could she produce—this was the *coup de grâce*—a passport.

And when *les flics* had apprehended her, they swore to Dick in broken English, she had refused to be (yes) touched or searched until she was in the presence of a certified representative of The United States.

So there she was.

Soaking wet buck naked—or so we were supposed to think—except for (possibly) her skivvies, yellow poncho and a pair of rubber thongs.

Every journalist needs to be adept at improv but believe me Lilith made an art of it. She avoided any act of trust in any government to aid or to protect her, or to aid and to protect The Press, in general. She used her passports—one from the United States, the other one from France—as garlics that could ward off vampires, but she didn't trust that any government could save its citizens at home, much less save them in foreign lands. She was opposed to any form, real or symbolic, of nationalism—which, as you can guess, made her tons of fun to be with in what we call "emerging" nations like, you know, for example, most of Africa, most of eastern Europe, all of western Asia and, christ knows, Puerto Rico, Wales and Scotland. Her trick—which was also tons of fun to witness—was to claim her passport, whichever one she happened to decide would serve her best in any given circumstance, had been lost upon arrival in a country. Sometimes, depending on the country, she'd claim to lose it after passing through that country's immigration—other times, she'd claim she'd lost the passport *at* immigration. That was always fun to have to watch. Many journalists assigned to travel, say, between countries that have been at war with one another, between Greece and Turkey for example, or between India and Pakistan or between Israel and every country in the world except the United States, try to find some smooth reason to justify traces of the enemy in travel visas, but Lilith is the only person that I've known who systematically lied, as a matter of policy, to every customs officer and immigration official she encountered. And, systematically, her lies were believed—not by everyone, only by the person, usually a man, who had the authority to stamp her papers and let her in. There was never anything in their transactions—and I watched her do it many times—there was never anything to suggest a possible exchange of favors, either sexual or monetary—on the contrary—what I saw was that they watched her very closely, watched her face, as she explained her story very slowly. What I saw were men reacting to her with a sort of awe, a form of respect, whether they believed her or they didn't (and I would guess most didn't).

This time, as it developed, she had, in fact, upon arrival by bush taxi into Yaoundé from Douala gone to the U.S. Embassy to report she'd lost her U.S. passport after landing at the airport in Douala (which wasn't true) and she now held a piece of sodden paper which someone at Dick's own office that morning had issued to her to prove it. But the lies —yes, there were several—that she was asking Dick in Chez Josette to validate that a) she was not in Cameroon as a professional photographer, b) she was a tourist, c) she was not on assignment with Agence France-Presse to get pictures of the victims of the explosion of the fart lake, d) her primary interest in the country was gathering recordings of Bamiléké music, and e-thru-zed) that she was not travelling with cameras, that she did not have a camera or cameras beneath her poncho, that—in fact—she had nothing on beneath her poncho because all her bags had gotten wet in the bush taxi, and that if it was necessary to be searched to prove that she was telling the truth, then she would agree to a search by a member of the free press, only, and she looked straight in the face of your obedient and enchanted servant.

Then she wrested her arms free of the policemen, held them out to her sides and waited for my hands to do her bidding.

No need, Dick protested and began to work some diplomatic hocus-pocus with the sheriffs but Lilith told him, "Don't. Insult. Me further," and I got to hear her voice for the first time (rich & throaty!) (deep & creamy!).

"*Bloody hell*," Duff was saying, "Noah, if you don't get your paw up there, you're the sorriest asshole west of Idi Amin . . ."

So I got my paw up there. My *paws*.

I put my hands under her poncho and moved them all around for everyone to see while I stared into her dark eyes and she stared back into my (so I have been told) nice brown ones.

There was a fucking Nikon fucking arsenal up there for christsake—42nd Street Photo couldn't stock the gear she had slung around her chest—I think there might have been an AK-47 up there, too—there were a zillion straps and caps and barrels—and some kind of waterproof affair at her waist filled with what were either hand grenades or cannisters of film—and (to my great disappointment) she was wearing a tee-shirt.

She was high-waisted, most long-legged women are, and

she had a broad ribcage for a woman which gave support to (yes) her breasts. There was no bra, so what's a guy to do? I didn't hesitate. First I touched one, then I touched the other, then I touched them both at the same time, cupping my palms around them. Each breast must have weighed (I reckoned) three-quarters of a pound (the right one was slightly heavier.)

Then, using my opposing thumbs for the purpose God no doubt had in mind when He created me from monkeys, I located her nipples and—only slightly—rubbed them.

Lilith didn't flinch.

Our faces were close enough that I could see the backdrop in her pupils and as I massaged her nipples I thought I saw a shadow there, life behind those curtains, but she didn't move, her face gave no reaction, though I thought I felt her heart rate quicken and I noticed then the flecks of red, two rubies, in her irises, one in each eye, red roses in a nighttime garden which would be the objects of my fascination for years to come.

I withdrew my hands with great effect, holding them up for all to see like someone in a sports event.

I looked at the two Yaoundé policemen. *Arrest her*, I said. I said it in Fulani. This woman's a danger to society, I said. I prided myself in knowing the word for "danger" in Fulani. She's a fucking terrorist, I said. They seemed impressed that I knew the Fulani word for terrorist and the Fulani word for fucking. That was the year I won the Nobel for Reporting. I frequently had two ejaculations every hour for twelve hours straight that year. I knew where Jimmy Hoffa had been buried and I knew where Amelia Earhart had gone down, but actually, "*This woman's telling you the truth*," is what I said, "There's nothing there," and that made me just as much A Hero in my eyes (and I hoped in hers) as if I had done all that other crap and leaped tall buildings in a single bound.

la porte de derrière

"You see, you *see*?" Dick dispensed, skillfully herding the two cops, his adjunct, Duff's person from the British Embassy and the Frenchman away from her, adding, "Now let's see if we can't come to some agreement over this . . ."

That left me alone with her (and Duff).

Why is it men like Duff are always smooth and charming at such moments while I stand mute and mucked up to my ukulele in pigshit? "You look positively ravishing, my dear, as usual, very Pucci-esque, that poncho," Duff simmered at her, "but you must be parched. Is it still pastis? *Pastis pour la gamine*," he ordered in an appropriately stylish language.

"You two *know* each other?" I blubbered in what sounded like (and was) total amazement, while *Come away with me into the night you incomparable creature* was what I wanted to be saying or—failing that—Can I buy you dinner? May I spend the rest of my life with you under your poncho?

But since my lie in her defense, my act of heroism, Lilith hadn't looked at me—instead she gave Duff a rough acknowledging embrace and waved a hand at the barkeep to refuse the drink, saying to him, "Éy, frère—la porte de derrière, où ça?"—then Dick was at my side again. "Well," he said to all and sundry, sighing with relief, "I think we've worked *that* out . . ."

"Yes," Duff's person from the British Embassy piped in, "damn clever, too. We've bought back the country with glass beads."

"Thank you," Lilith said.

"Don't thank *me*," Dick said in his best diplomatic service voice, "just make darn certain you straighten out this missing passport business at my office first thing in the morning. And if I were you," he added, playing against stereotype, I thought, "I'd slip out the back of here before those two policemen know you're gone . . ."

"She's already thought of that," Duff mentioned.

Then she smiled at Duff and smiled at Dick and smiled at the Frenchmen and at the bartender and left, never once casting a look or a smile or a wink in my beady direction.

"Who *is* she?" I begged of Duff when she'd left, fighting the impulse to follow her.

Duff ordered another Gala for me and another tumbler of gin for himself and said, "Don't even dream of it, old man . . ."

"But who *is* she?" I repeated.

". . . because she's swallowed head from every jackstraw from Texas to Tobruk."

Including *his*, his smirk was meant to tell me.

"Are you going to tell me," I bargained, "or do I have to let you go to Wum alone tomorrow while I hang around the Embassy all morning until she shows up?"

"You won't catch her at the Embassy tomorrow," Duff said, swallowing a quantity of gin, "she has no intention of going to the Embassy tomorrow. You'll have finer luck locating her in Wum . . ." He checked his watch, a showy Rolex. "Christ knows, she's probably halfway there by now . . ."

He studied me.

"Good god, Noah, don't look so pathetic . . . you *must* know her work—"

"Her 'work'?"

"Her photographs . . . she files for Agence France-Presse . . . did the Lebanon for them. Goes way back—the 70s. Boat people. Civil war in Chad. Iran–Iraq war. Sadat's assassination. Indira's assassination. She's lucky with assassinations. Miners' strike in the U.K. *Blitzkrieg* on Tripoli. Polisario. She did a portfolio for our colour supplement last year on Europe's gypsies. Hard to believe you've never met because she's been around for years in places that you've been around for years . . . uses a *nom de guerre* . . . '*Divi*' . . . initials of her surname, or something, *dee* and *vee* . . ."

"*She*'s . . . Divi?"

"She's Divi."

"I thought 'Divi' was a guy—"

"Everyone thinks Divi is a guy. That's the way she likes it . . ."

Several hours and a lot of bullshit later, after rehashing every war fought since the dawn of civilization and learning and forgetting far too much about the local tribes and tribulations from the assorted Embassy regulars at Chez Josette, I led Duff through the bead curtains of that estimable saloon out into the rue.

Part of my argument with the world, I suppose, is the irrefutability of my early years—when I was even more callow and less responsible for my actions and to my fellow men than I would become later—a large part of my discontent with how things are stems from my roots, from the fact that I am Southern from the seed, as Southern in my bent as Duff was (and is) non-working class and English. And there have been moments in my life I can recall so clearly (as if new) that I'm obliged to think of them either as headlines on the front page of my private paper or as chapter headings in the paltry epic of my life.

Coming out into the African night from that cramped saloon dense with foreign accents and tobacco smoke, coming out under the African sky into the rue with Duff behind me was one of those instances, exactly. It wasn't that the sky that night was more memorably beautiful or harrowing, as it often is in Africa—same stars, same galaxies—the moon had not yet risen. And it wasn't that the street, itself, was more distinctive than all the other reinvent-the-wheel Paris-manqué *rond-point* spokes the French imposed on far-flung cities that they colonized (it wasn't). And it wasn't even something in *the air* of Africa (which always makes me homesick for the South, don't ask me why). When I say that Africa is not my beat I mean there are journalists who've spent their lifetimes making it their language the way I developed what talent I was born with into an instinct for knowing what makes a breaking story unmistakably *European*. I never feel outside the culture in Europe—even places where the language is impossible for me, as in Greece, or Romania—I always find a way *in* through a gesture, through the country's art or through the music or, more and more these days, through a dissenter's p.o.v. of politics at the groaning table of shared cynicism. But in Africa—even in the north, in Egypt, Tunisia or Morocco—I, the thinking "I", am hostage to my senses much too often, living far too closely on my skin to be a fair reporter. Southern white boy syndrome—I am captive to my guilt in Africa, I'm too pissed off at history and I can't balance facts. I romanticize the whole damn continent for christsake like some great white fucking hunter. Nowhere else—not in India or China or Japan—do I suffer such a shift in my perspective as I do in Africa, and there had been times there when I'd been close to losing it completely—I mean really losing it—times in the north when I had gotten close to the Sahara, or times around the Horn when I'd seen a ship at sail or standing off that haunted coast. But that night in Yaoundé I was far enough away from both those circumstances when suddenly I walked into the rue with Duff into the yaw of something otherworldly.

Fucksake, Duff cursed, slamming up against me where I'd stopped dead in my tracks, "*Noah—?*"

I couldn't tell him that I felt as if a ghost had just walked through me or as if the world was one I'd never seen before. Once, through an interpreter, I was interviewing an Ethiopian *bright nausea elsewhere in the body.*

who told me he was an epileptic, so I asked the translator to ask him, near the end of the interview, what the legendary epileptic aura felt like, then I listened to the translator pose the question and I listened to the Ethiopian's response and then the translator said to me, in English, "He says it feels like a *bright nausea elsewhere in the body.*" *That's* something like the way that I was feeling—and I remember thinking about Dick having told me earlier that evening that some of the gas cloud victims had fallen down where they stood *after feeling a warm sensation*, and I briefly wondered if the carbon dioxide cloud had travelled all the way from Lake Nyos to Yaoundé, because I was very definitely feeling a warm sensation and experiencing bright nausea elsewhere in my body both at the same time.

"I'm *fine*," I said to Duff, patting all my pockets as a stall until the weirdness passed.

"You sure?"

He was looking at me funny.

"*Absolutely*," I assured him, having just discovered that my passport and my room key were missing from my right hand jacket pocket.

"Lose something?"

"Only my heart, Duff, old man . . ."

"What, *her* again? Thought we had exhausted that particular subject . . ."

As indeed we had (*he* had.) Among the many stories about Lilith I had pulled from Duff that evening—all of them untrue—was the rumor that she was the illegitimate daughter of Maria Callas and Onassis (the arithmetic was off by six or seven years) and the assertion that she was the kept woman of the CEO of Sony (happily married somewhere in Japan) and the certifiable truth (sworn on the grave of Duff's mother) that she was a Mossad agent married to a member of the

PLO. I didn't believe anything Duff had to say about her but what I couldn't dispute was the fact that I had my passport on me at the bar in Chez Josette earlier that night because I'd taken it out to show Dick where a Chad immigration official had once cancelled my visa from Nigeria at the border because he hadn't wanted Americans going to any African nations other than Chad to spend all those American dollars he thought every American was stuffed with—"You can't cancel a visa issued by another country, you idiot!" was my professional response, "Are you crazy? No one in his *right* mind comes to Chad *to shop*!"

I knew I'd had my passport in my jacket pocket and I knew I'd had my room key in that pocket, too, because, like most Americans, I take my room key with me instead of leaving it at the desk when I go out, as Europeans do, unless the key is some relic from Gargantua, like the keys from the Grande Bretagne in Athens, for example. I knew I'd had my room key in *that* pocket because I'd felt the room key there when I'd slipped the passport back, and I knew those two things were the only two things in that pocket because I always carry credit cards in my inside jacket pocket with my notebook and my pen and I carry local currency in my right hand pants pocket and my tape recorder, Kodak brainless, batteries and hard currency (dollars, marks and francs) in a leather ditty bag around my wrist. (What can I say—I'm a guy with a purse and a creature of habit.) Only three people, three people only, had stood close enough to me that night to pick my pocket and those three people, in chronological order of opportunity, were Dick from the Embassy, Duff . . . and the stuff of my dreams.

Duff was starting to lead the way up the rue to Place de l'Indépendance where we intended to engage a car and driver at the taxi rank for the trip to Wum. Both Duff and I lived by the journalist's tried-and-tested rule when it came to engaging a car and driver: *newest* car; *oldest* driver. The reverse can—and will—end in a disaster. Duff wanted to go on to a club called "Oxygen" ("*Hot*," he promised) which featured Afro-pop and prostitutes but the last thing in the world (or nearly the last) I wanted to do was spend the night with Duff and I was trying to come up with an excuse to cut myself loose from him when a large white Citroën passed us in the rue, came to a halt and tore at us in reverse.

'Duffy!" a woman cried. "Duff Diamond, is that you? I thought it was you but I wasn't sure then I saw it was you so I backed up—is that really you? Is it him?" she asked me.

I could hardly see her inside the car because of the way Citroëns are built, but she was definitely thin and coiffed and ditsy and thrilled to see Duff Diamond.

"Ask her who the hell she *is* . . ." Duff whispered.

"Uh, we'll have to see some I.D., m'am," I requisitioned.

"Oh, Duffy, you're so funny. Get in the car at once. You don't seem at all surprised to see me, Duffins . . ."

I opened the car door for Duff.

"Noah," he said. "I swear to you. I don't have a *clue*—"

"I'd definitely let the woman take you where she wants to. Duffins." As soon as Duff was gone and I started up the rue alone toward the *rond-point* of the Place, that eerie sense of otherworldliness returned. I'll tell you what it was like—it was like being in a horror movie at that moment right before the doom.

Or maybe it was Love.

I thought it *might* be love, but I suspected it was really only one half of my brain making a rebellion on its other half. Only later would I find out that I *was*, in fact, experiencing increased levels of testosterone and the first flush of mild psychotic symptoms of what is commonly called *luv*, but for the time being I concluded my state of mental disarray was my way of being angry with myself and with my job and with the fact I'd let the object of my desire stick her hand in my pants without my feeling it. I didn't want to have to deal with going through the exercise of bargaining a car to go to Wum to see the lake—because I didn't want to go to Wum. I was tired and pissed off and weirded out and I didn't want to see the fucking lake. I didn't want to face the fact of having come to Africa to file another body count report—I was fed up with body count reports from all continents, pissed off with having been dispatched by New York to write about a freak event in nature that killed people while they slept, when what I wanted was to write about what I saw in front of me in Africa—that the biggest freak event which had occurred here was the white man.

Where the rue opened out onto the expanse of the Place de l'Indépendance, I stopped, which is an asshole thing to do at night alone in almost any city but particularly in Yaoundé where unemployment among males was very high—about seventy per cent—and where the incidence of mugging was inching upward toward the extreme set by Kinshasa where you were relatively guaranteed to be set upon by thieves before you left the airplane.

A rootsy kwassa kwassa noise rose from the Place—part high-speed soukous, part Beti tribe triple beat, part penny whistle kwela music, part makossa licks, part balafon, part kora, part horn, part synth . . . man and his music, man and his *drums*.

Immediately I was surrounded by a rush of young men hawking goods or looking for *cadeaux* (pronounced "ay-cado")—*gifts*, street talk for a handout—and half a dozen heavily scented *fees*, short for *filles de joie*, street-walking prostitutes.

Across the Place, in front of the three-storey white stucco Hôtel de l'Unité, there was a line of taxis, so I made for that, leading my entourage which picked up in the number of boys and men but lost the prostitutes as we crossed the *rond-point* toward rue de Gaulle. Two blocks to the north, on Avenue Churchill, there was the British Embassy and behind it there was the German, so the bar and patio of Hôtel de l'Unité was popular with Anglos and with Saxons and with Teuts, and before his kidnapping Duff had said the taxi rank in front of the hotel was one of the best in town for hiring a car and driver, but the street scene in the Place, the sound and *souk*-ness of it, stopped me, once again.

Crowd scenes are a bitch to render into writing—numbers don't mean anything when read, that's why a picture is worth a thousand—so what you do, when you're reporting, is either paint it large, go for sweeping background color, or you look for those few details that reduce the mass to one archetypal human, or Everyman.

Or sometimes you just try to live your life without "reporting" all the time.

Sometimes you want to close down the manic rodent on the funwheel.

You don't *want* to make the mental note that to your left, under the skull and crossbones SIDA graffito, with a suckling on her depleted teet, there's a woman on the sidewalk trying to sell what appears to be a single dried-up boa constrictor skin. You don't *want* to have to try to identify the bushmeat on the kebab grill ahead of you (antelope? monkey? porcupine?). I've been in countless crowd scenes in my life—but never *not* as a reporter. Growing up, I never knew a crowd, the throng—several hundred strong—on Broad Street in Richmond for the Fourth of July parade loses its pressing significance compared to being in the middle of several hundred thousand people in Bombay for *Holi* or in Lahore on *Eid*. Some crowds are built for danger, others as resistance, like a dike, against impending force. The best ones are the ones with lots of women in them. The mean ones are the ones that rise from sticks and stones. The worst ones are the ones that come complete with uniforms. What I had around me in the Place was not a *crowd*, as such—more like a *throng*—and what I'd learned to do in throngs was put away my notebook and my pen and stop. So I stopped.

I've traveled with a lot of fellow hacks through throngs in many places and I'm the only one I know who always stops. I've seen a lot of hacks give things away when they're surrounded—money, candy and (yes!) condoms—which keeps the throng-biz thriving. I never give the throng-ees anything except my outstretched hand, a chance to touch me, and the chance for me to touch them, Journalist in Jesus mode. I watched a Brit I was on the road with once (a woman) when we were covering some new development in terror in Northern Ireland—I watched her throw coins at the children who came running at us, while she screamed at them, "Get away, get *away, you shites*!" It bothers me when I'm on assignment in the company of people like her who can't stand to be surrounded, can't stand the threat of being thronged by strangers, even children (*especially* by children), can't bear the threat of being touched. There's a school of thought, of course, which proposes that reporters need to put a lid on all the touchy feely aspects of their personalities, for the sake of Objectivity. But my response to that is *That's why there are wire services.* Wire service people are employed—no, they're *trained*—to go in, get the facts, *touch nothing* and get out. And that's why I was pissed off that I'd been dispatched to Cameroon. The fart lake seemed to me, at best, a wire service story. What was a guy like me—trained observer of political sophistication and subtle refinement—what was *I* doing humping up to Wum when I could stick around Yaoundé and listen to Radio Africa No. 1 out of Gabon and get the facts on the new soul makossa and bikusti music coming out of Cameroon (Manu Dibango, Sam Fan Thomas, Francis Bebey, and Les Têtes Brulées) . . . or—as the graffito to my left reminded me—I could hang around in Yaoundé and do a piece on AIDS.

I bought some cassettes from the street vendors, guaranteed to be both pirated and of poor quality, made some mental notes and put my newly-determined self into a taxi and let the driver drive me all around the back streets of Yaoundé before ascending, never out of second gear, up Mont-Fébé to my hotel. Now I had a plan, and I was satisfied—New York would throw one of its shitfits, what the hell—I hated doing lake stories, I absolutely hated them. Some beknighted goon in Gotham City had had the bright idea to send me up to Loch Ness when I first transferred to London, "for an update on the monster." *What "update"*? the thing's a *hoax*, was pretty much my attitude. Yeah, but it's good copy, I was told. So up I went, to the Scottish Highlands—my first fast-breaking Lake event. Took the night train up from London to Inverness, hired a car, drove south on the east shore of the Loch then north on the western shore along the "Loch Ness Highway" (A82, as I recall). Went to the Loch Ness Monster Museum in Drumnadrochit, admission three pounds fifty, interviewed the head of the Massachusetts Academy of Applied Science which maintains a year-round watch with sonar-triggered cameras—"We're not sure *what* it is. We're not even sure *if* it is."—rejected the idea of checking into the manorial hotel on eighteen acres in Drumnadrochit (pop. 542) at the paper's expense and exercised a less expensive option at a little lodging in Invermoriston which boasted 160 varieties of single malt behind the bar. Drank a lot. Visited the Loch (yup, it's wet), bought seven different tartan blankets at seven different roadside woolly shops, two for myself and the rest for my sister and her four children, bought five tins of chocolate-chip shortbread also for sis and the kids, bought a gun-metal grey cashmere turtleneck sweater for myself in Inverness, bought two bottles of single malt, turned in the car and took the sleeper back to London all for an expense to the paper (or, ultimately, to you, dear readers) of twelve hundred pounds for a thousand words of drivel which began something like, "First espied in the 18th century B.C. by a local monk, *Nessitera Rhombopteryx*, or 'Nessie', as it is called, is one of the world's most enduring unsolved mysteries . . ."

And anytime my bosses in New York start complaining, as they often do, about the cost of news, the cost of keeping bureaus open in places like New Delhi, I like to remind them they could run an office in Constantinople for a month on what my two-day jaunt to Scotland cost them.

That's why I hate Lake stories.

Monster in the Lake is right up there on my list of Big Shit along with *Statue of the Virgin Weeps* and *French Outlaw English Words* (again.)

When the driver dropped me at the Mont-Fébé, some sort of UFO seemed to be running flight maneuvers on the golf course (gads, Watson, a *Scottish* game!) in front of the hotel, but when I walked across the driveway over to the first tee on the hill above the city I could see it was only a band of merry Saudis playing golf in the dark by flashlight (now *there*'s the caddy job from hell . . .)

The desk clerk greeted me effusively—"Ay, Monsieur Noah!"—because there was, that season, an up-and-coming Cameroon tennis wizard by the name of Noah Yannick and the sound of my name, *Noah*, to Cameroonians seemed like a blessing oft repeated.

"*Tou ba ben*?" he beamed.

"*Tout va bien, merci*, but could you get someone to let me in my room, please? I seem to have come away without my key—"

"*S'ba*, Monsieur Noah! No problem—*tu'sho pour* Monsieur Noah!"

A bellhop was instructed to accompany me upstairs.

"Noah," he kept saying and pointing at me and grinning ear to ear.

Yup, I kept agreeing.

When we got to my room, he turned the key in the lock, flung the door back and pounded on it—*hard*—with the flat of his hand.

"Spirits! No spirits!" he said.

"Great. No spirits," I said, passing him five hundred Central African francs.

I closed the door and switched on the ceiling fan and a small light (the bulb was 15 watts.)

My passport and the room key were positioned neatly on the bedside table.

There was, of course, that chemical solution smell that I would come to know so well, but I did not interpret its true meaning at the time and assumed, instead, it was a less attractive aspect of Yaoundé's *ambiance*.

I always close the door between the bathroom and the bedroom in hotels because, if you must know, I'm afraid of lizards. I'm not afraid of them, exactly, I don't mind the sight of lizards in the bathroom if I'm dressed, but I sure as hell don't want lizards from the bathroom skittling over me while I'm in bed. So I always close the door.

I should have figured out what was going on the instant

the distance didn't seem to matter.

that I saw the passport and the key but it wasn't until I opened the bathroom door and saw all her negs hanging there like flypaper that I swung around and caught the sight of her slipping back into the room through the glass door from the balcony.

She leaned against the door, her head against the glass, and I leaned against the door where I was standing.

The moon had risen—I could see its light reflected in her hair, and on her skin.

She was barefoot and bare-legged.

She was wearing cotton panties which, in the moonlight, looked incandescent.

Above the panties she was wearing a pale tee-shirt with a Warholesque silk-screen image of Khomeini glaring in that charming charismatic way of his through the logo 'SURF SATAN'. It was a great tee-shirt. It looked incandescent, too.

We were standing about fifteen feet from one another but the distance didn't seem to matter.

We stood like that a while.

I don't remember what I was doing with my hands but she was using hers to fiddle absentmindedly with a small mirror, one of those travel jobs that are supposed to save your life out in the wild by focusing sunrays into a single pilot light on kindling, or by beaming up an S O S to rescue pilots from an ice-face on the Eiger.

Light bounced off the mirror when she moved.

A circle of white light—like Tinker Bell—skittered on the ceiling, back and forth, between us.

"Sorry I had to take your passport," she said.

"That's okay," I said (or something equally as stupid).

"It was just a matter of time before the police would come to search my room," she said, "so your key was irresistible. I had to take the passport, too, to find out who you were in case the guy downstairs stopped me in the lobby."

She jiggled the mirror (nervously, I thought) and a beam of light fell momentarily across my eyes reminding me (yet again no words were being spoken) of the interrogatory monocle of Charles Laughton's in the movie *Witness For The Prosecution.*

"I didn't know you were Noah John," she said.

The beam of light was shining right into my eyes.

"I didn't know you're 'Divi'," I said, without blinking.

She seemed to realize she was playing with the pocket mirror for the first time.

Without taking her eyes from me she threw the mirror on the bed.

It was a double bed.

"You're good at what you do," she said.

"So are you," I told her.

Without something to occupy her hands (she was never a *still* woman) she folded her arms across her chest.

I said, "Um, that, um, tee-shirt is gonna get you killed."

She smiled and said, "I'll give you one. I collect Khomeini tee-shirts."

"—gee, there must be tens . . ."

"—hundreds . . ."

"—thousands . . ."

"—millions . . ."

"Do you have a *name* that I could call you because I'd like to have a name that I can call you before I make my next move and 'Divi' is . . . 'Divi' doesn't make it for me as a name to call out while we're making love."

"My parents called me Lilith," she said. "My gear is on your balcony and we need to bring it in—" she started to add, but I had her head, her elegant small head between my hands.

I traced her eyebrows with my thumbs.

I kissed her eyes.

"Noah," she said, "there's a driver coming for us in six hours—"

Lucky for you, I said, six hours is my minimum.

in a body not your own

ENTER NOW into the sea of love.

One moment you are one thing—in the next, another.

One moment you are upright, stalwart and alone—in the next you are afloat, you are a couple.

One moment you're on dry land—in the next, surrounded, weightless, in a body not your own.

One moment you're determined to hang around Yaoundé, file two stories (one on music, one on AIDS)—and in the next some woman's standing in your underwear at the crack of dawn hellbent for Wum.

We hadn't slept (and I'll attest to every damn cliché about this newfound state—I hadn't felt that young in years!).

God—did I feel great!

Would you believe we spent the night just talking?

(Of course you wouldn't.)

But I'd never known such verbal fucking in my life.

In fact, I'd never known I *could* do both at once.

I mean—it wasn't like I found myself with Chatty Cathy, no—it was like we seemed to have stored up a lot of information that we needed to impart to one another.

And we only had six hours before the knock came on the door—and she had to pack up all her negs and clean the lenses and repack her gear—and, let me tell you, you would not believe how gadget intensive her profession is and all the shit photographers carry around while all us print guys need to do is sharpen up a pencil.

And she wasn't going to lose out on a photo opp to while away the hours with yrs. trly. (no way, not *this* girl) no matter how hard she'd fallen for me.

And (oh boy) was she ever smart.

Not Madame Curie smart, or Albert Einstein smart—but smarter than everyone else except—bless his bones, Edward R. Murrow—that I knew in this profession.

She was way out ahead of me, for instance, on the lake.

Her slant was simple:

DEATH—IT GETS TO EVERYONE

There were eighteen hundred or more dead from the gas cloud—and, since this was Africa—some of the dead were Bantu, some were Muslims, some were Fulani, some were Christian converts, some were Catholics.

"So who's going to bury them?" she'd asked me to consider, "and—possibly of more interest—*how*? With which god's blessing? Under which tradition? What Last Rites can the dead en masse demand?"

"Smart girl," I'd said, looking up momentarily from where I was plotting the coordinates of her elegant breasts, those heart-breaking parabolas, as we were propped on elbows, facing one another, side by side, in bed.

"You write it," she'd proposed—"I'll get the picture."

". . . and *then* we'll go to London?"

"No . . . then we'll go to Paris."

"Why Paris—I mean, besides the obvious sybaritic reasons?"

"Because there are direct flights to Paris from Douala, and because my darkroom's there."

"Can we make love on the direct flight from Douala?"

Opera People.

"—jesus, Noah . . ."

"—can we make love in your darkroom?"

We were interrupted exactly when she said we would be, at six o'clock that morning, by a soft rap on the hotel door and a loud male whisper, saying, "*Ma'selle Divi—*?"

"*—parle*!"

"'*Ci le mot ce matin—Air Tchad va go . . .*"

"*—merci, mon frère—donnez-nous dix minutes . . .*"

"Air *Chad*?" I said, coming fully to.

". . . only as a back-up," she said.

"—Air fucking Chad as a *back-up*? What's our first choice —Air Cuba?"

I was trying to get dressed—I couldn't find my underwear —and she was holding up two Khomeini tee-shirts. One said BIKINI AYATOLLAH. The other one said MOTORCYCLE IMAM.

"Nice—now you're trying to get us *both* killed."

She ended up wearing something moderately appropriate for visiting bush villages, but Lilith's clothing sense was as non-conservative as everything else about her. This might have been attributable to the fact that her mother—"Diva" —and her father—"Divo"—were Opera People. Or maybe she dressed so outlandishly because she never had to learn to dress in a becoming fashion because she looked so great in everything.

William Butler Yeats (another guy who loved smart women) wrote of his enchantment with Maud Gonne that they had only had the time to love, they had never had the time to know each other.

That was never true of me and Lilith—we got down to the serious business of knowing one another from the start—maybe because we were both reporters. We asked a lot of questions of ourselves and of each other.

From the start we worked astonishingly well together. And she was *fun* (take *that*, Wm. Butler Yeats—). Even when she was *The Ring* cycle incarnate, when her operatic *diva*-gations were larger than life, she was fun. She was the best company I've ever known. And she was certainly the most energetic woman I've ever met, both on the job and in the sack.

And she was beautiful—which was a bigger problem for her than she let on, I believe, because one of the keys of photojournalism is to deflect attention from yourself and from the camera.

She never wore a blush of paint or make-up, but she was a maniac for face creams. Her beauty was impossible to disguise. Her beauty was, I believe, so much a part of how she was in the world, the primary source, along with her intelligence, of her self-confidence—the reason (along with her intelligence) why she succeeded in her confidence tricks.

I never—ever—saw her flirt with anyone (not even me.)

She never used her beauty as a force that could manipulate, except to please me during sex, with the beauty of her body. She was not an exhibitionist, that way, except in bed. When she was working, she became a different person than the one who shared a bed with me—when she was working she could disappear like some women, passive bodies, can—and do—in sex. When she was working around people who weren't used to cameras, she became, I hate to say it, a near nothing, zen-like in the obliteration of her ego. She had the fiercest concentration I have ever seen—a trait, she claimed, inherited from her mother, the Diva, who once memorized the role of Senta in *Der Fliegende Holländer* in only thirteen hours.

From her impresario father, the Divo, she must have inherited her Fix-It genes, the genius needed to put up a circus or an opera on the road, the ability to find a last minute stand-in to sing Othello in Des Moines.

She was the best damn fixer I have ever worked with—she knew how and where to find the fastest mode of transportation, and best angle, the one person in a village or a city who could lead us through the alleys or the corridors to where it all was happening. She was not—as a photographer—as burdened by translation, by the added task of finding a translator before she could get to work—as I was. But every time we worked together on assignment, Lilith would come up with a local fixer for herself who was excellently qualified—more than qualified, in fact—for my own use.

And she was physically brave—a rare and always astonishing trait, a trait that one does not inherit, although I've known a lot of cowards and—to a person—they derive from other cowards. Bravery is individual.

Five hours, exactly, after that knock had come to our hotel door that morning, Lilith was leaning into the air from a helicopter with nothing to keep her from falling into Lake Nyos but me, at the end of the harness around her.

Her driver had taken us out to the end of the airfield in Yaoundé where there waited a heap of decrepitude the disrepair of which brought to mind that Edsel of the universe, that faded starduster of Han Solo's in *Star Wars* (whatever the hell she was called.) This machine—you should have been there to see it—was so battered and rusted it had to have been constructed in the sixties by someone with a serious misunderstanding of aerodynamics from a kit of spare parts which was missing its screws—or else it was a bit of military surplus picked up from the most miserably debased supply depot in the world.

In fact, it was Russian.

It was the biggest hunkajunk you could imagine.

It was a turbine 3-rotary blade Mil Mi-8, one of the few surviving examples of its questionable technology outside China and Albania.

And standing next to it was its own Han Solo, one of the coolest looking flyboys in a field which holds the record for producing cool-looking dudes, a man exuding mercenary suave (and a great humanitarian), Major Cecil Blades, U.S. Air Marine (retired).

I don't know if women come equipped with radar for scanning heat-emitting objects that come within the range of their beloveds, but men do.

Even before I got within ten feet of Cecil Blades my territorial border guards (good soldiers, all!) were in an altered state of Armed and Ready.

I hadn't even known Lilith twenty-four hours and already I was feeling jealous. That should have told me something.

Not that it was her fault (it wasn't). Cecil Blades was one of those guys—I can only think of astronauts and movie stars and maybe half a dozen baseball players—who epitomize the lanky cowboy philosopher-king who rides the range through all of us.

He was dressed like he was still in the Marines—Ray-Bans, flak jacket and camouflage—but as soon as he addressed us I could tell his formal regimental suit had been taken to the cleaners and forgotten.

"Copasetic," he noted, as I discharged the driver and helped unload Lilith's gear, "which one of you is talkin' money?"

"That depends," I said.

Cecil took a small calculator from his pocket.

All the service helicopters—mission teams and military rescue—had been commandeered in the necessity of finding and assisting the survivors, air-lifting the injured to safety, rounding up the dead. Up-country north of Bafoussam, in the vicinity of Wum and all around Lake Nyos, the rainy season was in full sog. The roads to the lake itself—dirt tracks at best, in a drier season—were unusable by even the best all-terrain vehicles, so the lake was virtually inaccessible, except by air. Chartering a prop presented problems of its own—namely that bush planes don't have the range per load that helicopters have, that they require greater landing space and that, airborne, they're always moving, which makes the subject of a photograph look, uh, *soft*—not Lilith's style.

She wanted to get in close on the lake—and she wanted to get in with *color* while the bottom chemicals were still churning—so she needed a chopper, though over water rotaries presented problems, too.

She had noticed all the oil rigs off the coast from her Air France window seat on the approach into Douala and she knew, from experience, that refineries and oil companies usually keep a fleet of choppers on retainer as trouble-shooters and eyeballers over spills and fires.

So she had tracked this wildcat Major down while I'd been swilling local brew with gin-gulled Duffins in Chez Josette the night before. Amazing woman.

She had promised Blades something like the fortune of the Grimaldis for the lease of his equipment overnight for an excursion to the cry-die up-country.

All we had to do was iron out a few details.

Like who was paying—and how much—and could the helicopter *fly*. I mean, there were books of the Bible that weren't as old as his machine looked, airframe-timewise.

"I've refitted her myself with a Kawasaki conversion," Blades said, failing to assuage my doubts.

"How much you weigh?" he asked me, then he added up

our weights plus all the gear, plotted the round trip course from Yaoundé to Lake Nyos back to the airport in Douala with a stopover in Wum.

"I have to charge you *in*surance for touching down in Wum," he said, and I noted his deep Southern inflection, "'cause they ain't no hangar there and I'll hafta spend the night with her myself, on shotgun."

He calculated the weight of fuel necessary to complete the mission, showed us the adjusted sum and said, "I take American Express." Lilith handed him her Agence France-Presse Gold Card.

Clearly I was working for the wrong company.

News costs money.

If Major (retired) Cecil Blades could charge a minor fortune for his air time in his heap of Russian crap, just imagine what it costs to keep a satellite up there, which is where all news is bounced from these days, for the sake of speed.

If it's news it cannot wait.

If it waits it isn't news.

If you wait you run the risk that someone else will make it news before you do.

We flew.

We were off the ground in thirteen minutes.

Chopper flight is always more exhilarating than bush planing, especially in cargo copters with the bays opened wide to allow the resident photographer to choose her views.

I scratched some notes about terrain—noting that as we headed north the ground got higher, greener, the sky got lower and the clouds got worse.

Major Blades had fitted out the cockpit with a nifty Sony intercom and I took the headset he offered me so the fine bones in my inner ear wouldn't be fan-bladed from the noise into fine mulch.

"You ever fly this route before?" I somehow managed to communicate with Cecil.

He nodded, affirmative.

"Where'd you train?"

He said something that I couldn't understand, until he showed me how to use the headset. Then, rather affably, he said, "Chinooks in Nam."

Chinooks—mo'*fuck*—I was as impressed as if he'd said he'd done a little brushwork on the ceiling of the Sistine Chapel.

"Is this baby legal?"

"Legal—? How d'you mean?"

"I mean—isn't she a piece of Russian classified?"

He flashed a smile in my direction.

"Don't believe everything you read in the papers!" he advised. He motioned with his chin toward the full fast rainy season yellow river down below, and its river falls, sending up a fog of mist and spume. "Sanaga River!" he instructed. "And Nachtigal Falls! At their most spectacular this time of year!" He cocked his head toward Lilith, aft. "Ask her if she wants us to go down so she can shoot the rapids—(that's a little *joke*, brother . . .)."

I went back and Lilith signaled "Yes!" to Blades and Blades swung us east then dropped into a low course on the water following the river as it ran above the falls. Then the river dropped away beneath us, like hot broth stirred into pearly froth.

Lilith shouted, "Hold me!" and I grabbed her by her waistband as Cecil dropped us parallel to the cascade (a really dangerous maneuver, I kept thinking) until amid the thundering water, we were face to face with our own rainbow.

We hovered there, suspended over those uneasy currents

until Lilith, flushed and soaking wet (again), ducked back inside the bay and sent Cecil a thumbs-up sign.

He swung us off the river, over land again, and shouted (I swear), "Hee-*haw*!"

Lilith smiled at me and began to wipe her lenses down.

"That was great," she said.

"Hey Noah!" Blades shouted. "Check through those boxes, will 'ya, and get us out some gas masks—And fix her to a harness, next time—I don't want to have to watch you lose her—"

I did as Blades instructed, then I sat down across from Lilith in the hold beside the open bay to watch the land.

Lilith had a Michelin map (Number 155) which wasn't very detailed and no help at all for navigating from our perspective, so I went forward to the cockpit and took the seat on the right hand of god and satisfied myself comparing the terrain below to how it figured on god's charts. *I am flying*, the brain tells itself—and I've always loved this part of being, fixing to a place, to an exactness, hilltop, shore or woman. I'm no artist of abstract conditions—what I need to know is where I am exactly, how I got there and how I can get out in case of fire.

"Space would really fuck me," I confessed to Cecil. "Outer space."

"Yeah it's freaky up there, a big black ocean," he agreed.

The first time I saw Africa it was from the air, flying into Tangier from New York on Air Maroc to go across the Strait one of those times the Spanish rattled swords along the border of Gibraltar.

And the first time I saw Europe, too, was from the sky—and Asia, and Australia.

But I had seen each continent before, in movies and in

photographs and paintings—I had pictured every continent's landfall through literature.

But places on the map, like women, cannot be realized, fully, except first-hand.

A map is rigid in exactness. A map does not mature through time.

I am flying, man insists, attempting to position his uncharted self within a plane.

This is where I am.

I am in love.

This is where we were in the beginning.

That is where we were when Love began.

GOD IS LOSING sleep over the cost of lives upon the parting of the Red Sea.

GOD IS LOSING sleep because of drowned Egyptians.

Five miles south of the airfield at Bamenda, still sixty miles away from Lake Nyos, Cecil hailed the tower on the radio to ask if it was safe, asphyxiation-wise, over the lake, and to file a provisional flight plan.

A World Health person told us, yes, air quality was A-okay but we should expect to see some human dead. If we found some human dead (he called them that) we should let him know, numbers and locations.

Then a Cameroon official came on the radio. "We are trying to assess what damage. Any count of dead you see will help. Livestock. Human dead. Number and location." There was a crackle on the line. Then he said, "Cattle in particular."

Cecil set his jaw.

"God is losing sleep," he said. "So we is countin' *sheep*."

There had been a downpour earlier, but as we started to ascend the higher elevations of the volcanic mountain chain —Cecil called each volcanic mountain a "ground obstacle" —we lost the rain but gathered clouds.

Cecil held to a height of only six or seven hundred feet above the ground, so where the gas cloud had rolled down the mountain from the volcanic lake, we could track its path by the white carcasses, bloated cattle on their backs, their legs extended like upturned nursery toys. The weird thing was, there were no carrion scavengers, no vultures—and if we had been down on the ground, we would have seen there were no flies on them, either.

The gas cloud had killed every living thing, except the vegetation.

When the lake came into view, it seemed to stun us all, including Lilith, because it was the color of dried blood.

The sun was high, and just as we approached, the sifting clouds exposed its pale white disk reflected on the surface of the lake like the negative of a dark pupil in a bloodshot eye.

"Tell me where you want me," Blades shouted to Lilith.

She had already shot a roll before the clouds blinked away the sun—then we played around with different angles for an hour with Blades doing fancy stuff to keep his downthrust off the water while I loaded cameras.

I was having a great time.

It was the best goddamn assignment we were ever on.

I filed two long pieces on it, with her photographs.

The first piece, about the lake, itself, made the front page of my paper two days later.

There is a legend in the hills around Lake Nyos about Mammy Water, it began. *A stone thrown in the water can be thrown back out by her, the legend says, as a bad omen. "Some mornings when you climb up to Lake Nyos," a local tribesman told me, "Mammy Water disappears and all that's where the lake had been are the ghosts of our ancestors, the shadows of the dead." The dead were certainly what you could see the night of August 21st* (I wrote.)

The other piece I wrote—a longer one about the cry-die—ran in the paper's Sunday magazine.

On the cover, in bright color, was one of Lilith's pictures of Lake Nyos, looking like that crimson eye.

On the inside, there were nine of her color portraits of the mourners at the cry-die—Bantu *fons* in their embroidered robes—the tall Fulani cattle-herder in his impeccably white robe—Father Denis, the officiating Catholic mission priest in Wum, his Celtic face fast-knit in grief—mourners sacked out for the night in a makeshift refuge inside the hold of Cecil's helicopter in the middle of a soggy field beside the Catholic mission.

Something happened on that assignment that set the standard for the way we worked, when we worked together.

From Cameroon, until she left me, I started writing *up* to Lilith's photographs, to try to match her standards.

She claimed I helped to make her better, too—but if you go back and look at Lilith's work from her years before we met until Berlin, you won't find any modulation in their quality.

She was great before she met me.

She was great while we were together.

She was great, again, without me.

I, on the other hand, was the better for her company, as was the first man for the first woman's.

Or maybe she had caught me at the bottom of one of those recurrent curves whose frequencies add bounce to one's mid-life cycle but fuck up the structure of self-confidence.

Or maybe I only *think* she sharpened my writing when what she really did was sharpen all my senses, raise the level of adventure, up the volume and increase the fun. Things *happened* around her, things happened *to* her more often than they did to me—things happened to *me* when I was with her, that hadn't happened to me before, things that vitiate conventions and enliven spectacles and circuses—and operas.

We were heading off the lake on a course for Wum—Blades and I had stopped counting the dead cattle once we realized there were going to be more than a thousand—when we spotted a stalled vehicle mired in the mud. I shouldn't say we spotted it—the driver heard us coming and was in the open waving his arms.

The driver was a grey-haired male, chubby, wearing one of those I-think-I-look-like-Hemingway-in-this safari suits that you see advertised for sale by mail in magazines like *Field & Stream*. His car, a Rover, was up to its door handles in mud. It was really fucked.

Going in to get a closer look at him posed all the targeting hazards for him as when the proverbial shit doth hit the proverbial fan.

"I sure as hell ain't landin' in no suck," Cecil observed. "Toss him the Bambi bucket and a hoist."

One problem with a helicopter is that you can't just let it idle at the curb while you jump out to grab a hot dog, so Cecil couldn't leave the cockpit to dash back and instruct us in the business of the Bambi bucket, and it fell to me and Lilith to unravel it.

"Fuck," Cecil was cursing. "Life is one long E-Vac mission . . . Find out what he wants . . . drop him down a message on the hoist."

I scribbled out a note in big black letters with one of Lilith's negative wax pencils, WHO ARE YOU? WHERE ARE YOU GOING? (". . . *très* Gauguin," Lilith wisecracked) and we lowered it down to him along with the pencil.

When the hoist reached him, he retrieved the message, felt through his pockets, started to run toward the Rover, slipped in the mud, searched through the Rover, emerged wearing a pair of thick-lensed reading specs, wrote out an answer, ran back to the hoist, slipped in the mud and waved at us to raise it.

IO SONO GIUSEPPE VERDI
VOLCANOLOGIST
the note read,
I GO AT WUM.

"*Giuseppe Verdi*?" I marveled at Lilith.

"Volcanologist?" she marveled back.

"How do you say, 'GET IN THE BUCKET, JOE,' in Italian," I asked as I scribbled out another note.

We sent down the bucket.

There ensued a sort of comic opera in mini, the sort of opera buffa that German composers, Wagner *und* Strauss, were convinced was the only kind of opera the Italians could compose.

Signor Verdi ran to the Rover and began to haul out what looked to be bottles of olive oil and bottles of vinegar, which he loaded with care into the bucket.

Then Signor Verdi attempted to load *himself* in. (As I said, he was chubby. Not as chubby as Pavarotti, but chubby enough to give Cecil aerodynamic concern.)

Halfway into the bucket he seemed to remember something back in the Rover so the process was reversed and then repeated (this time he hauled what seemed to be a mason jar of ripe tomato sauce).

As it turned out all these things were water samples from the lake, but saying they were water samples doesn't make it a good story.

Then he went back to the Rover a third time for what appeared to be a crate of wine (it *was* a crate of wine) which he placed next to the Bambi bucket, mounted, and climbed in.

Before lifting off, Cecil looked at us and said, "Baby, if that line snaps, we leave Cameroon one flat Italian pancake and *we split*, you hear?"

Lilith and I tried to winch the Bambi back into the hold but Signor Verdi was too *grasso* for us, so we kept a careful eye on him, like angels, from the bay door.

As we rose above the trees Signor Verdi gripped the bucket rim for all his life—but then, after a few minutes, when the sway subsided, he stretched out his arms and began to gesture at the landscape.

"What the fuck's he doing?" I asked Lilith.

'Hey what the fuck's he *doing*?" Cecil shouted. "Tell him to hold still!"

Lilith got down on her knees and cocked an ear toward Verdi.

"I think," she said, "I think he's . . . singing."

He *was* singing—fucking volcanologist was swinging in a bucket over Cameroon gesturing like a mad man, singing the "La donna è mobile" aria from *Rigoletto* at the top of his Italian lungs.

Lilith smiled from ear to ear at me and shook her head.

"My father hated that aria," she said.

She tucked her head onto my shoulder and put her arms around me and we knelt at the bay door, entranced.

"You should take his picture," I suggested. "This is probably a 'high point' in his career."

As she aimed her telephoto at him, Cecil banked the chopper slightly on its way down into Wum and the helicopter's shadow floated on the tree-tops under Signor Verdi.

"Noah," Lilith said, focusing, "look at him—what does this remind you of?"

I stared at Signor Verdi as he swung, his arms outstretched, christlike, from the helicopter.

"Aw*shit*," I said. "This is the front scene of *La Dolce Vita* —I wonder if Signor Verdi knows?"

I didn't wonder long, because as we lowered over Wum I saw firsthand the ways each person brings his or her own set of references, his or her own art pack, deck of bards, table of discontents and contents into every fresh experience.

The cries and shouts that rose from the crowd as we came down with Giuseppe Verdi on our tether onto some vacant land next to the Catholic mission that had been turned into a sort of chopper car-park were full of wonder, awe and terror.

There were six or seven hundred people there, standing about in tribal groups, when Cecil made our wind blow on them. Some ran, some stood, some hid—when the bucket was a few feet from the ground, it was surrounded.

We watched Signor Verdi being lifted out, and then he gave us a big wave and I winched his nest back in as Cecil took us over to an empty spot of soggy ground about a thousand feet away, and down.

It was two o'clock in the afternoon, and the cry-die was slated to begin, appropriately, at the setting of the sun.

Cecil locked up the controls and secured the bay doors—but even so, Lilith packed nearly all of her equipment onto her person.

"*Light*," she cursed.

"More like 'heavy'," Cecil said. "You goin' for the night?"

"Probably," she answered.

"Well you know where I'll be, but there's only one Paris flight tomorrow from Douala and it's at ten hundred hours. So get your asses back by o-seven hundred or you're fucked."

Over the next seven hours, until sunset, and through the

vigil of the night, I saw Lilith only a few times, crouching cat-like on the ambit of the crowd, or moving through the silent mass, a spectre among mourners.

Some peoples are not silent in their griefs, some funerary customs rage, as Dylan Thomas has admonished, against the dying of the light, some peoples ululate and rend their voices and their sleeves—but not the people who had come to mourn at Wum, survivors of the cloud that swept into their villages and killed their neighbors and their families. There is dignity in silence—but the silence that had gathered on that afternoon translated, also, as the sound of incomprehension. Some of the smaller villages—Cha, Isu, Kam, But and Fang—had lost more than half their populations in a single hour. In the larger market town, Lower Nyos, it was estimated that three quarters of the families living there had lost at least one of its members—and not all the dead had yet been discovered.

Outside the hospital in Wum—an ugly building in an ugly town—refugees had lined up to register with World Health volunteers the names of members of their families missing since that night, accepting, silently, the understanding that anyone still unaccounted for since then was most certainly dead. Two large boards had been assembled—one posting a list of persons missing; one posting a list of persons dead. On the "missing" board people were attaching tribal bits of sympathetic magic—and on the "dead" board people had begun to hang up beads and crosses, wreaths and reeds. This part of Cameroon was Anglophone, so I was okay on my own, without a translator, although the spoken English was almost entirely pidgin. But so great was their grief, few people were speaking. And the one person who was speaking most, out of necessity, was an Irish Jesuit, the guiding spirit of the cry-die, Father Denis.

We be ask God plenty question, I heard him tell a man whose wife and son had died, *Why this bad ting be?*

"He's in shock," he turned to me and said, his natural brogue restored, "We all are."

I attached myself to Father Denis and followed him around that afternoon as he went about the priestly business of seeing to the needs of the survivors, before he tended to the souls of the departed. Hundreds of refugees had come into Wum in the wake of the disaster, afraid to stay in their own villages until Allah, god or Mammy Water had been appeased and exorcised. They had come to Wum with nothing—and the Catholic mission's resources to house and feed them was severely taxed. "There's me," Father Denis said, moving rapidly down Wum's main thoroughfare, "the Red Cross, the World Health, the French, the Swiss, Allah and God, of course—plus a smattering of Camerooni officialdom—*versus* sin, starvation, athlete's foot, jock itch, crotch rot, worms, amoebic cysts, dysentery, giardia, hepatitis, typhoid, meningitis and all the various sexually transmitted hells Dante couldn't begin to catalogue, bless his heart, if he were still among us." We were standing in front of the (under the circumstances, unfortunately named) Lake Nyos City Hotel to beg bedding and shelter from the manager, when through the door came a newly showered chubby figure in a fresh safari suit...

"*Maestro*!" I exclaimed.

"Ah—*amico mio*!" he said, recognizing me. "Meester Hellcopter!"

He clapped his arms around me in an emotional embrace.

"*Dio, Padre*—this man, he save my life!" he explained to Father Denis.

"Father Denis—Giuseppe Verdi. Signor Verdi is a volcanologist."

(May I say the introduction sparked a twinkle in the *padre*'s eye?)

(It did.)

"I am a great admirer of your namesake," Father Denis said.

"And I, yours—*Father*," Verdi answered.

"Do you . . . sing?"

"Does he sing!" (Actually I didn't know if he was any good.) "Sing him something!" I urged.

Signor Verdi shrugged.

Then he stepped back and performed the first two verses of "La donna è mobile" (again), *bravura*-ing his way up to that final note (C above the middle C?) until he shook the bats out of the palm trees (the word "tenor" derives from Latin *tenere*, "to hold"—and Signore Verdi held that note about as long as it would have taken Father Denis to recite the whole Apostles' Creed three times.)

"*Musicabilissimo*!" the *padre* panted at the finale—a term I'd never heard before, but one which sounded, considering the occasion, apt and Joycean.

"Thanks God," Verdi demurred.

"Pray, will you sing a tune tonight? I'd be most grateful," Father Denis begged.

"—tonight, what is?"

"A funeral mass."

"I sing only Verdi. Is small promise I make to Gods."

"I'm the first to honour any pledge a man makes to God . . . Perhaps—if I may be so bold—you'd honour us with something from the last act of . . . *Otello*?"

Signor Verdi's eyes welled up. He insisted that we let him buy us a *rinfresco*, a *ristoro*, something that would serve to *rinfrescare* us, and although I readily accepted, Father Denis had to beg off to go on begging, so Signor Verdi and I retired to the nearby outdoor café—called (believe *this*) the Peace, Unity and Hygienic Restaurant—where he told me all I needed to know and more about exploding lakes and their volcanoes.

"Is make the best volcanologists in world, *i Italiani*," he assured me. "*Perchè*? I show you." He started counting on his fingers. "*Vesuvios. Stromboli. Etna. Messina.* Myself, I am *napoletano*, from the Napoli—the best. Sometime *i Francesi*, they are good. You know *i Francesi*?"

"—French?"

"—sometimes good volcanologists. Not as good as *i napoletani*, but pretty good."

"—but there aren't any volcanoes in France."

"—in Mont Pelée. Soufrière. In Martinique department. In —how you say—*Ca-reeb*."

There is a direct link between earthquakes and volcanoes, Signor Verdi told me. (I am translating freely, here—*very* freely, because his English was, at best, idiosyncratic, and I had learned what little Italian I knew in pizzerias and at the movies.) The earth is 4.6 billion years old but we (I think he meant mankind, and not merely the Italians) still haven't learned how the earth operates, nor have "we" learned how to prevent or to predict its massive disturbances (*i disastri*). Signor Verdi, himself, loved volcanos (I understand the word for Love)—you *had* to love volcanoes, he told me, because it was through volcanoes that water spewed, creating oceans, and gases spewed, creating atmosphere—it was volcanoes that created Eden, Signor Verdi said. He was soon sketching in my notebook, confirming my belief that all Italians *can* sing and draw and cook, and writing out the words I couldn't understand—in particular

MOHOROVIČIĆ DISCONTINUITY

otherwise known as *the Moho*—the shifting boundary between earth's mantle and earth's crust which he called *crostini*.

"Under Nyos Lake—is peep," he said.

"—'peep'?"

"Pipa."

"—pi*pa*?"

"How you say—pi*pay*? *Francesi* volcanologists, they don't believe pi*pay*. They believe, instead, the *tremolo* . . . a—how you say—tremor to make the *Lago* Nyos to *esplodere*. Me, I say is volcanic pipay underneath the *lago*. The *Francesi* say, 'No no no no no—*this-a not a pipay*.'"

". . . '*Celui-ci n'est pas une pipe*'?"

"—*appunto*!"

Lake Nyos is situated on The Cameroon Line, a volcanic chain ranging from Annobón Island in the Atlantic, northeast through Mount Cameroon toward Wum. Signor Verdi's theory, a contested one by the French, was that there was a volcanic *pipe* beneath Lake Nyos, connecting it to a magma source deep within earth's mantle. However, it was the lake's carbon dioxide composition—not the gases from the volcanic pipe—that had been the cause of the fatalities.

"Here," he said. "You stay. I get. I show," and he ran off to the hotel to bring me vials of water samples he had taken from the lake.

"You are go to Paris? You deliver these for me? To *I Francesi. Proof*," he argued. He showed me samples he had taken from the lake at varying depths. Carbon dioxide, escaping from molten rock into the ground water, had, over time, seeped into the lake and had been held in a dissolved state on the bottom by the gravitational weight of the water on the surface. But when the pipe erupted—or, as the French claimed, there was a tremor or a landslide under the Lake—

the mass of suspended carbon dioxide shot to the surface and erupted into the atmosphere.

A sample of water taken by him from the surface earlier that day still bubbled like a champagne inside the vial.

"It was just like cork from the *spumanti*, pa-pa-*boom*!" he pantomimed.

"Why does the water look like blood?"

"*Ferro*—is iron. From bottom. It is oxidize."

"Can this disaster reoccur?"

"Oh sure. Will happen many time. This is not the first. Over there—near *Lago* Victoria—*Lago* Kivu, worse a thousand times. *Carbona* dioxide and—how you say it—*metano*, the methane. Some *giardino de eden, eh?—in questo mondo* . . . some Garden of Eden, this world."

It had started to rain in heavy sheets. I took Signor Verdi's water samples and their delivery instructions with me and headed back to the mission, where more people had gathered in preparation to honor the dead. I milled among them, stopping to talk to a few when their eyes or a gesture invited me to. That's how I learned about Mammy Water and how I learned that, on some days, the lake disappeared. I sat with some Bantu, sharing a meal of cassava and maize with them. Then, at sunset, the Fulani muezzins called Muslims to prayer, people began to give voice to their grief, a sighing arose, and the cry-die began.

There was singing—some anguished, some hopeful, some Verdi, some plainsong, some chanting. There was dancing to drums. It lasted into the night, until—like all weeps and catharses—it exhausted itself.

Around two in the morning I made my way back to the chopper and found Cecil sitting up in an open bay door, wide awake. From the hold there was a dim light from a lantern. Inside, there were about thirty people, women and children, asleep.

the aroma of Southern tobacco

"It was raining," he said.

"It sure was," I agreed.

He shrugged. "They were standing out there in the rain, so I—"

I shot him a smile.

"Did you eat?" I asked him.

"I have my own mess. Where's your girl?"

"She'll be back in the morning."

I found a dry patch on the floor of the hold and stretched out beside him.

"I guess you two have worked that all out."

"I guess we have," I agreed.

"How long have you two been together?"

I looked at my watch.

"Uh, two days."

"—don't shit me."

I let him know with a look that I wasn't kidding.

"*Huh*," he said.

He let out a whistle.

"Well," he said slowly. "Son of a bitch. I guess when it happens, it happens that way."

He pulled out a pack of Camels and offered me one. I declined. When he lit up, the aroma of Southern tobacco cut through the damp swampy night, and I asked him, "What are you doing here, Cecil?"

"Just sittin' watch, my man."

"No—I mean how'd you end up in Cameroon?"

"No."

". . . 'no'?"

"That's not the question."

". . . it's not?"

"No, the question is not how'd I end up in the place that my people have come from—the question is, how did my people end up in Virginia? And you know the answer to *that.*"

"Where did the name 'Blades' come from?"

". . . oh, the first freeman. He was a tinker—you know, went around, did some farrier work, sharpened axes and saws, sharpened knives. 'Mister Blades', they started to call him. '*Why lookee younder ain't but Mister Blades*'—and shit like that. He passed it to his son, on down the line. My father moved us right on up the social ladder by sharpening lawn mowers. So I decided I would set my sights a little higher, set my sights on *high*-class blades—and it was either Air Marines or figure skating and, as well you know, we don't harvest too much ice down there in Tidewater."

"You ever think of going back?"

"Sure I 'think' about it. Race card too strong a suit back there."

"Ever married?"

"Nope."

"You ever want to?"

"Nope."

". . . sounds final."

"Well I'll tell you somethin'." He slid off the chopper and threw his cigarette into the mud. "I haven't seen too many reasons to have faith in man's condition," he announced. A mosquito caught him on the arm just then and Cecil slapped at it. I could see a smear of blood, even in the darkness, as he walked away.

I must have slept a little bit, but then I heard the women waking one another to evacuate the helicopter because of me, so I roused myself and hauled my ass outside, insisting, through my gestures that they stay inside, and rest in peace.

At o-six hundred Cecil woke them, got them out, and started going through his chopper drills.

I was so tired I could hardly stand.

At six fifty-nine Lilith appeared and Cecil said, "All *right*—let's do some flyin'!"

"Hey," she said to me.

"Hey yourself," I said and took her in my arms and kissed her.

There were two points of blood in her eyes—those two rubies I had noticed before. I would learn that when she was as exhausted as she was that morning, or as over-worked, her eyes looked like they were bleeding.

"Noah," she said.

Cecil snuck a peek at us.

"Do you know what we've got?" she asked.

"Yeah," I said, and shot a look at Cecil, "I know what we've got . . ."

"Fasten those seat belts, back there!" Cecil vamped.

"—an *exclusive*!" Lilith said.

"—5—4—3—2—1—and . . ."

"Didn't you notice?" Lilith shouted under the noise.

"—lift-*off*!" Cecil roared.

"—WE WERE THE ONLY JOURNALISTS THERE—!" Lilith cried, as if she were trying to get me to come to my senses. As if I was born yesterday. As if we were Adam and Eve on a new posting, instead of a man and a woman, newly in love, longing for good food and wine and a bath and a bed and a long fuck or two or two thousand, in Paris.

1986

ILE SAINT LOUIS PARIS

Firsts

I WOULD NEVER HAVE GONE TO GREECE *had it not been for a girl named Betty . . .*

. . . That's not me, that's Henry Miller, writing one of the great first lines. In fact, my favorite.

I would never have gone to Paris in August had it not been for a woman named Lilith.

And since we were flying First Class in the last two seats available that morning out of Africa, we drank champagne and played the lovers' game of Firsts.

It had been Lilith's guile, not surprisingly, that had secured us seats with no advance reservations on the already overbooked flight out of Douala. But to my credit, once I fell into the rhythm of her cunning, I was able to vanquish the initial resistance to our boarding the plane on the runway without tickets by claiming that Signor Verdi's samples of lake sludge and fizzy water were a matter of weighty scientific importance and timely significance to the future of research in France.

Lilith flashed her French passport and I flashed the samples and Cecil flashed his flyboy stuff and the purser let us board without vetting us through immigration because—why else? —we were mud-caked and disgusting but, like him, we were First Worlders needing a way out of the Third World.

As far as I was concerned, we were getting out, getting from the preface to the text, from the accident of place where we had met to the incidents Love needs to shape its axis.

Now it starts, I thought. *Now* is when we start as lovers, not back at the Mont-Fébé in Yaoundé, but *now*, here, on this airplane and in Paris.

Little did I know that love is always starting over, reinventing its dimensions. There is no first day of creation between lovers, there are days and days of making love, inventing it, of shaping it, of making it exist while living it.

Creating love is unlike any other function of creation because its form is immaterial. Can you see it? Can you touch it? Its existence, at the least, is in the mind of the beholder. Its existence is confirmed, at best, in tenderness and by avowal.

You make love like you're playing with death, I had to tell her at the end of our acrobatic first night back in Africa.

"Playing, yes, but not with death."

"With what, then?"

"Playing with what's after death."

If one believes in God—and I don't—then I have to think that that god must be the reflection of one's life, as each love is a reflection of both lovers.

A bitter person will create an unforgiving god, a guilty person will create a god of mercy. Only psychopaths love for the same reason or the same way every time they take a lover. So it was her newness that I loved at first, not her youth, her newness. Blinded by and burdened with the visions and perceptions that any man my age has acquired about Women, on the flight to Paris I got down to the tedious exactness of conducting a serious discovery. I played, for hours, with her hands, for instance, committing to my memory for future use all their lines and muscles. I circled 'round her wrists, I cuffed them with my fingers, I focused my investigation on her forearms. I instigated a champagne-soaked archeological dig into her life and history. Lovers, after all, are the first and only witnesses to the event called Love—lovers are Love's first reporters. I've been asking questions in my sleep for what seems my entire lifetime, so I held her hand and led her through the game of Firsts.

FAITHFUL CORRESPONDENT (ME): First things first. Tell me your favorite first line of a poem.

LIL: Rage.

"... *sorry*?"

"'*Rage*, Goddess, sing the rage of Peleus' son Achilles ...'"

"—*fuck*, a classicist. I would never have suspected ..."

"—yours?"

"'Now to the come of the poem, let me be worthy & sing holily the natural pathos of the human soul ...'"

(blank expression)

"Ginsberg."

(blank expression)

FAITHFUL CORRESPONDENT: *Allen* Ginsberg.

"Never read him."

"Never *read* him?"

LIL: Favorite first line of a novel?

"No, no, this is my game, *you* go first ..."

"'A screaming comes across the sky.'"

"Good one."

"—yours?"

"'I never would have gone to Greece had it not been for a girl named Betty ...'"

(blank expression)

FAITHFUL CORRESPONDENT: Henry Miller. *The Colossus of Maroussi.*

"That's not a novel, Noah."

"First memory?"

"Sucking."

"Falling. First time in an airplane?"

"When I was two years old. 1958."

"1966, when I was twenty. First time in Paris?"

"Same trip—in '58. That's when Divo and Diva brought me home from Brooklyn."

"Brooklyn?"

"I was born in Brooklyn. But 'home', for them, was Paris."

"My first time in Paris was in August '66, before my senior year of college. First . . . movie?"

"De Sica's *Umberto D.* I saw it with Divo."

"—that's the one with the old man and the dog?"

". . . that's the one."

"I *love* that movie!"

"So did Divo. Not a kid flick, though. I thought Divo was trying to lose me, after that. I identified with the dog."

"Mine was *Bambi.* My mom took me. Another rotten choice. Bambi's mother buys it."

"You identified with Bambi?"

"Who else would you identify with in 'Bambi'? You identified with a *dog* in *Umberto D*—"

"I was only five years old. Why identify with *anything* you see in film?"

"Because that's the magic of the moving picture, *shweet*-heart . . ."

"—*is* it? Who do you identify with in *Casablanca*?"

". . . oh, please, do you need to ask?"

"Who do you identify with in *Kagemusha*? In *La Règle du Jeu*? In *Birth of a Nation*?"

ME: Don't you ever go to films in color?

(Big smile. Accompanied by a swallow of champagne.)

"I'm color-blind, Noah."

"*Whoa* . . . rare in a woman."

"Very rare."

"Where?"

"—'where?' On my retinas."

"I mean, where in the spectrum?"

"Across the band."

"But you *can* see some, right? Colors?"

"Yes, I think so. Brown. Brown is thought to be the most mysterious color, did you know that? Because it's not isolated in the spectrum. Your eyes are brown, aren't they? Even if they're not, they are to me."

"Do you know you get two red points in yours when you're tired?"

"I've been told."

"Can you tell the color of my shirt?"

"I would guess it's tan."

"—and blood? What color does that look to you?"

"A color value that I recogize as 'red'. *And* 'green' . . ."

"So you never shoot in color."

"I always shoot in color. But my film is always black and white."

"I interviewed Ansel Adams, once."

"—well, *he*'s not color-blind."

"No, I mean, so I understand about those shades, those shadow values. The zones. He drives this big old white sedan with a California license plate that says 'ZONE V'."

"—well, I'm glad you told me that in case I ever find myself behind him on the highway—otherwise I would have thought 'ZONE V' referred to the erotic."

". . . and he fries his prints in his kitchen microwave. The whites. It keeps his whites from drying down, he says. From dulling. Do you do that?"

"I don't make art prints, Noah."

"But did you ever think you would?"

"No."

"Is there a darkroom in your house in Paris?"

"Yes."

"I know I asked you before, but . . . can we make love there?"

"Yes."

"Have you made love in it before?"

"Yes."

"Was it the first darkroom you made love in?"

"No."

"Where was the first?"

"At my teacher's."

"*With* your teacher?"

"Sure."

"Was he your first?"

"Christ, no."

"When was your first?"

"At fourteen."

"Where?"

"The Plaza. New York City. Don't look so pathetic, Noah."

"Who was he?"

"A man. First tragedy?"

"Your last two answers."

"—seriously."

"Boy stuff. Dog died when I was nine. Yours?"

"Parents died when I was seven."

"I'm sorry."

"First time under fire—?"

"No. I want to know your first love."

"My first love is myself."

". . . first time *in* love. Romantically."

"Never."

"—'never'?"

"No."

"—you've 'never' loved?"

"I don't think so."

"—you don't think so?"

"No."

"—jesus, that scares the crap out of me."

"Why? It should encourage you."

"—how can you *not* have ever loved?"

"Because," she said. "There has to be a *first* for everything. Doesn't there, Noah?"

Her hands, I should tell you, were astonishingly strong, with tapered fingers so enlarged at the knuckles that she couldn't wear rings. What I hadn't noticed yet, because I hadn't seen her hold a pen, was that she was ambidextrous in all manual pursuits (pub darts, speed dialing), except in writing, in which she was decidedly southpaw. Her left arm was slightly more muscled, and her overall upper body strength was, for a woman, way above the norm. She was five feet, nine inches tall. Her blood type (listed in her French passport) was A-negative. She was born in Brooklyn, New York, on the 14th April, 1956, a birth day tailor-made for a child of operatic parents, she explained, because it was the anniversary of the day Lincoln was shot and the sinking of the *Titanic*. Also listed in her passport, which I read through page by page with her permission to reconstruct where she'd *been* all my life, was her full name: Lilith Luciana da Vinci. Her passport photo resembled Jean Seberg (if she'd had dark hair) in *Breathless*.

"*Da Vinci*?" I said.

"Yeah—get it? *D*a *V*inci, 'D.V.', Divi. *C'est moi.*"

"—but it's like belonging to a family called Einstein . . . or, Verdi. Or Pythagoras."

"It's just a place name."

"—*I* know it's a place name. But it's not Beltville, is it? Even if it's as common a name as pigshit in Tuscany, it just happens to be a name that's shared by the most divergent thinker of his age, probably *the* most universal genius of all time . . ."

"So? What's your point?"

". . . if my name was da Vinci I'd fucking use it."

"It's a blood thing. Divo didn't approve."

"—a 'blood' thing?"

"—between the *toscani* and the Neapolitans. Divo was from Naples. His mother was from Naples. His opera blood was *napoletano*. Caruso was his distant cousin. Da Vinci was his father's name, a northern name, so Divo dropped it. Have you been to Vinci?"

"Sure—everybody there has red hair and is left-handed and claims they are direct descendants of the great Leonardo, and the drive north from Vinci over Monte Albano to Pistoia is one of the most beautiful in the world."

"Is there something I should know about you and landscapes? Because I'll tell you right up front, I don't do them."

"I know you don't. I don't think I've ever seen a photograph of yours that didn't have the human figure in it, dead or alive. That's why I was surprised back there with Cecil at the waterfall . . ."

"—there were women washing clothing at the bottom."

"—there *were*? And by the way," I said, speaking of washing and clothing, "where do you get these things?" We had both washed up in the First Class heads and changed our clothing, and she was wearing a clean Khomeini shirt which read, "QUM ÇI, QUM ÇA".

"I shop at The Fascist Outlet," she told me.

Then I asked her to explain how and why Divo and Diva had come to call their only daughter "Lilith".

She would always say that she was not a natural storyteller, which wasn't true—she was a gifted storyteller; rambling, true, often losing a story's thread or starting on a story only to abandon it, unfinished, in favor of another unrelated one which had intruded on her memory, but she owned the visualist's magic lantern, the ability to shadow and to shape, to develop in the listener an animated mental image. That eye which framed and cropped the details of her photographs also guided her selection when she spoke—she wouldn't tell you everything, sometimes she wouldn't tell you the important thing, but everything she told you you could see, in black and white.

She did not so much describe her parents, as she seemed to light them. Only later at her Paris flat, a large apartment on the Ile St-Louis she had inherited from them at age seven, could I compare the sense of them that she imparted through her stories to the way they were, the way they looked, in portraits and in photographs—and when I saw their photographs I knew at once that I was seeing people I had come to know from her descriptions. They were, in many ways, so much alike they could have been mistaken for twins, instead of having taken one another as husband and wife. Both of them were small, he was five feet, she was four feet ten, which did not limit Divo's career prospects (he wore lifts, as did his cousin Caruso), but her height severely compromised Diva's standing in leading soprano rôles because she was almost invariably obliged to sing her arias into her tenors' crotches, at approximately the same height as their penises, which would have made for great burlesque, but which made for unintentionally comic opera, especially in the *bel canto* rôles. Her stage career was therefore brief and limited almost entirely to the rôle of Cio-Cio-San in *Madama Butterfly*, for which she didn't have to stretch. But she became a brilliant and meticulous *maestra*, along with Divo, who accepted only two or three students every year and owned the most respected musical instrument repair and restoration studio in the 4th *arrondissement*, a little shop called Orphée in the rue du Pont Louis-Phillipe. They knew everyone in Paris opera in the forties and the fifties, and everyone knew them. But of all the geniuses who crossed his threshold, no one came close to claiming Divo's respect and adulation as did the *diva di tutte dive*, The Callas.

From the moment Divo first saw Maria Callas in Serafin's production of *I Puritani* in Venice in 1949, he became obsessed with a grand plan to commission an opera written expressly for her.

"My parents loved each other, and they loved opera, and they loved Maria—and that was all the love they had in them," Lilith told me. Unfortunately La Callas never repaid their love in kind. Divo was a little person in the grander constellation of real stars—and he was from the south, a little coarse despite his dandyisms, an easy weeper, like Caruso: common. In his suit to woo Maria, Divo was up against an insider's insider, the elegant film director, Luchino Visconti. No one ever whispered that Visconti's family might have had Black Hand connections, as they whispered about Divo's.

Divo was a puppet-maestro, Visconti was a genius. And

soon after she started working with him at La Scala in Milan in 1955, La Callas fell in love with Luchino, and she had no time, no time at all, to hear of grand plans from a bantam *napoletano* in a pair of platform shoes, even when Divo and Diva went to petition her in person in Milan.

They were in the first tier of La Scala on the night of January 8, 1955, for Maria's première in *Andréa Chérnier*, when, on the final B of the "La mamma morta" at the end of the third act, Callas lost control and let the note go wide and the local *tebaldiani* went wild and pelted her with boos and verbal raspberries. It was, according to Lilith, who had the story from Divo, *una vergogna, un delitto.*

"Divo and Diva blamed the fracas on Tebaldi's claque," she told me. "Divo said Tebaldi had the galleries papered with her fans, but who knows about these things. Divo liked stories that pitted women against women, woman against woman, cat-fight stories. I think in some way, it excited him. He used to pinch his face into this look of horror when he said the name 'Tebaldi', and I'll tell you, the whole time I was growing up, even after Divo and Diva had died, I believed the phrase *i tebaldiani* was the universal word for all shits and monsters because of the way they used to spit it out. But if you listen to the live recording of that night—I have it at home, I'll play it for you—you can hear that Callas was attempting to achieve a deeper pathos in the word '*lamore*' on that high B and that the audience response was undeserved."

"—do you sing?"

"Oh god no, if they hadn't died when I was seven, to this day I'd be a lasting disappointment to my parents."

"—because I better tell you right up front that you can fit the sum of what I know about opera through a needle."

"Me too."

"—oh come on. It doesn't sound that way."

"—well, I had seven years of intense indoctrination, so I still retain a bit of it. Plus, I still live in that house."

"Are they going to greet us at the door?"

"No, not you. Me. They're always there to greet me. Them, and Maria Callas . . ."

So (she went on) the next day, January 9, 1955, after Callas's disgrace at La Scala, Divo and Diva went back to Paris inflamed, obsessed and otherwise in an operatic hissyfit over the need to find an heroic subject for their opera for Maria—and one week later, while buying salt beef from M. Goldenberg in the rue des Rosiers, Divo heard the Jewish legend of the woman known as "Lilith".

"He went looking everywhere," she said, "and finally he found someone at the Brooklyn Academy of Music in New York who knew the legend well enough to write the libretto, and then he and Diva moved to Brooklyn and they worked on the idea for a year and nothing came of it and they didn't get an opera for Maria by that name, but they got me while they were there, and so they called me Lilith."

"—they got you instead of the opera?"

"—yeah. Instead. So here we are. What else do you want to know? You're Noah, I'm Lilith. Two names from the Bible."

"—except . . ."

"—except you never heard of 'Lilith' in the Bible, right?"

"Right."

"—chick God made for Adam before Eve."

"—wait."

"—really."

"There's a woman before Eve? In the Bible?"

"How drunk are we, Noah?"

"Well we're re-writing the Christian canon so I don't think we're very sober."

"—well, she's in there. Black and white. Adam didn't like

She wasn't blond.

her because . . . whyever. She wasn't blond. So God sent her out of Eden to a cave beside the sea, and He created Eve."

"—is this true?"

"I swear, it is the skinny."

"—you have this on good authority?"

"I have this on tape. It's in the Talmud."

"Can I quote you?"

"—only if you get the spelling right."

I knew less about Talmudic legends than I knew about *bel canto*—but, hell, if love wasn't about learning, what was it about?

Soon after that—or maybe even during that—we fell asleep, Lilith's head against my thigh, my head thrown back against the seat, our hands entwined, my arm around her pelvis. We slept a needed sleep for several hours, then I woke up, as I always do from a fear brought on by a change of altitude, as we approached Marseilles. Lilith didn't stir. I touched her face. *Neat head*—I've said that about her, but every time I woke anew or saw her after having been away from her for any length of time, even a day, it was the neatness of her head, the bone of it, its sheerness and its neat ears—and the fact that her hair was cropped—that brought me close to tears, reminding me each time I saw her of the way I felt when I *first* saw her.

We were scheduled to be on the ground for only half an hour in Marseilles, but after those passengers not going on to Paris had disembarked, the plane was boarded by two *douaniers* and a cop. Lilith slept right through this, or pretended to, turning on her side and nuzzling her face between my legs as I presented both our passports.

"*Quelque chose à déclarer*?" I was asked.

"No," I said in English.

"*—haschisch*? *—kif*?*—héroïne*? *Vous parlez français*?"

"No," I said, again, in English.

Through the fabric of my trousers, I felt Lilith exhale hotly on my thigh.

"You come from Cameroon, yes?"

"Actually I come from Petersburg, Virginia. It says so right in there," I said, pointing to the little book of mine stamped with the spread Union eagle that he held between his hands.

"How long in Cameroon?"

"Three days, two nights. It says so right in there," I said, again, pointing and pretending to forget my exit visa wasn't stamped.

The other guy—the cop—said, "Did you practice sexual intercourse while in Equatorial Africa?"

"—*what*?"

Lilith moved her finger, slightly, on my leg.

"Intercourse," he said. "You know this word? Did you practice sexual intercourse in Africa?"

What is this? I thought, a remake of *The French Connection? Did I pick my toes in Poughkeepsie?*

"With an Equatorial African," he said, "of either sex, just answer yes or no."

"No."

"'No', you did not?"

"*No*, I will not answer. What is this *about*?"

They were poking through our stuff by then, and Lilith's play-acting as *La Sonnambula* was wearing a bit thin, when they found Signor Verdi's sample case containing vials from the red lake.

"What is this?"

"Water," I explained.

"—*wa-ater*?"

"—*red*?" another asked.

"—not *blood*?"

At that moment the woman named in honor of the opera that was never written for Maria Callas awoke, and there ensued a drama—full of accusations, guilt, revenge and resolution, all in French—that would have made her parents proud.

In the end, the *marseillaises* marched away with Signor Verdi's sample box, some beads, and two carved Bamiléké ritual masks of questionable provenance confiscated from some guy in Coach. "Are we going to have to go through this again at Charles de Gaulle?" I asked Lilith.

She was staring at the backs of the departing *gendarmerie.*

"What's it like landing back in England on a flight from Africa these days?" she asked me.

"—don't know, haven't done it for a year," I said. "Why?"

"Would U.K. public health inspectors ask you about sex?"

"—these were 'health inspectors'?"

"Two were. The other one was *l'impôt indirect*, excise. I flew through here from Libya four months ago and there was only Monsieur Excise, then, without the health police . . . of course, Libya isn't 'equatorial' . . ."

"You did the Libya thing in April?"

"Yeah—didn't you notice in my passport?"

"Oriental chops and Arabic are two writings lost on me—were you there when we bombed Tripoli?"

"What's with this 'we' shit?"

"—me and Reagan."

"—on my birthday, too. Kinda made me feel real homesick for the nation that gave birth to John Wilkes Booth . . ."

"I almost lost my job on that one.'

"'Almost' isn't good enough."

"—did a piece that questioned Thatcher's skirting NATO letting Reagan's F-111's refuel at Lakenheath. My paper killed it."

Lilith looked at me and said, "I would have quit."

I hesitated before telling her, "I have nothing in my life, except my work."

"—what else is there? If your work is compromised, then what's the point?"

We were taxiing for take-off, and I took her hand.

"You're a fucking ballbuster," I said.

"—yeah, I'm named for one."

There was a look of seriousness about her that I hadn't seen before, the corners of her mouth turned down and there appeared two deep short furrows on her brow. "Did you ask anybody any questions about SIDA in the last three days?" she said.

"Is that what you think that was all about? AIDS?"

"I think we should find out." She looked at her watch, a man's Rolex, extremely showy, perhaps to compensate, I thought, for the fact she wore no jewelry. "—two hours to Paris," she announced. "I'm going back to sleep. I have to work tonight." She shot me a look. "Shouldn't you be writing—?"

"—you have to *work* tonight?"

"—just going in to make some prints."

"—'going in'?"

"To AFP."

"—we're not going 'home'?"

"*File first*," she said. "That's my motto."

"—yeah? Well my motto is QUIS ME AMAT, AMAT ET CANEM MEUM, but I can file from a craphouse in Cracow, I don't need to 'go into the office' . . ."

"—it'll only take a little while. There's a bar across the street, you can wait for me there. Then we can have dinner. Go to my place. Take tomorrow off."

"Two days off," I bargained, "and a down payment right now to appease me."

I was coming

She slapped a pillow into my lap and slid her hand beneath it. It was her left hand, the strong one. I closed my eyes. "Don't get too excited," she warned me in that really really winning way of hers that I was coming to adore, "I'm not wearing gloves."

Mac

I wanted to be a poet because I was reading Ginsberg

thinking myself so cool
too cool for love

too cool
too poor
too beat
to be believed

those were the days

when everything you wanted you could get for free.

THE NEW YORK TIMES PARIS BUREAU can be found at 3, rue Scribe, and our bureau is five doors down. You can walk in from the street on any day of the week and be greeted by a resident din of careless efficiency, lorded over by and in spite of my hands-down favorite person in this business, unrivaled squash opponent, brother-in-arms across The Sleeve, Mister Paris Bureau Chief to my own London Chief —a man, a Catholic, a monument, a Glaswegian, who, like Kierkegaard, had read theology but, as he, himself, was fond of saying, "did not take orders": the incomparable Mac.

He was standing at the far end of the newsroom from his

office when he saw me enter and we clocked each other, step by step, as we did on squash courts, down opposite walls of the long room, silently watching one another, 'til he led the way into his office, circled 'round his yacht-size Louis Something desk, plunked down in a Louis Something chair, opened the bottom left-hand drawer of the Louis Something desk and withdrew two triple dram glasses and a jeroboam-size jar of the Macallan.

"—*aye*," he said, dispensing the elixir, "if they havnae gone and sent in me best wee bonny as The Hitman. Do your bidding, Judas. I always knew me days wuur numbuur'd."

"It's good to see you, too, Mac."

"So I'm finished, then? They're giving me the sack?"

". . . no, not at all, I—"

"—I knew it, I knew it, I knew it as soon as the rumor reached me that *The New York Times* was moving Alan Riding here from Mexico, I knew that I was standing on the gallows then . . ."

"—Mac, I swear, you're more secure here than I am in London, I'm just passing through on my way back home from Camer—*wait*, where'd you hear that? That's ridiculous, *The New York Times* would never transfer Riding out of Mexico, he's too good . . ."

"—the boy can write."

"—the boy *does* write."

"—that's why I'm worried. You know how our humps operate in New York."

"Don't I ever."

". . . every administrative tactic they initiate is predicated on a fear of 'The Paper of Record'. Is the Big Hump still dressing like a *Times* man?"

"Yep."

"—with those goddamn dayglo braces?"

"—'suspenders', Mac, 'suspenders' is the common useage."

"—fucking suspenders. I don't know why *Times* men think they have to dress that way. Lorna says it's because their dicks won't hold their trousers up."

"How is Lorna?"

"Fabulous. Keeps me suspenderless, as you see. And the boy—how's himself? You'll stay with us, of course. I'll ring Lorna. We'll all go out for supper. She'll be thrilled . . ." He reached for the phone, looking over at me. "Oh," he said. "Oh. Oh. *Oh.*" A smile broke out—it bloomed—across his face. He cradled the receiver. "Anyone I know?"

"I think so, yes."

"She lives in Paris?"

"Yes."

"A journalist?"

I nodded.

"English-speaking?"

"Sometimes."

"Good god, you haven't trysted with the Amanpour from CNN—?"

"—'trysted', Mac? 'Like we did last summer'—?"

"—be *something*, to coax a connoisseur such as yourself to Paris and in the dead of August."

"We'll see."

He took his glasses off and rubbed the bridge of his nose between his thumb and his forefinger, a gesture that was so French, so much instinctively a *geste* of French *intellos*, of the intellectuals, that I wondered if Mac knew how many of their traits he had adopted as his own. You spend hour after hour sitting on stiff chairs at press conferences, observing, always watching as a journalist, until unconsciously you take on as your own a protective coloring, the gestures of the objects of your notations. It was that time of day, anyway, when such reflective gestures are a reflex, so maybe I was making too much of it. It was the time of day when, if I was on the desk in London and Mac was in Paris, I would pick up the phone to him, or he to me, to carp about the humps, bullshit, tell a joke, commune, dismiss the politicians and generally, specifically, *bond* malewise. I trusted him in everything professional, every aspect of our job; and I envied him his marriage. I envied the sexy way he and Lorna were with one another after twenty years, two kids and half a dozen postings. He was, of all the many types of men who fill the pages in this business, the only truly happy man I knew. He knew that as a Scotsman working for a U.S. paper he would never get a plum job in the two important bureaus, Washington and New York. He knew the highest rung on our paper's so-called ladder of success he could aspire to, as a final roosting place, was the London desk. And he didn't want it. He'd already had Sydney, Hong Kong, Tokyo, Beijing and Moscow, and he was happy as a clam in Paris. He had a furry, burred command of French, his lust for it and all things French no doubt augmented by his early training on the short leash controlled by Jesuits—and even though they were now both atheists, he and Lorna had pledged, upon their births, that they would never let the daughters of their Catholic blood be raised or educated back in England. So he is his happiest in Paris—but distracted, too, by the anxiety contentment brings, that he might lose it.

He slipped his glasses back on, looked at me, and said, "I want for you what you want in this, Noah."

"I know you do."

"—but I've seen a lot of men our age do stupid things. Not even bachelors. Married men."

"Let's drop the subject."

"—okay."

"—she's not *that* much younger, Mac."

Even as the words tripped off my tongue I sensed the trap, too late, and I saw that he knew that I knew that he'd set me up, the Jesuitical scumbag, and that I'd fallen for it, I'd revealed *a fact*, despite a vivid effort on my part at concealment. "Oh, you *are* good," I conceded.

"How much younger is she, Noah?"

"Ten years. And that's all you're getting on her."

"—*ten years*? What do you two talk about?"

Five different things happened, then, all at once, to spare my cultivating a mild anger or resentment at that last remark —his phone rang, his number two asked him something on the intercom, his office door flew open and there entered a woman in a work-blue frockcoat with Mac's dry-cleaning, another woman with a pencil in her hair who said New York needed to know a.s.a.p. about my length, and another person, a stringer whom I'd never met but who wanted to be introduced to me because the humps were thinking of hiring him full-time on a share basis among Mac and me and the miserable Fleischman in Frankfurt.

Mac cupped his hand over the telephone receiver and said, "—Boot says I'm supposed to tell you he's sitting in New York with his—excuse me, Jill, this is a verbatim—dick in his hand, waiting for you. What do you need, Noah? You want my machine?"

"I'll plug in outside—"

"—and he's shouting for photo."

"—tell him it's coming from AFP in an hour, and tell him it's the photographer's exclusive . . ."

I turned to head into the newsroom to file, then turned back to squint at Mac, who hadn't moved.

"—*gotcha*," he said.

"—you bastard . . ."

"Now I know who it is."

"—you Society of Jesus s.o.b . . ."

"—blessing, my son. Go for it. Everyone who knows her says she is a veritable sweet piece—excuse me yet again, Jill —*of work*."

As it turned out, it wasn't Lilith who got bogged down with work that night, it was yours truly with the humps and Science Desk half-humps who thought they owned the copyright on exploding lakes, and Boot, anal retentive hump, mucking with my style. "Do you really want to write, 'a fusillade of demands for scientific, and a godly, explanation'?"

"Do I really want to 'write' it, Boot—?"

"—yes."

"—no, I typed it that way just to waste your time. What's the problem with it?"

"'Fusillade' and 'godly'."

"—fusillade and godly in the same sentence, or the use of 'fusillade' as an English word, or the use of 'godly' in the lower case?"

"—yes."

Spend your life like this. On top of never being home. Yes, there are still rags (the *Guardian* in England, for example) where journalists are paid to *write*, but writing's only one half of an equation; it is nothing, comes to nothing, is worth nothing, if it isn't read.

"Good piece, Noah," Mac assessed three hours later. I had written two: a bleeder for the next day and a heart-stopper about the cry-die for the color supplement on Sunday. "Lake Nyos plays the AIDS virus. Hell of a metaphor," he said.

"You think that's how it will be read?"

"Hell, no. It will be read as a straight chronicle, man on the scene at an unexplained phenomenon, a natural killer, an act of God." He smiled a haggard smile. "Now, get out, go, go. You're late. Go meet your woman."

I had called and left a message at her office—no phone in the darkroom—and she had called me back and we had arranged to meet for dinner at her local, Chez Julien, in the rue de l'Hôtel de Ville, sometime between nine and ten.

"—they keep a table for me there," she said.

"—under what name?" the reporter in me asked.

Mac and I were about to leave his office together, when he saw me staring at the floor and the reporter in him asked, "—*what*, what is it, Noah?"

For the previous three hours, coming, going, working, we had talked over a range of things, the Syrians, Algerians, Tunisians, Reagan, Thatcher, Mitterand, the ecu, Chunnel, Libya bombing—but then finally I had to ask him how to buy a condom in this city.

"I haven't had to swim with boots on for twenty years," he bragged, smiling ear to ear, "but here, take this—" He opened a file cabinet and shot me a consumer study of French condoms. "I wrote a reader on French condoms last month, but Boot killed it."

"—ever the prophylactic, our man Boot. They're called *préservatifs*?" I marvelled, trying to translate the study as I read it. "I thought 'condom' *was* a French word."

"Stick with these," he told me, pointing to the brands classed TB for *très bon*.

The *préservatifs*, twenty-eight brands in all, had been rated in a dozen categories—*surface*, *couleur* (who the hell can think a green condom is sexy?), *ârome*, *odeur* and *rupture*.

"—they tested each one of these three hundred and fifteen times?" I beggared from the fine print of the survey.

"—dark and lonely work," Mac agreed. "But someone's got to do it."

We walked into rue Scribe together where he put me in a taxi. "What'd you tell Boot?"

"About what?"

"—about where you're going to be the next few days."

"*—nada.*"

"You know you can count on me for cover, cowboy."

"—yes. I know I can."

"God bless you, son, in all the sins you are about to overtake and undercover."

As the taxi sped me around l'Opéra I looked back at my friend through the rear window.

A light was shining from above, anointing him with radiance like a sovereign's brass, a knighthood on his head and shoulders, only, his body falling under its own shadow. *Light*, I thought —here I am in the city that exploits its name, if not its substance —and, like Love's goon, I began to hum a hokey "Light" tune with the reverence I usually reserve for Bach and Dylan. I mean, could anybody ever really *light up* someone's life?

And I thought of Melanie just then—not another woman, just my sister. I thought about the time, when she was nine or ten, when she was picked to go on *Kids' Bible Quiz* on the radio with a chance of winning a bike or a free trip for the family to Virginia Beach to go hear Billy Graham live in person. Take the bike, Dad and I told her, but she didn't get a chance to choose because she flunked on her first question.

And now for a chance at the Schwinn 3-speed, Melanie John—according to the Book of Genesis . . . what is the first thing God created—?

"An egg," my sister said.

". . . er, nnnnnnnooooooo . . ."

"the chicken?"

Have to call my sister, I was thinking—let her know that for the first time in his life her big brother was finally coming 'round to seeing Light, the First Act of creation, for the fundamental and eternal miracle it was.

l'Opéra

Voilà la poésie ce matin et
Pour la prose il y a les journaux.

There—poetry this morning and
For prose, there are the papers.

—Apollinaire

If friendship teaches *réalisme*, then work will teach you *sur-réalisme*. If War teaches *symbolisme*, then love will teach you who you are, Love teaches *existentialisme*.

From the moment I entered the taxi at l'Opéra, it seemed I was infected, evidencing symptoms of the virus of nostalgia, a veritable retro virus, *nostalgie*, recombinant bug which makes you long for a place or time which was never yours.

From the instant I entered the taxi and looked at the streets through its windows I was infected by Paris at twilight in summer, a low-burning fever brought on in me not by cinematic memory this time, but by the memory of photographs, Atget's photographs of Paris, and by the memory of poetry I'd barely read.

"*Américain*?" the taxi driver safely hazarded, since he'd heard me say goodbye to Mac in English. Nationalism will teach you *cubisme*, I thought. "You *visitez*?" he said.

"I visit."

"*Elle est très belle ce soir, Paris.* I give good ride, we pass by river, '*voila la poésie*'." He turned to me. "Apollinaire," he said. "You know?"

"*Le polonais.* Inventor of the word *surréalisme.*"

". . . '*les pihis longs et souples*'," he quoted, "'*Qui n'ont qu'une seule aile et qui volent par couples*'." He craned his neck to catch a look at me in the rearview-mirror and kissed his fingertips, a gesture of élan. I hadn't understood a fucking word he'd said.

Or maybe love's a virus, attacking some as virulently as a toxin, while others seem immune to it. Admittedly, I was ready to fall prey, I was in a weakened state already on my way to meet my lover as we doubled back toward Place de la Madeleine, but when we turned into the rue Royal and Place de la Concorde opened out in front of me, sun setting across the river beyond the Tour Eiffel, I was, as the driver was trying to explain, like a *pihi*, a long and supple bird, real or imaginary, which has only one wing and can fly only when it's in a couple.

"*C'est belle, non*?"

"*—si belle,*" I agreed.

If you have to get a taxi driver who's a talker, better he's a poet than a right-wing stalker.

Along the Quai des Tuileries with the Louvre looming to the left, a pale green light, a gloaming, came glowing down the river casting eerie shimmer on the kings' keep.

"*Le bateau-mouche,*" the driver nodded. "You know these bateaux-mouches?"

"*—truc touristique, n'est-ce-pas*?"

"*—pas fatalement. Sont un peu romanesques, crois.*"

Even though Cary Grant and Audrey Hepburn made it look stylish and *romanesque* in the movie *Charade*, what could possibly be romantic about a boat ride on a river under floodlights with six or seven hundred other people? Cary Grant and Audrey Hepburn didn't need the Seine for that scene (after kissing her for the first time he opens his eyes to see a floodlit Notre Dame behind her and ponders, "What's *that* doing there?")—Cary Grant (whom I resemble not at all) and Audrey Hepburn (whom Lilith resembles a lot, except for her tits) could have played that scene in sleeting rain on the Erie Canal and it would have seemed just as romantic. And what's romance, anyway, but a ghost town or a set of props fronting for real meaning in the stead of an abandoned notion? Dinner by candlelight in the corner banquette of a quiet Paris restaurant where you are always welcomed, where the chef comes out to clasp your hand and the proprietor offers you wine from his private cellar. A slow stroll home after an heroic brandy and a meal the exquisite details of which you will remember, heartachingly, for years to come when you are stranded somewhere where the only meat is either goat or rooster and the only vegetables are onions, turnips, cabbage or—worse—manioc. Pausing, several times, for a series of slow kisses, first on one of the best bridges over the Seine, then on the island's quai under the windows where Baudelaire wrote *Les Fleurs du Mal*, then on a bench facing the Left Bank, then at her doorway, then on her stairs. She lived, it evolved, at the top of a house I had dreamed of, at the top of a house I had actually stopped and admired from the Pont St-Louis each time I had come to Ile St-Louis and Ile de la Cité. Perhaps that's the nature of romance, its real stuff: that it's a waking dream, that it's a dream's embodiment. I couldn't believe where she had led me —I, who've been known to go everywhere. I couldn't believe I was watching her unlock the door, turn and pause on the marble stairway with its turned iron balustrade. I, whose clear clinical sight is unsparing, whose sentimentality stops at the door with the quick and the dead, whose emotions are bottled and stoppered. When she opened the door and led me in there, into a remembered Atget photograph, I was knee deep in a wet dream, neck high in a lotus. A swath of yellow light from the stairwell cut a path through the darkness of the foyer and bathed us both in amber, but as she reached to turn the light on in the apartment I placed my hand on hers and said, "Keep it dark." I held the hall door open as she felt her way across the murk to the river-facing windows and began to roll the shutters back and up. Slowly, one by one, the planes inside the room revealed themselves, mirrors and the reflections from the glass-framed photographs. I began to see the slow curve of a grand piano in the corner, the backs of chairs, a divan; and I let the hall door close behind me. This was, I thought, the most beautiful room, other than a cinema or places built expressly for religion, that I had ever been in. Its ceiling was at least six meters high, as were the windows. Lilith moved through a double French door into a room which was the mirror image of the first, and began to lever back the corrugated shutters at the windows. As she opened the first window I could see the back wall of this room revealed, high and wide, made to seem higher and wider, vast, by the absence of furniture except for a chair, an Ionic column and, freestanding, center, a large frameless bed, boxspring and mattress draped in white bathed in moonlight. This was her bedroom—a bed on the floor, a Greek column, a chair and three ceiling-high windows looking out on the Seine, with a view of canal boats, the rive gauche, the Panthéon and Jean Ravy's fifty-foot aft flying buttresses of Notre Dame. As I'd done on our first night together, I approached her there, where she was, in that light by a window.

"Let's take a bath first," she said.

There was a claw-footed copper-lined tub through a door in the corner into what was once a rectangular hallway or larder connecting her bedroom with a room at the back of the apartment, facing a courtyard, which served as her kitchen. We moved, choreographed by embraces, through the tedious work of disrobing, to searching for matches to light the candles, to filling the bath, to finding a bottle of Meursault-Charmes in the fridge and finding my last English Fetherlite from Boots, the Queens' chemists.

I washed her.

I wrapped her in a large bath sheet and carried her back to her bed.

I had been making love to women in my mind and in movies, since my first winter of nocturnal ejaculations when I was eleven. I came to love the warmth of jism—sput, sput, sput—on the sheet and on my legs, and later in my hand when I learned to masturbate. I used to draw my knees up on the pillow by my head and try to blow myself and watch myself come into my face only it was never me, it was a girl, a woman doing it for me. Every time I'm with a woman I recall the hopelessness of self-love, the pathos of that first desire, and I thank her in my heart *thank you* for being real, for being there, a lumpen childish thing to do, no doubt, to start out making love by being ravenous but grateful. Thank you woman's thigh and woman's belly, woman's breast, your woman's ass, your flesh, your woman's nipples. And I am reminded of the old game that the emirs play inside their tents and marble halls to feed you well then sit you down and pose you this one question: If you were the First Man and Your Creator came to you and said, My Son I wish to make you a companion for eternity, but only one, which one do you want, a man or a woman? The conundrum, we are told, is that the First Man, knowing only his own image —Adam knowing only Adam—would of course choose only Adam, choose what was known to him, himself, rather than the unknown woman as companion for eternity. But what makes Our Creator the one God before all other gods, the answer goes, is that He knew. He didn't ask. He didn't go to Adam for a taste survey and I have always been extremely grateful for the packaging and the design of Woman but I'd never seen its fundamental parts combined to such a pitched effect as I did in Lilith's body. Her head, small and neat—I've already written of—I could palm it in one hand. She had broad shoulders, like a swimmer, a clavicle that rose beneath her skin between her scapulae like a coastal ridge or like the time-rubbed smooth roots of a Buddha tree. Her nipples grew hard at a touch, or sometimes even at a breath, or sometimes even if she caught me staring at them. Her pelvis was the center of her strength. You can feel a woman's strength when you are in her, feel her muscles in and out, the muscles of her lower back and abdomen, her ass her thighs her vaginal canal the crowning ring of muscle of her cervix. A woman's pelvic strength is always a surprise, for me, because so many women are so weak there like an emptiness behind a curtain, but Lilith was a pounding surf a fucking thunderstorm a pelvic strength that challenged like a riptide, needed to be fought against, and as she'd done on our first night, she seemed to withhold her own pleasure, or take added pleasure in delaying it to tempt me with it, drive me toward it, compete with me, almost, to test which of us could hold out longer but I didn't want to play that way, some people say that making love is only ever about power, but I never thought that's what it *only* ever is—*Lilith* I heard myself say I'm going to come and *now*, Noah, she said and I saw her open up, I threw my head back and poured into her Noah's flood, the room began to burn white, white jism, as floodlights from a *bateau-mouche* on the river swept through our open window roving over us, a searchlight, as if we were two escapees with no shelter but each other, towing darkness in its wake and neither of us had the strength to speak when it was gone until she whispered, "Noah. Speak. It feels like we have died."

the thing of interest

THE FIRST PHOTOGRAPH I ever made was of the ceiling of my room back in Virginia when I was lounging on my bed and tripped the shutter of my new Box Brownie by excited accident, in 1953.

After that I got progessively better but never brilliant. Timing got better, the films got faster, equipment got slicker, but I still treasure that shot of the ceiling. That, and the pictures I took in Paris during those next magical days. I can't remember why I even unpacked the camera from my bag—except, possibly, because the sun was on her in a certain way, or because she was heartstoppingly beautiful that morning, emanating light, radiantly gloriously fucked. Some men immortalize their trophy moments—big, bigger, biggest fish. I caught, instead, the light of love that never lingers, that flame of happiness which sacrifices its own heat as kindling to a momentary look. There is nothing better I have ever done that put that look on her. There is nothing I have written that is finer than the look of pleasure written on her face as I toiled, slowly, toward achieving a perfection.

Did she ever take my picture?

Yes, but only as the secondary subject, only as a prop, an undifferentiated foreground in a depth of field that yielded something huge or something happening or, her standard canvas, an event in history. In the photographs she took of me I am not the thing of interest, I am not the first thing that you see. In the photographs I took of her she blots out an entire world. In the photographs she took of Adam that I later found, he is staring at the camera (her) with a look that seems to be a look of tender anguish or despair, which proves the camera lies. It lies, and so do we, as spectators, we lie to ourselves when we believe that we can capture time, that diamond watch, or capture love or capture rapture snapped and shot and fixed and flawed and faceted in a heart-shaped setting. Does any household of the middle class not contain the lie, that essential photograph? Whether it's the nine foot fish or a photograph of Uncle Buddy in his uniform or it's on the box of Wheaties or staring from the pages of *The Times-Dispatch* every household has a photo somewhere, usually a photo of a wedding, or a Royal or a pope or a dead person. People of the middle classes even take possession of the lie, the essential photograph, one step further—they carry at least one in their pocket, in their wallets, on their person. I would even speculate that you are who you carry, you are known by what you frame—a good reporter can assemble a still life, a quick biography, sketched from the collected snapshots in a person's home. Snapshots first, then the bookshelves (if there are any), then the larder, then the medicine chest, then what's hanging in the closet tells the good reporter all he needs to know.

She didn't own a dress.

She had a tux, a burka (black) and a baby-blue djellaba but no skirt and not a single dress. Her medicine cabinet showed all the symptoms of the world traveller: Lomotil, Benadryl, iodine crystals, Flagyl caps, calamine lotion, Halazone tabs, vitamins and condoms. No perfume. No Tampax. The most extensive array of face creams put together outside the pharmacy—Clarins, Chanel, Lancôme, La Prairie—but no make-up. No frightening "feminine hygiene" products. Zovirax.

Her larder was empty, except for three bags of pistachios from Teheran, several 4 oz. jars of U.S.S.R. Malossol and four 10 oz. tins of Iranian beluga caviar on the top shelf of a fridge otherwise packed out with white Bordeaux and canisters of film. She had inherited Divo's music library, including scores and dusty libretti covering two walls of the salon, which appeared archival, intact and untouched, perhaps for decades. On the third wall, there were "her" books, photography books, poetry and fiction. The fiction was in French and English, but the poetry was all in French and I'd never heard of most of it (*Misérable Miracle*? *Epreuves, exorcismes*? *Cravates de chauves*? *L'Antitête*?). As for Lilith's fiction, for a girl she read far too much Mishima and Tanizaki. But it was her volumes of photography that dominated her booksheives—all four volumes of Atget, Berenice Abbot, Muybridge's *Complete Human and Animal Locomotion*, Hausmann's *Je ne suis pas un photographe*, Walker Evans, boyhood photos of Jacques-Henri Lartigue, Roger Fenton's photographs of the Crimean War, Brassaï, Daguerre, Cartier-Bresson, a collection of German and Swiss anatomists, most notably, Fritz Lang's *The Language of the Human Face* and Ernst Kretschmer's *Körperbau und Charakter*—and, for me, perhaps the most revealing—the collected Matthew Brady.

But it was what was on her walls, what had been chosen to be framed, what was on display for her eyes to fall upon day in, day out, which caught me by surprise.

To begin with, there were no paintings in her house, and only a single mirror (a full-size one propped against the corner in the bathroom, facing the tub). Everything else, with the exception of one framed document and a single framed newspaper clipping, was a photograph—and all of them were black and white.

Starting at the place of prominence, on the piano, there

was a photograph of Maria Callas with Aristotle Onassis. "Per Divo, con," was written across the top of it in a sweeping hand.

"'*Per Divo, con*'? 'Con' what?"

Lilith shrugged.

When she shrugged her breasts didn't move but her abdomen tightened as if she were shrugging not from her shoulders but from her hips.

"Divo was begging Maria for a signed photograph," she started to tell me but I interrupted and said, "Shrug again."

She did, and her breasts didn't move.

"—so knowing how much Divo detested Onassis, she took this photo off her piano and broke the frame on the parquet floor of her apartment in front of him. It was very upsetting. Broken glass frightened Divo. It always did. Broken glass sent him into a panic. Then she picked the photo out of the pieces of glass and Divo started to cry because he was afraid she'd cut her fingers. You have to understand—my father did a lot of crying. And he couldn't stand the sight of blood, which, let's face it, plays a crucial rôle in a lot of operas. Blood and crying, blood and tears. So she started to write, '*Per Divo, con*—' then she stopped and looked at him with that Tosca look that she had. '*Con* what?' she said. 'With what should I sign this to you? What emotion do you want today? What sentiment?'"

"—*oof*," I said. I think I was probably nibbling on some part of her at that moment. "She would have made a *great* Lilith . . ."

"—the best."

"—the second best."

"—poor Maria."

"—poor *Maria*?"

"—what Onassis did to her."

"—she did to herself."

"No. She didn't. He ruined her. Ruined her career, then married that Kennedy woman. Thank goodness Divo died before he had to live through *that* . . ."

"—'that *Kennedy* woman'?"

"—that Bouvier."

"—you mean *Jackie*."

"—some names you never speak."

"Are you serious?"

She was.

She could talk about Qaddafi with more equanimity than she could talk about Aristotle Onassis and his crimes against Maria Callas. He was her one real prejudice, there was no logic to her response to him, hers was a learned hatred acquired, unchallenged, from her parents. I came to understand that she guarded it, kept it, so to speak, as a keepsake of them, the one real living thing that they had left her. Everything else was a form of memorial, but the heat generated in her by a dead Greek tycoon was stirring and alive.

"—so if you hate him so much, why have you kept the picture?"

"—because I don't see Onassis in it. I don't even really see the Callas. I see the story I just told you."

"—picture worth a thousand words?"

"Sometimes a word is worth a thousand pictures."

"What word is that?"

"—'rue', for one. 'Woe', for another. 'Humility'," she said.

On the wall next to the piano there was a framed newspaper clipping, about a thousand words, slightly yellowed, from the *New York World* dated 12 March, 1910. "Black Hand Death Threat for Caruso", its headline said. "Divo's," Lilith said, as if I hadn't guessed.

"—was he *alive* in 1910?"

Leonardo, actually.

"—born in 1916. But his family kept Caruso cuttings by the boxload."

"Why this one?" I asked, reading the subhead, Army of Police Guards Him as He Sings.

"—because of what it meant to Divo about artistic freedom, I guess. I don't know. Or maybe because he believed Caruso refused to be blackmailed by thugs and acted with courage. Or maybe Divo just liked the cartoon . . ."

"—jesus, what's *this*?"

Hanging beneath the Caruso article was a small document, passport size, in a gold frame.

"Divo's brother worked in Hollywood. He was a painter."

"—*uncle* Divo?"

"Leonardo, actually. He was hired to design this."

It was something no less than magnificent. It was the most beautiful piece of Hollywood junk I could imagine—Victor Laszlo's *carte d'identité* from *Casablanca.*

"—how much?"

"How much what?"

"How much do want for it?"

"It's not for sale."

"I might have to steal it from you."

"I keep it because of the importance of the photograph—the way P h o t o g r a p h i e is printed on it. It means a lot to me.

"—it means a lot to *me.*"

"—but you've only just laid eyes on it.'

"But the love affair was instantaneous."

I think I was falling in love with the package—her, her address, her house, her dead parents, her copper tub, her Greek column, her windows, her view, her piano, her books and—not the least—the fact that she'd lied to me. Again. Because what I turned to next was a series of framed prints, thirty-six in all, of what I had at first mistaken to be original Atget photographs of Paris but which proved to be, on closer inspection, a collection of eighteen Atgets side by side with Divis, eighteen of her own prints, studies of the same Paris streets, the same sites Atget had photographed seventy years before under different light.

"—*liar*. I thought you told me you don't do 'art' . . ."

"—are these 'art'? They're what I do in my spare time when I'm in Paris, which is hardly ever . . ."

"There aren't people in them."

"There weren't people in Atget's either. Or if there were, only rarely."

"I've never seen a photograph of yours without a human figure," I recalled.

"When I come home from trips, sometimes, home from Ethiopia or the Gaza camps, for example, I don't want to see another human figure, ever, no less 'immortalize' one. So I pretend I'm Atget and go out and hunt down buildings . . ."

"I'm impressed."

"—why? Because I appropriate someone else's work?"

"—no, because you respect it enough to modernize it."

". . . 'modern'," she murmured, and led me toward a final group of photographs. "Are these 'modern' enough for you?"

"—fucksake," I said when I realized what they were. "I *know* these places. I used to *play* there . . ."

"—'play'?"

"When I was a kid. I've actually stood right *there*, right on that spot . . ."

"That spot" was a long Confederate trench in Matthew Brady's photograph called *Dead in the Hole*, a portrait of Confederate dead outside Petersburg, Virginia, in the earthworks of Fort Mahone, otherwise known as Fort Damnation. It was one of his most famous field photographs, and I remembered having studied it in high school, it and the accompanying text, written by Brady himself for a slide show and lecture tour he made after the war.

"This picture is a good view inside the rebel Fort," Brady had written. "The trenches all along the line were found to contain many dead Confederates just as they fell. You will notice that no (2) two men have fallen in (the) same position . . ."

Lilith extended a finger and touched a soldier in the trench in the Brady photograph. "The convention, then, in Brady's time," she began to say, "was for the photographer to title the photograph and append a little narrative to each . . ."

"—I know."

"Do you know what he wrote about this one?"

"—yes. 'No two men have fallen in the same position' . . ."

"Well that's pretty fucking 'modern', don't you think? I mean, that's the sort of specificity Eliot was after in *The Wasteland.* Or Yevtushenko in *Babi Yar.* Specificity in carnage. That's why war poems are like extreme close ups: they resurrect on detail . . ."

"Did you ever write?"

"—write what?"

"Poems. 'Little narratives'. Anything."

"—no, I hate to write. Too passive."

"—*passive*? You?"

"—no, writing is. I don't get its risks."

"—it's 'risks'?"

"—it's thrills. I mean—what's in it? Where is the excitement? It's a basic sit down job."

Excitement, for her, I was to learn, was a sort of job description, a categorical prerequisite, like salt, of which she needed to maintain a daily minimum requirement. The jones was in the job, no bones about it, I had seen enough suicides waiting to happen in the field by photographers who wore their cameras like bulletproof vests. Hers was not a risk-for-risk's-sake disposition—she wasn't out to show that she could cut it with the boys or prove she was the hottest long shot, longest hotshot on the track. The danger seeker really only ever seeks his self-destruction; but, then, so does the narcissist, and Lilith was the least self-absorbed persona I had known in our profession. She sought out situations which blasted any sense of lasting safe-ness, of security; she gravitated toward tense circumstances, looking for the sort of tension which could snap at any moment—quicksand, ice floe, precipice, a slippery ledge, the dangerous liaison—any place, either physical or of the spirit, which was *insecure* was heaven to her. How, you have to wonder, could I have viewed the evidence, inspected all the clues and failed to see the light? I didn't get the whole Maria Callas thing, for instance. Lilith had a sort of altar of the mind around the singer which I should have found peculiar but which, instead, I failed to register because I'm not an opera buff and because, to tell the truth, I tend to lump the cultural hype of Callas in with other opera queens as a phenomenon dished out for male homosexuals. Sure the woman had big eyes and an expression of emotion that added wallop to her voice but so did Judy Garland and Piaf and, admit it, you'd get a bit suspicious of anybody in the final inning of this century who kept a framed picture of Judy Garland in her living room and played "Somewhere Over the Rainbow" as many times as Lilith played the soundtrack of Callas' 1953 La Scala performance of *Tosca*. It went with her everywhere. "So what's with fucking *Tosca*?" I finally asked late one night in some hotel somewhere when she climbed into bed with Callas on her Discman. "Everybody fucking dies," I complained, "three characters—number one gets shot at the command of number two. Number two gets stabbed by number three. Number three throws herself off a building into the Tiber. What's so great about that—?"

"Passion."

"—*passion*?"

"Principles—passionately held."

"—bullshit."

"No one dies for principles anymore."

"—double fucking triple fucking bullshit."

"Would you?"

"—what?"

"—sacrifice your life for principle."

"Depends."

"—on what?"

"—how old I was."

"What *would* you die for?"

"—*nothing*, are you kidding? Maybe, if I had a kid . . ."

"You don't think there are principles worth dying for?"

"—like what?"

"Like freedom."

"—freedom to do what? Bear arms? Expose myself in public? Declare my clear belief that there is no god as God but some people call him Allah? No. Would I enlist with others against tyranny? Maybe. We exist—have existed—under the protection of so many interlocking freedoms it's impossible to isolate a freedom without cutting loose another. If you're asking me what I'd do or who I'd be if this were 1937 in Bavaria or last year in Johannesburg I can't answer. I can't play Let's Pretend. I think it's fatuous. Worse—I think it's smug."

"—but being Southern . . ."

"—being Southern . . . what?"

"—staying out of Viet Nam the way you did . . ."

"—I stayed out of the *army*, sweetie, not just Viet Nam . . ."

"—on principle?"

"—on luck. And what does 'being Southern' have to do with it—?"

"It must make you wonder which side you would have taken in the Civil War."

"I would have gone to Cuba. What would you have done?"

"I would have bound my breasts and gone to work for Matthew Brady."

My paper, like most, has a logo—ridiculously pompous and heraldic—and a motto which makes New Hampshire's "Live Free Or Die" sound like Chamberlain's statement after Munich. This motto is printed under the newspaper's name on all the office stationery and it, too, like New Hampshire's, begins with the imperative "Live". I was in the habit of x-ing out the motto or altering the command to suit my mood and this series of fake mottoes ("Live, fast and die."—Jung) became a not-so-funny running joke between me and Lilith, along with her Khomeini tee shirt slogans. One afternoon she called me in London from some other time zone, I think it was Islamabad, and I said, "Hey I'm glad you called, seriously, I'm stuck, I need a motto," and she said, okay: *Live like a man and love like a woman.*

"—my god: but: that's *you*," I told her.

"—fucksake, Noah," she shot back, laughing at me from a foreign country, "actually—it's *you* . . ."

Live like a man she did, in her imperiousness, her assumptions, her freedom of movement—in those regards, in the way she lived, I always thought of us as same-sexed, I never thought of her as a woman, of her as a gender that was different from my own. Her strengths—her bravery, her confidence—allowed me to think that in a lover she might welcome—what can I call it?—*a change of pace*: some indulgence: some cosseting: so I pampered her. I pampered her by taking care of her, doing things for her she'd never do herself, because I didn't understand the part that danger played for her, in and out of bed. I am a slow and thoughtful lover, I believe—though you never know the truth, if there is a truth, about your end of the mating game. But unless you're in it only for the exercise, you discover how to find the clues true intimacy brings. I thought I had reason to believe straight from the start that she and I were startling, better than the average, maybe made in heaven, matchless, part of something big. I thought she wanted what *I* wanted; I thought we wanted the same thing. I don't know—given the chance—I don't know if I would do it all again the same way. I've thought about that a lot—about what I might have done to make things different, make it turn out different, in the end. And the truth is, it wasn't poker and it wasn't chess; it wasn't war games or a dress rehearsal: it was love, on my part, pre-programmed for mess.

But in the beginning there was Light—there was passion and delight, obsession and abandon, revelation, rebirth, all the horny, corny chaos of identity in drift: puberty all over again. Those first few days in Paris it seemed like I was living —this sounds crazy—living through my fingers, on the stimulus of touch. I couldn't keep my hands off her—not just my hands—I couldn't keep my *self* away from her. All my senses were on Sense Alert—sense of balance, sense of decency, sense of humor, sense of touch, of smell, of taste.

. . . and Christ did we eat. All we did was eat and make love. And fuck and eat. And talk and love. And talk and eat. *A consummation devoutly to be wished* pretty much describes those days—I don't think we ever dressed, or if we did, we only dressed to go outside to eat. I don't remember being dressed but I remember eating. And talking longingly about those satisfactions, bed whettings, anticipative titillations that food, alone, or food *qua* lust inspires. We talked about foods that we missed in the field, foods that we'd nearly died eating, foods that are so bad they're no longer food, foods that are so bad drought victims wouldn't eat them, foods that are jokes, foods we despise and detest, foods we ingest without joy, joyless foods giving rise to great longings for far away foods and home-cooking; foods that we love. She said, "—every time I'm in India I get crazy for pasta."

"—and cheese," I concurred.

"They have cheese in India."

"You call that 'cheese'?"

"In Poland my craving is salad."

"In Poland, for me: grapefruit."

"In China I really miss corn."

"—in Japan, too. Ice-cream and corn."

"—but in Japan I can have soup for breakfast."

"You like soup for breakfast?"

"Second only to oysters," she said.

I was in heaven. Heaven because, I can finally admit it, there are few things I'm good at—in fact, maybe only three—and one of them is cooking. She didn't cook. Not only didn't she "cook", she had real genius for avoiding any culinary exercise, she couldn't begin to construct vinaigrette, deconstruct béchamel or make coffee. She couldn't make coffee, a fundamental skill, one would think, of modern life, like driving, or understanding how to use an elevator. When she was on the road, she ordered out, she lived on room service, take-aways and street food, and when she was at home, in Paris, she did the same. There was a café downstairs next door to her building, Le Flore en l'Ile, which sent up anything she wanted, when she wanted it, coffee in the morning, espresso late at night—and she took advantage of it, as a resource, more like a New Yorker would, than the average *parisienne*. There was a *cafetière*, rather ancient, and an old tin *filtre* in her kitchen—along with a trove of copper and enamelware and Tuscan pottery inherited from Divo—long since entrusted to the sadness of disuse along with the gas stove which hadn't been turned on for thirteen years.

So I took charge—I assigned myself to KP duty, scrubbed her pots and got her stove to work and swept her off her feet with a flood of lusty soups for breakfast, pappa al pomodoro, avgolemono, carrot soup with lavender, velouté de Saint-Jacques with vermouth. Every loving culinary drop, you see, was part of my grand plan to pamper and seduce her through the sensual art of feeding her in bed.

I went to Paris almost every other weekend through that fall. Thanksgiving coincided, or almost did, with the opening of the Musée d'Orsay, so I ordered smoked turkey from Virginia and stuffed it with Louisiana cornbread and broiled oysters. I had been alternating her soup breakfasts with fresh oysters all fall, ever since September, ever since "R" for Romance had reappeared in the names of the months. I fell in love with her neighborhood—and she fell in love with mine, in London. I got to know the shopkeepers by name—*Louis* at Ulysse, the oldest and best travel bookshop in Paris, at no. 35, rue St-Louis-en-l'Ile, where I could find any foreign newspaper I wanted and every travel guide to any country that I needed; *Louis* at La Ferme Saint-Aubin, the crèmerie at no. 76, where I bought terrine de lapin à l'armagnac and pur chèvre and fromage blanc; *Louis*, *fleuriste*, at Patrick Allain's where I bought anemones and poppies; *Louis* at Jean-Paul Gardil, *boucher*, where I bought volailles fines and pigeon; *Louis* at Les Vergers de L'Ile St-Louis, the greengrocer, where I bought frisée and chanterelles; and my favorite *Louis*, at Aux Rougets de l'Ile, three blocks from her house, where I struck a deal to pick up a nickel tray of three dozen shucked oysters every morning to carry home along that ancient Seine-surrounded street, to feed her, in bed.

When we were in Paris, we made love and ate and read and walked and tracked down Atget sites together. When we were in London, we made love and drank at local pubs and read and ate less well. And slept outside under the stars in the communal garden on warm nights.

For the next two and a half years, in fact, it seemed all we did was work and make plans to meet somewhere to be together to eat and read and cook and drink and love each other. She had the key to my house, I had the key to hers. Sometimes, between assignments, she would stay at my flat when I was somewhere else—sometimes I stayed at her place when she wasn't there. Little by little, we made both places "ours". Her place had a tub—mine had a shower for two. Hers had a view—mine had a fireplace. Hers had the Seine, mine had the garden. Both felt too small to contain too much future, but both held what we had, a future on hold, for the while. And I knew, from experience, from observation, from reading the best books, that to last, love must change, love must grow. I knew that what we had could not last, but I believed it would shift from comparative to the superlative, expand and enlarge and encompass our lives. But then it all ended as unpredictably as it had started. Just as suddenly as she had walked into my life one evening in Cameroon, she walked into the street to hail a cab one night in London and what happened next may as well have been the sun colliding with the earth because some uncharted maniac behind the wheel of a Mercedes ran her down. And the man that engineered the accident, that uncharted maniac, was Adam.

1989

ARUNDEL GARDENS LONDON ENGLAND

THE ACCIDENT

ON THE MORNING OF THE ACCIDENT I was on the phone with a New York night desk hump called Swizz who wanted me to feed him current English Law concerning bats.

The English are more than slightly batty, Swizz maintained, everybody knew that, but was it true they had a law protecting bats, making bat assassination a felony along the lines of fratricide? Swizz needed to know this in the worst way for some reason at four o'clock in the morning Eastern Standard Time because Swizz was a rewrite man and all rewrite men are, by nature, insomniacs. "Most people don't know this," he was crooning in my ear, "but bats are inadvertent pollinators. Inadvertent—with their feet. They eat insects that feed on flowers and they transfer the flower pollen with their feet while they're feeding and all the flowers pollinated by bats' feet stink like shit, don't you think that's interesting? I mean, things that bats come into contact with by accident come up smelling rotten. Even things that are supposed to smell sweet, like flowers. It's like that vampire story where the guy turns into a bat and flies into that woman's bedroom to suck her blood and turn her into a creature like himself. Rotten, man. *Nasty* little critters."

Until that morning I had probably focused my mind on the subject of bats no more than five or six times in my life—each of those times being prompted by the actual appearance of those nasty little critters overhead, usually in trees. The first time was in Delhi, twenty years ago. I was walking down a Brit-built tree-lined street about the width of Piccadilly, when I noticed bags hanging in the trees, black bags the size of ten-pound sacks of potatoes. *Strange fruit*, my Southern background made me think, *strange fruit hangin' in them trees*—but they were bats, fruit bats, nasty fearsome fucking *loathsome* critters. Next time was in Rome when I saw tiny brown-caped Capuchin-type creatures flitting home to roost at dawn in the belfries of St. Peter's. And once, soon after Reagan was elected, there was a shakeout at the paper and all of us were called back to New York to kiss the new Big Hump's ring and I spent a night with an old girlfriend who was living on Tenth Avenue behind Lincoln Center near the monolith that is AT&T's Mother of All Transmissions and this old girlfriend had a balcony on the twenty-second floor that looked out on the Hudson and the AT&T building. After making love I went out on the balcony to do that thing of communing with the cosmos after orgasm, and I saw a nervous black apostrophic form against the backdrop of the city, a bat, trapped in the urban canyon by a sonic beam. "It will fly itself to death," the old girlfriend said, expressing sorrow for the bat, but I felt less pity for it than for the shocked schlemiel its shriveled corpse would fall on on his way to work the next day, so my thoughts and feelings about bats —to the extent that they existed—tended toward the macabre, or the dismissive.

Since the accident, my thoughts and feelings about bats are

different. Since the accident my thoughts and feelings about bats are linked to Adam.

Even now, at this remove, and praying that he's dead, I find it hard to find a way to fit him in my narrative, I want life's story to exclude the episodes where he appears.

You shouldn't trust me on this subject.

This is where it starts to fall apart.

When I start to think of Adam my powers of description fail—I seem to need to find his likeness somewhere, find a force of nature that he's like—a plague, a curse, a snake, a bat. Maybe it is better to pretend it doesn't matter, the tawdry lives of three not extraordinary people. In the sum of things two of us, at least, would hardly be remembered; but not Adam, Adam must be remembered, his name must be spoken as a token of the evil that was done, it must be written, added to the list of fascists, rapists, racists, criminals against humanity and tyrants: you see how quickly I become insane, like a man possessed—or worse—like his opposite, like a man who has been *dis*possessed.

Of what did Adam dispossess me?

Of trust; of a certain future; of my love.

To what extent was I his co-conspirator?

Fully.

To what do I owe my present state of despair?

To my cowardice.

To Ulysses S. Grant.

To the Army of the Potomac.

Sir! I should have said to him, *you insult my honor*! You are on my land and you are on my woman—you are a mangy blood-letting crotch-sniffing cur and I will run your clotted heart through with my Excalibur, my wisdom and my justice and my pen tip which is mightier than any sword but—fuck it—I did not do him, I was not the doer, I was done, I was the donee, I was run down, run over, left behind fucked re-fucked and forgotten by a master of such deeds as have withered the hearts of new-born children.

Put this spin on it: the third planet of a star system in a far corner of a galaxy collides with catastrophe without warning, a comet hits it, and it sinks, unremarked upon, from existence. It doesn't die, it is annihilated. It does not receive a cancellation notice, no omen shakes its mystics, it mistakes its earthly probabilities for the promise of eternity, and when tomorrow never comes no hymns are sung no ditches dug no monuments constructed no intervention is demanded and mankind and its divinities are no longer separated between what was once a Heaven and what was once The Earth. It wasn't War. It wasn't people dying in rice paddies, it was just the end of one man's love affair, or the beginning of another's.

This is how it happened; or, this is how I could have prevented it from happening, judge for yourself. Or blame it on the Sultan of Oman.

The Sultanate of Oman in London is at 167 Queen's Gate between Hyde Park and the Natural History Museum, and for some reason in the second week in January, 1989, I and the London correspondent for *Die Zeit* were asked to go around to the Sultanate at 6:30 one evening for an in-depth briefing-with-mint-tea on Oman's official position in those eternally shifting sands known as The Middle East.

Lilith had flown in the night before from waiting five days at the border trying to get into what was once called Burma but which is now called the Republic of something else and she was feeling shitty and out of sorts and worried that her old giardia had kicked in again so she'd made an appointment to have the blood work done at the Mutuelle de Médecine Française Polyclinique on Harrington Road which is more or less right around the corner from the Sultanate of Oman and only several blocks from our favorite French restaurant in London, Hilaire. So I made a reservation for us at Hilaire for eight, only eight came and went and there still had been no briefing from the folks from Oman while *Die Zeit* and I sat sucking mint tea until, finally, at eight thirty-five I left, briefless, and Hilaire, being Hilaire, had given up my reservation to a couple from Duluth who couldn't tell the difference between Damon Runyon and rognons au Pernod. Lilith was mildly furious with the world anyway so she took it out on me. It wasn't a fight, so to speak, it was one of those slow horizon-blacking burns that couples have when one or the other of them is pissed off about something not quite perfect fucking up the love affair, like working late, or working half a world away, or working too many hours at something stupid or at something brutally insignificant in some sultanate other than the commonwealth of Love. Usually she and I could walk it off or talk it through but that night the slow burn slowly burned, she wouldn't let it go, even when I pulled the rescue remedy of suggesting La Brasserie only four blocks away in the Brompton Road as a moderately okay second choice for some français cooking that night. Walking there I could feel her simmer, but every time I asked her if there was something on her mind she answered, "No." She simmered through South Ken, past the tube station, along Pelham Street, past the intersection where the crowning structure of the Victoria and Albert Museum shone under its spotlights like a folly of spun sugar. She simmered through the dark green doors of La Brasserie, across the three-color tile floor in shades of tan into a banquette beneath the yellow walls facing the long zinc bar. She simmered through her omelette and her frites and her salade de Roquefort and two bottles of the mayor of Sancerre's mouthfilling vin rouge until, the wine working its standard miracle, she said, "I'm sorry, Noah."

"—want to let me in on it?"

"—if I could, I would."

"Okay."

"—but I can't."

"Why not?"

"I don't have the details."

". . . of—?"

"I feel knotted up. Anxious. I don't know why."

"—is it . . . us?"

"I don't think so. I don't know. I think we're fine the way we are."

"—you think we're 'fine'?"

"Yeah. You know. I think we're fine."

"Maybe I don't 'know'," I said. "I mean—I think we're more than 'fine'."

"—you know what I mean."

"—in fact, I can't imagine anything 'finer'."

I should have stopped there, but instead I said, "Can you?" and she said, "Yes," and the next thing I knew she was pushing back the table and I was standing up and throwing fives and tens and twenties on the tablecloth and she was heading for the door, her trench-coat swinging from her shoulders, her Doc Martens squeaking on the tile, and I was staring at her head, her dark neat head as she pushed against the door, the cold air reaching me a moment later as she kept going straight across the pavement, out into the street, her head turned to the left to hail a taxi, out into the street before she had a chance to know what hit her.

I saw the front end of the black Mercedes strike her on the right side, strike her hip and thigh upending her backwards over its hood so the right side of her head struck its windshield and shattered it, then she kept on going, though the car had stopped, she kept flying with the speed she'd picked up from the moving car, she flew headfirst fifteen or twenty feet, her arms outstretched, across on-coming traffic, until she landed on her stomach in the Brompton Road.

The whole thing must have lasted a few seconds though it seemed much longer and I already knew from covering armed insurrection under fire that everything that's said about slo mo is absolutely true.

She wasn't moving, but she wasn't dead. She was bleeding from her head.

People came from nowhere—everywhere—the waiters ran out of the restaurant, then ran back in, then ran back out again, with towels. Someone called an ambulance. Someone said, "Don't move her." Someone else said, "The thing to hope is that it's not the spine." "She stepped right out in front of him," someone else was saying, "not his fault at all, poor man." I kept talking to her, saying all the things she loved to hear—"Lilith, Elvis lives. Lilith, the Stones were nine times better than the Beatles. Lilith, Wegman's models are all *dogs*. Lilith, Mac was right, terrorism is declining because after Reagan bombed Tripoli the Syrians said, 'Holy shit, if that's what Reagan will do to a country that *isn't* funding worldwide terrorism, imagine what he'll do to *us* . . . Lilith, can you hear me? Lilith? We're going to be just fine . . . we're fine . . ."

Later I would blame myself for never noticing the way he took her by surprise, for not preventing his positioning himself that way, crouching down above her head while I was kneeling by her in the road. I didn't see him, and I should have seen him. I should have noticed his approach and stopped it. I should have put myself in front of her so that when she regained consciousness, I, not he, would be the first one she would see, the first man who would look into her eyes.

He was wearing a black velvet jacket, black jeans pegged over a pair of cowboy boots and a tee-shirt that read BEEN THERE DONE THAT.

His hair was the color of an ostrich egg.

His eyes were the color of night.

When she awoke her head was face down and she told me later her first thoughts were,

I'm going to die,

and,

I'll never see my love again.

"It was such a strange thing to think," she said.

"—who did you mean by 'my love'?" I asked her.

"—that's what I mean. I didn't know."

"Did you mean me?"

"No—because you were there, I knew you were there, I could hear you. Then I looked up and saw lights . . . and saw Adam."

When she awoke she lifted her head and stared at her hands which were in front of her face and covered with blood from her head wound

"Lilith?" I said. "Can you hear me?"

Somebody said, Tell her to wriggle her toes.

Somebody else said, Ask her to name the days of the week.

She lifted her head and stared at her hands; she lifted her head and looked right up at Adam.

He covered her hands with his hands.

Only then did I see him—not so much him, but his hands on her hands, with her blood between them.

Then everything happened at once.

The ambulance came, they lifted her onto a stretcher, they asked her her name, they asked her the days of the week, they asked her to wriggle her toes, they asked her the name of the current Prime Minister.

They asked me who I was and I said, "Her fiancé."

They asked me where she lived and I told them my address in London, while Adam listened.

At some point—I think it was as the police were arriving and the paramedics were loading her into the ambulance—I finally put it together that the man with eggshell-colored hair and the bad tee-shirt must have been the one who had been driving the car that had done this to her, so I hit him. There was nothing good about the punch except the way he took it—it was, otherwise, a bad punch, the kind of punch a drunk throws, wide, ill-conceived and self-pitying. I hit him in the face and hurt my hand but I made his nose bleed.

He laughed at me.

He put his hand, already bloody from the blood on Lilith's hands, up to his nose, then shook his head and laughed. Then he looked at me with an expression not easily forgotten. It was the expression of someone willing to wait a long time for revenge.

I turned away, never expecting to see him again, and climbed into the ambulance. As the door closed, I saw the lacerations on Lilith's head and I heard a sob heave out of me. I took her hand and said, "I think we should get married. I'm serious," I said.

Lilith squeezed my hand and said, "*I'm* the one with the skull fracture here, Noah."

In fact it wasn't a skull fracture, it was a concussion, but she took twelve stitches, and while she was being sewn up my beeper beckoned me to call New York, a normal occurrence when I'm in London since New York doesn't care about the difference in the time zones or about the fact that I might possibly have a life which might allow me to be doing something interesting around midnight like sleeping, or making love. I considered not answering the call but I knew what would happen if I didn't, so I did. If I didn't they would send somebody looking for me, usually Mac, who, to their way of thinking was in the neighbourhood by virtue of the fact that he lived in Paris. So I called New York, and I got Boot. And Boot said there were rumors that Mandela was going to be released from prison within the week. So Boot said, "You have to go to Jo'burg ay-ess-ay-pee."

"No."

"—'*no*'?"

"Lilith was just hit by a car, so I can't. I'm calling from the hospital."

"Ha, ha," said Boot.

"They're stitching her head up right now."

"—*trop drôle.*"

"So get Ivy to go."

"Ivy has never *met* Nelson Mandela . . ."

"—so now Ivy can. Chance of a lifetime. Whose rumors are they, anyway? Botha's or the ANC's?"

"The ANC's."

"—forget it."

"You gotta do this, man. You're the only one who can do it."

"Ivy can do it from Delhi, I'm saying—"

"—since when does Lilith getting hit by a car mean you can't go anywhere?"

"Since I almost saw her fucking die is since when. Since it occurred to me that she might actually get killed, in her line of work. Since three hours ago. Since I asked her to marry me. That's since when."

"—well, I hate to be a prick, but you've had more than your share of personal time since you met Lilith. More than Mac gets, even. And he's a family man."

So I flew to Jo'burg in the morning.

I flew to South Africa having sat up all night, after bringing Lilith home from the hospital, sat up all night at the foot of the bed, our bed, with her feet in my hands, staring at her. She had been wearing suede pants and a black turtleneck at the time of the accident. At the hospital, they hadn't undressed her—at the hospital their major concern had been her head. They looked the rest of her over, made their assessment and got down to the business of x-rays and stitches. But she had minor scrapes on her body and blood had dried into the lining of her pants, into the weave of her sweater, so I had to cut the clothes from her, scissor her out of them. She was doped up so I carried her in from the taxi, over the threshold, light as a feather, a weight, for a woman, that should be called a perfect Cordelia. I put her down on the bed and started to cut her clothes away. Through the drug she kept saying, "It's your kind of story, Noah, it's perfect for you, I wish I was going."

Then she asked for some music.

"Play *Tosca*," she said.

She fell asleep and I sat at the foot of the bed, not really watching her—it was too dark for that—listening to the night and her breathing. After a while she woke and said, "Fucking christ, everything hurts. Morphine's worn off, have to pee. Lift me up, Noah, will you, please?"

Some things make me cry, remembering them.

When she was in my arms, she said, "Lucky you, you'll fly over the desert."

"—I can't leave you like this. I'm not going, you can't even walk."

". . . I can walk. Promise me someday I'll do the desert."

"—can't even pee."

". . . I can pee. It's the drug. I can pee, I can walk—promise me next year I'll do the Sahara."

"Next year you'll do the Sahara."

". . . no, the Sinai."

"—the Sinai."

"—cross it on foot."

"—on fucking foot."

I never dream of the desert, myself, but she did—a landscape she went to, while dreaming, and once, when I asked her to explain its hold over her she answered, "All light, no shadow."

I wish love were like that.

Or maybe I don't.

All light no shadow renders everything flat.

Darkness is deep—why is that? What's the reason behind that illusion?

I ask too many questions. It's a habit. The truth is I don't give a fuck if reality's flat, or if the earth's flat, or if only the meek shall inherit flat earth. I ask questions I don't really care about hearing the answers to—that's what she said, in the end. She said, "You want to know what the problem is, Noah? The problem is you ask too many questions you don't want the answers to."

Is it hot enough for you?

Did you have a nice time?

Can I get you another?

Asking is easy—the answer is hard. What I had tried to be able to tell her was that my work hadn't formed me, I wasn't "a type", a "journalist" type, I was a person who could make sense of his life only by asking himself why when who what and where.

Why did she leave me?	(Adam)
When did she leave me?	(The next day)
Who made the first move?	(He did)

What was he thinking? (I have to have her)
Where did they have their first fuck? (In my bed)

There are some things you don't need to know.

For example: How many angels dance on the head of a pin? People of good mental health know that angels blow horns and pluck strings, Annunciate, fall and occasionally weep, but angels don't dance. They don't cut God's rug, atoms dance on the head of a pin, but angels do not. Some people spend sleepless nights at computers checking and re-checking, running facts through, facts about angels and facts about pins about stainless steel pins about stainless steel density and how many molecules fit on a flat or curved surface the size of the eye of a fly, what was he doing in London, where had he been going in that black Mercedes, and *who* can prove, anyway, that angels don't dance? Some people, see, are obsessed. Some people, like me, are obsessed not with seeking the truth—that's too tarnished a grail—but with seeking a re-creation, with finding out how the other half lives, how people wake in the morning and take up the threads of their lives, how and why people act as they do, how and why people love, why the people we love love other people.

I cry too much—that's another thing she said, in the end—I ask too many questions and I cry easily and she didn't like seeing men cry.

Stripped of its love an affair is a monstrous thing to behold, a virtual Omaha Beach to survive or be slaughtered upon.

It got ugly.

It got ugly between us, most notably in Berlin in November—but from the night of the accident until I saw her again ten months later, she dropped out of my life, she disappeared. In her stead, for a day, there was Adam.

my familiar

Returning to Heathrow from anywhere, but especially after a long haul, always gives me a lift. As airports go, it's my familiar. I've spent more time hanging around there than hanging around any other, I know the Yardies there and the people in charge of security and the lady who changes the money.

But arriving back from Johannesburg I was anxious and edgy—I hadn't spoken to Lilith all week. Part of the problem was South African phones, but even when I'd gotten through to the flat there had been only my own voice in response on my answering machine. And Mandela, of course, hadn't been released and wouldn't be until January the following year, so that was a bitch because I'd been reduced to doing one of those stories-about-the-missed-story which I hate like hives. And an additional bitch was that on the plane I'd discovered that Holden, my yuppie twelve-year-old deputy from Harvard who'd gone to school with the publisher's son, had filed three pieces in my absence from the London desk, the first one on the eternally news-worthy future of fox-hunting in England, the second on the history of cement and the third about an eighty-six-year-old pixie expert from Sussex. "*He seems to know everything but everything seems to be all he knows*," was one of the key sentences in this last report. That, and, "He is currently studying the number 5040."

So although it was great to be back in the jaws of the long English winter, I was feeling a loss of control over events in my life, feeling semi-pissed off and unsettled, plus I was still dressed in a seersucker summer-weight suit.

It was a Saturday morning—so that was a bitch, too, because the sky god at Heathrow dumps fifty planes on the ground at the same time every Saturday from the U.S. of A., India, Yemen, Malaysia, Dubai and Toronto—all bound for the same immigration line.

So I clocked another hour and a half of my life on earth at Heathrow that morning, ringing Lilith from a phone in the baggage hall and getting my voice on my answering machine. I left a message. "Hi, baby, it's me. I'm at Heathrow. I'll be home in a bit. I'll bring coffee," it said. Not only did I get to record it, I got to play it back later that day.

My flat occupies the two lower floors of a Georgian house on the north side of a quiet street one block from the Portobello Market in a neighborhood of which I am intensely fond and to which I am homefully attached because it's like living in the Village in New York or on the Ile-St-Louis in Paris. Everything I need or want when I'm in London exists within a fifteen minute walk from my front door—restaurants, art film house, travel bookshop, produce stalls, walk-in clinic and an ATM across the street from my favorite pub—plus the antiques market every Saturday.

The neighborhood was crowded with tourists that morning and I had the taxi drop me at the corner so I could buy coffee, milk and croissants. While I was at it, I bought her some flowers.

It was a gorgeous January day, sharp and bright.

I had my house key in my hand and when I reached to slide it in the lock my hand was shaking from the cold. When the key touched the lock there was a short-lived spark.

Tosca was playing on the stereo.

There were dishes in the sink; there was the careless litter of a take-out curry on the kitchen counter.

Through a wide arch one passes from the kitchen to the sitting room at the other end of which there is a corridor leading to the bedrooms, my work room and the garden.

I walked into the sitting room, toward the stereo to turn the volume down.

But there was a man sitting on the sofa, facing me, wearing

my silk bathrobe, the one Lilith had given me at Christmas.

He scared the shit out of me.

He had his feet up on the coffee table, and the robe was parted at his thighs. The robe was small on him. I could see the half sacs of his testicles. His penis was dark purple, like a fruit.

He waved his hand and said, "Not *my* pet piece of music, I assure you." He smiled. "I'm a Wagner man, myself."

"—what the fuck . . . ?" I started, but the question died.

His eyes were what made me remember him—his eyes and his hair.

On the night of the accident his hair had looked silver, now it was the color of weak piss.

His eyes were unmistakable, cloaked and menacing. Their leer, I would later learn, was the result of an eye muscle disease, a symptom not of his malice or his lechery but of a degenerative disorder, a morbidity of small specific muscles in the vastness of his body, as if the effort of holding up, controlling his monumental façade had resulted in subtle but hazardous structural fissures.

"Surprised to see me?" he asked, already reading the answer.

"You're in my robe," I said. It was a stupid thing to say.

"Ah, yes," he said, glancing down, "—that, too. That, too," he repeated, gazing back at me. As if to let me know my robe was not the only thing of mine that he was in.

The puzzle pieces there could only fit to form a picture that I didn't like the looks of and didn't want to see—and I was having a rough time believing I was not up to my knees in deep whatever.

I tossed my gear into a chair and moved through the hallway to the bedroom where I thought I would find Lilith.

The bed was all torn up but empty, and her suitcases were lined up on the floor before the closet.

Hanging on the closet door was his camelhair coat, pale suit, dark shirt and an ivory satin tie.

He was on his feet, going toward the stereo when I came back in the room, and I had forgotten that he had about three inches on me or else I would have swung at him again.

"Where's Lilith?" I demanded.

"—look, I really am awfully sorry about all this, old boy," he said in that way that people have, especially, certain kinds of English people, of claiming to be sorry when in fact they're busting out in spores of joy. He had an English accent but, like most Americans, I'm deaf to English accents, capable of finding Cockney in a crowd but incapable of all that consciousness of class they tie themselves into severely fucked up knots about. But he wasn't English, I could tell, he was just the sort of Anglo-sucker who might try to buy himself a title.

"—we weren't really expecting you to be back quite this soon . . ."

WHERE'S LILITH it sounded like I shouted.

". . . oh . . . gone, said something about the stitches coming out. Shouldn't be that long, I should imagine. She goes to those Frenchmen in South Ken, does she not—?"

"You're history, bud," I told him from the door. "When I get back you're gone, you understand? You're outta here. You're yesterday. You're last year's news."

Just calm down, I tried to tell myself, pushing through the tourists on the street to find a taxi—*christ*, I hate Americans in London, why the hell do they come here? Thousands of them, buying Wales's wedding china, picking over pewter whatnots, marveling at junk that has Sale of The Empire all over it. Two particularly well-cut specimens from some sundashed suburb in I would have said either Connecticut or Texas had just bagged themselves a cab to haul them and their newly-acquired authentic Victorian shitpot back to their hotel when I closed on them at a trot, shouting Hey there, hey there, hiya, hiya, gotta have this cab, I gotta have it, Press Emergency—

"*Nice* people, Americans," the cabbie smiled as I slipped in, "most of 'em'll give you the shirts right off their backs—where you from?"

When I didn't answer him he shot me a look in the rear-view-mirror and christ knows what he must have seen across my face because he turned a half-turn in the driver's seat and asked, "You goin' t' be all right, mate?"

I nodded and gave him the name and address of Lilith's clinic in South Ken and he must have thought that I was about to die on him because he got us there in no time.

But I should have called, that was another stupid thing, I should have called ahead and made them keep her at the clinic 'til I got there because just as I was paying off the taxi driver I saw Lilith further down the street, getting into a taxi of her own.

It was unbelievable—it was like, I'll tell you what it was like, it was like that scene in *Doctor Zhivago* when Omar Sharif spots Lara getting on the tram or already in the tram and the tram starts to move and he starts to run after it and he has a fucking heart attack and dies that's what it was like, in retrospect. I didn't die but I didn't run, either, *I didn't run fast enough*, I didn't know, of course, that I wasn't going to see her again, that weighty fact hadn't fallen on me yet, but I didn't get there soon enough, I didn't call her name loud enough, I didn't run, I let her slip away, oblivious of me, oblivious of my running and my shouting as if I were Zhivago, too, an impotent pain-stricken man falling down among a crowd of people, dying, with the vision of his love before him, in plain sight.

And then I couldn't find a taxi.

And then when I found one we got stalled for twenty minutes between Queen's Gate and the Hilton on Kensington Road. So when I got home, she was gone. Everything was gone. She was gone, he was gone, her suitcases were gone, all her clothes, all her bathroom junk, all her face creams, all her books, all her fucking operas, *Tosca*—everything.

There were two messages left on the answering machine.

The first one was me—"Hi, baby, it's me. I'm at Heathrow. I'll be home in a bit . . ." The second one was in French. It was Jean-Luc, the London chief for Agence France-Presse. He was looking for her, so I called him.

"Noah, *zut*, you sound like what is shit—"

"—where's Divi?"

"—*you* don't know?"

"Has she called you?"

"Not for weeks, the last I heard she was in Golden Triangle . . ."

"—*Burma*, yeah, that was two weeks ago. Before the accident."

"—'accident'?"

"She was hit by a car, someone ran her down here in London last Monday."

"—*dieu* is she all right?"

"I think so. I don't know. I've been in Johannesburg."

"—this was a car, what runs into her?"

"—yeah."

"—whose?"

"What?"

"Whose?"

"—whose what?"

"—whose car was it?"

"*—who?*"

"—yes, who was driving it?"

"—fucksake. That's right. I wasn't thinking. Thank you, Jean-Luc. I can find out who he is from the police report—"

But as it turned out, I didn't need to trace him.

I wandered back into the bedroom, badly shaken by the violence of its mess, by the evidential horror of the well-slept-in bed.

I lost some time that afternoon, the first lost hours of what would come to be lost days and weeks. I think I stripped the sheets at some point but I don't remember what I did with them. But I do remember, later, standing in the bathroom, standing at the toilet for a pee. The seat was up and propped there, camouflaged against the porcelain and facing me, was an expensive-looking calling card.

ADAM PENTRÚ

it read,

MINISTER OF TRADE
BUCUREŞTI
ROMANIA.

First he almost kills your woman, then he does her in your bed. Then he leaves his forwarding address where you'll find it when your dick is hanging out. It took me a long long time to learn how to believe it, but *that's* the kind of man she left me for.

I FELL APART.

I fell apart—over time—over nations—in a way that would shame General Motors, every broken part breaking down into even more parts to break down.

A calamity of mind beset me. To use a shopworn phrase, I was not my former self. What's more, I didn't know my former self. There was no former self.

There had been an act of violence in me. On some internal plain a holocaust had rained. The cost was stunning. The cost was everything that had made me happy.

My job did me a favor—it saved my life. It was as if, the way the stories broke that year, newsgathering became a stroll along the midway of a funfair, one thrilling event after another. We journalists only had to stand and take it, History, down in shorthand. Breaking stories were not hard to get—but it was hard to get *all* of them. For me it started as a year when everything reminded me of something I had seen or done with Lilith. That's what sadness does. It robs you of your wonder and usurps surprise. It unfurls an isolation like a tundra, yokes the mind to drag a furrow of self-pity, burrows in the backbone of determination like a feeding worm. Receives no guests but memory's ghost, the solo reminiscence. Weeps pints and walks the nights. Plays sentimental songs. Sadness is a boozy amber liquid. Sadness writes bad prose but oh can sadness sing. I became addicted to laments and heartaches of the music of my roots, country music duets in that Appalachian harmony that sounds like single sorrow singing for itself across a chasm.

In other words opera for a short attention span, so fuck her.

I did a lot of Tammy and George Jones after midnight with the amber liquid burning in the belly. One morning in February three weeks after she'd walked out on me I woke up with my face against a car window focusing on boulders in a green meadow through a misty dawn. I had no idea where I was. I had no idea how I'd gotten there. I had no idea whose car I was sitting in, or if I'd come to wherever I had come to on my own in a loaner or if (the horror) I had stolen it. No keys, no papers in the glove compartment, just a box of Kleenex on the back seat. Nothing in the pockets of the manky suit I'd slept in but a pack of matches that had 'Tootsies' written on it. I was thinking *deep* shit getting out to take a pee but the grass was wet, the car was stopped atop a hill and I took one step, landed twenty yards away beside a giant standing stone.

Avebury, I realized.

I was sitting in the middle of the largest and second most famous henge in England (yes, I was still in England), sacred site for thousands of years onto which I had in a semi-conscious state driven a possibly stolen car. I vaguely remembered being somewhere and needing to "go hug those stones." I sat there a long time, unable to move. That was the morning I relived each moment with her, a riotous montage, a nightmare of recall. I could smell her. I could feel her. I could taste the way she tasted after I had come. I could see her up close in the dark knowing her too well to lose her lines to shadow. See her moving so quick like the light on water. See her hands. Her eyes. Her mouth. But only silence, a flock alighting on the meadow, birds in hedges, tractor coming down the road.

Mac got on a plane and came over from Paris that same day after I called him. Walked me around the cold grey streets, drowned me in coffee and diet cola and put up with me while I talked him to death. "Lose the country & western," he said at the end of two days. But I didn't. For the first week that Lilith was gone I went looking for her—I littered the bureau with E-mail, I hounded Jean-Luc and the AFP crew with a vengeance. After two weeks Jean-Luc showed up at my office and said, "You must stop this. She is fine, people knows where she is. She wants you to stop this."

"—*people*? What people? Who knows where she is? You?"

"Please, if you will, Noah, don't shoot the messenger."

"—people are hiding her from me, Jean-Luc, and I don't know why . . ."

"Give it up, as they say. *C'est fini.* Walk away."

"Have you seen her?"

"*Non.*"

"Would you tell me if you had?"

"Yes."

"Where is she?"

"Don't asks this, Noah. She is taken what you call a leave. Indefinite."

Sadness is a glass you can't look into without seeing your reflection so he couldn't hold my gaze and looked away.

Pinned to my office wall I kept a Hammond world map, same full-color map I stared at every year in grade school when I was bored. Through the years some names have changed but all the country colors have remained the same and I order up a new one every year for sentimental reasons and because it helps me concentrate. And because the incidence of boredom in my day when I'm behind a desk hasn't *everybody else already knew.*

decreased much since I was eight. When he couldn't bear to look at me Jean-Luc turned and stared upon The World. He looked at it for half a minute, then he looked down at his hands.

"You won't tell her it was me," he said.

I shook my head.

I waited.

He stepped toward the map, looking at it, buttoning his coat. He tucked his winter scarf into his coat that way that Frenchmen do. He slipped his gloves onto his hands.

Then he drew a finger to the map and touched it down on Paris, where he tapped it once. He drew a straight line east-southeast across the map through France, Germany, Austria, Hungary and Transylvania, then let his finger rest on Bucharest.

"I have never been," he said, "but they say it was a second Paris in its day." He looked at me. "But once you have had love with Paris what's the point? Right, my friend?"

I can't imagine what I looked like at that moment.

"There are only two reasons why anyone goes to Bucharest these days," he said. "And fortunately for us we are not vampires, for one. And two, we are not under the spell of a Romanian."

Even after he had murmured "*Au revoir*, my friend," I stared in disbelief at the place he'd pointed out on the yellow-colored fist-shaped country on the map. It had taken me two weeks, despite the evidence, in spite of all the dropped hints from my friends, it had taken me that long to realize what, it seemed, everybody else already knew. "The personal is *not* political," Boot would keep insisting through that year, "not for journalists it ain't. Keep your nose wiped and your butt high and deliver what you see not how it fucking feels inside your belly." But Boot rode shotgun on a desk in New York

City and had long forgotten, if he'd ever known, that revolutions can indeed occur, that they devolve one person at a time and we were all caught with received opinions up our asses, our assumptions in the toilet as events rolled on that year and I was not the only cuckold on the planet, whole nations up and left their cozy bedfellows, people left discarded principles at boundaries all over Europe they tacked footnotes to their texts which started Oh, and by the way, everything you've read for twenty thirty years should be forgotten. The little personal desertion in the corner of my heart was about to play out big time in the world and I threw myself into its movements rooting for the broken-hearted schmucks who hoped they could create a bright new future on the altar of their desecrated histories with no more than spoken promises, blind trust and one forsaken image, of an *Eden* that no one here on earth had ever really known.

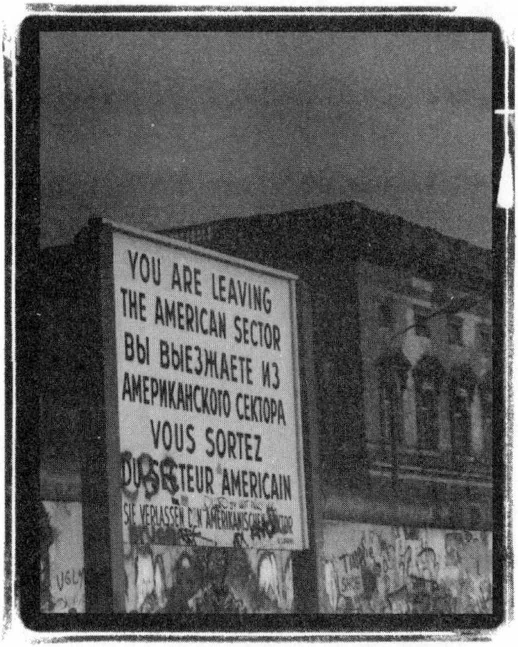

1989

EAST AND WEST BERLIN

Our father

Oh, life is a glorious cycle of song,
A medley of extemporanea;
And love is a thing that will never go wrong;
And I am Marie of Roumania.
—Dorothy Parker

CLAP, IF YOU BELIEVE IN FAIRIES.

When my sister and I were growing up in Virginia after World War II there were only two books in our household that our father hadn't sold or given away to charity when he came back from Germany. One of them was the Bible and the other one was *Gone With The Wind*. Our mother refused to see them leave the house for no more laudable a reason than she had named her son after a leading character in the first and her daughter after her favorite female character in the second. Our father, an early and voracious reader until the war taught him that literature was a futile and insignificant expression, thought our mother's reasoning was stupid but he loved her so he let her have her way. Even when she died from polio when Melanie was five and I was seven, he kept those books there on her bedside table although I'm sure he never touched them. All in all he must have parted with a thousand books because I can recall the bookshelves in the front room in the background of our Thanksgiving pictures being filled with them and those shelves—bare throughout my adolescence—covered all four walls. What makes a man destroy a book—well, not destroy books, exactly—destroy his love of reading? Our father hadn't outlawed reading in the house, Melanie and I were free to read, to frequent the town library—but he did not, would not, engage his mind, he swore, with the printed word after what he'd seen and done in war. Our father. He became an expert at using his eyes not for reading but as signals of his inner vacancy, for staring blankly, staring past me and my sister, staring at plates or out windows or at walls or TV. After he came back from the war if television hadn't been invented, he would have sat every night on the sofa anyway and stared at some mote in the room, so you have to hail progress, progress buttressed the pretense that our father was normal. After Mom died he hauled Mel and me into the kitchen one night for a serious Talk. Melanie was five, as I've said, I was seven, and up until then she hadn't spoken. There was nothing wrong with her, physiologically, she'd passed all the tests with her larynx and brainwaves. She read—she read like a demon so we knew she had language and sometimes when she was excited she wrote in the air, backwards, so you could read what she'd written looking at her. She was such a weird kid I had to love her. She was the first girl, the only girl, I ever loved. And for me she has never grown up even though she's a mother now of more kids than it's righteous to have. But back in the kitchen that night with our father soon after the funeral she still wasn't speaking when he called us in and told us that Mrs. Boddy who'd looked after mom in the iron lung would

be staying on as our house-keeper. Now children, he started off saying, your mother's dead and nothin' can be done about it. But if she was here today she'd back me up in sayin' there are two things you need to know to make your individual ways against the world. The first: Don't never admit you know how to type. And second, don't never learn German. Since he wasn't looking at us anyway, Melanie scrunched her face into a quizzical look. Later she appeared at my bedroom door in her pyjamas and said, "Have you noticed that our father doesn't like the German?" To my knowledge these were the first words she had ever spoken and before I could overcome my stun she was peering at me, in my face, writing out, "What are the German?"

Well, indeed?

"At times," she said to me when we were talking after Lilith had walked out on me, "we got all the way across to each other."

"I remember," I agreed.

"When was that, exactly?"

"After mama died."

"Oh, yeah. And did you and Lilith ever get all the way to each other?"

"I thought we had. I guess not."

When she was about seven or eight Melanie appeared again one night beside my bed while I was sleeping and turned a flash-light on into my face.

"Did you ever read this?" she demanded.

I couldn't see a thing.

She climbed onto my bed and sat down on the pillow by my head and opened up a book and aimed the flashlight on it.

"You're in here," she said.

"'Genesis'," she read. "'Chapter Six. Number Nine: This is the account of Noah.'"

She looked over at me with that dead serious look she had like all of world peace was hanging in the balance, and said, "'Number Ten: Noah was a righteous man, blameless among the people of his time, and he walked with God.

Eleven:

Now the earth was corrupt in God's sight and was full of violence.

Twelve:

God saw how corrupt the earth had become, for all the people on earth had corrupted their ways.

Thirteen:

So God said to Noah, "I am going to put an end to all people, for the earth is filled with violence because of them. I am surely going to destroy both them and the earth."

Fourteen: blah blah blah.

Fifteen: blah.

Sixteen: blah.

Seventeen: blah.

Eighteen:

"But I will establish my covenant with you, and you will enter the ark—you and your sons and your wife and your sons' wives with you."'"

She looked at me again with that carved in granite look like she was posing for Mount Rushmore.

"So what's your point?" I said.

"'Chapter Seven'," she forged on. "'Blah blah blah blah, blah blah blah blah, blah blah blah blah, blah blah blah.

Part Twenty One:

Every living thing that moved on the earth perished—birds, livestock, wild animals, all the creatures that swarm over the earth, and all mankind.

Everything on dry land that had the breath of life in its nostrils died.

No thanks to you.

Every living thing on the face of the earth was wiped out; men and animals and the creatures that move along the ground and the birds of the air were wiped from the earth. Only Noah was left, and those with him in the ark.'"

She shined the flashlight in my face again and I grabbed it from her and turned it off.

"So?" I asked her in the dark.

"You didn't take your sister," she said. "You took your wife and your sons and your sons' wives and the animals along, but you didn't take your sister."

"Jesus, Melanie, it wasn't *me*—"

"Your name's Noah isn't it?"

After that she went on talking like a normal person but she became seriously frightened every time it rained. This was in the days in the United States when even first and second graders routinely practised crawling underneath their desks In The Event Of and families weighed the option between building a bomb shelter or adding on a carport. But Melanie knew the bomb story was a cover up, that when Annihilation dropped from the skies it would fall upon the earth a last time in a liquid guise. When it rained, she sat vigil and began to count. And when the rainbow came and the dove returned an olive branch she would look at me as if to say, Well. I survived another one. No thanks to you.

Which is the story of how I never learned German.

And the story of how I came to participate in the ritual of keeping vigil with my sister as a penance for the failings of that first Noah my namesake, who would let his sister and his mother and his father drown, and with whom I have not a single thing in common except our sex and one four letter word. Even after Melanie outgrew her fear of forty days and forty nights of flood, I continued to find rain, the sound of it, a sluice between what once was and what was coming. If you believe, as I do, the slate is washed clean every night, that the earth, itself, does not distinguish one day from another, then you begin to listen for the sound of rain and understand the nomad, you begin to understand the need to manufacture myths of Transformation.

"Was she—*is* she—anything like me?" Melanie had asked soon after Lilith left me. "—because Jason says the reason that I married him is you and he are two peas in a pod."

"Jason and *I*?"

"—both of you have ship captains' names and before he got dressed after his vasectomy Jason sat there in the cubicle and cried."

"—I've never *had* a vasectomy, Mel . . ."

"I know but if you had you would have sat there in the cubicle and cried. Although in your case maybe before, not after."

"—she *is* like you. I guess. A little. Fiercely independent. Walks that walk. Tomboy. Nothing glamorous."

"—I'm not trying to put Freud on the shelf at K-Mart, Noah, just going for some insight. What was we hate the color of his guts like? A stallion, huh?"

"—it's a shame you ever started talking, Mel, it really is."

"—I mean, from what you say, it sounds like they were only about sex. Which is good news when you think about it."

". . . thanks."

"—I mean, because if that was all it was, they won't last. Two months, tops. I've been there and I've done that."

"I hate that expression."

"—what was her father like?"

"Not like yours."

"I mean, was there a conflict? A daddything?"

"You watch too much American TV."

"I mean, aside from sex it might have been a power-thing. What kind of sexthing was she into? Equality? Submission?"

"—I can't talk about this with my sister, Mel . . ."

"Do you want me to put Jason on the phone?"

"Once, and only once, just once, she asked me to blindfold her."

"—tie her up?"

"—not tie her up. Christ. Blindfold her."

"—just blindfold?"

"—jesus."

"—did you?"

"—no."

"—that was a mistake."

"—yeah well I'll remember that for future reference."

"Don't get huffy."

"—huffy, fucking shit."

"I didn't ask you to talk dirty to me, Noah."

"—people shouldn't know about the sex lives of their families."

"Didn't you ever wonder about mom and dad?"

"—no."

"—that iron lung. And *Mrs. Boddy*. Didn't you ever wonder if dad and Mrs. Boddy got it on?"

"—this isn't helping, Mel."

"—sorry, Noah, nothing will. She did the worst thing she could do. Why in godsname do you want her back—?"

Because I'm empty without her. Because she likes oysters for breakfast. Because she's brave. Because the bed smells like her. Because her nipples get hard just by looking at them. Because she gets goosebumps in the darkroom when the print burns to perfection. Because she never cries. Because she never manipulates facts through the lens simply for an angle.

Because she's color-blind. Because she's tone deaf. Because she speaks every language on earth through her silence. Because she doesn't snore. Because she knows exactly where to be and how to get there. Because she is ambitious only in her work and about that she is tireless, uncompromising, stubborn. Because before I had the chance to tell her where it was, she had found the spot a half an inch below the head of my penis where the nerve lays hidden and hair-triggered. Because when she left she took a passage from my history. Because I was afraid that I'd forget the way she looks. Because, as if I'd lost the key to my genetic code forever, when I found her passport with her picture in it in my shaving kit one night, I sat down and cried.

The duality of lovers, inside/outside, is the thing, when the breach occurs, that can drive either one or both of them toward desperation. I am in you, one lover has informed the other, I love being in you. Inside/outside the lover comes to know the one he loves, the rhythms of her body her positionings her aspects all her attitudes her avenues of thought her frames of mind and when and where she'll weave and feint or shift and move. She had left me all the prints she'd made for me of the photographs of hers I'd asked for. Photographs not of her, by her, inside/outside, the point of view from which each one of them had been immortalized in time had been inside her head, my lover's head, and through my lover's eyes. This is the way that Lilith moves, I'd learned from making love to her, from studying her photographs: this is where she'll go: and this is where she'll stop and freeze to capture something. A writer's moves are different, not necessarily seeking such close range. Even in the dark I'm seeing, she once told me; *especially* in the dark. She used to look at other people's photographs as if they were dispatches. See, I would have been two feet further back. See, look how this has fucked with the horizon. Can you read your paragraphs before you write them? she had asked me once.

You mean while the news is breaking? Absolutely.

I print pictures that way, too. While they're still inside the camera. In my head.

She had made her first still photo in her head, she'd said, while being blindfolded. It was her opera debut. Debut *and* finale because the only tune she could approximately carry was "Amazing Grace", a dirge, and she sang it pretty horribly. But Divo and Diva had had high hopes for her and as soon as she was old enough Divo started using her as the half-caste in *Madama Butterfly*. Butterfly was the only rôle Lilith's mother could really bring off at her height so Divo trotted her around in it whenever and wherever he could, and as soon as Lilith could more or less get up on two pins he cast her as the boy named Sorrow, the bastard babe of Pinkerton. Lilith was a girl playing a boy in an opera where her own mother played her mother except as a Japanese woman singing in Italian. It was usually very late at night when Lilith was brought on in the final act and blindfolded as Butterfly rips her own guts out with her father's sword—inscribed TO DIE WITH HONOR WHEN ONE CAN NO LONGER LIVE WITH HONOR—while singing about love. That's opera. So when she asked me one night for the blindfold it was innocent, I thought, it was something going back to something good and straight, a time when she was playing in the bosom of her family on a stage, planning stills behind her eyelids only she could see. But even though it was spoken in a moment of playfulness between us, the request came at a time when blindfolds reminded me of hostage-taking so I said no, not thinking what it might mean to her, only thinking of what it meant for me.

Both of the people that I've told this story to—only Mac

and Melanie—have told me that not doing it for her was a mistake. If you had a problem making love to her, seeing her blindfolded, Mac advised, you should have put the blindfold on the both of you. If that isn't love, what is?

"Is that the Scottish definition?"

"—what? 'Love is blind'? Nay. Drunk is blind. Love is being two or nothing while pretending to be one. Love's a sneaky transformation. But after all this, could you take her back?"

The opportunity did not arise.

Even though she changed the locks in Paris, she had my London key, she didn't have to knock, which drove me crazy every time I came home from being elsewhere, hoping against hope to find her there.

You don't know what it's like when someone simply disappears from your life.

I started watching pictures on the services, unsigned, unattributed, in case she was trying to elude me, filing incognito from the field—I knew her inside-out, I could spot a Divi . . . blindfolded . . . and I couldn't believe, nor could Jean-Luc and everyone else she had worked with, that Lilith would take "a leave". It was impossible. Her whole life was her work—and, at the time, I meant that in the cruelest way. Nothing else mattered to her. She lived for her work. It was *all* that she lived for. But from the moment I saw her get into that taxi, the trail went cold.

. . . which left me with only one option.

For a while, I didn't want to know any more about Adam than I already knew. Maybe that doesn't make any sense—but, believe me, I couldn't have handled it.

Then one night I was working late in the office on a story and was using a program that searches a name out of old clippings files—and without really thinking about it beforehand, I did it. I typed in his name, hit the SEARCH key and waited. As simple as that. And up it came, the response, as instantaneous as if Peter Pan had begged it to clap, if you believe in fairies: Adam had been at Duff's college at Oxford.

"*Duffins*—!" I hooted five minutes later in my best bray down the horn. "Noah John, here—"

"—ohmygawd I thought he was dead."

"I need a favor."

"—course you do."

"—skinny on someone at your school at Oxford."

"Sorry, we don't eat our own—and anyway, didn't you leave me lost and stranded somewhere? Where was it? Fuck. Guinea-Bisau—?"

". . . *moi*?"

"—no, no, Cameroon. Absolutely. Cameroon . . ."

"—'fraid you've confused me with a blond in a limo. Need you to draw me a straight line connecting Oxford to the current Romanian Trade Minister."

How did it evolve, I wanted to know, that an orphan of the war from a small town on the Black Sea got out of Nazi-occupied Romania and into the arms of academic elitism in the city of dreaming spires only to go back to the country he had fled, behind the iron curtain? Call me a pig-eating capitalist but the conventional wisdom about Romania then was that it was a police state whose citizens subsisted on a diet of grey food, plum alcohol, fear, shit and suspicion. People were dying to get *out*, so why would anyone go *back*?

Duff wanted to know what was in it for him so we worked out a trade and two days later he delivered.

"He liked porn, that's all I could come up with," Duff reported. "No friends. No women worth remembering. But if you needed a something to wank off on, his was a selection of salaciousness *de première odeur* . . ."

"What kind of porn?"

"That I don't know. Classics scholar, so imagine. Degenerate Roman. Published a few poems in the *Vulgar*. Not very good. I'll fax them to you . . ."

It wasn't difficult to find the men who'd been to school with him but it was difficult to find someone who could tell me how he passed his weekends, where he spent his summers, who his friends had been. No one had specifics. "He was good at Latin," constituted the consensus—"it was easy for him, you know, being from Romania—they're all descended from the Romans there, aren't they?" No one admitted to knowing anything about his dabbling in pornography—in fact, no one admitted anything. Except for what I learned from Duff I came up empty on his years in England. People simply closed, a recurring symptom in the English and the one which distinguishes their insularity. They talk a lot—christ knows, all you have to do is turn on their radio or count the number of column inches they devote to columnists as opposed to straight news—but they say substantially little. Information communicated per hundred spoken words in England weighs in at about ten per cent, so, like Hamlet's dad, the average foreign listener gets an aching earful and a tortured response, if one at all, to his entreaty. What I wanted to know, and what I wasn't finding out, was how Adam got to Oxford in the first place—how he got to England. This took a lot of legwork in my so-called leisure time, but finally I found someone who'd known him when he was an adolescent at Uppingham before Oxford who told me that he remembered Adam only because Adam, who had not been good at sports, bragged to him that he didn't need to play team games because he believed team games debased man as super-man, and that the true test of manhood was only to be found in a contest where life, itself, was in the balance. Adam claimed he knew this for a fact because he, himself, had tested death. His English was very bad when he first arrived at Uppingham, and the other boys made fun of him, but he fought off their ridicule by bragging—bragging in Latin class, for example, that he came from the same town on the Black Sea where Ovid had been exiled by Augustus Caesar—bragging in private to my informant that he had actually *killed* someone and had avoided punishment by assuming the victim's identity and escaping on a ship that was torpedoed during the war and that he had been lost at sea for seven days. "Every time he told this story," the informant told me, "the other lads and I would beat him up. I mean—if you're going to tell a tale, you ought to make it credible, at least. We had to beat him—don't you think?—just to make a better liar of him. Finally, of course, he gave the story up. They all do, eventually . . ."

Except, what the lads all thought had been a lie turned out, after weeks of digging, to be the only scrap of truth I could find out about him. He *had* survived at sea after the sinking of a ship, but of which ship and in which sea took me a long time to discover. In the years I had narrowed the possibilities to—between 1939 and 1942—a hell of a lot of boats were going down in a hell of a lot of waters around Europe. Families were being divided along with towns and cities and nations, borders were being renounced or reclaimed, and children and babies were being shipped by desperate parents to safer spots on the changing map. War was coming to Europe, again. Trying to track the course of one life through that mess was more than daunting and I looked for every excuse, any excuse, to move in on my subject, to get Boot to let me go to Romania. *No* was the repeated answer, "not in the shape that you're in."

"What shape is that?" I wanted to know.

"Look in the mirror," Boot told me, but I was afraid to. I threw myself into my work and used what small skills I had for nursing the story on Adam, deluding myself all the while that it stood for something more stately than just the excitement of coondogging my rival. And maybe it did, in the end—but in the beginning, my motive was simple. I wanted her back. Or I wanted revenge.

So I went on with my search, discovering, along the way, something I should have known all along, something my years in this business should have taught me, or maybe *did* teach me without my realizing it: people vanish in war and people's histories vanish when they're not put to paper. Without a paper trail—birth certificate, *carte d'identité*, passport, work permit—a person is lost in the crowd, statistically nonexistent. A person who stays under the radar by chance or by method, then, remains freer, truly free, of the state, of surveillance, of history—and the spectre of untaxed, untaxable hordes must scare the shit out of governments. Searching for Adam made me aware of how much of a record I'd made, how much was on file about me, including my fingerprints, blood type, phone number and genealogy. Computers, of course, made the invasion of privacy issue worse; but, that said, after slogging through forests of paper at the halls of records, I started to wish the invention of silicon chips had come in with the wheel.

The aid agency that had placed Adam in England had folded at the end of the war, but, finally, after a lot of false starts and dead ends, I found his name on an old Red Cross list of refugees transferred from Budapest, and the Budapest list led me back to Constantinople, where a boy with his name had been bivouacked with the Red Crescent after being rescued at sea by Turkish fishermen near a village called Şile. The boy, calling himself Adam Pentrú, claimed to have been on the refugee ship *Struma* out of Romania when it was hit by torpedoes on or about 24 February, 1942, in the Black Sea. *Bing*, as they say in church halls, fucking-*go*.

As catch-of-the-day, for Turkish fishermen, a boy was more worthless than an unexploded floating mine or the flotsam of an airplane fuselage or rotting parachute silk, especially if the boy was hypothermic and near dead, which Adam was. But they saved him anyway, with that logic that some people have in wartime that by saving individual specimens of mankind they can contribute to the future greater good of all humanity.

According to the Red Crescent report to the Red Cross, the boy—who understood no Turkish—repaid the fishermen's efforts by nearly dying on them so they turned him over to the local imam who was the first to write his name down and the first to make a notation next to it that I did not immediately understand. I got in touch with my friend Ülkü the Turkish Language Bureau Chief at the BBC World Service and described the circumstances of the ledger entry and the fact that it was later given to the Red Crescent in Constantinople, along with the boy, who was put under the protection of the British High Commission there and interrogated about the sinking of the *Struma*.

"He survived the *Struma*?" Ülkü asked.

"You know about the *Struma*?"

"Famous sinking. Not as titanic as the *Titanic*, but still famous in the lexicon of sinkings."

"Waltz me through it—?"

"—with pleasure."

During the war, Ülkü's uncle, Amca Osman, had been high up in the branch of Turkish military charged with policing the waters between the Black Sea and the Aegean—the Bosporus, the Golden Horn, the Sea of Marmara and the

Dardanelles—but especially the Bosporus, Europe's back door. In the autumn of his years, his wartime experiences weighed heavily on Amca Osman and he was given to sitting late into the night on the balcony of his *yali* on the Asian side of the strait, drinking *raki*, cracking walnuts with his knuckles and disparaging the British to his impressionable nephew. The story of the *Struma* figured prominently in this litany, and although many of his stories lost their rub in tedious recital, the lustre of his anger always banked when he began to talk about her. It was that rare thing in the Black Sea—a converted cattle boat for the transport of refugees. Berthed in Constanţa, Romania, she had been flying neutral colors, Panamanian, when she embarked for Palestine on the 12th of December, 1941, five days after the attack on Pearl Harbor, with seven hundred and ten refugees from Germany, Poland, Czechoslovakia and Romania aboard. While she was still in the Black Sea, the United States declared war on Japan, and Germany declared war in turn on the United States and its territories and protectorates, including the Canal Zone, Panama and the *Struma*. German submarines patrolling the Black Sea would have harassed her anyway, but the timing of her mission was, to say the least, unfortunate. Her only hope, once she officially became a ship under enemy registry, was to attempt to run to the Bosporus before being attacked in open waters—which she did, successfully reaching Constantinople on the 16th of December. But the British, who still controlled the mandate in Palestine, were pressuring the Turks to turn back all refugee ships bound for the Holy Land because it was not in the British interest to offend the Arabs there. For more than two months the *Struma* and her human cargo were kept in quarantine in the strait while the British and the Turkish military dithered. Finally, in February, the British High Commissioner in Palestine sent a cable to Ülkü's uncle's commander stating categorically that Jerusalem was under no obligation to receive foreigners, especially "enemy nationals from enemy-controlled territories" whether they were Jews or not, and suggested that the presence of such "nationals" on a ship in such crucially strategic waters as the strait in wartime should be construed as a clear and present danger. So on February 22, the *Struma* was escorted back up the strait to the Black Sea. Two days later she was sunk. Seven hundred and nine people died not counting the crew. There was only one survivor.

"I would like to meet this man," Ülkü told me.

"He's a Romanian."

"I'm not surprised."

"There's one thing I don't understand . . ."

"—what's that?"

"On this paper the imam from Şile filled out for the Red Crescent, there's a mark in closed parentheses shaped like a small 't' after the boy's name. What does that mean in Turkish?"

"—small 't'?"

"—yes."

"But you're joking, Noah."

"No."

"Look at it again."

I looked.

"Is it not shaped like a cross?"

Earth to Noah:

"Is it not the sign, not just for Turks, but everywhere, that symbolizes 'Christian'?"

"—But how would the imam—?"

"Perhaps the boy was wearing a totem, for disguise. It was war. Jews were hated. Or else, perhaps, upon examination . . . Circumcision is a sacred rite in Islam, too, you realize."

"Everywhere?"

"This is not my specialty, my friend, but I believe it's only on the part that matters—"

"—no, I mean, in every Muslim culture? In Romania, for instance?"

Because I knew that Adam wasn't circumcised. He'd made certain that I'd seen that for myself in my own house.

So—what was he? If he had been a Jewish refugee wouldn't he be circumcised? (Not necessarily, I found out: to forfeit the rite of circumcision often meant that parents would rather keep their son alive than jeopardize his future with a cut that would set him apart for the rest of his life, especially in Romania . . .) And if he hadn't been escaping from pogroms against the Jews in Romania why had he been aboard the *Struma*?

"He might have been a gypsy," Ülkü told me. "They went after gypsies in a big way, too, those Romanians did. Still do. But you can always tell a gypsy when you see one . . ."

"—what the hell does that mean?"

"Can't you?"

"No."

"—from their *eyes* . . ."

"Jesus, Ülkü, what a load of crap—"

"We have them in Turkey, too. Everywhere they have these gypsies. Except in North America. And in Far East. Green eyes, gold, or black—and a blond child in every pack as proof that they steal children."

"Tell me you're not serious."

He told me.

"Are you serious?" Holden charged, swanning into my office as I put the phone down. "I just heard you're not going to Paris to cover the bicentennial—"

"Do we knock? Did anybody ever teach you knocking?"

"—in New York they don't knock."

"In New York they don't have doors."

"—you're right."

Bright kid, but flawed. Twenty-seven—whiz-kid with vocabulary, dry as dust with its delivery. Speaks fifty-seven languages, and all alike. Like this? With an inflexion? Likes "to deconstruct the moment"? Likes to formulate "the etymology of the event"? He is astonishingly sophisticated for his age (all the whiz kids are these days), but his patina glossed a pocky knowledge and a rusty education: there were holes in it? Like—major holes? He was not as bad as one assistant I was sent one summer from New York who every day would proffer up a witless gem along the lines of, "Sorry, sir, but the only Berlin in Germany I can find in the phone book seems to be in the GDR . . . ?" The holes in Holden's parachute were not as large as that, although he was given, daily, to at least a single *charmant* construction. Such as:

> Good morning, Holden. How are you?
> I'm not really sure, sir, I think I need a CAT-scan
> or something?

In effect, Holden's smarts settled on a level somewhere between the elevated knowledge of all the things clever people have known since time immemorial and the slippery slopes of things that morons will never get, not ever.

And I can't forget the day he asked me, "What does it mean if it says the 'Tet Offensive'? What's a 'Tet'? Do they mean 'Pet'?"

'So if you're not going to Paris, can I go?" he asked me.

"No."

"How, about Blackpool? Can I go to Blackpool?"

"To do what?"

"Snooker, sir?"

"—snooker?"

"—Finals?"

"Are you good at research? Did they teach you how to research at that fancy school you went to? Because I need someone to—"

"Harvard. It's called Harvard, sir? It's not called 'that fancy school'."

He got me, that time, Holden did.

"—do some digging down in Swansea on a vehicle registration. Black Mercedes. Just your cup of tea, I bet—"

"—because I thought New York could really use a deconstructed piece on snooker finals?"

"Well, Holden, I'll tell ya, one of my guiding principles in life is that all of us are gonna hafta stand before St. Peter one day and St. Pete is gonna say—"

"I don't believe in the concept of St. Peter, sir."

"—he's a metaphor for Death, Holden . . ."

"Oh . . . Okay . . ."

"—St. Pete is gonna say, 'What have you done with all your talent, Holden? Written cream pieces about snooker—?' "

"Nothing wrong with snooker, sir,"

"If there's nothing wrong with it, then why write about it?"

"—sir?"

IF THERE'S NOTHING WRONG WITH IT WHY WRITE ABOUT IT?

"To report it?"

"*—snooker?*"

"—the What of it, the way it happens."

"*News* happens. Sport is made."

"Are you saying, 'Sport is war without war's virtues,' sir?"

I sent him to Northern Ireland.

That was my job, as his boss, as his mentor, as his hero and as a potential father figure. Send him off to frayland. Let him lose his milk teeth on Falls Road and write his lilywhite off about The Troubles. Except he didn't, 'cause he couldn't. Faced with something more intuitive and bloody than the games men play with tapered poles Holden's knowledge failed him and he returned to London after seven days with all the smooth airs of a man with rabies. I'd suddenly started feeling quite paternal toward him. Especially since I'd found out the Mercedes Adam had been driving when he'd run Lilith down wasn't registered to the Romanian legation. It wasn't even registered to a Romanian.

"Cement," I said to Holden, smiling. "You did a piece on *cement* a while ago when I was in South Africa . . ."

"Are you going to send me to *South Africa*?" he asked, a little panicked.

"Not if you're a good boy," I pledged.

The Mercedes Adam had been driving the night of the accident was registered to a German company called Zement.

"—do you speak German?" I asked Holden.

"Of course," he said.

"—*zement* does mean 'cement' in German, doesn't it?"

"Well, it does, yes, sir, etymologically, at its most literal—"

"—German cars, German wine, hell, German lederhosen—but 'German' cement? Is there an export marked in *cement*?"

"Well, it does need a lot of lime, sir . . ."

"Find out everything you can about this company. I want to know who owns it. I want to know what it manufactures. I want to know when it was incorporated, where and why. And if you're very good, Holden? I promise I'll pull strings to get you somewhere within pissing distance of a Princess . . . so you can deconstruct her."

"Not Diana, sir."

"—not Diana?"

"York, please, sir. Those teeth? I think I love big women . . ."

Next day he was back with a full file.

". . . Zement *is* a German company, sir, but not German German, *Swiss* German? It's a trading company, only, in the GDR with a sales office in Berlin? *West* Berlin, that is, but corporate headquarters are actually in Zurich. That's in Switzerland?"

"—I *know* where Zurich is, Holden."

"—New York could really use a piece on Zurich . . . ? Needle city there, these days, I hear?"

"—wipe your nose, kid, Zurich is the Frankfurt bureau's. Unless you want a transfer?"

"Oh, no, sir, why should I want to go to Frankfurt just because I speak the language when I'm having so much fun with you?"

He tossed the Zement file onto my desk.

"Not sure *where* the product's coming from, sir, but 'the product' is your basic med-tech stuff—sixth largest independent supplier in Europe—that means 'non-nationalized', I think—"

"—I know what 'independent' means, Holden."

"—in the *Blut Produktion* field, *die Bluterkrankheit* market—*das Hämoglobin, das Plättchen . . .*"

"And what, exactly, is *that* when it's at home?"

"Blood. Blood products, sir."

". . . 'blood products'?"

"Individual constituents in the blood which can be separated out and marketed along specific lines? Clotting agents.

Immuno-suppressive factors. Hemoglobin. Platelets? To say nothing of the trade in your standard just-plain-blood, as we used to know it."

"There are companies that trade in blood?"

"Sure. There's a trade in human organs. Blood's an organ. Not so long ago there used to be a trade in humans . . ."

"—there still is."

"—there *is*?"

Just for the hell of it I said, "You done real good on this—let me buy you dinner."

"Let *me* buy, and it's a deal?"

I suggested Khan's which is cheap and loud, but he opted for the Standard, where the curries aren't as good, but where it's quiet.

"So where'd you go to school?" he asked, starting to go man-to-man with me over two Kingfisher beers.

"Chicago."

"Really? Wow. All those heavies. Bellow."

"—but I didn't finish."

"Really? No degree? But you seem so smart."

"—back then, Holden, public education was a head start. Thanks, in part, to Sputnik . . ."

Even as he looked at me, before he said it, I could hear it coming:

"—what's a 'Sputnik'?"

Dad and Melanie and I would go out and stand in the yard at night before our bedtime, Mel and me in our pajamas, and Dad would point up to the travelling light and marvel, "There it goes, there it goes, that's a satellite, kids . . ."

"Is it going to *fall*?" Melanie would whisper.

"It *is* falling," Dad would say.

"Is it going to fall on *us*?"

"If it does, we'll hear it comin'."

"What *is* it?"

"It's a kind of ark."

"—like Noah's?"

"No, that one way up there is empty. 'Cept for gizmos—guns an' cameras."

I think that must have been a pretty awful thing to tell a little girl—okay to say to me, I was a boy, I had that guns-and-gizmos chromosome.

"You get on okay, then, with your father?" I asked Holden.

"Oh yeah sure absolutely he's the greatest," he said, his face reflecting the brick red of his tandoori. "You—?"

"Well my sister says we could have stood more Romeo, less Timon . . ."

O no, I thought, don't ask What's Timon? but he didn't. Instead he said, "Yeah—I had a professor who said tragedy teaches us how to die, comedy teaches us how to live. And I always thought Romeo was pretty funny . . ."

He started to laugh.

"And I had another professor," he said, "whose, like, stock answer to every question was, 'Think of it as a sausage.' "

I don't know why, but I started to laugh, too, thinking of things as sausages, thinking of work as a sausage, of love as a sausage, of me as a sausage.

"Comedy," I told Holden, "doesn't teach you how to live. Nothing 'teaches' you how to live. Comedy reconciles us to our insufficiencies," that's all. We have a good laugh, then we wake up in the morning and feel like shit all over again. We slouch through tedium and boredom, longing, though not consciously, for renewal. We halfway listen to the drone of politicians, wishing they had tics that might distinguish them from one another. Dictators, only, keep us alert, and then one day we're watching yet another army in police action against the citizens that it's enfranchised to protect and a skinny slip of youth about Holden's age walks out into a square before a file of rolling tanks and stands unarmed in front of them, pleading, and we wrench ourselves awake, believing for an instant that what we're seeing is believing, that what we're seeing is belief incarnate, or incarnate hope incarnate courage or incarnate desperation, and we weep self-recognition. The human river is both deep and wide. Why it courses, from where it courses, how it holds its course I do not know. But I know that something changed in me in the next four months, starting with four weeks I spent in China with the students in Tiananmen Square. Whether or not it was because, in the beginning, they were committed to non-violence and in the end were violence's victims; or because, as a Caucasian, I was conspicuous, looked up to; or because I had been despairing over Lilith in the months before Beijing —I don't know why I came away from there feeling as I did, I only know that some thing happened. I had seen people die before. I had even had the experience, in Lebanon, of living through a scene from Erich Maria Remarque's novel *All Quiet on the Western Front* when I was on one side of a street with my Lebanese translator and there was another journalist, a photographer and a female civilian on the other side of the street and we were all crouched down in doorways under a cross-fire. A burst of shots sprayed across the pavement on the other side of the street and I saw the woman double over and I ran across to her. I can see her face, even now, because I had to brush away her hair, I had to touch her neck to try to find a pulse, but I couldn't find one. Before I could understand that she was dead, there was another burst of sniper fire behind my back and I turned around and saw the recessed doorway where I'd been sheltering across the street disappear behind a cloud of dust and ricocheting plaster as if it were exploding. If I had stayed there fifteen seconds longer, I'd be dead. My translator was dead. The woman whose hair I held between my fingers was dead. So before Beijing, I had seen the dead, a lot of dead, too many. And I had seen much younger dead, I had seen children die. I had seen a child killed for the first time in 1976, in Soweto. And in 1982 I had seen tens of them, hundreds of them, deformed by hunger, deprived by famine of all individuation, in Ethiopia. So I had seen the young destroyed. And I had been in crowds, too many crowds, all kinds of crowds before. And even though I still hoped at every turn that I might run into Lilith on assignment, by the night of June 3rd I knew that that probability had been decreasing for four months and was by then so small as to exist only in my mind. By then I didn't even know what I would say or do if I encountered her again, all my speeches had been iterated to infinity, all my anger targeted at darkness. Then, that night, I was in the square, at the edge or in the middle of a human river and everyone was silent, listening, waiting, weighing their own futures on the balance of the whole, while a disembodied voice harangued from the loudspeakers, a chant, almost. I had wandered out when it got dark without my translator so I kept pointing to the loudspeakers and making puzzled gestures until several Chinese students who spoke English attached themselves to me. What does it say? I asked. It says the same thing, many times, a student told me. It says, *Go home. Go home, stay alive.* It says, *Go home and save your lives.* Everyone knew that night that the army was on its way; still, nobody moved. 'What do you think is going to happen tonight?" I asked the students. They looked at one another and at me and then one of them answered, *We're all going to die.* And many did; too many. Others were killed later that month after having been tried and found guilty of their convictions. But on the long flight back to London I found myself doodling those words over and over, *go home, stay alive.* I was routed through Hong Kong that time, instead of through Tokyo, and since I always have to make my own airplane reservations, I had put myself yet again in the lose-lose situation of either flying home one way which would take forever or flying home in the opposite direction which would also take forever. And because I like touching down in California about as much as I like sitz baths, I decided to go west, fly back over Asia, with a touch down in Bahrain. If you've never touched down in Bahrain you've missed an airport retail shopping glut surpassed only by Schiphol (the best) in Amsterdam, and Rhein-Main (for cameras) in Frankfurt—but the truly memorable part of touching down in Bahrain is what art people call its "installations". The Bahrain airport "installations" change irregularly, sometimes every month, sometimes once a year. The last time I had been there, I had been with Lilith on the way from Paris to I can't remember where; Kabul. (As Holden would say, That's in Afghanistan?) The installation in the airport that time was titled (I kid you not) MESOPOTAMIAN BOOTY, and Lilith and I got a case of Terminal giggles over it. In order to provide an answer to the eternal question, "What the hell is This Thing?", each exhibit had its own description card typed in Arabic (which neither of us could read) and English (which the typist clearly did not speak). The first item's card read, ITEM ONE: MOOFLON WITH WHEELS. Next to it, with no attempt to explain the disappearance of Items Two through Six, was ITEM SEVEN: ALTAR WITH KNIFE AND UTERUS, which was followed by ITEM SEVENTEEN: BOWL WITH MAN AND COMBLIKE ANIMALS. The man of Item Seventeen was your average nursery school stick-figure with a big round head and what appeared to be a *rake* planted in his cranium. He and his identical twins were the dominant figures on all the rest of the artefacts, and I was about to start to get serious and stop giggling and tell Lilith that I had seen figures like these before in the petroglyphs on the hills outside Taos, New Mexico, but a man from our plane who had touched down with us came up behind us, lamenting, "*Mais c'est tous en anglais . . .*" He turned to Lilith and said, "*—parlez-vous français?*"

"*Un peu,*" she lied.

"*—pouvez-vous traduire pour moi?*"

"*Oui—'Aucun sait,'*" she pretended to read from the card, "'*quand les rakeheds vins—*'"

"*—'les rakeheads'?*"

"*—'vins sur la terre pour la première fois . . .*'"

NO ONE KNOWS WHEN THE RAKEHEADS FIRST CAME TO EARTH—

On my touch down from Beijing the exhibit in Bahrain was sponsored by the indigenous pearl-fishing industry and the installation was titled, in English, HOW WE IN BAHRAIN PERAL FISH: THE HISTORY OF PERALS.

I stood there and missed her, and thought about perils —stood at the window and looked out on a post-midnight landscape colored by sodium lights and I thought about home, about Beijing and dying and loving and saving your life. So I rang up my office in London:

"—Holden? What are you wearing?"

"*—sir?*"

"*What are you wearing?*" I asked.

". . . where are you calling from, sir? Are you safe? Is this urgent—?"

"Bahrain, and I just want to know if you're wearing a suit."

"—this is a phonecall about what I'm wearing?"

"Because if you're wearing a suit, Holden, I just want to

tell you they're great, you have wonderful suits, we've seen them, we love them. But you don't need to wear them to work every day. On days when you're not going out to meet Mrs. Thatcher, take it from me: lose the suits. And for christsake lose those suspenders."

". . . sir? . . . are you sure you're all right?"

"And lose the 'sir'. Don't call me 'sir'. Don't call anyone 'sir'. And pick me up at the airport. And don't wear a suit."

Fuck it, I thought. Save a life, any life, if you can't save your own. I'd like to think I saved Holden's, a little after Beijing. I'd like to think I helped make him something he might not have been. And by the time in late November when I was getting Boot to hold two front page columns every day for six days in a row for Holden's exclusive dispatches from Prague, I knew I had created a good kind of monster because Holden was having himself photographed with the Civic Forum in Wenceslas Square sporting a two-day old beard and a sweatshirt that had SID VICIOUS WAS BLAMELESS BUT SICK written on it. God knows what he's up to right now. Probably interviewing the last rakehead left on the planet who just stumbled out of the jungle in Borneo. Or acting behind the scenes in a top secret peace process. Or negotiating the release of a hostage. Or discovering an heretofore unknown prime number. Or, like me, travelling on yet another airplane, another journey, and hoping, like me, that this one won't turn out to be like all the rest. But most likely, wherever he is, he's thinking of it—whatever it is—as a sausage.

The Wall

ON NOVEMBER 8th, 1989, I turned forty-two. I was covering the demonstrations in Leipzig where Melanie tracked me down and woke me up at some ungodly hour:

"—happy birthday. How 'ya holdin up?"

"—been better. I've been younger, too. The Politburo resigned today. Everyone thinks The Wall is coming down . . ."

"Great news. What Wall?"

". . . so I'm going to Berlin."

On November 9th I went to Berlin and The Wall came down.

On November 10th and 11th thousands of East Berliners visited the West, many for the first time.

On November 12th I ran into Lilith.

Even though I was definitely older than I'd ever been, in the preceding autumn weeks I'd been working harder than I'd ever worked and had spent more time on the road than I'd ever spent since I had started in this business. I like falls —if I had to pick a favorite time of year, it would probably be fall, and that particular fall had been especially melancholy because I was in those ancient forests at the heart of central Europe, watching chestnuts hardening against the coming cold, watching meadows try to hold their dark green edge of summer which succumbed, protesting first in a blaze of orange, then going red as blood, then moldering to shades of purple that were both the hues of European royalty and of quiet resignation; watching game rise over border crossings where a line of Trabants in the mist of morning stretched, the cars identical as clones, like ghosts in single file to the horizon, indecipherable in their outward sameness, each one ferrying its own inreplicable and unreported history. And I missed Lilith, I missed seeing her on the periphery of crowds, circling 'round and circling in.

There were a lot of photographers on the Trabant Trail from East Germany to Hungary and Czechoslovakia in the early autumn and for a while, in October, I shared a car with a German one, a woman, from Popperfoto, just so I could watch her work. I think she thought I was coming on to her so one morning at the border checkpoint near Karlovy Vary in Czechoslovakia, when we were sitting together in the front seat of a rented Mercedes trying to stay warm with a Thermos of watery junk that was supposed to pass for coffee, I said to her, "I used to be in love with a photographer," which didn't come out exactly as I'd intended, because once I'd said it I realized it really *did* sound like I was coming on to her so, like a jerk, I added, "—and boy, I'll tell you, never again!" and she said, reciting every syllable with her precision-driven accent, "Yes. I know just what you mean by 'never again'. I used to be in love, once, with a man."

I was having no luck making conversation with women anymore because the day before that, I had offered half a sticky-bun (they're called *moučníky*'s in Czech) to a woman journalist from the Hungarian news service MTI and I had thought she said, "No, I shouldn't, because it makes me fart," when really what she'd said was, "No, I shouldn't, because it makes me *fat*," and I said something in reply like, "With all this soft coal air pollution, believe me, no one will notice one little fart," which just went to prove my sister's long held belief that I spent my time with women acting either like a cad or a buffoon.

And you can convince yourself quite easily, when you're on the road, that you're not lonely because you're asking questions all the time, making people talk. But invariably where you're staying has no water or no running water or no hot water or no electricity or no electricity at night or no electricity for anything moderately electric, like a light bulb, like a light bulb brighter than an egg, and you end up staring into a bowl of bright pink soup for dinner, brighter than the light bulbs, a kind of brightness only beets can generate day after day and soup after soup, and you find yourself grateful that at least the soup isn't cabbage and wondering why the hell, at your age, you're alone *and* uncomfortable.

And why your socks are wet.

Your socks haven't been dry for three weeks and the countryside, let's face it, is beautiful but smells like pig.

I missed the comforts of big cities—Western ones. I missed phones that worked so I could call anywhere around the world whenever I wanted to, when I couldn't sleep, when I was lonely, if I wanted pizza burrito sushi or curry or to find out what the trade laws were in blood, if private companies in South America, for instance, could ship blood in those plastic bags it comes in to Liverpool or to Cannes or Nice for transfusions or to hospitals and hemophiliacs in Luxembourg or Dresden or Romania.

I talked to anyone I could that autumn who knew even something slight or sketchy about blood—about blood banks, about transfusions and donations. I'd be waiting at a border crossing or standing at a demonstration with my translator and I'd just ask someone, a soldier or a street cleaner or a student, "Have you ever donated blood?" and if they said "Yes," I'd ask them where and when and how it had been done. I made a point of visiting donation centers everywhere I went, in Budapest, in Prague, in Leipzig—but these were state-controlled blood centers attached to hospitals administered by the state, and I needed information about free market blood, the Western kind, the blood of capitalism and free enterprise.

So I was eager to get out of the countryside, away from secondary cities and shoulder up to a bustling he-man place whose ethos was materialistic and whose icons were consumers: West Berlin. Except every time I tried to get there that autumn something happened somewhere else that kept me from it, until the day after my birthday when it seemed the entire media population of the world descended on it, including Lilith. And the strange thing was, I was so caught up in the general disbelief and mass euphoria, that the thought of running into her wasn't even remotely on my mind. Sod's Law, the English call this, Sod being short for Sodomite, I guess because it takes you from behind.

I told Holden in London to book two rooms for us and get on a plane to West Berlin and meet me there. I wanted him with me because no journalist above the salt should miss this story, and besides, he spoke the language. He got us two rooms at the Inter-Continental on Budapester Strasse, between the Brandenburg Gate and Kufürstendamm, and when we met up the next morning I told him to go out and play, go out and bring back all the human stuff and I'd cover the predictable, thank you, just the facts, m'am, who and why and what and when and where and how the boys and girls and General Haddock (no, not a character from "Tintin" but the U.S.A.'s top military man in West Berlin) were responding to the fact that *die Mauer* had *gefallen*.

What was routinely referred to as The Fall was, to say the least, every reporter's wet dream but it was also great street theater, live drama, a good party, a cause for celebration for most, a cause for concern for others, a vivid experience, regardless. But christ, the nights were cold. The thing I always forget about Berlin is that there's no elevation to break the north wind on its hoot down from the Baltic—it never looks cold in the pictures, that's why I always forget how cold it can be but, let me tell you, it is a city where both men and women still wear fur coats for warmth, not status; a place where birds freeze on the wing, ink ices over and there's nothing to do for it except to keep moving or keep drinking, and that's pretty much what everyone seemed to be doing.

Next day, I interviewed the general Haddock and picked up some moderately interesting background for a piece I'd file later that month about cold turkey, about the fun and farce of stuffing a "real" Thanksgiving dinner down the throats of far-flung regiments, about the lengths some people go to for an *echt* can of pumpkin or a box of Bell's seasoning. Military enclaves as studies in provincialism fascinate me, anthropologically; and I find their use of language thrillingly Dadaist (where else will you hear a weapon venerated for its "maximum lethality"?), but the Big Story in Berlin was not whether the Four Powers would be pulling up their stakes and breaking camp in the near future, but whether or not some mythic shapeshifting was going to occur in the form of a United Germany, so I gave short shrift to what Boot wanted me to do which was to "put the Tulsa angle on the foreign news", and decided, instead, to buck the traffic and go over to the East at Checkpoint Charlie.

I couldn't help but notice all the oranges.

Where were all the oranges coming from—Israel?

Food is a detail so fundamental to existence it's often overlooked by journalists unless it's the issue, as in a famine or a siege, soup-kitchen conditions which generate bread-line reporting and photographs of mournful kids with their fingers stuck in bowls of shining, almost seraphic, rice. In East Berlin, through the—what else can I call them?—*grey* streets under the lowering grey sky, amid the grey detritus of a failed idea, people carried string bags filled with oranges. Oranges everywhere—a canvas of uninterrupted dullness, save for orange dots, an excess of them, as if some mad decorator had run amok with dreamy tangerine. One hundred Deutschmarks per adult and a string bag full of oranges were the details of this transit, this transaction; transformation. And you had to wonder where the years had gone, and what utopias had died, to be reduced to such small beer, so little booty.

Of course I didn't write that, that's what columnists are for—at least in the American tradition.

I took the S-Bahn to Friedrichstrasse station on the West side and walked to Checkpoint Charlie and stood there, trying to make my eyes do tricks, see through the trick of time. THEY CAME, THEY SAW, THEY DID A LITTLE SHOPPING was a fresh graffito near the billboard that announced VOUS ARE LEAVING DEN AMERIKANIS CEKTOPA in four languages; and I thought of my father for some childish reason. I thought dad would not be happy with me at this moment. Dad would not be keen on my being in Berlin, in Germany, keen on its unification, or *re*unification—but he had taken his prejudices and his reasons, unspoken, with him to his grave.

Waiting to come through from the East was a long line of pedestrians and a shorter line of Trabants. I changed some Deutschmarks for some Ostmarks, sublime in their detailed drawings of factories and grain combines, and walked over, heading up Friedrichstrasse towards Unter den Linden. I had gone no more than a hundred yards before the time warp happened, as it always did for me in East Berlin: you could stand there in the street and smell 1945. You could see 1961.

The boundary The Wall cut through the city was a time line, too, and all along it there were places where a moment stopped, where time had stopped, where a street ran into a brick wall, where tram tracks curved into a barrier, tucked beneath it to emerge somewhere in a different world—or not —who knew.

I walked up Friedrichstrasse to Unter den Linden and stood for a while staring up at the Brandenburg Gate from that side, at the Quadriga, that swashbuckling work of copper horses bridled to a chariot commanded by Victory, no less, a goddess who seemed to get around a whole lot more in previous centuries than in this one and who looked, as depicted by her creator, about as sexy and transcendent as a pickle. I slouched around a while, walking all the way to Alexanderplatz, stopping to talk to anyone who would stop and talk to me, including three stiffs, not together, who were operating their own black market currency exchanges. Around sunset I went back across the old checkpoint, interviewed some British soldiers dispensing styro-cups of free tea to the cold and thirsty from recycled (I hoped) Army fuel drums, ate some dinner at a beer hall (a rather interesting goose soup with prunes thickened with goose blood to start, followed by a pared down minimalist *Schnitzel*), and I was back in my room with a good bottle of Mosel at ten o'clock. I had just turned the TV on and settled down to read when Holden came a-knocking out-of-breath and bright-eyed at my door.

"—it's fantastic our there! Isn't it fantastic? What are you doing in? I just came back for warmer clothes—I can't believe what's going on out there . . ."

"Sit down, son, your eyes are glazed, are you on drugs?"

"—was Woodstock like this? Why aren't you out there? What's that you're reading?"

"I'm reading what's known, in Germany, as 'the phonebook', Holden . . ."

"—the phonebook? Really? That's a good idea . . . Why?"

"Zement."

"—oh yeah, Zement . . . that old zement thing. I forgot to tell you—since you've been away so much. I've gone ahead and done some work on that."

"—you 'forgot' to tell me . . ."

"—yeah." His attention moved, as it was like to do every nineteen seconds, to the television in the corner of the room. "O geez, is that . . . no, it can't be . . . is that *Bewitched*? Holy cow and that's the original Darren! This can't be CNN. Why aren't we watching CNN?"

"Because CNN would tell us how Helmut Kohl is reacting to this while he's in Warsaw. Because CNN would give us too much news. *What more* did you find out about Zement?"

". . . oh, um, yeah . . . Zement . . ." He focused back on me: "Chief plasma supplier to the Swiss Red Cross, no less. And West Germany gets some antihemophilic concentrates from them."

"That would be . . . what? Human blood or artificial—?"

He looked at me with something close to doubt, or pity.

"What do you mean by 'artificial'—?"

"Manufactured."

"—what planet are you from?"

"—can't 'manufacture' blood?"

"—parts of blood, yeah, sure, but not the cocktail."

"—so where, exactly—pity me, here, Holden—does the blood come from?"

"—well, bone marrow, actually . . ."

"—no, no, Zement's. Where do they get the 'cocktail'?"

"Donors."

"Who? Where? What—?"

"—okay, okay: walk-ins, mostly. They offer a small cash payment plus they give out soup and bread or coffee and a doughnut, depending on the time of day."

"Do they have a collection unit here?"

"—why ask me, you're the one with the phonebook—oh, I get it. You can't read the language . . ."

"Numbers, as I recall, and addresses are fairly universally translatable—"

I started leafing through the phonebook.

"—is this why you're not going out? You're working on Zement?"

"—what is this? Twenty Questions? I'm not going out because I'm old, Holden. And because I want to be out in the morning before the sun comes up so I can go to Kreuzberg."

"What's in Kreuzberg—?"

"Three hundred thousand Turks. Delivered here by the East Germans. Accounting for a greater percentage of Berlin's population than the Jews did back in 1933. Service workers. I want to watch them go to work. I want to ask them what they think about the prospect of the job market being flooded by East Germans . . ."

"Do you speak Turkish?"

"Do I look like I speak Turkish?"

"—jesus, what channel *is* that?"

"American Armed Services Network."

"—and now they're showing *Hogan's Heroes*? That's a little tasteless, don't you think? Geez. Bob was murdered, you know."

" 'Bob'?"

"The actor who plays Hogan."

"... no, I didn't know. *Bingo*: Zement: Wagner Platz, 27 ..."

"... that's their sales office."

"—how do *you* know?"

"Because I phoned them there. I phoned that number, like, four months ago. Voice mail. They never called me back. Look in the Yellow Pages. Under *Blutbanken*."

I handed him the book. "*You* do it ..."

"... seven of them. That's an awful lot for a population this size, don't you think? Four of them are hospitals. You want to meet up some time tomorrow and go check them out together? You'll need someone to translate for you, anyway ..."

"—you're suggesting we go out and *work* together?"

"Yeah."

"Okay. Meet me in the lobby. Noon."

"... *great*!"

He tore the page out of the phonebook, folded it and stuck it in his pocket.

"—and in case you're entertaining any thoughts about this, get this straight," I told him: "—*you* play Hoffman, *I* play Redford."

"—you're too old for Redford. You're more Hackman."

"—thanks, and you're Tom Cruise, no doubt."

"—no, they'd cast a woman for my part. They'd have to. This would be the scene where I've come to your room and we end up—"

"—outta here."

"Hackman and Juliette Binoche, I'm telling you."

I didn't give him the satisfaction of my asking who Juliette Binoche was, mostly because I didn't care.

"—you file yet?" he asked.

"Twice," I answered.

"Two different stories?"

"No, I fucking forgot I'd filed a first time . . ."

". . . bastard." His eyes moved to the TV again. "What is this—'Domestic Violence Helpline Number'? In the Army—?"

"—that and Alcohol Abuse Hotline. And where to dial to order your Thanksgiving turkey . . ."

"—they're saying they're going to open up the Brandenburg tonight. I think I'm going to be awake all night . . ."

"—what am I, your confessor?"

"You used to be my boss."

"—*I* did?"

"Now you're just some cool ol' dude I'd like to be like someday . . ."

"No you wouldn't. You don't want to be like me, I haven't gotten laid since January."

"—you see? See?" He started walking backwards toward the door. "—*that's* what you say that makes Juliette Binoche finally sleep with you . . ."

"—*who's Juliette Binoche*?"

There was a *This Week in Berlin* entertainment guide on the bureau and he tossed it at me, saying, "Juliette Binoche," then he left. The guy who plays the whacky Nazi on *Hogan's Heroes* was staring at me from the TV through his monocle. I turned *This Week in Berlin* over and stared at the photo on the cover of a woman with big eyes and dark hair. My heart stopped. Binoche. Juliette. French actress. Dead ringer for Lilith.

The tricks the mind can play:

When I saw her coming toward me across no man's land in the cold grey mist of dawn the next day, I thought she was Juliette Binoche.

I had left the Inter-Continental around five-thirty in the

morning, thinking to grab a cab with a driver who spoke my lingo and have him drive me around Kreuzberg until I spotted some kind of place where workers gather to have breakfast. But once I got outside I had the urge to walk so I headed up through the Tiergarten, sticking near the road, since it was still dark, toward the Brandenburg Gate, which had become the TV satellite trucks' news center because, backdrop-wise, it made great television. All the American and French and British trucks were there but only the Americans were still awake, or up that early, feeding live to their affiliates in California and Hawaii, and I ran into Rick Davis, a guy I knew who worked for NBC and he hauled me into their truck and fed me coffee and a perfect three-minute egg with slices of Westphalian ham on pumperknickel. Guys who cook tend to discover one another on the road the way guys who drink and guys who like to go to strip joints do. The first time I met Rick I was with a troop transport somewhere in the desert during the Iran—Iraq war and he came up to our truck at our destination in the middle of nothing and I mean nothing, clutching a package of spaghetti in one hand and three tomatoes in the other and said, "Anybody here have any garlic?"

We sat around and compared notes for about a half an hour, then I stood up to leave.

"Where you headin—?"

"Kreuzberg."

"—on foot?"

I nodded.

"—that's quite a trek. Here, take my hat. It's cold out there."

His hat was a Stetson and I would have looked like a prime asshole in it, but I said, "—a Stetson?—in K'berg? Why don't I just paint 'Marlboro Man' on my forehead and ride in on a Harley—?"

"—you're right. Here . . ." He rooted around in some bags and came up with a knit cap like the kind Tony Curtis wore in *The Boston Strangler*, but I took it because it would keep me warm.

"Let's have dinner later," Rick suggested. "Somebody told me about this place out in Charlottenburg that serves only wild game and it's that time of year—venison, partridge, pheasant, rabbit, bear . . ."

"—bear?"

"—you've never eaten bear?"

"—there are a lot of things I've never done. That doesn't mean I need to do them."

"—pick you up at eight."

"I'll have somebody with me."

I could see Rick struggling to ask, so I said, "Not Lilith. Not a woman. Pup of mine I'm paper-training."

I'm going over all these details—Rick, the egg, the hat, the bear—because of what took place soon after that, the ferocity that was about to seize me, as if, boiled down, those few preceding hours could render up a specimen, a sample of the potion that, as one had done for Dr. Jekyll, transformed me.

I've thought about it now for almost two years, relived the guilt and shame of it like some undead Inferno figure condemned to reenact the worst of sins again, again. I've stripped it down as if it were my job to clean it and inspect it, daily. I was walking south along The Wall, the Reichstag was behind me, Tiergarten to my right. I really don't remember any specificity of thought—I was worried about deadline, but I always am. I remember thinking how the 9th of November in this century in Germany would now be re-enshrined not as the date of Kristallnacht and all its horrors, but as the date The Wall came down, and I think I might have said aloud, "One event will hide another." I remember noting to myself how the sun was rising from the East, and then immediately thinking what a stupid ass I was for thinking in clichés. And I remember looking over at the nearly bare trees in the Tiergarten, black-barked, watching the fog dissipate upward among them, and lamenting the fact that I'd never learned to identify trees, especially European ones, in winter, without leaves. And the ground was hard, harder than cement because the dirt around The Wall was bare of vegetation, packed and frozen. And there were no birds, I remember thinking how strange it was that I hadn't seen a single bird since I'd been in Berlin. And there were rabbits, dun-colored and fast-breathing, dozens of them, not in the Tiergarten where you'd expect them, but running helter-skelter in the open desert which had been carved out years ago beside The Wall. This was not the dreaded no man's land within The Wall that the East Germans had created, this bare stretch was something else, a sort of planned futility of hope; a wasteland. There, in that artificial wasteland, from the end of the Tiergarten down to Potsdamer Platz, and inside The Wall in no man's land, that swath between opposing look-out towers with their searchlights and gun-emplacements, rabbits had been buggering and bunnying for years with that fast-breeding frequency they're known for. And I remember thinking that it was right along here, on the other side of The Wall, in no man's land, that Hitler's Chancellery had been, and his bunker. The Wall at Potsdamer Platz had been breached the day before, literally plowed down to take the strain of traffic off Checkpoint Charlie, so it was possible to walk across the widest point of no man's land, which I decided I should do —I'll never understand my reason—even though it was out of my way. I think I did it because I knew that within the hour it would be jammed with traffic, Trabants and Wartburgs coming over not only from East Berlin but driving in from all around East Germany. I wanted to get a sense, while it lasted, of what it had been like to try to escape, what it had been like to try to run that gauntlet, that death trap, so I left the dirt track that had been made the day before and wandered in, doubling back in my direction, north again, The Wall to my left this time and in the distance, a couple hundred yards away, there was a group of gypsies, camping, blue smoke rising from what seemed to be a lean-to jerry-built from plastic bags and bales of wire, and there was a woman moving toward both them and me, with something hanging from a dark strap on her shoulder. Her hair was short and dark. She moved with easy confidence, stopping now and then to take a photograph. She was wearing what appeared to be grey sweatpants and a shearling coat. I had bought that coat for her myself, bored to tears with nothing else to do but shop, covering some Commonwealth affair in New Zealand.

I pulled the hat Rick had given to me from the pocket of my coat and shoved it down over my forehead and dropped, instinctively, into a squat, about two feet from The Wall, so my figure would appear anonymous from a distance, a hunched figure digging in the earth.

The air was so cold my lungs burned, and my heart was racing.

I tried to watch her without making it seem that I was staring at her, but I was afraid that if I looked away, she'd disappear all over again. So I kept my head low, my eyes smarting with cold.

She was walking toward me, but not at me, like that final scene in *The Third Man*—only, unlike Joseph Cotten, I wasn't going to let the woman pass me by. I remember, in those agonizing moments, pretending that I was digging in the rubble. I could hear her footsteps crack the veil of hoarfrost on the frozen ground, coming toward me.

It was violent, from the start. In part, I think, because, although I took her by surprise, as soon as she recognized me, looked me in the eyes, she panicked. She had always been as fast as light, quick-witted, triggered for a fast response, her arms and legs had always been extremely strong—especially, her arms. I had her by one wrist and I was saying, "Lilith—" as she swung around and recognized my voice and saw my face, and suddenly I needed all my strength to keep my hold on her like holding fast to turbulence in weather. *Why*? I kept repeating, *why*? I was afraid she'd scream so I had to clamp my hand across her mouth and push her up against The Wall. Just tell me *why*, I said. I had her pinned with all my strength, my arms, my legs, my hips.

"Noah," she said once. "Noah," she said twice. "Don't do this—my camera . . ."

I smashed the fucking thing against The Wall. The Wall was strong. It broke the glass inside her lens. She was wearing cashmere at her neck, a blood-colored scarf I'd never seen before. I pulled it up and wrapped it tight around her eyes, blindfolded her, before I pulled the sweatpants down inside her coat and felt her stomach, flat and warm beneath my hand and fucked her, fucked the woman that I'd said I loved, fucked the woman that I'd said was my redemption, fucked the woman for whose life I would have freely pledged my own.

The last time I saw Lilith she was running like a rabbit over no man's land.

1989

BUCHAREST ROMANIA

Denk ich an Deutschland in der Nacht,
Dann bin ich um den Schlaf gebracht . . .

That's not me, that's the poet Heinrich Heine:

If at night I think of Germany,
then I can no longer sleep.

I TRIED TO CONVINCE MYSELF THAT WHAT HAD HAPPENED HADN'T HAPPENED, that what had been had not been, that the man who had performed that violence was not I, that the woman was not Lilith, that the truth was lies, that love is always Love now and forever, that rage is but a minor trait in man and not his trademark, that mankind is distinguished by its acts of goodness not its savagery and despoliation, that The End will never come, that Santa Claus was coming, that pigs fly, the check was in the mail and I will live forever in eternity if only I confessed my sins.

But I told no one what I'd done.

The horror of the act existed only in my memory and

Lilith's. Its exclusivity coupled us. That's the way a rapist thinks. She asked for it. She wanted it. Man's ultimate power is violence.

Except, violence isn't power, violence is the absence of it, violence is the shrill stuff that fills the vacuum when power is in jeopardy, it is power's disappearance. Try telling that to any of its victims.

Get your mind around this, Noah, I kept having to instruct myself after that morning in Berlin: It is the worst thing you have ever done. I knew it was the worst thing I had ever done but a wall partitioned me from it, me from the man who had committed it, a wall partitioned me from me, perhaps that's what real heart/break is, a factious self, a self in pieces.

I had never done anything like it before, the idea of harming a woman being so alien to me that I had only rarely in my lifetime raised my voice at one and then it had been over the political and not the personal. I never shouted at my mother, maybe because she died before I got either the chance or a cause. I shouted at Melanie when we were teenagers, but only once since we've been adults and that was when she told me Jason wanted her to quit her job to stay at home when their first kid was born, toss over two years of law school, her law degree and an associateship in a Richmond firm to breast-feed so I said are you *crazy*? and she said butt out, it's not your business, and then I said Jason was a revanchist troglodyte and she called me a sick-brained traitor to the South and then we started shouting at each other. And Lilith and I had only ever had one screaming see-red set-to and that was late one night in Paris about courage. I had said I didn't think putting one's life at unnecessary risk in the line of work as a journalist was any act of bravery. I had said I thought that kind of journalism was an act of egoism, of showing off. I was making a late dinner for us at the time and we were in the kitchen, the second-worst place after the front seat of a moving car to have a fight. There had been a brief, heavy silence after I had made those opening remarks during which my mind began to catalogue sharp objects within sight and then, kaboom. First she said, "You're joking, right?" When I told her no, I really did ascribe to Tina Turner's view that we don't need another hero, she went into a crescendo the likes of which even Beethoven would have heard. The only other time we even came close to fighting with each other was once, when we were in a car, of course, in fucking Jordan or somewhere and we had passed a woman walking on the road carrying about six dozen babies on her body and Lilith said, "Another brood-mare. Like your sister," so I had to stop the car. "You . . . don't . . . ever want to say that about Melanie ever again," I told her, "even if you're thinking it. And you . . . don't . . . ever want to think it." I think she must have weighed the odds real quick because she said, "Okay," but I couldn't drop it so I had to say, "I mean, do you even *like* women?"

"—what do you mean, do I 'like' women? I *am* a woman."

"No you're not, you're a man with a uterus and ovaries."

"No—*you're* the man with the uterus. *I'm* the man with the clitoris. A *functioning* clitoris, by the way."

"—is that another swipe?"

"At what?"

"—at *whom* . . . forget it."

"No—at whom?"

"Forget it."

"No, you thought I was saying I think Melanie doesn't enjoy sex, didn't you? Well, I wasn't."

"—that's not what I was thinking."

"—oh well then you were probably thinking I was talking about yours."

"—*my* clitoris."

"—yes."

"My clitoris functions very nicely, thank you, the only problem I have with my clitoris is that you're always trying to prove that yours is bigger."

"Well it is, so can we go now? Or are we going to sit in the middle of this fucking desert and . . . aw jesus, Noah, *put that thing away*—"

I think we must have made love under every meteorological condition on this planet except in the middle of a sandstorm and that was only because you have to be truly insane or Lawrence of Arabia or both to try to make love in the middle of a sandstorm. We did it in a hurricane on St. Kitts under a house. And we did it in a monsoon in Karnataka State in India. We did it in a sleeping-bag the night of the eclipse in Poland while all the dogs for miles around were barking. We did it under water (not my favorite), in the snow, and by the light of the midnight sun in Sweden.

You'd think we would have learned to love with all the love we made, but the truth is, I don't know what we learned.

She was so fucking funny.

I never knew anyone so ferocious in her work and yet so quick to make a joke. You'd think we would have learned a better punch line than the one we gave it, what with all the jokes we made, but I couldn't laugh about the two of us together now if my life depended on it. Love and laughter—I remember them. And maybe that was part of why I did it—to stop her laughing, to stop *them* laughing, stop them laughing at *me*. One excuse may hide another, but no excuse can hide my shame.

Sometimes I tell myself I never knew her, that she duped me, and in addition to researching who and why and when and where Adam was, I went back into the archives about her, about Divo and her mother, about how she got her first job, where and how, who knew her where and when and everything she'd ever told me came up certifiable except for one impossible to deny omission:

She had forgotten to inform me that she had a history—no, a pattern—in and for the death-defying.

Of course she *had* informed me, countless times, every time I saw her on assignment, working, every time I saw the photographs she brought back from the brink of some disaster—I must have asked *How did you get these?* a hundred times, or meant to ask a hundred times, but never, not once, ever, in our time together did it ever dawn on me to ask, "Lilith . . . do you *like* to put yourself in danger? Do you have some *need* to—?" It never occurred to me, but there it was, in photographs on the streets of Managua, photographs of members of the Shining Path, of war-lords in Somalia, male prostitutes in Paris, municipal tyrants in Naples, Moslem separatists in Kashmir: men with guns, more men with guns, men with guns who shot civilians, men with weapons, men with knives, men in face masks, men in uniforms, more men in uniforms, men in uniforms with weapons, men in uniforms with weapons standing over corpses. There were other types of photographs as well—all her famine work with children, all her careful re-creations of Atget's photographs of Paris—but the overwhelming evidence was that Lilith wasn't just a photojournalist, a correspondent, as I was—Lilith was a *war* correspondent and I hadn't ever seen it, seen the pattern of it, 'til I laid her whole life's work from the AFP archive out in front of me.

"Geez—whose are those, Don McCullin's?" Holden asked me one day, looking over my shoulder.

"No."

"—geez, *someone* who gets off on danger . . ."

"—say that again?"

". . . what?"

"What you just said."

"—what did I just say?"

"'Someone who gets off on danger.'"

"—so?"

"—so what would that person see in me?"

"—'see' in you?"

"Why would the person who took these photographs be attracted to me?"

"Whose *are* these? These are Divi's, aren't they—?"

"Maybe."

"—well they are, it's right here. 'dee-eye-vee-eye', why are you torturing yourself this way?"

"*—just answer*, Holden."

"Well for one thing: you're safe."

"I'm 'safe'."

"—you know, steady. Standard. Cuddly. You're going to send me to some godforsaken corner of the earth if I continue in this vein, aren't you?"

"—no, no, go on. Am I really that boring?"

"—no, I mean, well . . . no. I mean . . . you're no Ernesto Hemingway in Spain for the *Toronto Star* . . . but, hey, who would want to be, I mean, the guy fucking shot himself through the mouth, right? What I mean is, you're not dangerous, you know what I mean? That's why people talk to you. You're safe. That's what makes you great . . ."

". . . don't fucking patronize me, Holden—"

"—you do the job better than anyone I know but at the same time there are certain parts of the job that you refuse to do. Like go to Monrovia. Like expose Colombian drug cartels. Like stand too close to Sadat after Camp David . . ."

"—you mean, like *die*."

"—that, too."

So I began to think that what she left me for was not for safety's sake, but for more danger. And maybe that was part of what compelled me in Berlin—to prove to her, to prove to myself, that I was dangerous. But I'm about as dangerous as dust: tell *that* to the victim: read *that* riot act out loud to my dead love affair.

What remained was to discover just how dangerous Adam was—then, maybe, I could wean myself from my obsession onto a higher horse of moral outrage, smug superiority, disgust and fundamental mental health.

So it was with no small personal delight that a month after Lilith ran from me in no man's land Boot called in the middle of the night to tell me to get the fuck as soon as possible to Timişoara. "That's in Romania," he said.

". . . actually, Boot, you harbinger of springtime, it's in Transylvania—in the *Banat*, really—but, wait: are you telling me you're *sending* me to Romania—?"

"—to Transylvania."

"—but you're *sending* me?"

"All things come to those who wait."

"Even Romania?"

"—especially Romania. And every other kinda shit . . ."

"—for how long?"

"For how long what?"

"—am I going? You do understand, don't you, that I'll need some time in Bucharest to—"

"—*no*."

"What?"

"You cover what goes down in Timişoara, *period*. You don't fuck around on personal vendettas while you're wearing my credentials."

"—funny, but I always thought of them as *my* credentials . . ."

"Correct me if I'm wrong but it's my received opinion that your press card has this paper's name on it."

"—correct *me* if I'm wrong but I'm still a journalist without my press card."

"—*are* you?"

"—jesus, Boot. What are you afraid I'm going to do?"

"He's the Minister of Trade, Noah."

"—so?"

"He's the Minister of Trade of a Most Favored Nation. So back off. Stick to the fucking story."

"—and that is?"

"—Tokes. The Calvinist. Budapest broadcast a speech of his today. The Romanians are going to evict him from his church tomorrow. Could get violent."

"—yip-pee."

"—normally I'd say go through Hungary, but that's the border they'll be paranoid about and where they'll hassle you the most, so book yourself through Belgrade—"

"—what do *you* care how I book myself?"

"—because, my pussy-pie, I care about getting you a translator so you can understand the fuck is happening before you file your copy, *comprenday*? And since every other English speaking gringo in this business is going to require lingo-aides, the best ones will be snapped up by the time you get there so I thought I'd do us both a little favor and get on the job while you're still napping, I'll arrange to have her meet you in Moraviţa, you'll see it on the map, first town once you cross the border from Yugoslavia into Transylvania."

"—'her'."

"—you heard. Eva, with an 'E', Deserdnú—'undressed', backwards. 'Eve Undressed'. Don't thank me."

"Obviously you've never seen what passes for a 'woman' in Romania—"

Shall we just say that this woman was a knockout and leave it at that because, like most men, with the exception of William Shakespeare, I'm an idiot when it comes to describing beauty. A beautiful woman falls out of assembly into parts in my hands, ankles, ear lobes, cheekbones, eyes and voice —o fuck it: tits and ass. I'm much better describing landscape, which, let's face it, at its best, reminds us all of Woman, even when it's barren arid flat or the Hungarian Great Plain through which I found myself driving the next day from Belgrade toward the Romanian border in the northeastern reaches of what used to be called Yugoslavia but which is now called godknows what, some outer ring of hell. I had wanted to rent a small innocuous car, a Yugo, maybe, or a Renault 4 which wouldn't draw attention at the border, but the lady at the Hertz counter at the airport must have seen me coming because she put me in a stretch Mercedes the color of which can only be described as map green, that green that lives on maps and nowhere else in nature. The border checkpoint at Vatin was an easy drive of seventeen miles over flat land and I was waved through, without either a hitch or a search, by the two Serbs on duty. Then I sat, the sixth vehicle, behind a small truck full of weird dark green squashes of some kind, freckled with orange, in a stalled line of traffic and I stared through the windshield at the place that had lived in my imagination since Lilith had left me. Usually this was the part I like best about travel—the sudden arrival of Place, that intersection of one's expectations with the panoply, usually less than splendid, of the real, the mundane, the dusty, the rusty, the littered, polluted unpretty unavoidable world. Few places are, in reality, what you hope they will be when you get there—fewer, still, exceed expectations: New

York City does, for me, at least, flying into it from the ocean, over Staten Island and Miss Liberty; and Paris always does, stepping down from the Air France bus from Charles de Gaulle airport onto the sidewalk beside the Arc de Triomphe at the Etoile; the Grand Canyon does; and the Acropolis. Rivers almost never do, and certainly the Danube doesn't, if it was ever blue its azure days are long gone and it was as puddingy and umber there in the countryside between Romania and Serbia as it was in those gay further western cities that had so elevated it in myth and song. Once you write about a place you fix it; then it disappears, and your written words remain as ghost towns, or worse, play things, toy villages, not history but a science fiction. Why write about a disappearing place when there are photographs to tell it better—and, anyway, Boot always excised the scenery wherever I included it, his method following on a sort of step by step reversal of the way God created earth, first to go were all the beasts of the earth I might mention other than Man, the cattle and creeping things, then the birds and sea creatures, the sun moon and stars and then grass and seeds and trees and fruit. Boot liked me to write about things Man has made, which is, I suppose, the way to describe what we call News as opposed to, say, what we call weather. So that's what I did, marveling all the while at all the ways Place shapes populations, shapes its indigenous myths and superstitions, shapes Man. I had read everything I could get my hands on in those last ten months about the place that stretched before me, a nation relatively new in its formation, a bastard born from spoils of war, cobbled together as only that unlikely old pair of boots, Churchill and Stalin, could do—bit of this, a bit of that, eye of a newt, bones pilfered from graves and hey presto, like Frankenstein's opus, noble and savage, this monster, Romania.

By one of those circumstantial flukes that keep conspiracy theorists flushed with proof that nothing ever happens by accident, I had never come to Romania in all my years as a working journalist—neither had Lilith—missed it and Bulgaria, Albania, all of the USSR and, strangely, Denmark. The USSR was, of course, the private backyard of Ivy's bureau in Moscow during those years but there was no particular reason why I shouldn't have been sent to the other four countries to satisfy Boot. I was in Europe when the Ceauşescus stayed at the White House—a surreal event, if ever there was one, after which Elena Ceauşescu was said to have called Rosalyn Carter "Mrs. Peanut-head"—but I was in London when the Ceauşescus came calling to collect the dictator's knighthood from Queen Elizabeth, the Brit-head, and I had gotten close enough to the Romanian leader and his leaderene to see that they were short, mean-looking and butt-ugly. A man's eyes will tell you how his character's been formed, but with a woman I have learned to watch her mouth—and the leaderene had lips like leg irons. In Romania parents frighten misbehaving children with the threat that if they don't shape up, then *vin minerii—the miners are coming—* but, personally, I'd take a shaft full of miners any day over being anywhere close to Elena. But according to official propaganda, she and her husband were both much loved—even though there was the growing evidence of a dissenting point of view:

> "Good news and bad news, Comrade Socialist Vlad!"
>
> "What's the good news, Comrade Socialist Radu?"

the hood

"The good news is the sainted
mother of our beloved leader
is still alive!"

"Amazing woman! She must be at
least 110! What's the bad news?"

"*She's pregnant again.*"

"Good news, Comrade Socialist
Vlad! Have you heard that our
beloved socialist government
has put Romanians on the moon?"

"Amazing! But can moon support
human life?"

"*Not any more.*"

I was hoping to obtain my entry visa at the border, and in what I thought was a slick move, I'd inserted Adam's calling card into my passport, which, after waiting and watching the cars behind me pass through, I was beginning to regret. The first Romanian border guard had taken my passport with the card that said

ADAM PENTRÚ

MINISTER OF TRADE
BUCUREŞTI
ROMANIA

tucked inside, and had disappeared into a cinderblock building at the side of the road. After forty minutes a second guard had emerged, motioned me out of the car and proceeded to search it, under the floor mats, under the seats, under the hood and under the chassis, while I stood there, consciously keeping my hands exposed, out of my pockets, only too well aware that I was being watched by the guards near the door of the building. Then a guard with a dog which looked like a doberman only fatter had come toward me and let the dog sniff my shoes, and then the dog sniffed all over the car. Then a fourth guard came up and said, "Very big car," looking at me, not at the Mercedes. I said nothing. I've learned that the best thing to do while going through border checkpoints anywhere on this planet is to stand perfectly still, remain perfectly quiet and to recite to oneself in one's head very slowly all the lyrics to all the Bob Dylan songs one can remember, and to limit one's answers to *yes*, *no*, and *hard rain's a-gonna fall*. Border guards the world over are notorious for possessing zero sense of humor except possibly those in Antarctica where they're probably really glad to see you.

"Very big car for one person," the guard elaborated, so I said, "Yes," and he said, "You will follow, please, me," and led the way into the cinderblock building where there was, as there always has to be in those kinds of places, the guy who you can tell is the party official because he's official in both manner and in dress and he looks like a real party animal. He was seated at a table on which there was a telephone with a frayed fabric cord, a letter opener, my passport and, to one side, face up, with his index finger resting on it, Adam's calling card. "You wish visa?" he said. "Yes," I answered. He nodded slightly. I was presented with a form by a guard who also gave me a ballpoint pen, the retractable point of which was permanently retracted. The form was in Romanian. "Purpose of visit?" I was asked, "Pleasure or business?"

"I am a journalist."

"Yes. We know. How many U.S. dollars you are bringing?"

I had nearly two thousand on me, which was illegal, so I lied and said five hundred, and he indicated that he'd like to see them on the table. I reached for my wallet where I had separated out five Uncle Bens, and handed it to him. He looked it over, looked inside, looked at the picture of Melanie's kids and, eyebrows raised, looked back at me, handing me the wallet, and said, "You will change these U.S. dollars for Romanian *lei*, please, here, now." A guard brought him a cash box. "You will spend these Romanian *lei* on Romanian goods while you are in Romania," he said—which, interpreted, meant that I was going to get the visa. My heart beat a little faster. "Romanian *lei* do not leave Romania," he added, a sentence that was begging for an ironic observation, but I bit my tongue. He had me sign the visa form, if, in fact, that's what it was, then stamped my passport, counted out the funny money and that was it. When I left, the only things remaining on the table were his elbows, the telephone, the letter opener and Adam's card. *Good*, I thought, getting in the car, if they haven't called him yet, they'll call him now and by tonight he'll know he'll have to deal with me. But I was wrong, he wasn't even in the country at the time, he was in Teheran paving the way for Ceauşescu's imminent arrival there to finalize a trade agreement. Toying—only briefly—with the idea that they'd bugged the car while I was separated from it (behind-the-iron-curtain paranoia on my part: it was clear, on second thought, that they didn't have that level of technology) I started to whistle "Santa Claus Is Coming To Town" as I crossed, officially, into Transylvania. There were only ten days left, 'til Christmas.

A mile down the road, exactly as Boot had arranged it, I pulled up beside a barren-looking café and a woman came out, carrying her suitcase. *O lady*, I thought, I hope you have a big strong jealous husband.

"Misterjohn?" she asked, leaning toward the car window on the driver's side. She was blond, the real stuff, straight and long. Dark eyes. And tiny, like a doll.

I showed her my passport, and she showed me her identity card, and then she got in.

"Is not far, Timişoara," she said. "Thirty-nine kilometers. Straight road. One turning, only."

She was all of twenty-something but she knew (of course she knew) what Sputnik was.

"Why do you ask me—?"

"It's a standard operating question."

"—'standard operating'—?"

"—for journalists."

"I have been translator for many journalists before now but no one has ever asked me—"

"—for Bureau Chiefs. For London Bureau Chiefs. For London Bureau Chiefs in December."

She smiled and oh shit she had good teeth.

"There are different standard operating questions for London Bureau Chiefs, depending on the month?"

"—yes."

"This is very useful information. I am in debt to you. I must educate myself to learn answers to these questions. What is the standard operating question for, oh, the month of March, for example?"

"—March? Oh, um . . . What is meant by the term 'Tet Offensive'?"

". . . 'the term'? But this was military action in the Vietnam—"

"—well done. You know more for someone from Romania than a lot of people your age know in the United States . . ."

"—well, there are reasons we would know about the Vietnam here in Romania. And Sputnik. In life there are reasons, and then there are reasons . . ."

"One reason may hide another, hey?"

"—well, that would be sure road to madness . . ."

"—or politics."

"—*and* politics."

So she was smart—or maybe only cynical. Everyone in the big R was cynical, even the children—especially the children.

"—but *we*," she brightened, "are on road to Timişoara. Would you like for me to tell you about Timişoara? I have much knowledge about all Transylvania. Perhaps I should tell you, first, I am student of Political Science at University in Bucharest. I speak Romanian, of course, also Hungarian, French, English and little Russian, as one must, because when I was girl—I was born in Constanţa on Black Sea—and when I was girl my father he took me to edge of sea and points to left—'See that? *Russia*!' He points to right—'See that? *Russia*!' He points between. 'See that? *Russia*. Everywhere you look—*Russia* . . .' So I learn Russian, too, in case some day, God help me, I should need to swim . . . I should tell you also that I expect cash dollars, yes? All meals, you pay. And I have own room in hotel. For translating Romanian newspapers I charge nothing extra. Same for Romanian TV. I work very late into night but sometimes I get little tired and give only, how we call it, high-lights, not word for word. I am not big eater but then, as you will see, is not much to eat anyway. Wine is good. If you like wine, I will help you what is good wine—"

"—you're from Constanţa?"

"On Black Sea. Very famous. Place of Ovid's exile. Many poems written there in Latin by the famous Ovid. Miserable poems because he was very miserable—"

"I'm interested in finding out everything I can about a famous person who might have been from Constanţa—a man called Adam Pentrú. Forgive me if I'm not saying the name right . . ."

"You are saying name right."

A decided chill had entered her voice.

"—you know him?" I asked.

"Everyone in Romania is familiar with that name."

"The Minister of Trade."

"That is one of his titles."

"Can we get to him?"

"What do you mean?"

"—in Bucharest. Does he give interviews?"

It was uncommonly warm for the time of year—a factor which would weigh significantly in the events of the ensuing days—and a previous snowfall was melting in the fields, its run-off wetting the road's surface, sending up a spray of sludge from tires. I turned on the windshield wipers, which slapped and whirred, and she rolled up her window.

"Why do you want to meet this man?" she asked.

"I've already met him."

"You know him?"

"He's stayed at my house."

"Excuse me, but I find that difficult to believe."

"—I kid you not."

"I'm not saying you are kidding. I am saying there is some mistake."

The truck in front of us was transporting saw-cut logs and random woodchips bounced from time to time onto our hood.

"—you don't want to talk about this, do you?"

"I am saying it is not my job as translator to help foreign journalist collect information about members of Romanian government. I should not be asked to do it."

"They don't bug cars," I told her.

"And Elena Ceauşescu is great beauty. And foreign journalists do not carry tape recorders. I am translator. There is nothing here for me to translate, Misterjohn. Until we get to Timişoara."

Having learned that one can't argue with a woman or with anyone, for that matter, while one is driving through a spray of sludge with woodchips dancing on the hood through a goddamn foreign country in a goddamn foreign car (why is it *always* a Mercedes?), I pulled off the road and stopped.

And lo and behold the car that had been trailing us since I hadn't noticed when pulled over too.

"Oh boy," I said, watching the black Dacia in the rearview mirror, "so it's going to be like that. Who are they watching, me or you?" I ventured, like I didn't know.

"I hope you have to pee," she said.

"—you hope I have to what?"

"You call it 'pee', make water? You have stopped the car. One of us must now get out and make some water. *Real* water—they will check."

She looked at me, I looked at her and then, with an expression that could have sunk a thousand ships she hauled her dainty self from the Mercedes onto a melting snow bank, turned her back to me and squatted. Either she was wearing one of those do-hickies with the snaps down there or she wasn't wearing underpants. When she stood some twenty seconds later to adjust herself, steam rose.

And sure enough, before they resumed their tail, two men in black trench coats, the urine stain inspectors, got out of the Dacia to relieve themselves, but only temporarily, of their suspicions.

She didn't speak to me for nearly fifteen minutes until we hit a T-junction and she said, "No, no, turn right, turn right—"

"—but the sign says—"

"—turn right, turn right. They've changed the signs . . ."

"You're a *gold mine*, do you know that?"

When she wouldn't answer me, I told her my life story,

including how I'd almost won the Pulitzer each year since 1973 and ending with me punching Adam in the face in the Brompton Road in London ten months earlier.

"—she lived, your friend?"

"—yeah, she lived."

"She was not paralyzed or hurt?"

"—she wasn't paralyzed or hurt."

"So you do not go to Timişoara to report what happens to the priest Laszlo Tokes."

"—that; but something else, as well."

"You call this 'a agenda', I believe."

"—*an* agenda. Latin word."

"I think your Mister Boot should have told me Misterjohn was coming here with *an* agenda. There was also television job from U.S.A. but television crew is three times work and they work translator very hard. Still, if we are fortunate, we will find you someone else in Timişoara for translator. And I will find someone without *an* agenda."

"I'm sorry," I said. I was remembering a poem by the Romanian dissident Ana Blandiana about her fellow countrymen: We are more like plants than people. *We are vegetable people. Who has ever seen a tree in revolt?* "I've been stupid. I wish you'd change your mind," I said to Eva.

"I won't know you long enough for that to happen," she told me.

She was wrong.

Maybe it was something in the water that made her change her mind—the Romanians are skilled in crafting rumors which they then accept as fact, and one of the many rumors to be born in both Bucharest and Timişoara during the week to come was that the water had been treated with a soporific to sedate the revolutionaries—so maybe it was something in the water, or maybe it was something in the air, in her seeing for the first time in her young life someone shot and killed before her, or maybe it was when the army turned the water cannon on us and the force knocked her to the ground and rolled her over and I had to put myself inside the torrent, put myself between its force and her so she could breathe, maybe that was when she changed her mind and decided to stick with me, a stranger, through her nation's revolution. People do things without reason when the bullets start to fly. And I forgot the other reason I was there, completely, once events started to unfold that night in Opera Square in Timişoara. I forgot, completely, about Adam, the man who had made me a reluctant quasi-expert, compared to other foreign journalists, on a country I had never even been to before and wouldn't have wanted to visit even in time of revolution—especially not in time of revolution—if it hadn't been for him because by Christmas day, by the time the kangeroo court in Tîrgovişte tried and sentenced the Ceauşescus to death and shot them in front of someone's video camera, I was revolutioned out, baby; I was overly revolted. Docility, undue respect for authority, a sense of personal superfluity, comfort in conformity, an atmosphere of deceit, distrust, anxiety, suspicion, superstition—all these the dictator demands of his constituency, and I had seen the inert weight, the burden of it, attain critical mass in China earlier that year where its spontaneous combustion flared briefly like a comet through our sky then disappeared into oblivion; and in East Germany, where it transformed itself into a brand of history. What happened in Romania was neither the defeat of an ideal, as had been dealt the Chinese students, nor a transformation, as had occurred, for better or for worse, for Germans. What happened in Romania was that something only seemed to happen, like some sleight of hand manipulated by a fist inside a velvet glove. The docility, the superstition and suspicion were so deep inside the bone—perhaps even in the water—the rural majority and most of the urban population were so profoundly malnourished, badly housed and numbed by meagre living conditions in decaying buildings with no available heat other than wood or the odd bits of coal, and little or no electricity during the winter months when it was most needed, that the energy generated in the protests on the streets of Timişoara and Bucharest during the last weeks of that year exhausted the country's reserves. When the light of the New Year dawned on the nation it seemed to fall over the land with the same unnoticed effect as the rays of the sun through a crypt where the undead lie sleeping—nothing much had occurred; except prolongation. But I didn't know that then—nor, certainly, did Eva, who had much more at stake in the moment, much more to gain or to lose than I did. I had nothing to gain. What could I gain—an exclusive?

On Monday, when things had moved too far in a direction that Ceauşescu didn't like, he did two things—he ordered all the borders closed, nobody in, especially no foreign journalists; and, confident in his tactics of containment, he flew to Teheran.

The Securitate, or the Army, either one, would have certainly expelled me, if they had found me, but after our first night, Friday, in Timişoara, the two Securitate flatfoots dogging us lost us in the crowd and never picked us up again because Eva had friends at the Polytechnic where we found a floor to sleep on instead of registering at a hotel. And once the border was sealed, I found myself in the very rare position of being, for once in my spotty career, in exactly the right place at exactly the right moment for a breaking story.

And, miraculously, Ceauşescu's government, in his absence, didn't try to jam Radio Free Europe—and they didn't cut the phone lines.

Boot kept saying, "It's a goddamn miracle," when he wasn't chanting, "Pulitzer, Pulitzer," as a mantra.

"There's nobody here with a camera, though, Bootsie—"

"Well I'll tell you what—just this once, to make up for not having a picture—I'll let you wax."

"—birds of the air *and* fish of the sea?"

"—no birds. What fish? Aromas and what's in the gutters —shit like that. This could be 'Mr. Pulitzer' calling."

"—a reason to live."

"—not for *you*, asshole. For the paper."

And for once, too, I actually thought I had a feel for what was going on—something I rarely have when reporting other nations' politics, although I don't admit it. Put me back in the South, back in Alabama, Arkansas or Virginia even though, by choice, they're not my beat, and I can read chapter and verse everything a Southern politician says between the lines, how a joke is used as reference to another joke or how innuendo is twisted through the wringer and hung out to dry alongside other laundry. But put me somewhere else, no matter how long, it will never be my element. I'd been writing on the British system for almost twenty years and I felt piglike in a poke most of the time, a lament I frequently took up with Mac who, as a Glaswegian, shared my porker's nose for dead wood and truffled up the wrong tree with me, frequently, on our forays into the Parliamentary jungle. But I actually thought I got it, got it right, got it better than I usually did, in Romania—not only because my timing was accidentally perfect and my translator was both brave and brilliant, but because I'd soaked myself in all its lore while soaking in self-pity—and I had it in my skin. The issue Friday night was the classic divide-and-conquer tactic used by tyrants since before the dawn of modern nations—except the film of it was playing backwards, instead of *un*making itself, the shattered glass was un-breaking, its scattered pieces reuniting. Every dictactor relies on setting factions of the population at each other's throats—that's the first instruction on the box: sow distrust. Sow fear. Sow prejudice. The issue in Transylvania, a long-standing one which went back centuries before Ceauşescu's time but which he did everything to exploit, was one so overworked in human history that you'd think our ancestors would have declared it dead long ago. It's called Get The Fuck Off My Land Or I'll Blow Your Brains Out—or, to put it more enterprisingly—Possession Is Law. The Romanian-speaking Romanians (who comprised the minority in the region) thought that Transylvania, as part of Romania, should be Romanian in character and, therefore, Romanian-speaking; while the Hungarian-speaking Romanians (who were the majority) thought that Transylvania, which until the last war had been part of Hungary, should be an example of Hungarian culture and language; to say nothing of what the German-speakers of the region thought, nor the Gypsies. They were all on the same bread rations, all without meat, all equally unemployed, all equally miserable.

Any student of history could have told you what was likely to happen:

Either a greater threat would come along to unite them, albeit temporarily; or a charismatic figure from the region would emerge—either way, something-bigger-than-all-of-them was waiting in the wings to happen. And it did. A man refused to leave his church.

Expressed that way it sounds so simple.

But we have to take these actions one, by one;

An old lady with tired feet takes a seat on a bus restricted to "whites only".

Somewhere else another lady takes a drink from a "restricted" fountain.

Elsewhere, a priest refuses to evacuate his church.

Only fools believe that history isn't accidental—Rosa Parks and Miss Jane Pittman can't have been the first to act defiantly against the Southern segregation that oppressed their race—I'm not trying to diminish the importance of their individual acts of conscience, but others died and went unnoticed for such acts—others had been beaten, silenced, burned out, lynched, imprisoned, exiled with their acts forgotten, gone for nothing, disappeared. An individual act is nothing in its isolation, it's an act of private piety, a kamikaze mission for the soul unless—until—it catches in the safety net of witnesses who take it up immediately, without thinking, which then transforms it into something selfless. Few worse fates await us than to face a crowd that feeds on hate, but to stand and watch its opposite assemble, a crowd which gathers from resolve, in silence, on a prayer, without a chance—that comes as close as I have ever been to witnessing a miracle. The best crowds are vigilantes, in the true sense of the word. The best crowds are silent. And they never panic.

That's the kind of crowd that came out of the houses and the factories, the classrooms and the shops on Friday afternoon to gather outside the Calvinist Reformed Church where its pastor Laszlo Tokes was confined to house arrest in the government's attempt to evict him not only from the church, but from Transylvania, too, where he had become a potent spokesperson for Protestant Hungarians. Until that afternoon, only individual members of his Hungarian-speaking congregation had smuggled food and fuel to him inside the parsonage, but that Friday everyone in Timişoara who listened to the radio knew that time was up for pastor Tokes, Friday was the deadline the government had set. Friday was the day—*vin minerri*—that the Securitate were going to come to take him.

By the time Eva and I entered the square in front of the

church there were about five hundred people there. Within an hour there were more than a thousand. Around four o'clock Tokes appeared at a second storey window, clutching his Bible, making gestures of appreciation to the crowd, when a group of people near Eva and me started singing a song that was taken up through the throng, not by everyone, but by most, a song that sounded more like an anthem than a hymn and suddenly Eva was clutching my arm, stretching up on her toes to speak in my ear, "—is *Romanian* anthem—! —is *Romanian* singing, not Hungarian! Here, like in Poland —*Solidarity*!"

Tokes, in his window, stood silently, nodding, and placed the Bible over his heart. It occurred to me that maybe he, like me, couldn't understand the words to the song so I shoved my notebook into Eva's hands and scrawled,

—DOES TOKES SPEAK ROM?

—DOUBT, she scrawled back.

—WORDS TO SONG?

—DOUBT.

—WRITE, PLEASE

I watched as she wrote,

DESTEAPTĀ-TE ROMÂNE
(WAKE UP, ROMANIAN!)

DIN SOMNUL CEL DE MOARTE
(FROM YOUR DEATHLY SLEEP . . .)

ACUM ORI NICIODATĀ
(NOW OR NEVER,)

Wake up, Romanians

CREOIESTE-TI ALTĀ SOARTĀ
(MAKE YOURSELF ANOTHER FATE . . . !)

Her hand was shaking as she handed me the pen and her face reflected that same brightness of hope and burgeoning belief that I had seen burning on the faces of the students in Beijing; and, believe me, I didn't want to be there when the tanks arrived, again, as I knew they would . . . and I didn't want to tell her what was going to happen, when they did.

Wake up, Romanians, from your deathly sleep—fucking weird refrain for an anthem, I remember thinking, not exactly in the class of glory glory hallelujah or god bless america, or, even—translating loosely from the French—let's go, children of the fatherland. Who or what was ever woken from a "deathly" sleep other than Lazarus and Sleeping Beauty and a score of breeds of hibernating bears . . . ?

. . . *Dracula.*

Welcome to Transylvania, Noah, I warned myself: don't stick out your neck.

But I did—I ended up doing things in the course of the next week that, in retrospect, were really crazy—unnecessarily, insanely dangerous. By the end of the following week the street battles in Bucharest became so intense, so explosive, that a lot of foreign news crews landing at the airport got off their planes, took one look and said fuck this, jack, no way, we're outta here. Five foreign journalists were killed in Bucharest by New Year's Day—one, a Belgian photographer working for Associated Press, was shot through the back of his head by a sniper in front of the Inter-Continental Hotel where I and the rest of the pack were bivouacked. Not that press corps fatalities outweigh the deaths of civilians, but—forgive this cold statistic—the number of civilian casualties of war took a quantum leap from the last century into this one, then tabled out, once it became accepted warfare during World War II to bomb the shit out of the enemy whether or not that enemy was military or domestic, whether or not that enemy was pointing a weapon up your ass or sitting knitting in her kitchen in her own house listening to Christian hymns on Radio Free Europe. The number of fatalities among the press skyrocketed during the last half of this century, proving that we are going into places we have never gone before, that we are going in in greater numbers and that we are going in with the insane illogical conviction that because we are observers, not combatants, it's a given that we'll come back out, unscathed, untouched. But the alternative—keeping a safe distance—runs counter to the contract a free press enters into with society. Of course, people like Ceauşescu—and Ronald Reagan in Grenada, Mrs. Thatcher in the Falklands and General Schwartzkopf in the Gulf—would love it if the press would disappear or, barring that, if the press would only print what they are told to. So we keep going in with the logic that the more of us there are the better, but there are some events which can't sustain the weight of hundreds of news gatherers, and the ultimate absurdity we face, which I hope will never happen, is that the army of the media will have a greater troop strength on the ground than the army of the people's revolution or, christ knows, more people on the ground than the U.N., for example.

But that night in Timişoara the foreign press attendance was light, much lighter than I'd thought it would be, probably because, given Ceauşescu's record for putting down dissent, no one anticipated that the demonstration would become so large without the Army taking what were known as measures to restore the peace. The only other foreign journalists I saw that night were two young stringers for *Time* and *Newsweek* magazines, both about Holden's age, some Hungarians and, god bless them, a string of French, who had been canvassing events in Europe that year more heavily than any press from any other nation; and, of course, everybody's favorite aunt, the Beeb.

Around nine o'clock that night a BBC soundman told me they had stated the number in the crowd at 30,000 in their broadcast and I asked him, "How the hell did you arrive at that?"

"Experience," he told me. "The rumor is the tanks will come at midnight," he added.

"Set your watch by it," I told him. "And the men on foot behind the tanks will aim their rifles at your knees. *Experience*," I added.

What struck me most that night—aside from that when the Army did arrive they acted without tactics, and, thank god, they didn't shoot—what struck me the most and what I wrote about throughout the week to come, was that the organizing voices in the crowd were coming from the young. They moved among the people, touching them, speaking over and over the same few words. "What are they saying?" I asked Eva.

"'*Ramanaptā-te á stradā, impreunā.*' Stay in streets. Stay in streets, together."

"When I was in Beijing in June," I told her, "the government broadcast the opposite: 'Save your life. Go home . . .'"

"Here the people say, 'If we own the streets, the Army cannot own them . . .'"

"That's what 'the people' said in Beijing, too."

"Here is not Beijing."

"I hope to god it's not. Eva. I really do."

That night the Securitate and the Army, both, seemed to lack direction and, several hours after midnight, the Army withdrew and the crowd dispersed in celebration of what everybody knew was victory.

When the news reached Ceauşescu he upbraided his Commander of the Army, General Milea, for being a traitor. Four days later, after Milea had hesitated, again, to give the order to open fire on another crowd, this time in Bucharest, Ceauşescu, newly returned from Teheran, had Milea summoned to his office in the Central Committee Building in Bucharest and had him shot, right there, outside his office, in the corridor.

There are times when I am taking down the facts of all these stories (in this case, the man's name, his place of birth, his age at death), when I'm taking down these facts of what are being called, unfactually, "suicides" and "summary dismissals" and "disappearances", when my hand cramps up and I realize I'm holding my pen so tightly that I've made a fist around it—and there are other times when I miss Lilith, when I miss love, when all the shit comes down, when the truly evil get to me and I believe they are at large, undead, and taking victims, energetically.

It got really bad real fast in Timişoara.

On the 16th the Securitate broke into the church and forcibly removed Tokes and his pregnant wife in separate cars to an unknown destination.

That same night the Army, shooting from tanks, opened fire on the crowd, killed god knows how many, and set up checkpoints cordoning off parts of the city.

That's the night they closed the borders.

The rumors that began to circulate in Timişoara then were more absurd than any I had heard elsewhere under siege: the water was, of course, *still* poisoned; the Air Force was going to bomb at night; radioactive isotopes were being introduced into the city; Ceauşescu was going to sell the country to Iran—or, worse—he had already sold it to the Chinese; the PLO was going to attack tomorrow.

"The 'PLO'," I asked Eva, thinking maybe I had lost a little something in translation, "as in the Palestine Liberation Org—?"

"They are very big here," she informed me. "With Syrian. Many Libyan. Many PLO. The Securitate train them."

We were sharing a packet of Bombay mix I had found in my rucksack. It was our dinner. We had slept about four hours in the previous three days.

"Is like for cosmonauts, this food," she noted. "Is nutritious?"

"—absolutely."

"Tastes nutritious."

"So you're staying with me?"

"—'absolutely'."

"—*why*?"

"You make nice husband."

I froze.

"Is joke," she said. "But similar in chance of lifetime."

"—for what?"

"To go with you. I think perhaps you are not staying Timişoara long?"

"—they might not let me out."

"—they will be happy to watch journalist depart."

"What will Ceauşescu do, do you think, when he gets back from Teheran?"

"Call peoples' rally. Organize counter-demonstration."

"—rent-a-crowd, that's what I think, too. Where—?"

"Bucharest. Is safe for him. Is large. Is made for television."

We were sitting in the dark on the floor of a second storey corridor of the Polytechnic, hunkered down for what seemed to be an endless night outside a lav which stank and had no toilets that flushed, although the drains of the urinals were unclogged and there was, miracle of miracles, a single tap that still produced spasms of cold and "poisoned" water, but no one could figure out how to turn it off.

We were both dead tired but I knew neither of us was of a mind to sleep—we had spent the day, at some considerable risk, at the city's two main factories, the ELBA electrical works and the *Solvent* petrochemical plant where strike committees, mostly female, were being formed. The women there had not been afraid to talk to me about conditions in the workplace and in their homes, and I had liked them, lots. I had liked their guts.

"What are you thinking?" Eva asked.

She was sitting very still.

"I'm thinking about the car, actually. What the best thing is to do with it . . ."

"Oh," she murmured.

"I don't want to have to take it into Bucharest."

"No," she murmured.

"And I don't want to have to drive it back to Belgrade."

"No," she sighed, again.

After a brief pause she said softly, "I will ask Sorin and Andrei to drive car back to border. Telephone car rental in morning. Say, 'Too bad, Army shooting at us, take your car at border, or insurance pays.'"

"—or *Noah* pays," I said, "but thanks. Good plan. Above the call of duty."

"You will give Sorin and Andrei—"

"—something, yes. You'll tell me what's appropriate. Eva . . . what's the problem?"

"Back is hurting."

"—water cannon—I *hate* water cannons. Always hurts the worst the second day. Come here, I'll give you 'Noah's Rub' . . ."

She hesitated.

a towline

"Come on, come on," I said, "christsake—"

Within two minutes she was fast asleep across my legs, her head turned toward me, cradled on her folded arms, her breasts, such as they were, small weights against my thigh. She had bound her long straight hair that morning into a single plait, which I lifted off her spine to knead her shoulders. She was very light, her bones were light, she was more bone than flesh, more bone than muscle; bone, no fat. Once she was asleep, I put my head back on the cold tile wall and found I had no place to rest my hands. After a while I lifted up that plaited weight, heavier, in fact, than I suspected her whole body was, and hefted it and wrapped it, silky smooth, around my hands and, helpless, held it, like a towline, through the night.

Unless they're truly insane, like Hitler—and let's face it, most of them have been—the only "nice" thing you can say about dictactors is that they're predictable.

When Ceauşescu returned to Bucharest on the 21st of December to find some of the people of his fiefdom behaving as if they owned the place and had a right to determine its fate, he rounded up the usual suspects and invited thousands of party regulars to Bucharest to demonstrate their loyalty in return for a day off work, with pay.

Vin minerii—not only did the miners come, factory workers from the state-owned fertilizer plants, petrochemical plants and oil refineries came—all delivered to the dictator's doorstep, predictably, by trains laid on by the state-owned railroad.

And the Army came.

And because Ceauşescu was, if not insane, then truly deeply paranoid, he had built his own private information-gathering army of thugs, the Securitate, because he couldn't trust the other, the official, Army. And *they* came. *They* came to everything, in Romania. *They* were everywhere, the Securitate, listening in, checking up, bribing, intimidating, interrogating —no dictator can exist without his private *corps*, every dictator has one, a secret service whose first allegiance is to the leader, and whose fealty has either been built into them from a young age, as in the case of Hitler's Youth, or it springs from faith—as in the boys who go to war to die for the Ayatollah—or it has been bought. In Ceauşescu's case, because he lacked both personal charisma and a self-perpetuating dogma, his loyals had been bought. They'd been bought, first, with a blank check for unrestrained abuse of power and, second, more deliciously, with foreign gizmos, battery-operated toothbrushes, electric can-openers; and foreign goods, like *food*. And the person at the top from whose replenishable larder all this booty had trickled down into Securitate agents' pockets was the chief provider, the quartermaster general—*Adam*—the Minister of Trade.

I didn't know that then, I didn't know, coming into Bucharest on a night train on the 20th from Timişoara with Eva and the loyal factory workers from PAROM, the state-owned woodpulp factory, how corrupt a corrupt system could become. At his show trial on Christmas Day, Ceauşescu would be accused of genocide, of systematically starving 23 million people, but his crimes exceeded what is corporeal, he and Elena and their corps of bought souls bled a people, robbed them of Place, en-crypted their fate to a Futureless time, engendered the undead and fulfilled the prophecy whose shadow was long but whose features could cast no reflection —that this was the soil from which the first vampire had sprung.

No small irony, then, that what happened that week

depended on what TV-people call "live feed"—when the crowd started throwing shoes and potatoes at him, when Ceauşescu lost control of the crowd he lost it big because, as always, he was being televised, live, to the nation and when it went terribly wrong, as it did, his whole world was watching.

TV as History—people believed it, but they *couldn't* believe it—people in Bucharest watching him on TV left their homes to come out and see for themselves. And yet four days later when the video of the Ceauşescu's corpses was shown on those same TV screens and replayed at intervals all day long on Christmas Day, people refused to believe they were dead. "Dummies" was the rumor. "Wax dummies", "balloons", "plastic dolls", "stand-ins", "body doubles"—all these phrases were used, these and, "*They're not dead*, they've taken the money and gone to China." Some rumors had them living in Iran, others had them living in Libya, but all the rumors made them undead. All the rumors kept them alive, sharing, in myth, that restricted topography where Elvis resides—on the same street as Hitler and Hoffa and Earhart and Mengele—but, believe me, they were dead and so were their dogs. Only what they gave birth to persists and survives.

On the fifth day of the Bucharest uprising, after the revolution and after the counter-revolution, after the National Salvation Front had declared itself the new government of the people's Romania, after the Ceauşescus had been murdered, I gave Eva the day off to go visit her mother and father and I went to take a look at the dictator's office in the old Central Committee Building. It was the day after Christmas, and it was finally very, very cold. I walked from the Inter-Continental through the University quarter where the heaviest fighting had taken place. I had to stop a lot, to sort out my thoughts, to try to get my bearings. Eva and I had spent much of the previous five days trapped under fire on these very streets, often in the dark. Now there were candles burning on the pavement, candles held upright in balled-up wads of bread, amber-colored church candles stuck in loaves of bread to mark the spots where people had been killed. On some blocks, especially around the School of Architecture, the whole sidewalk was aglow with them. I didn't want to be there. Buildings bore the marks of sniper fire—head height—and lower, heart high, gouges made by Army mortars. There were bloodstains in the strangest places, scattered on the undersides of bare tree branches, splattered over windowpanes. I had bloodstains on my jacket, three or more, front and back, from christ knows where and whom. The smell of blood—that's what you remember. I think of it as shameful. I call it the smell of shame—anything to call it by some other name than what it is. Warm, alive, it smells the way your piss does after eating fresh asparagus. But on the dead it smells like shame. Fires were still smoldering—the University library, where half a million books had burned, still hissed in ruination—the whole city smelled of cordite, wax, wet ashes, shame. I wanted to go home. I wanted to forget the things I'd seen and stop the ringing in my ears, I wanted to be somewhere else, somewhere where the world was not like this one, where the world was not this world. But first I had to find someone. I had to locate Adam.

We may never know what it was like before the revolution, but when I saw it, Ceauşescu's office in the old Central Committee Building had transformed itself into a zoo. Taxi drivers-turned-heroes of the revolution, gawkers, filchers, ambulance chasers and hangers-on of every stripe were lifting, looking, lounging and looting everything they could, rifling through files, peeking behind paintings, sitting on the desk, pretending to put calls directly through to Arafat and Deng.

"Who's in charge?" I asked a likely suspect and was told,

"People of Romania." I spent all day trying to find anyone who knew someone who had a clue about how I could get hold of anybody with some information about the former Minister of Trade. Finally I found someone who told me where his office was. The office doors—big double ones with large brass handles—were thrown open, off their hinges. The reception room was stacked with packing cartons. In the central inner office there were, I counted quickly, seven men in seriously ominous attire, suits like only Eastern Europeans made, dark and square with baggy pants and stingy pockets.

It was clear that I had crashed some kind of party, so charmingly I asked, "Anybody here speak English?"

"Who are you?" one of them replied.

"I have an appointment with the Minister," I tried.

"You're lying," I was told.

"—true," I said.

"American?"

"— and damn proud of it."

"What do you want?"

"I want to see the Minister."

One of them nodded at another who nodded at two more who came toward me in what was a not-so-friendly effort to remove me.

"Wait, wait," I said. "Wait—"

I scrawled my name on a blank page in my notebook along with the name of my hotel and the message URGENT underlined.

"Give this to him," I said to the guy who'd done the talking. "Make sure you give this to him," I repeated.

The smallest guy in the room, the one who looked most unassuming suddenly shook his fist in my face and started shouting, "Filthy American Senate cancel Romanian Most Favored Nation Trade Status—!"

Something told me he was also going to shout that the International Monetary Fund was owned by Jews, but he didn't. He shouted that the *World Bank* was owned by Jews. Bigotry, too, in its narrative form, is always predictable. It's not the book but its changing covers that surprise you.

I went back to the hotel and slept.

There is always a longing and real need, when you're on the road, for deep sleep but there's never time and, worse, never the peace of mind. So there's only one thing to do: work yourself until exhaustion drops you—and that's what I had done.

In no time at all I was having the classic foreign hotel room nightmare, dreaming someone was pounding on the door, and it appeared, once I got my eyes open, to be that time of day known the world round in those latitudes as *morning*.

It also appeared I had slept fully clothed, including my boots, and my feet hurt like hell, my soles did, when I tried to stand up.

Don't open the door a voice in my head from the nightmare was warning *they'll shoot you.*

I opened the door.

A grey man in a grey apron was standing there.

With his left hand he thrust an envelope at me. With his right hand he asked for a tip. Because I was groggy I gave him a five dollar bill.

Inside the envelope was the page from my notebook I'd written my name on. At the bottom of the page, written in black ink, was the instruction,

Str. Decembrie + Str. Academici 7.30

Fucking cops and fucking robbers, I thought. I looked at my watch. I was already fifteen minutes late. It was 7.45.

I got to the intersection of December and Academici Streets

in fifteen minutes, dallying only to pee and drink mouthwash. One corner had a burned out Army tank cantilevered up on it, one corner was deserted save for me, and the other two had been turned into shrines decked with candles. Kneeling at one of them was a kid in a denim jacket and jeans. When I came up behind him he turned around and said, "Mister John?"

I nodded.

"You call for taxi, please?"

"*In a revolution*—?" I said, but I stepped out into the street and waved for a taxi and, almost immediately, one came.

When I opened the door to the back seat there was a man sitting there dressed in jeans, too, with a big smile on his face.

"Now what?" I asked him.

"You get in," he replied.

"People are kidnapped this way."

"You have my word," he assured me.

I took two steps backwards, away from the car, leaving the door open.

"You know—" I started to say, then, I stopped.

I looked up at the sky.

I had started to say *you people really amaze me*, using "you people" as a pejorative.

"—fuck's going on?" I asked, instead.

The man in the back seat leaned toward me. "You do not recognize me?" he inquired. He clapped a hand on the taxi driver's shoulder. "—and my brother-in-law? From yesterday?"

The brother-in-law, now that he'd mentioned it, *yes*—one of the men who had hustled me out of the Trade Office yesterday.

"Radu Dan," the brother-in-law said, thrusting his paw at me, by way of introduction, through the car window.

"Drago Apostol," the man in the back seat announced and stuck his hand out for a shake, too.

"What's this about?" I said, refusing their handshakes.

"Pentrú," the guy in the back seat responded.

"What about him?" I said.

"Please get in, Mister John, you are drawing attention . . ."

"—*what about him*?" I repeated.

"We'd like to know what your business is with him."

"—who's 'we'?"

"You see, Minister Pentrú has disappeared. Into thin air."

"I don't believe you."

The man in the front seat, the driver, turned to the man in the back seat and spoke a few words to him, anxiously, in Romanian.

Then the taxi took off.

Right, I thought:

This is a stage that I've wandered onto, by accident, while a play is in progress. I don't know what play it is; and I don't know my lines.

I turned around to look at the kid by the shrine, for a cue and a clue. He was gone.

Think of this, I said to myself, *as a sausage*, as some kind of borderland where you wait to move from one Place to another, from the real into a fantasy, or vice versa. So I stood there a while and did some Dylan lyrics in my head, waiting for something to happen. Nothing did. At the end of the *Blond on Blond* album I walked back to my hotel. In the lobby a young man accosted me and said, "Mister John?"

"What's it to you?"

"Are you indeed Mister John?"

"—who's asking?"

"—sorry. Beg pardon. I am Drago Apostol."

"—and I'm Marie of Roumania, buddy."

"—sorry?"

"You're the second 'Drago Apostol' I've met today and it's only . . ." I looked at my watch: ". . . it's only nine fifteen and I can't wait to see how many more 'Dragos' this day has in store for me . . ."

"—but *I* am Drago Apostol . . ."

"You have I.D.?"

He *was* Drago Apostol, although he didn't do his picture justice.

"—is this your date of birth?" I asked him, pointing to some numbers on the card. He nodded. My rapid math said he was thirty.

". . . so: what can I do for you, Drago?"

"Take walk, please."

"I've already had mine thank you."

"Please. Outside."

"Not until I—"

"—is confidential. Is about our mutual acquaintance."

"—'our mutual acquaintance'."

"*—please.*"

On closer inspection I realized the reason that his face was not as pretty in the light of day as it was on his I.D. was that it bore the puffy tell-tale signs of a day-old knock upside the head.

"Okay," I said.

We walked in silence for a block, then he said, "Is not far," and we walked another fifteen minutes without saying anything before we stopped beside a light blue Dacia and he told me, "We are lucky, they not follow us." He motioned me to climb inside the car but I refused. There was a low cement wall nearby where I preferred to sit.

He was very nervous.

"I am—I was—personal chauffeur for Minister of Trade," he began.

I waited.

"Day of twenty-one December, day of helicopters on roof, Minister goes off in helicopter, different helicopter than Ceauşescu. Day of twenty-two, no, twenty-three December, Securitate come for me, say, 'Where is Minister?' I say, 'I don't know, I am driver only.' Many questions. Keep me long long time. But I am not to frighten of them and I tell them nothing. Then yesterday they come again and take me. They put—" He spread his hand over his mouth.

"—'gag'," I said.

"And—" he said.

He put his hand over his eyes.

"—'blindfold'," I admitted.

"—take me somewhere under streets, beneath the ground. Then they ask me, 'What is business of Minister with American at Inter-Continental Hotel called Mister John?' What can I say? I have never met you. Then they show me picture. Ask me, 'Do you know this man—?'"

"—'picture'? What kind of picture?"

"Not too good."

"—of me?"

"Of you. Like this . . ." He measured out about two inches with his thumb and index finger. "Black and white. Like made from copy machine."

I felt inside my jacket, then produced my passport photo for him.

"—is same!—but only not with color . . ."

He looked at me, expectantly.

"—*so*?" I said.

"So," he echoed.

He seemed to indicate that we were in agreement, although about what I didn't have a clue.

"You have news for me?" he asked.

"—do *I* have?"

"Yes. About Minister."

"I was hoping to get news from *you*."

"—from *me*?"

He suddenly looked scared.

"—listen, listen," I assured him, "this is strictly personal. You understand 'personal'? Whatever the Securitate want with him is their business—I just want to ask him a few questions. I have a little score to settle. But it's strictly personal . . ."

He nodded as if he understood but I could tell he didn't.

"So you don't know where is Minister?"

"—don't *you*?"

He looked bewildered.

I think I probably did, too.

We sat in silence for a minute while I watched steam rise off the street in front of us.

"Let me ask you something," I finally said. "Are there . . . are there *a lot* of people missing—from Ceauşescu's government, I mean."

"—no. Only Minister. Rest are still the same."

"—still in office, you mean."

"—yes."

"—there is the chance, you know, that he was . . . that he met with some kind of accident. Did he have a woman with him?"

"—'woman'?"

He looked scared again.

"Foreign woman," I pursued. "Dark hair. Thin. Big eyes."

"Minister would never be with foreign woman here. Not allowed. If Ceauşescu would found out—"

"American," I said.

I watched him as he wrestled with some problem, worked his hands.

"Thirty-five years old," I said. "Speaks French. Likes opera. Named Lilith."

He studied me.

"—how do you know about this woman?" he finally demanded.

"She's my friend. How do *you* know her?"

"—I drove him to . . . Sometimes I drive woman, too."

"—you 'drove him to'? You drove him where?"

"—nobody knew. Nobody allowed to know. Extremely secret. To her house."

I put my hand on top of his.

"Take me there," I said.

"She's not there, I have already—"

"Take me," I repeated.

He hesitated only slightly, then we both stood up.

We drove through the city, west I thought, although the driving wasn't easy, many streets were closed, still barricaded —but the further we maneuvered from the center, the easier it got, the more like normal driving, outside the ruts of war.

I was not in good shape.

My heart was racing and I wasn't thinking straight.

Drago, too, was worse for wear.

"You like car?" he asked at one point, patting the plastic dashboard.

"It's a nice car," I assured him.

"Gift from Minister."

"Is this the car you drove him in, on official business?"

"Oh no," he scoffed. "Official car is big. Mercedes. This one private car. For private. 'Strictly personal' . . ."

He turned to me and smiled.

"He trusted you," I led.

"I am his son."

He smiled at me, again, and said, "Which you say—'adopted'."

"He 'adopted' you? What does that mean?"

"—from child. From boy."

"—you lived with him? He raised you?"

"I was orphan, he was orphan. For me, he made father. Many orphans in Romania. Perhaps some day I, also, am be father . . . like Minister."

"Who taught you English, Drago?"

"Minister. Is good, no? Very interesting. Mrs. always say I talk with English 'very interesting'."

"—'Mrs.'?"

"—your friend." He stopped the car. "Here is house," he said, and pointed.

We were parked in what appeared to be a part of Bucharest which must have been a neighborhood of quiet elegance once, although "neighborhood" suggests a certain coziness and a proximity to other houses which the residences, sitting on at least an acre of land and set back several hundred yards from the tree-lined avenue, did not possess. A pebble driveway between two crumbling stucco pillars veined with moss and damp led from the street to a large three storey structure painted yellow, St. Petersburg yellow, the color of a dying flame, with ornate but rotting wooden shutters and a red tile roof. The shutters were bolted and the house looked uninhabited.

"Mrs. has, which you say—'apart'?—behind. At rear. Second floor. Extremely private."

"Who else lives in the house?"

"Is no one. Once was prince. Is finish. Which you say, 'the monarchy'."

"—a prince lived here?"

"—small prince. Many princes in Romania. This one small. Unimportant. From some other country. But nice house inside. I have been with Mrs. once. Through window."

There was a wide, wooden staircase leading to the second storey along which ran a covered balcony in the style of a Spanish mission or of a tenement in Katmandu. In the center of the wall there was a single, large, carved wooden door.

"Is not lock," Drago told me.

"—you've been inside?"

"Door was open."

I turned the handle and pushed against the door and her aroma welled up all around me in the entrance like a presence.

Drago must have sensed my emotional response because he hung back like a shadow as I moved from room to room.

It is not a good idea to trespass on the place where someone else has loved your lover. It is not a good idea to walk into the room where she had recently been living and view the bed. It is not a great sensation to verify that she's erased you from her life.

Lilith's 'apart', as Drago called it, was about the size of her Paris flat and, eerily, laid out along the same lines, although draped differently, with heavy claret-colored curtains and, at such a distance from the Seine and its reflecting water, far less light. The interior was dark and it seemed heavy, a heaviness interpolated in the furniture of carved wood rounded out and shaped with tapestries and cushions in the Romanian version of Asian kilims, with red, as stark as blood, the dominating color. The art on display, such as it was, was distinctly nationalistic, iconographically reminiscent of a vision once experienced of a mythically orthodox Romania where saints with long pale beards, incandescent lives and long pale hands were venerated. There were no photographs anywhere. And except for the CD player, stereo, TV and VCR in the main room, there was nothing to suggest anything modern about the place. Three of the picture frames, one in the entrance, one in the main room and one in Lilith's bedroom, had been draped with plain black cloth.

"Whose idea was this?" I asked Drago, lifting a corner to peer behind, thinking I'd find a Warhol or a Stella or a Cartier-Bresson.

"Was like," Drago said. "Was always."

I lifted the cloth up the whole way to show him what had been hidden. It was a mirror. In it, he seemed to shiver. "Old custom for dead," he explained.

In her bedroom there was evidence, among other things, of a rapid and unplanned departure—the doors of the armoire were flung open, hangers strewn on the floor, drawers pulled out: but everything was gone, all her clothing, all her personal effects packed by her or by someone else, but obviously packed up in a hurry. Even in the large tiled, tapestry-hung bathroom every trace of the personal had been removed, except in what seemed a glaringly obvious omission, all her face creams. Lilith lost her self-control when it came to face creams, and if there'd been any doubt before I saw what was on display on the shelf over the bathroom sink that she'd actually been living there, this collection was enough to prove her tenancy beyond a shadow because there were a dozen different jars of different shit, some with inscrutable Romanian names and some marked "Gerovital". "Is famous face saving," Drago told me, noticing my fascination. "Pure Romanian. From thermal spa on Black Sea. With, which you say, 'fetus placenta'. Very expensive, not cheap. People fetus placenta, not sheep."

"'People fetus'?" I repeated.

"Which you say, 'baby soft'," Drago said.

I lifted one of the jars, unscrewed the lid, looked at the glop it contained and smelled it. It smelled waxy. Then I looked to see if the ingredients were printed on the label. "What does it say on here?" I asked Drago, handing it to him.

"'Special Cream For Eye For Night'," he read.

"—no, the other stuff," I told him.

"'Produced and', which you say, 'manufactured exclusive on Black Sea, Romania. Distributed exclusive by Zement.'"

"'Zement'."

"Yes."

"Does that mean anything to you?"

He shrugged.

"—you've never heard of it?"

He shrugged again.

"It's a company," I said. "A non-communistic concept. And your Minister either owns it or controls the stock . . ."

"—Minister has many business. Trade. Is job."

"—oh yeah? Does the Minister of Health keep consultation hours? Does the Minister of Education teach—?"

"—is different with Romania trade. Is necessary. Good for nation."

"'Good for nation' that shit like this with human placenta in it gets sold for export with the profits going solely to the Minister of Trade?"

"Puts Romania on many faces. Makes beautiful. Is good for nation."

"Was the woman who lived here beautiful?"

"—she is Minister's, I never look."

"—all men look, Drago."

"—okay sometimes I look. Like this." He turned his head. "Which you say, 'sideway'."

"—and?"

"—what see? She is little sad, I think. Women very beautiful when sad."

"I don't think so," I informed him.

"Gypsy women," he elaborated. "Can want man and sing when sad"

"—like *Carmen*," I said, going to the bureau where the stereo was set up and starting to pull open all the drawers.

"—for what you look? Is strictly personal. Is private. Not advisable . . ."

"I'm doing what reporters do, Drago," I said, rummaging about. "I'm looking. You want to find your Minister? You have to look . . ."

"—but here? For what?"

I popped open the CD carousel to see what she'd been playing last. It was *Tosca*.

"It's what the Securitate does," I told him, moving from the main room to her bedroom, "you keep searching until you find something. You *will* find something because you're searching for it even though you don't know what 'it' is . . ."

I turned down the bedclothes and felt through all the pillows. I looked under the bed. I looked under the carpet. I pulled the black cloth off the mirror. I pulled out drawers and ran my hands through them. Then I pulled a chair from beside the bed to the front of the armoire and stood on it. And there it was, maybe, if not the whole story, at least things that I knew had belonged to her, things that I knew were important to her, things she would not have forgotten or left behind by mistake: her camera bag, her battered hand-stitched leather briefcase and a cache of *livres de poche* bound with an old leather strap.

I brought them down and placed them on the bed.

Drago looked scared. "—oh, oh," he said. "Not good to look. Is personal . . ."

The camera bag was empty save for two rolls of unexposed T-Max 400 past their expiration dates and four of her Khomeini tee-shirts, washed and folded. One of them, the FATWA MORGANA one had a rusty stain on it down the front where her blood had dripped when someone threw a stone at her and hit her in the head when we were caught in a communal riot while covering the fortieth anniversary of the independent democratic state in Delhi. "Not a brilliant thing to wear," I had advised her when she'd put it on that morning, "in fact, downright insulting."

"To whom?" she'd said.

"To some," I'd answered and she'd looked at me as if I'd just hatched my stunted life from that rotten egg called political correctness.

"We're guests here," I reminded her.

"No, we're not. We're reporters here," she'd countered.

I sat down on the bed.

In unison I unsprung the two brass locks of her briefcase, then lifted the lid.

Out sprang the story.

Few things reveal themselves so thoroughly, spring materially into being like recovered gold unsprung from some encrusted deep-sea hold, a treasure in a chest, the furies from Pandora's box.

The photograph on top was a portrait of an absolute, a picture, black and white, which neither encompassed nor created any light of hope which could relieve its agony. It was what it was: a portrait of a naked child, a girl, unwashed and near starvation, lying in her own mess on a soiled sheet, shackled to a rusting bed in what appeared to be a ward of some sort filled with more beds in the background with more bodies on them. The girl is on her side, a bony shoulder, pocked with scabs, pointing upward, her face atop her bony arms. She is staring at the camera and her eyes are dead. Lilith must have been a foot or so from her when she took the picture and—because I knew her, because we had had this conversation countless times—it must have been as morally despicable to her to take the girl's picture in that helpless state as it was for me to force my sex on her at the Berlin Wall. But the worst was yet to come—there followed prints of children, infants, in unimaginable despair—babies, three babies to a cot, showing signs of extreme malnutrition and disease—more children shackled to their beds, stony, impassive adult females dressed as nurses standing guard near them. On the back of each print there was a brief notation written in Lilith's hand—a line noting the place and date. The earliest date seemed to be the 14th July, Bastille Day, 1989—the latest one, October—and all the places, there were five of them, were listed either as "hospital" or "orphanage".

Drago had shrunk back against the armoire, away from the bed, as soon as I'd opened the briefcase. When I started to show him the photographs, he gripped his shoulders and shook his head.

"'Tatari Hospital'," I read from the back of one, "where is that? 'Mures Orphanage'. 'Colintina'. You know these places?"

"—not good," he said.

"—are they hospitals? Where are they? You must know—you must have driven her there . . ."

"—not good," he repeated.

"—very not good," I concurred. I held up the first photograph, the one of the girl, and pointed to her. 'Buftea'," I read off the back. "Is that near here?"

He nodded.

"You know the way?"

He nodded again.

"Take me."

At the bottom of the briefcase there was a notebook which I paged through briefly to determine what it was—a diary, of sorts, describing all the photographs. I took it out and put the photos in the case and locked it and stood up.

"Let's go," I said to Drago, but he was looking doubtful.

"This will help find Minister?" he said.

"I don't know," I confessed. "I don't know what this will do, but I know you have to help me do it."

He searched my eyes with his.

"You have father?" he asked.

"Good father," I said.

"—good man?"

"Average man."

"—many children born here without average father. Many average orphans in Romania . . ."

"Show me."

He closed his eyes, then opened them and nodded.

He gripped my wrist and told me, "You are just like her."

Driving out, I didn't speak to him by choice; driving back, I couldn't speak, could not have spoken had my job or life depended on it.

What the vanguard saw, storming into Dachau, straying into Buchenwald, how they reconciled themselves, reconciled their species, to the horror they encountered, how they lived thereafter with the knowledge of that evil, with the stench of it forever in their nostrils, with the stain of it forever on their waking vision, in their nightmares, on their memories—every journalist, or maybe every person prone to making sense of history, every visionary, every tin-plate skinhead, every military crackpot, each evangelist, each saint attempts to wrap the mind around apocalypse, imagine the impossible, the end of ends, the death of anything and everything that's good. No one ever wants to see it, that would be too much, the human mind rejects that as a sane selection, but everybody plays with the idea of envisioning it from the point of view of an observer; hence, as a survivor. Try, I dare you, to describe it in the language that we take for granted, watch what happens to the words, 'hi', 'how are you', 'have a nice day'. Lilith wrote to me maybe twenty times in the years we were together—funny narratives spiked with local highlights, market gossip, travel, lively tips and kvetches. Hers was always a good eye, whether with a pen or with the camera, but she didn't have the patience for protracted storytelling, nor the natural equilibrium for a balanced view. So the diary that she wrote about the orphans in Romania—more a book of revelation, really—was all the more affecting for its exacting use of language, its restraint. It was she, to my knowledge, who first translated the Romanian word used to describe abandoned infants with AIDS as "irrecoverables"—a word in English which, unlike the Hindi "untouchable", implies the state-held view that every person born within the state existed to fulfill some state-deigned rôle, to work and breed within the state, for the state and by the state—and if they couldn't, if they were born with defects or if they acquired a deficiency in childhood, an immune deficiency, for example, then they were less than refugees, less than unemployed, less than homeless, less than worthless—they were irrecoverable. And Lilith was the first, to my knowledge, to use the term "AIDS babies" and to describe how AIDS had come among the newborn in Romania. Like the reporter's search for reasons to events, the search for the AIDS equivalent of Typhoid Mary, the First Carrier, the primary infector, the Source, the serpent in the Garden of Eden, was part of the epidemiologist's job, part of disease control, and the artificial borders of our man-made nations define the spread of the disease in ways that, surprisingly, reveal the nature of that man-made nation's soul. There are some countries, for example, where the introduction of the disease into the population was absolutely non-sexual—such as Greece—and other countries, such as France and Italy, where the disease was introduced both through sexual transmission and through tainted blood. In Romania the disease was spread entirely through tainted blood transfusions, and it became endemic in its newborn orphan population for reasons which could have happened nowhere else but in a suspicious, peasant-mentality driven, Dracula-inventing, Ceauşescu-producing state. With his kingdom's population falling, his impoverished workforce dispirited and disinclined to fuck for procreation, Ceauşescu outlawed all forms of birth control, including abortion, in 1966 and enacted a system by which all women, factory workers as well as rural peasants, were subjected to routine gynecological examinations every other month to guarantee that they weren't cheating their beloved leader out of unborn future subjects. Untold numbers of unwanted pregnancies occurred, resulting in untold numbers of unwanted children whose overworked underpaid parents could not afford to keep them. Someone in Ceauşescu's coterie, one of his advisers with an eye for profit and a knack for problem solving, saw a way both to save the children and to save Ceauşescu's population program by providing state-sponsored parentage in the form of orphanages, hundreds of them, one for every town or district with a population greater than a thousand. In the hands of a compassionate or tolerant society it might have been a bold enlightened move, but in Romania it was a program of far-reaching state-sponsored cruelty. In some districts the children were kept in abandoned warehouses with no heat, no electricity. The women who were hired to look after them were women to whom political favors were owed, women who had spied for the state on their neighbors, women who had been good communists, women who, on the whole, had no training in childcare. Healthy children were routinely culled out and sent to superior facilities. Infants who showed signs of frailty or illness, babies exhibiting lethargy or "bad color", were treated to the age-old Romanian tonic of 'micro-transfusion", a tablespoon or two of blood transfused to the infant once or twice a week to kick-start a sluggish system. Even healthy children got this treat. Perhaps there is a sound medical reason for this practice, I don't know, but by modern lay standards, it sounds medieval and appalling. The blood, unscreened, unfiltered, was obtained, as most blood was in those parts, as a form of *baksheesh*, a product provided by immigrant service workers for a small sum or for a meal or for a week's work visa. Where or when, precisely, AIDS entered the Romanian blood supply will never be known but it is almost certain that the Typhoid Mary in this case was a carrier from another country who donated blood for money sometime in the early 80s. And that's all it took to start the epidemic among infants—that, and the peasant practice of bi-weekly micro-transfusions with unsterile needles, that and the all-encompassing system of state orphanages, the brain-child not of Ceauşescu, but of one of his Ministers, a man of far more evil genius, in the end, a man who understood—because he had inhabited them, both—the empty corridors of orphanhood and the long corridors of power: *Adam*.

Even having read through Lilith's notebook, I was not prepared for what I found that afternoon. After an hour's drive, we approached what seemed to be an out of season camp or spa constructed entirely of wood surrounded by fir trees at the end of a packed frozen mud driveway half a mile from a pig farm on the state road to Buftea. As our car approached, shunted between icy mud ruts, two black skeletal yellow-fanged fuck-looking dogs attacked us head-on, followed by a female individual, formidable and thick, who in any country would be called the Frau, the Matron, bitch, or the Prime Minister.

Drago went pale with fear and indecision.

"She's seen this car before?" I pressed him.

"—yes."

"—and she's seen you before?"

He nodded.

"—then we'll be fine," I said. "You'll do the talking, I'll wave money."

As it was, I waved a lot of money—since the start of the revolution, no one had come to this facility with food or with supplies of any kind or with instructions, and Frau Matron bitch was ready to leave the mewling little bastards to their already cruel fate, shackled in their own shit to the rusted bedsteads without food.

Drago refused to leave the car so I stuffed all the *lei* I had in my pockets in the woman's hands as she dogged my steps, jabbing at me with her blunt thick finger, cursing me, no doubt, detailing every past complaint and every present grievance in that sing-song ancient language, striking me from time to time around the head as if I were one of her defenseless charges until, thoroughly disgusted with her, disgusted by the place, I grabbed her by the square knot of her headscarf and recited in her face the universal words for Fuck Off.

If I had stayed more than ten minutes in that place I would

have become a different person, I know I would have, I would have become someone who could tolerate a sight that must turn every human being's stomach.

I've never vomited at the sight of anything before, although I've been with people who have done that, greenhorns, ninnies, weakshits in the field who vomit when they see somebody killed or see somebody's legs blown off—I don't vomit at the sight of blood or shit or tanks or water cannons, or ordinary death, at people dying out of ordinary violent causes because we are such shits to one another, as a species—but I lost my cookies there, tossed my guts the same way as any novice would viewing an autopsy or straying into Buchenwald, though I'm loath to draw comparisons among the genocides that man has made, each one is vile, no one is viler than the other. That we have come to take such acts for granted, as part of war, as a price that tyranny exacts, as a cost efficient way to trim the population while birth control and abortion are still decried in many quarters as a crime, that we can canonize one form of death as justified, turn our backs on parts of our native world with the meagre justifications that their ways are not ours, their ways are barbaric, backward and outdated, that we can exempt ourselves from the hubbub of the whole brutal biblical koranic pantheistic atheistic polyglottal horde as easily as rolling over on our side in bed—that we don't bleed when others bleed, that our needs are narcissistic and, therefore, self-destructive, that we are fatally more territorial as a kind, in pride, than lice or lions, that we behave as if there were some other life, elsewhere, more perfect than this one, toward which we aspire in our prayers, such prayers exempting us from action, beatitudes exempting us from other attitudes, platitudes exempting us from coming to, each one, our own definitive conclusion, what goes around must come around, if at first you don't succeed, all you need is love, walk softly and carry a, Rule Britannia, Merry Christmas, Happy Halloween, he who laughs last laughs longest, there is no god but one god, there is no life but this one: that we live our lives as squanderers, as if the gift of it was expendable, is our first and only sin, and always has been, from the beginning we have cast our covenant, our promise, to the wind.

Don't get involved in the story used to be the rule, the guiding principle of journalism until involvement evolved into the story, the phenomenon of the far-flung reporter taking precedent over, becoming newsier than, what was to be reported. For myself, old-fashioned stick, I like to keep my voice under the fray, not betraying my prejudices, if I have any, and I seem to have developed more as I've grown older. But not this time, not with this story—it took me six false starts, my hand shaking as I wrote, as Drago drove us back to Bucharest—six emotionally high-pitched starts that I knew were wrong, that I knew would never find their way into print in any moderately respected paper, until, telling Drago to stop the car and let me out near the burned out Bibliothèque, I sat down on an upturned vendor's cart that had been used by students to transport the dead and wounded and wrote the story square on, toned down, dead-toned as I could make it about eight- and ten-year-old children who had lived their lives in pens, who had never learned to walk, who, at five or six or nine years old still acted like six-month olds, still rocked their torsos back and forth still knocked their foreheads endlessly against the structures that confined them. I wrote about the blood transfusions, about filthy needles, about babies with sarcomas, using Lilith's notes to back me up, trusting them because there was no earthly reason I could think of not to. I wrote it, then I phoned it in from the press room in the Inter-Continental, knowing full well Boot would cut its bleeding heart out, as he should. And to his credit, or perhaps to mine, he did exactly that, extracted the bare facts and ran them blind without a byline then built me a box beside it where he let me wax, as he would put it, "like a Goodman or a Quindlen or some other skirt in pants." Then I did something I thought I'd never do: I walked. High noon on a breaking story and I couldn't Coop it, couldn't strap the gunbelt on, couldn't face the fucker, couldn't put the badge back on. What I wanted more than anything was a reborn innocence—but that was lost forever, I suspected, so I'd settle for a week somewhere beside some ancient salty water, the Red Sea, for instance, sleeping solitary underneath the stars, counting the Pleiades, staring down the backs of dusty mountains into Jordan or some other holy land over clear blue water where, from history's deep uncertain keep, flying fish would break on the horizon, silver, two by two.

Could I really come to trust that Lilith had come to Bucharest to get this story, that she had gone with Adam in the first place because she had been following a lead?

And pigs fly, Noah, I repeated to myself.

But clearly she had assembled the documentation on the Romanian orphans with a purpose in mind, and I had to conclude that her purpose had been exposure, exposure through publication.

In the bar at the hotel I made a swift assessment of the pack—it was cocktail hour, every hour was, and the place was chockablock with some of the best this hackwork has to offer. In the corner at a table by himself, nursing seriousness and a Dr. Pepper, I spotted the very essence of high-minded gloom, Sid, from *US News & World Report*, and made a beeline to him.

"Noah," he said, looking up, not smiling.

"Sid," I said, placing Lilith's briefcase on the table.

"Don't tell me," he said, frowning toward the briefcase, "Hitler's diaries. At last."

"Come up to my room," I said.

"You must be joking." He gave me a thorough going over. "You're not joking," he concluded and hauled his small but weighty self up from the table.

As we made our way across the lobby toward the elevator we were shadowed by a not too subtle bird dog type in a clown cop suit who trailed us like a bad reputation into the lift. Sid, shaking off his gloom for the occasion, punched the buttons to each floor, then turned to our fellow traveler and, offering his hand, said, "Hi. Sid. Coming with? Why don't you invite ten more, we'll make a *minyan* . . ." He zeroed in on a pin on the guy's lapel and said, "That the microphone?" then cleared his throat and coughed into it. Getting out on a floor which was neither his nor mine he said, "Do you have scotch?"

"Sorry, no," I said. "I've just come from Timişoara . . ."

"Am I going to need a scotch for this?"

I nodded.

Five minutes later he was at my door with a quart of the Macallan.

It didn't take us long, about an hour, to sort through Lilith's notes and photographs and to sort through all the arguments between us why we shouldn't—but we would—use her material.

"What I don't understand," he finally said, as it was growing dark outside, "is why—"

"—don't ask."

"—you're walking."

The scotch was taking its effect, so I said, "I just hafta get outta here."

"That's what we all say."

"But *I'm* saying it. This time. I hafta get a life."

He looked at me a long time.

"I hope what's happened to you never happens to me, Noah," he finally said.

"I hope so, too. I hope so, too," I repeated.

I laid my hand on top of his.

"—oh fuck you're not going to kiss me, are you?" Sid said.

"—no, I'm going to ask you to take Eva."

"—'Eva'?"

"Eve."

"—okay. Who's 'Eve'? Not an orphan, I hope—"

"—my translator."

"I have one."

"Not as good as this one."

"—what about this Drago person?"

"—hopeless."

"What's so great about this Eve?"

"—she's smart. Thinks on her feet. Needs the work. Doesn't know I'm going . . ."

"—oh, man, you haven't fucked her have you?"

"—nothing like that. Not even close. I just feel . . . I owe her something."

"Okay," he said. He stood up. "You'll tell her to get in touch with me." I handed him the briefcase, and he sat down again, meticulously emptying it and handing back to me Lilith's notebook and the case itself. "I'll have to talk to legal about these," he said, holding up the photographs.

"I know you will," I nodded.

"—and I'll have to give both you and her joint credit . . ."

"—that's up to you."

He stood up, again.

"When are you going?"

"—tomorrow."

"—where?"

"I don't know."

"—you won't disappear on us?"

"I'm tempted to."

"What about this Pentrú character, what do you want me to do about him?"

"Find him."

"—and Divi?"

I stared at him.

"—Noah?"

I hadn't thought of her as "Divi" for months—even as Sid and I had sat there, going through her notes, looking at her photographs, I had called her Lilith, not even registering that throughout our conversation he had called her by her working name.

"Lilith, Sid," I said. "Her name is Lilith . . ."

Suddenly there was a lot of movement in the hotel corridor outside my room and someone started pounding on the door. Sid slid the photographs inside his jacket, picked the briefcase up and, for some amazing reason out of some perverted reflex, placed it on the chair he had been sitting on and sat on it.

I opened the door and in swept Eva, balancing a cardboard box, a suitcase and six or seven plastic shopping bags of different pastel colors.

"—you didn't told me you are in hotel!" she started, "I am asking all day through the desk—"

She tumbled in across the threshold, box first, suitcase, then the bags: "—I bring Christmas feast, much wine, you'll see, my brother and his friends have find much looting—oh." She suddenly became aware of Sid, who stood up in the face of her grand entrance.

'—sorry," Eva said, blushing slightly, but unruffled, "you are making business?"

"—no," I said, as Sid said, "Yes."

"Eva, this is Sid," I said. "Sid, this is Eva."

"—Eva, yeah, Eva, yeah," Sid said, clutching the briefcase. 'Well, I should be going—"

"—no, please," Eva said, "much food. Is Christmas. Feast."

"—oh 'Christmas', yeah. That *goyim* thing. No, you kids have fun, I have to, ah, you know, I have to go and file—but, listen, Eve . . . you have a card, or something? Business card? Noah here tells me that if I need a translator you're the best there is—"

Briefly, Eva looked at me, confused, but I slapped an arm around Sid and said, "I'll tell her to call you, Sid, if she needs a job," and moved him toward the door.

On its threshold he said, "Br'er Noah—" and shook my hand.

"Br'er Sid—"

"I owe you one."

"Just do it justice, kid . . ."

"My word," he promised.

He looked briefly back at Eva then at me, then he stepped into the corridor and headed, swaggering, in the direction of the not so subtle guy in the dark suit smoking a cigarette beside the elevator.

I closed the door and when I turned around Eva said, "You won't believe it, close your eyes," and when I told her that I couldn't she reached into a plastic bag and handed me a melon.

"—is real!" she bubbled, "is real melon! Smell! Isn't it fantastic! Here—" She thrust a bottle of red wine at me and cleared the coffee table of the debris I had accumulated and began to place a fantasy upon it, two squat candles, two round plates, a tin of caviar, a string of dates, a bowl of olives, pita bread, tomatoes, tangerines, halvah, pistachios—

"—*desert* food," I marveled.

"—is fantastic, yes? Is from PLO."

"—is from *what*?"

"—from PLO. My brother, he and friends have find below ground place that was the PLO's, where Palestine Liberation was in train with Securitate—you like? Is real caviar—from Caspian, better than from Black Sea—"

She was like a kid and nothing could have made me spoil her mood except the certain dread necessity of having to inform her of the truth. It could wait a little while, but it couldn't wait until the morning, as I wished it could.

"—sit, sit, sit," she was encouraging me, "did you work today? What did you did? My mother and my father send you greetings. They thank you very much for saving life of daughter. They thank you also for the dollars . . ."

We ate the caviar off the ends of wooden matches, and we folded the unleavened bread around slices of tomato, and she watched me as I sawed the melon open with my Swiss Army knife, confessing to me, "I have never tasted." I handed her a crescent of its mint green honey-scented ripeness and as she put her mouth to it I told her, "I've been called away."

"—'away'?"

"—to another story."

She blinked and put the melon down, her lips still wet with it.

"—'away'?" she said again.

"—yes. That's why I was recommending you to Sid, he's got this story that is going to need—"

"—you're leaving?"

"—yes. Tomorrow."

"—but you're coming back? You're coming back here? To Romania?"

"—no. I'm not coming back."

For what seemed like too long a time to have to bear her silence, she said nothing. Then she said, "I'll never see you? After this?"

"—that's right. After this, you'll never see me."

It was hard to tell what she was thinking, because she sat so still. Then she took a breath and I could hear the sadness rattle in her chest. We sat in silence as the small flames sputtered on the overfatted candles and then, with that exquisite timing practiced only by dark gods and suicidal comics, all the lights went out in a power failure everywhere in the hotel. I stood up and went over to the window to see if power was out elsewhere in the city, if Ceauşescu was sapping his already weak system of its vital juices from the grave; but outside in the University Square yellow sodium light burnished the damp street from globes on those few lamp posts that had not been shot out. Behind me I heard Eva rise and go into the bathroom. From somewhere, outside, I could hear the sound of water dripping. I put my head against the window pane and closed my eyes. After a while I could sense someone behind me and I turned around. Eva had unloosed her hair and was standing there, the candlelight behind her, pale and pearly-looking as the Botticelli Venus, her small breasts nesting in her hair like sea eggs, her skin the brightest surface in the room. "Oh geez," I said as she came toward me, "Eva, Eve, don't do this, honey . . ."

"Please," she bargained, "please make love to me."

She was such a small light presence, almost insubstantial —her skin along her shoulders, down her back was dry and dusted with dry hairs like the skins of certain fruits and she had a strange ashy aroma the scent of clean but stubborn poverty washed in unscented soap. Her hair smelled, oddly, of chlorine and ripe melon. There was not the slightest impulse in me to make love to her and she began, clumsily and awkwardly, to fondle me as one who doesn't know the difference between massage and sex. She lifted her face up and tried to kiss me but I took her by the shoulders and pressed her back, away from me, and she began to cry. "It's not you, honey, it's not you," I said, "please don't cry," but she put her hands up to her face and lay down on the bed and put her head down on the pillow and curled her frail white form into an infant-like position and went on weeping, softly. I stood and looked at her a while and then I went across the room and blew the candles out. I stood there, too, and looked at her, then I moved over to the door and turned the light switch off in case the lights went back on. From wherever I stood within the room and looked at her across the bed she appeared like some strange form that I had woken to, some new form arrived from heaven, and I think I must have slept at some point in the night, but I don't remember sleeping. I remember standing there and wishing I was somewhere else. I remember sitting there, the yellow light outside the window falling on the slight curve of her body as her breathing slowed and I remember that no matter where I moved in the room, from whatever angle I looked at her she remained this strange form, this innocence, a shape so unlike myself that I could neither touch nor comprehend her. And I remember feeling as the biblical first man must have felt beholding his first woman, that first stranger, knowing neither love nor sex, not knowing sex from love. And I remember thinking through the night, to get me through, Soon it will be morning. Wait. Don't move. Do nothing. Stay awake. Pray to anything within your reason. Pray for children. Pray for orphans. Pray for women. Pray for Melanie and Lilith. Pray for Eve. Don't let the bad thing come. Don't let the bad things come and get her.

But everything I thought and did back then was too little, and too late.

1991

ARUNDEL GARDENS LONDON ENGLAND

pieces in their pants

DON'T TELL ME YOU HAVEN'T SEEN THESE PEOPLE—if you fly, you have. I'm sure you've seen them —they're the people on the gangplank, standing there, watching you as you come off the plane. Normally you wouldn't give them any notice beyond a casual glance because you're glad to be, at last, where you set out to be—until, that is, one of them falls in with you as you de-plane, and starts to walk along beside you down the ramp, real chummy-like, the first thing in the morning on your way to Customs.

"Noah," he says, amiably, giving a nod of the head.

"Twev," I acknowledge, in greeting.

You can always spot a Yardie, after you've met a few—you can spot them by their necks, the way they hold their heads. I have a theory that this has to do with the way they have to hold their spines because, unlike the FBI who pack their pistols in their armpits, the kids at Scotland Yard tote their pieces in their pants, over their right buttock if they're right-handed, over their left if they're left, but to either side, one way or the other, of the coccyx bone. I've had the efficiency of this particular placement demonstrated to me and I can see how it cuts down on the draw time over the FBI-across-the-chest reach, and I can see how it increases the exactitude in target hitting, what with its straight-arm reach as opposed to the FBI swing-arc approach, but the truth is, having to pull their pieces from their pants means Yardies increase the odds of shooting themselves in the ass under fire, which they frequently do.

Detective Sergeant Trevor Herron, however, to my knowledge, had never plugged his own gluteus maximus with anything as base as lead—his career as a law enforcement officer was full of holes of quite another kind, to wit, he had been taken off a plum anti-terrorist detail and assigned to a shoe leather job at Heathrow as a warning that he'd better get his private life under control, keep his fifth wife and not divorce and marry for a sixth time. This upset Trev profoundly, as he boozily confessed to me one night, and were it not for his invested pension he would shove the whole lot because this time, this time, he had told me, he had found the perfect woman.

"A tragedy," had been my assessment.

"Fuckers," had been his.

Trev speaks with what in England is called "the Winchester 'R'", a speech impediment sometimes affected for a posh purpose that only the English can appreciate, which we Americans who watch TV would most commonly associate with Barbara Walters' pixie whistling.

"Been over to the Pearly?" Trev now asks me. Although he's hardly Cockney, this is one of Trevor's stabs, for which he's famous in the force, at Cockney back-rhyming, "Pearly" meaning to imply the Pearly Gates, which rhymes with *States*.

"No shit, Sherlock," I say, hoping to impart my deep respect for his genius at deduction, seeing as I am merely one of about two hundred of us getting off this flight direct from JFK.

"Buy you a coffee, then?" he offers, "after you've collected your luggage?"

I stop and stare at him, which means I'm staring down at him, because Trev is all of five foot six, at the low end of the Yard's required stretch.

"What is this about, Trev?"

He looks sideways down the ramp and whispers, "Not here, Noah . . ."

"—because, you see, I don't *have* any luggage," I gesture, holding up my carry-ons which consist of a soft kit with my razor in it and EVE, the portable unit Boot arranged for me to write with, sound asleep now, snuggled neatly in her cushioned case.

"Buy you coffee, anyway," he says.

"Had my coffee on the plane," I say. "And I'm in a hurry."

"—got a date?" he says.

"—no, but you know how it is—a job's a job."

"—oh absolutely," he agrees.

"—so let's find out why yours has brought you out so early in the morning as my official welcome lady . . ."

He puts a palm on my back and ushers me along the concourse, saying, "Well now, this isn't what you'd call 'official', Noah, it's just that a, uh, a, uh, pwoblem has awisen which is wather delicate and they asked me, unofficially, to have a word with you because they know we're fwiends."

"—'they'. Who's 'they'?"

"The word is it's the Guv who's asking, actually."

"—who, Browndown?"

Trev nods.

I'd had a run-in several years ago with the Guv, Trev's boss, a creep called Browndown who resembled in the flesh

Alec Guinness impersonating a boiled onion. I'd begun to write a piece about the incidence of membership in the Masonic Lodge among the ranking officers at Scotland Yard, and Browndown put a No Talk order out among his foot soldiers—but, still, Browndown wasn't one to take his winnings and forgive. Browndown didn't like me; and he was a man who cultivated grudges in the steamy heat his power generated as a by-product.

"Tell Browndown he can call me at the paper, if he wants to ask me something," I tell Trev. "I'd rather deal with Browndown 'unofficially' than have him lean on you. I *like* you. Sometimes."

"It's about, ah, this Womanian," Trev says, and I decide real quick not to pretend that I don't know what he's referring to.

"What about him?"

"—he's dead."

"—I read the papers, Trev."

"He was murdered."

"—what's this got to do with me?"

"Why have you weturned to London, Noah?"

"I live here, Trev, in case you have forgotten."

"I mean now. Today. You changed your flight. We pulled your Bwitish Aiwway wecords."

"I got an overwhelming longing to hear *Gardeners' Question Time*."

"—sewiously."

"I'm working on a story."

"May I ask what that stowy is?"

"Not where I come from you can't, but I suppose in this country you could throw me in the Tower for life if I refuse to answer, or revoke my residency . . ."

"Your wesidency has been mentioned."

I blink.

"I'm just passing that along," he says, "because I think we understand each other, man to man."

I don't answer.

We are passing down the corridor that leads into the immigration holding pen and I look at him and say, "You going to flash me through?" Trev shrugs and says, "Okay." Then we go downstairs and he walks me through Customs, too. In the Visitors' Hall we take two seats like ordinary tourists in the smoking section while he lights up a cigar and says, "It's about your girlfwiend, actually."

I listen.

"Heard fwom her?"

I shake my head.

"When was the last time?"

"November the twelfth, 1989."

"—long time."

I nod.

"—you seem fairly sure about the date."

I nod again.

"—and nothing since?"

I shake my head.

"—no word?"

I stare at him.

"—no letters? Phonecalls?"

Shake my head again.

"—well, that tallies, actually. Appawently *we've* had her since about then."

"—'we've'?"

"Her and him—well, it was him we had, he bwought her along."

"—what do you mean you 'had' him?"

"I'm not at liberty to—"

"—you 'had' him in custody?"

Trev nods.

"Not us, actually, not the Yard. It was another, ah, division that had him in pwotective guard. We've only just been called in on a consultancy since, ah, since his misadventure . . ."

"—wait a minute, are you telling me Pentrú's been murdered *while* under protective guard—?"

"—yes."

"—are you serious?"

"—yes."

"—this isn't another attempt at your famous sure-to-backfire-in-your-face fucked up policy of disinformation?"

"—no."

"Well then, you boys are in deep shit, aren't you?"

"I wouldn't be too quick out of that particular gate, if I were you."

"Why not?"

"—because this wasn't a political assassination."

"—what, don't tell me, he accidentally threw himself on top of an IRA car bomb?"

"—because all evidence points to a cwime of passion."

"—*what*?"

"The girlfwiend did it."

The speed with which I'm on my feet surprises even me and I don't know what you get in this country for whacking a policeman but I'm willing to whack straight up to the Top Cop: "—you miserable cocksucking sons of bitches if you try to cover your incompetence by hanging a bum rap on her I'll have your royally commissioned dicks uprooted and diced before you feel your zippers slide, I'll plaster this on every news service you can think of before your guys in wigs can get their curlies on to stop me—"

"Well at least I can tell the Guv you didn't know . . ."

"—'at *least*'?"

"—he was certain that you knew. Especially when word came down that you were coming back today."

"—when 'word came down'? What do you guys do? Spy on the airlines?"

"—we put out a list. Hourly. Like the shipping news."

I sit down again.

"— and now I'm on that list?"

"—not for the first time, I might add. Computers," he says, picking tobacco off his tongue, "you have to love 'em. They don't dwink, but then again, on the plus side, they don't ask you to mawwy them. Does the girlfwiend have any fwiends in the UK she might twy to contact, other than you . . . ?"

"Lilith," I tell him.

He takes out a notebook and starts to write.

"That's her name," I tell him. "Not 'the girlfriend'. Lilith."

"—fwiends?" he repeats, his pencil raised.

"I don't know."

"—how 'bout where she used to work?"

"—I told you, I don't know."

"—key to your flat?"

"I don't know."

"—telephone the same? Yours, I mean. Haven't changed the number?"

"No."

"—changed the locks?"

"—*no*."

"Weason I ask is, *I* always do . . ."

"I know her, Trev—what you're suggesting is patently—"

"—you *knew* her, Noah, by your own admission you don't *know* her, you haven't heard fwom her for two years so you don't 'know' her. You *knew* her. People change. People change a lot. *Especially* women . . . Appawently the evidence is—"

"—fuck your evidence."

"—understand, no one's shedding cwocodiles over the untimely demise of this particular chawacter. Word was he was a weal pwick, but loss of life is loss of life, and murder in this countwy is still a cwime. Against which accusation, I believe, the little lady is entitled to her best defence, but first we have to bwing her in—and we will, we will . . ." He looks at me. "Guv wanted me to take you home but I convinced him that was unnecessary. Tomowwow morning will be soon enough."

"—for what?"

"We'll have to keep a man in your house until we find her, Noah."

"—why not now, then?"

Trevor shrugs.

"—what's the huwwy? Even if she contacts you, what can you do? This is an island, after all. I pwevailed against the Guv to let you have a night alone . . ."

"—bullshit."

"I told him if she contacts you you'll let me know. You *will* let me know, won't you, Noah?"

"No."

"Think about it."

"I don't need to think about it."

"Take the night to sleep on it. I believe the term is 'access-owy after the fact'."

"—there are no 'facts' here, there are only accusations. You people stink like last week's garbage in this and you know it . . ."

"See you in the morning, then," he says. "Eight all wight with you?"

As if they don't have someone there already, I consider.

I never know what to think about policemen, although I know what they want me to think—they want everyone to think that they run a tiptop organization and that all of them are chess enthusiasts and MENSA members. The ones I meet are the mouth organs assigned to the press, but still they wouldn't know a queen's gambit from a transvestite.

But am I supposed to try to think of Adam as a "good guy" now, someone a good guy government would place under protective guard, just because some flatfoot offers that suggestion?

I have to try to get my mind around this. Adam's dead. I have to start to try to think of ways I can help Lilith. I have to start to try to stay at least one step ahead of Trev.

Lilith will come back to get her U.S. passport, she will have to, it's her way out, she's never used it in this country, I've never seen her use it anywhere in Europe because her French one gets her through the European Union immigration channels like greased lightning. When they're looking for you, when they want to try to stop you leaving the country, do they put you on their list by name or by your passport number? Who knows these things? In her French passport, the one she always used to enter England, her name is Lilith L. DaVinci. In her U.S. passport, the one that's at my flat, her middle name is first because some dipshit back in Brooklyn fucked up on her birth certificate and reversed her first two names and typed in "Luciana L. da Vinci", thank god. Or do they send your photograph to every immigration outpost by computer? She'll need a lawyer. She'll need the best damn lawyer we can find, that's not a problem. Either stay and get a lawyer or get out. Maybe she's already out. Or maybe she's already got a lawyer. What would I normally be doing? Stopping here to put a call into the office. Stopping here and calling Poppy. Poppy first. Poppy has the basement flat in the house directly behind mine across the communal garden and for years she's kept a key hidden outside her door for me in case I come home at three o'clock some morning having left my house key in some hotel room in some godforsaken country somewhere, as I'm more than likely to do five times out of ten. The system has worked for years—I let myself into Poppy's house having called her first to let her know I'm coming—walk through her flat, out her back door across the garden, which is locked on both street sides, over to my place where I keep a key to my rear french door hidden, not too intelligently, in the bird feeder. Poppy is the surviving half of a husband and wife music-hall act that played the fish and chips circuit in the fifties until Poppy had "the accident", never explained to me, developed either gangrene or frostbite, the story varies with the season, in her "lowers" and had both her legs amputated at the knee. "I'm thinking of making a comeback," she's fond of saying, "me and Christ. Whatd'ya think? He'll need a cripple for his act . . ."

I call her from the cluster of phones by the fresh-squeezed orange juice and nut wallah in the main hall.

"Hello, sweetie," I say, "it's Noah, I'm back. I might be passing through—need anything?"

"—just to be remembered in your speech in Stockholm, luv."

"—don't get it."

"—the Nobel."

"—lost me."

"—the one you're going to win in physics. Is it physics—? For disproving Newton—was it Newton? Maybe it was Leonardo. I always get the lot of them confused, they're all either red-heads or left-handed. Who's the one that said time can't travel backwards?"

"Einstein. Maybe."

"—well there you are, then."

"—where?"

"—aren't you at the airport, luvvie?"

"—yes."

"—and didn't you come through here without a sound around three o'clock this morning?"

I blink.

Lilith, I think.

"—didn't want to wake you, sweetchops," I lie.

"—well come around and kiss me later and apologize. Or come around last week. Bring 1956 with you. Ta, for now—"

I hold the phone receiver to my chest.

The thing the doctors tell you about stress-related illness is that any kind of stress can bring the symptoms on and right now my hands are killing me, not my hands, my wrists like there's some kind of Middle Ages screw device, a corkscrew of torture, trying to join my elbows to my palms.

I call Mac in Paris, and for once the hour's time difference works to my advantage because he's sitting at his desk this early in the morning.

"—what in hell are ye doin' awake at this hour?" he says.

"I'm back in London," I tell him.

"—so are ye gonna be a TV star?"

"—what?"

"Did they make you an offer any man of my principles would refuse? Tell the truth. How much?"

"Mac, Lilith's in trouble."

Silence.

"I'm still at the airport—the Yard was here to meet my plane. Apparently—I don't own the skin on this—they had Pentrú over here, under some kind of protection program, 'though that doesn't make any sense to me yet. Then they end up with a dead man and they're claiming murder. Worse, they're saying Lilith did it."

"—I hae me doots."

"—me too. This dick informs me they intend to crawl inside my pants tomorrow morning if they're not already on my tail. So listen. I'm pretty sure Lilith got in through the back door to my house this morning. But obviously she can't stay there. If we need to, can we use your brother's place in Dunoon?"

"—I'll do it straightaway. What else?"

"Don't call my house. Don't tell your brother what I'm on about. Don't even tell Lorna. Have you ever—do you know anyone—if you had to pull a runner off this island what's the way to go?"

"—Ireland. By the boat. All the islands off the west. Otherwise, Plymouth to Santander. Santander's always good but if they catch you then you end up in a Spanish gaol. Harwich to the Hook of Holland is the least patrolled. And once you make the continent—"

"I know."

"But if it were me, I'd tell her stand and face the fokkers."

"—voice of reason."

"—always."

"—suitably jesuitical."

"How are the hands, by the way?"

"—fokked. I couldn't pull a trigger that's for sure."

A pause.

"You never could."

". . . you take care, Mac."

"—*and* you."

I go outside and join the people queuing for black cabs. Maybe she won't be there—except for needing her passport, except for needing shelter, why should she be? Why would she come to me, after what I did to her? My life's beginning to be dangerous. I'm needing to forget more shameful things, more horrors, than I can easily keep hidden from myself. Maybe this happens to all men, I don't know. Maybe this is the price experience exacts.

"Here on business, sir?" the taxi driver asks me.

"I live here," I tell him.

"Why is that?"

"—why do I *live* here?" he nods. "Where do *you* live?" I ask in response.

"—not in London that's for sure. Couldn't pay me."

"—why is that?"

"—the fiddles. All the graft. What do you do for a living, then, if you don't mind me asking?"

"I'm a journalist."

"Oh, well then, you don't have to deal with foreigners that come here to take your job from you."

I don't know how to answer that, so I don't.

"This your place of choice, then, or did you have to come here?"

"Place of choice," I answer.

He shoots me an eyeball in the rearview mirror.

"I know where I'd go, if I had me chance."

'Where is that?"

"Phoenix, Arizona. Seen some pictures of it—beautiful. I bet if I took this same cab here you're riding in over there, I'd make a fortune. What do you think?"

"Everybody owns their own cars in the United States. They don't ride in cabs. It's in the Constitution."

I let him drive past my house so I can look in all the cars parked on my street for evidence of some surveillance, but I don't spot any. Getting out at the corner I give him a large tip then walk to the Midland Bank ATM on Portobello Road and take out all the cash my deck of plastic will allow me.

Then I walk home.

Strange feeling, walking into known surroundings where you know another may be waiting—feels like the game we played when we were kids, when we summoned presences, played with higher powers to create companions who reside in our imaginations.

The first thing I encounter inside the door is a terminal moraine of accumulated mail carpeting the kitchen floor like scattered runes—magazines, solicitations, overdue utility bills easily recognizable in their envelopes of crimson borders.

Like a giant I step over the debris, soundly close the door and turn the key.

The house is quiet and every noise I make resounds.

She's here, I know. I don't know how I know it, but I know.

My hands are killing me.

I realize now that I've been clutching the handle of the EVE case as if it were the handle of a lifeline, salvation in a crisis, and although she isn't heavy—she weighs about eight pounds—my right hand is frozen on the handle in a spasm of clamped pain. When I pry my fingers loose they look white and bloodless and the pain tears through the sluice of my wrist like a piranha on a monkey's ass.

And my hands are shaking with a junkie's jive, from the shoulders down.

Shit, I mutter.

I kick the mail and do that little trick they've tried on me in physio of Talking To My Body, telling my muscles to relax as if they're brats strung out on sugar highs but the only things that ever work for me in attacks like this are straight-forward painkillers and a posture of abject supplication.

Please, God, I'll be good.

I eat three Solpadeines, then take a fourth one for good measure, wash their acrid taste back with a cup of water from the tap. Then I clear my throat and go into the sitting room.

The room is dark, the curtains drawn, blond watery light shimmering in bands across the floor from the edges of the window.

I turn on the radio, World Service, low, and when I sit down on the sofa I pick up a faint aroma in my house of candle wax, of soap.

Sometimes when I come back from long weeks on the road I can walk into my house and smell a curry that I'd made three weeks before, smell the turmeric and coriander. Sometimes I walk in and the house is holding weather that's occurred while I've been gone, the smells of weather, sharp metallic colds and spongy lilac damps. This time the house is holding soap. My soap. Hers, actually—the house is holding the aroma, her aroma, of the soap she used, a finely-milled clean-smelling something from the Dead Sea she brought back from Jordan, faintly scrolled with desert fragrance, the soap I started using when we lived together, the soap I went on using for all the reasons you can name after she had left.

Nothing else smells quite like it. It's the scent that I associate with Lilith's skin.

I exhale, try to clear its traces from my brain, hold my hands in front of me and spread my fingers, watch them shake.

In front of me, on the coffee table, the red numerical display on my phone console tells me there are thirty-seven messages in store for me. From memory I dial my doctor, punch the speaker button on the phone and slump back on the sofa with my head against the cushion and my palms pressed on my eyes. When the number's answered I say, "Hi," without moving. When I press my fingers in my eye sockets the blind dark of my inner vision floods a ruby red. "It's Noah John," I say. I move my fingers and see scarlet nebulae, wine-dark protozoa, cartwheel on my field of vision. *How can we help you, Mr. John*?

"My hands are killing me again," I say.

Would you like to see the doctor?

"Yes."

Doctor isn't in his surgery today. Will tomorrow do?

"Sure," I say.

Tomorrow will do fine.

Inside my head pinwheels of bright color, starfish galaxies, are turning, weightless, through eternity, while *How is two for you*? the disembodied female voice enquires.

"Great," I tell it, "two is always great for me."

Two tomorrow, then, it answers.

When I take my hands away from my closed eyes the smell of Dead Sea soap intensifies as if the pressure of my palms against my head had stopped it wafting over me.

See you tomorrow, Mr. John, the voice is saying.

Bye-bye, followed by the telephonic sound of Disconnect.

I open my eyes, lean forward, blink.

Everything in front of me is flooded with that slurry light, the unfocused vision of a waker from a dream, a drunk, a lotus-eating drug-taker. Everything is swimmy for an instant, and the aroma is intense. Then through the marbled light she makes her entrance, spell-binding, the way her form appears, this time so pale, so still, like Sorrow, and I'm struck as dumb and caught as short-cocked as I was the first time I lay victim to the lightning, her weather, to the drama of her entrance.

This time is even more dramatic.

She is standing in her bare feet dressed in the cheap cotton Japanese kimono I keep in my bathroom, the one I bought myself after I got rid of the robe she'd given to me, the one I wanted to burn, the one Adam had worn.

She's wearing this thin cotton kimono, tied around her waist, this thin kimono which ends just below her knees, and I can see her legs are pale, really white, and smooth like she's just shaved them, and she looks like she's still damp, like she's just had a bath, and she's clutching this wadded up white bath towel around her hands and it's got circles of bright blood on it like poppies that you see in fields in Spain from trains, and her skin, her neck, is very white, her lips are pale, her face is very pale, her eyes are huge and I stand up and she lifts her hands inside the towel like she's about to say something but then she stops and leans against the wall and stares at me and lowers herself down until she's sitting on the floor and I move across the room and stand there, over her.

Her head is shaved.

Not a neat job, either—like a kitchen job or like a mob's work, like the work an angry mob would do on a traitor, on a whore, on a collaborationist.

What the fuck—? I start to say.

"—the drain is clogged," she says.

I stare at her.

"—in the sink . . ." She points with the blood-stained towel back down the hall toward the bathroom, then adds, "My hair." She looks at the towel as if she's noticing the stains for the first time and says, "My hands have opened up again."

Jesus this is just like you, I want to say. No, I want to scream it at her, want to say There is a major fucking problem here and you're fucking staging *Aïda*, fucking hauling elephants onto the stage.

"Lilith—*shit*," I say. "Shit . . ."

I crouch down across from her in the hallway, both of us unconsciously nursing our wrecked hands.

"I know," she says.

"You know what?" I say.

"You don't want to talk about the fucking sink."

"—damn straight."

I can see her hands move inside the towel like she's balling up her fingers in its fabric.

I bite my lip and tell myself I'm not going to ask her how she got cut up. I'm not going to ask her anything, until she opens up.

She presses her hands inside the bloody towel into her lap and I say, "Try and not get fuck all over another robe of mine, will ya?"

She lets out a little puff of air like a prize fighter absorbing a body blow and says, "I need my other passport, Noah, where is it?"

"'Hello,' to you, too, baby," I marvel.

"What did you expect?" she marvels back.

"—some kind of explanation wouldn't go amiss. Go ahead. Give it your star treatment. You're a pro. Start at the beginning. 'Once upon a time . . .'"

She stares at me.

"The police are after me," she says.

"—I know."

She doesn't blink.

"Did you kill him?"

"—*no*."

I look down at the bloody towel and then back into her eyes.

"—well that's a pity, honey," I say, the old anger fighting with the old desire.

"Is he dead?" I ask.

She nods.

We sit there, words in some foreign language coming softly to us from the radio.

"I didn't think you'd be here," she finally says.

"—no, shit, for some reason, you never think I'll 'be here', where I live. Peculiar, ain't it? This habit I fucking have of showing up where I'm 'least' expected?"

"—like in Berlin."

"—no, angel, *you* were not expected in Berlin . . ."

"—why keep using all these luvee names, why not just fuck with me and get it done with, Noah?"

I become aware that we are touching, that her bare feet are resting, lightly, on my leg. I look down at the place where we are rubbing on each other and the sight of it, the shock of it, is physical.

"Jesus," I murmur.

"I'm sorry," she says.

"I don't believe you, Lilith."

"—you don't believe I'm sorry?"

"—I don't believe you're sorry, and I don't believe I can believe anything you say."

She looks away.

". . . I don't know what I'm going to do," she says. "Can you believe that?"

She looks back at me.

Involuntarily my hand has found her ankle, those narrow rounded bones, and I'm remembering how fast she runs, how all her weight comes down like a hammer on these tiny bones, and I lift my hand from them with the deftness of a sudden realization and I touch her head, her skull, instead.

Her eyes widen with my touch.

"—what do you *want* to do?" I ask her, knowing if she asked me the same question that I couldn't answer, couldn't fall back on the easy answers I had used as my support for years, the arguments I had constructed for the peace of mind that could be found through work, through loyal friendships, through enduring love—*fuck all that* is running through my mind, I am staring in the face of the irrevocable, either entering a terrifying new world where the signposts aren't in any language I can read and understand, where the only landscape is forgiveness—or else she and I are going to commit and re-commit the same mistakes, chain ourselves to that brand of History who's second name has always been Annihilation.

Before we say what we are *going* to do we need to know what we have *done*.

And I don't know what we have done.

Once I thought that we had made a paradise together but I'm not so sure of that right now. I'm not so sure that what we made together was a kind of love, I can't remember it, I can't remember what it felt like even though the shock of her, of touching her, reminds me.

I run my palm over her scalp and down, around her head.

I touch her cheek and find a new thin line of sadness near her mouth where one had never been.

All the while she's staring at me and I see that soul-searching look she always had, that spine-tingling look of pure submissive vulnerability, the one that tells you, as a lover, that she's willing to surrender all she has to try the ecstasy your hands, your manhood, is suggesting. She stares at me, her gaze unflinching, daring, and I see, again, those two beacons of her own fear, those two distant lights, blood dots, those rubies in her eyes that gave me my first signal on the day in Cameroon when I first met her—and I want to kiss her, but I don't.

"—please," she begs.

I shake my head.

I put my fingers to her lips, instead, and she takes them in her mouth.

Christ, this woman I am thinking . . . Every time.

"—I've been . . . locked up . . . for so long," she says.

"—what do you mean, 'locked up'?"

"Locked up," she repeats. "Caged. Kept. Spied on. Guarded. By him. With him. Because of him."

"—'By' him," I say.

She nods.

"In Romania," I say.

She nods.

"—but it didn't start there," I say. "It didn't start between him and you in Romania."

She shakes her head.

"—it started here," I say.

She nods.

"—*right* here," I say.

She stares at me.

"—are you telling me it started here against your will?" I say.

"—no," she answers.

"—you went with him because you wanted to," I say.

She nods.

I close my eyes.

"Jesus," I say—"How could you do it? In our bed. How could you *do* such a thing?"

I hear myself sound like every sanctimonious broken-hearted bastard I have ever heard.

I hear myself sound like my sister, christ.

—I sound like my *mother*.

"I don't know," she says.

"You 'don't know'?" I say. "I'm sorry. But you have to."

"—why?"

"—'*why*'? Because I was going to marry you, I had just asked you to marry me. Then you invite a stranger in and sleep with him in our own bed while I'm away. And then you disappear—like that—out of my life. For months, for years. For fucking ever. What did you think that would do to me? Did you think I'd chalk it up to ol' Experience? You fucking ruined me—no, look at me, goddamn it. You made me into someone I despised."

"—I did it. Just because."

"—sorry, no, that's not an answer."

"—he came here. I let him in. After the accident. The day you went to see Mandela . . ."

"—you 'let him in' . . ."

"—I fell for him, okay? What do you want me to say? I never acted like some icon Virgin fucking hausfrau—that was *your* idea of me, never mine, you knew what you were getting into, vulgar reference *meant*, when you ran your hands all over me the moment that we met, so how could anything I do surprise you? Do you think it's legal only when you call it 'love'? Do you think it's sanctioned only when the rules are broken on the side of 'Right' . . . ?"

"—too much has happened, Lilith, someone's fucking *dead*. Someone's dead who—one way or another—killed *a lot* of—"

"—*I* know what Adam did. I know what Adam *was*, better than you do, believe me, better than you ever could. I lived with him, remember? Longer than I lived with you."

I blink several times and ask her if she loved him and she answers, "Jesus, Noah, get a life. Get fucking *two*," and starts to fret about her bleeding hands inside the towel.

I clamp my hands around the towel to still her movements, and I tell her, "We're not finished talking, yet."

She goes still and says "—okay."

Shoot me.

"Romania," I prompt her, "when and how . . . and *why*?"

"*When*," she answers, "right away, that day. *How*—a stupid question. *Why*—I'd never been. He promised me a lot of things. He promised me an inside take on Gypsies, inside take on dissidents. He promised me that he was 'living for the end of tyranny' . . . 'working for the revolution'. And I took my freedom as given. Shoot me. I'm a sap."

"—so you got there . . . and?"

"—and he had to hide me. I mean—I was a foreigner."

"—you were his whore."

"—I was, first, in their view, a 'capitalist'. And—second—a journalist. I am never anybody's whore."

"—oh really? I saw the place he 'kept' you."

"—I know you did."

"—how do you know?"

"—you published my photographs."

"We gave you a credit."

"—which almost got me killed."

"—by whom?"

"—by him."

"—but he must have known what you'd been doing, that you'd been going to the orphanages . . ."

"—no. Drago was discreet. It was a stroke of luck. Drago was the only person both of us could trust—and Drago lied to him for me. Not 'lied', exactly . . . didn't tell the truth."

"Did you sleep with Drago, too?"

"—fuck you."

"Seriously."

She leans her head against the wall.

"Sex doesn't have the premium you think it has, in countries where there isn't anything to eat." She looks at me. "But you know that. You used to know . . ."

"Why didn't the Frau Mengele characters at the orphanages turn you in?"

"I just told you."

"—you bribed them?"

"—easily."

"How did you know you could trust them?"

"—I didn't. It was worth the risk."

"Did you know I'd find the photographs?"

"—christ no. I never thought you'd come to Bucharest. I didn't think you had the guts. Not after Berlin. I thought you'd ended your campaign against me in Berlin."

"—I see your high opinion of me as a journalist has improved a lot with age . . ."

"—are we competing?"

"—me with you? Hell no, sugar. There's no contest. 'Divi' died in bed right here in this apartment the day she let the serpent in."

"—don't be an asshole, Noah."

"—and she's even shaved her head in penance for the treason."

"Why is everything a Bible allegory with you? The cops are on the look-out for a woman with dark hair."

"—and being bald won't grab attention?"

"People on the look-out notice only what they're looking for. First Rule of Photography . . ."

"—from someone who used to know. Did you leave those photographs behind on purpose so someone, if not me, could find them?"

"I didn't leave them, they were left there, overlooked."

"—by?"

"—whoever did the packing."

"Why did you stay with him, once you knew what he was up to?"

"—story, Noah. He became the story."

"—you fucked my life up for a story?"

"Not at first."

"Oh thanks . . ."

"—and to tell the truth, your rôle in this never really featured as an object of my interest."

"—double fucking thanks. So you just erased me."

"I just left you to your own devices."

"—I mean, from your heart."

"—my 'heart'?"

"—oh, right, I keep forgetting 'heartless' is your middle name, as shown in all your photographs . . ."

"—unlike yours, my heart is *only* in my work."

"—well, that's your privilege, precious. Hack work's heartless when it's at its best. So I save my schmaltz for daily life . . . *What* story, by the way? What *is* the story about Adam?"

"If I tell you will you help me?"

I study her eyes. The two red flecks of blood in them are fire bright.

"I help old ladies cross the street for christsake—what makes you think I might help you?"

She gives a little smile, her first.

"He got me into Bucharest without a visa," she starts. "He was amazing—"

"—I don't need to hear this part."

"—no, I'm serious. As a kid he was amazing—the things that he survived."

"—yeah, yeah, Nazis, shipwreck, what a guy. You didn't actually buy into all that crap about the *Struma* did you—?"

"—what 'crap'?"

"—about him being a Jewish refugee. He wasn't circumcised."

"—no shit, Sherlock, I keep my eyes wide open during sex, remember—?"

"—so who was he?"

"—Gypsy orphan."

"—how romantic. And 'Adam Pentrú' was—?"

"—a Jewish boy he stole the name from in Constanţa."

"—what does 'stole the name from' mean?"

"—maybe killed or maybe didn't . . ."

"—left for dead, though, one way or another . . ."

"—then the ship went down."

"—that part checked out."

"—and he was picked up first by Turks and then the British."

"—from whom he learned how to de-bone a kipper with a fish-knife and a fork at public school—Cut to the chase."

"—they turned him."

"—into what?"

"—a little Englander. An operative for England."

"—spy?"

She nods.

"—my ass."

"—it's true. Why else would he go back to Bucharest from Oxford—go back to work for the Ceauşescus?"

"—so you land in Bucharest and he just, what, he tells you he's a spy for England?"

"—something like that, yes."

"And you believed him?"

"—yes."

"—*why*, for christsake? What kind of proof was there to—"

"None."

"He must have been *some* fantastic bonk for you, then, baby."

"—he wasn't bad. He had—"

"—I *know* what he had."

"—his charms."

"'Charming' is the word *reserved* for bastards, Lilith."

"He wasn't half as interesting in bed as you."

"—oh thanks, that's great to know, but don't let that put you off fucking other spies and murderers . . ."

"He was afraid of mirrors."

My turn to give a little smile.

"And—don't tell me," I beg, "—he used to climb into a pine box around sunrise every morning."

"I mean he was really afraid of them."

"Mirrors," I repeat.

"—weird, huh? His whole life was built with mirrors but that was what he feared. To look himself in the face."

"—so *was* he a spy?"

"—oh absolutely. He hated the Romanians."

"—who *didn't* he hate?"

"Drago."

"—who could hate Drago?"

"—the new régime hates him I'm sure. Was he okay when you saw him?"

"—a bit beaten up, but who wasn't? You missed all the fun."

"—so I heard."

"Where did the two of you go?"

"He had a car, then a plane provided by the Brits. Things moved more rapidly than planned. He didn't know, to the minute, when it would come. The moment to move against Ceauşescu—to murder him. He had several plots in motion all at once."

"—I don't buy it."

"—buy what?"

"—that the revolution happened according to 'a plan'. That Ceauşescu's death was pre-arranged."

"I don't either."

"—you *don't*?"

"—but the Brits did, and that's all that mattered to Adam. He thought that they thought that he was a genius. Because of the way things turned out, he thought he could get away with it, take all the money he'd made and escape, fool the Brits into believing he'd masterminded a coup, he thought he had succeeded in fucking them all . . ."

"—but he hadn't?"

She shakes her head.

"—not by a long shot," she says.

"—fucksake don't tell me the Brits double-teamed him," I argue.

"They did."

"—must be the first time they got something *right* . . ."

"They're not stupid," she says. She stares at the towel in her lap. "They're just provincial . . ."

Her voice trails away.

"—and after Bucharest?" I prompt her.

"Eden."

"—what?"

"'Eden'—that's what they called it."

"—who's 'they'?"

"That was its codename."

"—what's 'it'?"

She looks at me, hard, like she's deciding to answer, or not —like she's weighing the odds and weighing the truth.

"I did try to leave him, to get away—I want you to know that—while we were still in Romania."

"—but let me guess: there were no Jews left for you to steal a name from."

She looks back down to her hands.

"You had a chance in Berlin," I remind her.

"He had me watched."

"Well I hope they enjoyed what they saw."

"Why are you being like this?"

"Being like what?"

"—like a fucker."

The chimes of Big Ben strike the hour for news on the World Service and I look at my watch.

"Adam's dead," I say, tensely. "And in an hour or two I suspect the police will arrive . . . And . . ." I look toward her hands in the towel. ". . . either you're breaking out in a sainthood with stigmata, or those hands are bloody as shit with his murder . . . And so far, my darling . . . despite your story . . ." I start to fold back the edge of the towel—"I think you have left me still in the dark."

One look and I say, "Christ can you get up?" I lift her. "Can you stand? Are you faint?"

"Don't get nursey on me," she argues, "I hate it."

"Count your blessings," I tell her, "I usually puke at this point."

We get to the bathroom and she says, "I told you—"

"—*fuck*," I say, seeing the problem.

"—it's *clogged*."

I sit her down on the edge of the tub and I sit beside her, on the toilet.

Someone had wrapped both her hands up, expertly, in surgical gauze which is soaked through with water and blood.

"Start talking," I say as I reach for the scissors and begin cutting away the wet layers.

"One thing that's good about not being able to see the complete range of colors," she says.

"—*is*?"

"You can't see it."

"—see what?"

"—the color of blood."

I look up and admit, "I forgot."

"Maybe that's why I can see people bleeding to death without getting sick to my stomach."

"—like you see people bleeding to death every day," I concur.

She starts to shake, first her hands, then her legs, then her body.

"Hey, *hey*," I say trying to calm her, "what's going on, are you cold?"

I wrap a bath towel around her.

"Who bandaged your hands?"

"Kevin," she tells me.

"—well that Answers All."

"One of the agents—only a driver—with us in Eden."

"—he did a good job."

"—they're nice guys."

"—what kind of 'agent' we talkin' about?"

"The Intelligence kind."

I had started to peel the last layer of gauze from her palm but I stop what I'm doing. I'm holding both of her hands in my own. I look in her eyes.

"You're not kidding," I say.

She shakes her head.

"If I didn't know better," I have to say slowly, "I'd say you were crying."

I strip the last layers of gauze from her palms and say, "Fucking A—what kind of hellthing can do this to you?"

"—a shattered mirror."

"—the size of Montana?"

"—it *was* a very large mirror."

"—who was driving it?"

"That's very funny," she says without smiling. "Adam was driving it. Same as last time."

She folds her hands over mine and caresses my fingers.

"—don't try to seduce me," I say.

"I don't have to try," she assesses.

Her fingers are sticky with blood.

"Put your hands under the faucet," I tell her, and we both lean forward a little, over the tub, as I turn the bath water on.

The kimono, of course, does that thing that kimonos all generally do.

Oh shit I hear myself say.

And I would have thought, at my age, no single part of a woman could ever again be *this* simply breath-taking to behold.

In spite of myself, I touch my cheek to the back of her head, closing my eyes, thinking it might be like nuzzling a breast or a newborn, but the skin there feels head-strong and taut as a drum.

Like a colt, she shies against me with the back of her neck.

"What goes on in you—inside of you—when we get this close?" I whisper in her ear.

"A kind of blindness," she answers.

I feel her heart pounding.

"—what else?"

"A suspension. In time."

"—and what else?"

"A drift. In my hearing."

"—do you like it?"

"It scares me."

"I'm not going to touch you," I whisper, from behind. "You want me to, but I'm not going to. You know why not."

"I didn't kill him," she says, which isn't what I expected to hear.

I move away from her slightly, turn off the water and turn her to face me.

"Then why are you worried about the police?"

"Because. A lot of things."

"—let's hear them."

I start to look for some gauze to rebandage her hands.

"*Now*," I demand.

"They think I was working with Adam. In the black market. For Zement."

"—were you?"

"—no. Never."

"—so why would they think it?"

I find the gauze and sit down again, near her, and examine her hands.

"—some of these should have had stitches," I say.

"—that's what Kevin said, too, but you don't visit the ER when you're in Eden—Didn't we used to have a whole box of those butterfly sutures you brought back from Holland?"

"—we left them in Paris . . . hold still."

"—fuck Noah *ow*!"

"—what the fuck is this 'Eden' you keep bringing up?"

"Where they kept us. The latest safehouse. They kept moving us around. But that was soon going to stop. What *is* that shit—?"

"—diaper rash ointment."

"—why do you have a tube of diaper rash ointment in the house? And does it look like I have diaper rash on my hands?"

"No but it's better than toothpaste for cuts and those are our only two choices. Talk to me: *Zement*."

"—a gold mine."

"I know."

"—blood, blood products, placenta-based face creams above line. Below line—human organs, crude oil, black market, christ knows."

"Why do they think you were working with him in Zement?"

"Because he told them I was."

I look at her.

"Why would he do that?"

"To keep me with him. Blackmail. He makes them believe I'm his partner, that I know how and where the Zement profits are stashed, then I can't escape. They can't let me go because they think I have the money—and *they* want the money—and they threaten to tell his old friends, the Securitate, where I am, if I try to escape."

"—from the *Brits*, we're talking about. If you tried to 'escape' from the Brits—a major ally of the country of which you're a citizen—*both* countries of which you're a citizen, but especially the U.S. of A. Are you crazy? Why didn't you just say *fuck this* and walk to our embassy? England can't hold you for shit on the word of some fucking Romanian without any proof—even *with* proof, for all that I know."

"This is *Adam* we're talking about, not 'some fucking Romanian'. There was proof. He made sure he had proof. His kind of proof—counterfeit. Manufactured—but proof."

"What did he have?"

"*Photographs*—what else *would* he have on me, what other proof could provide such an ironic twist?"

"*Your* photographs?"

"—photographs *of* me."

My hand shakes, a little.

"—what kind of photographs?"

The question sticks in my throat.

"—not *those* kind of photographs for christsake since when are you such a sex maniac?"

"I think I was always a sex maniac."

"—here's what he did, which even *I* never figured. He smuggles me into the country, into Romania, without a visa, without showing my passport, which I think is damn clever at the time except that it means I can never get out on my own without showing some dick on the border how I got *in*. So there I am, in Romania, and he keeps my passport anyway, for some ka-ka reason he makes up—and I can't speak the language—and, officially, I don't exist—and I want to take pictures. I *need* to take pictures. So things fall apart pretty fast. Between him and me. I discover that I have no freedom of movement—*me*—can you see me cooped up? I took fucking pictures of tree bark. Then I ran out of film. That was a red-letter day. I snuck out of the house and hitchhiked to town and got on a train going west to the Hungarian border. I made a scene at the border. He sent some henchmen to bring me back but not before I drew a lot of attention to myself which caused him embarrassment. He was terrified the Ceauşecus would find out because they despised all Americans since Jimmy Carter. One thing led to another, the details would bore you, but eventually I won his permission to travel a little, from time to time, to take pictures—with the proviso that while I was traveling, wherever I went, I'd do favors for him, deliver some papers to—so he said—his British 'drops', so I did. Deliver the papers. He had me shadowed, of course, the whole time, as well as having me stay with 'a guardian'. And he had me photographed doing these errands for him—and of course, the people to whom I was delivering stuff were all Class-A super-wanted-for-crimes against planet earth kinda shits."

"How much money do you figure he syphoned through Zement?"

She makes an *oof* noise.

"—maybe none. Maybe a couple hundred million in sterling. There were so many rumors . . ."

"—but did he have money, or not?"

"In Bucharest, he lived like a pasha."

"Did he brag there was money in Zement?"

"—to me? All the time."

"Did he say where it was?"

"—sure. In an icebox, 'under the Alps'."

"*Did* you ever try to get out through—excuse the expression—ordinary diplomatic channels?"

"No. Not in Romania—pretty soon after I arrived I started to peg the story on the orphans. Ask me what first tipped me off."

"—the face cream," I tell her.

"I hate you."

"It shows."

"—and once the Brits brought us here, things just got too weird."

"How long has he been in this country?"

"—six months."

"Jesus, Lilith, you've been in a safehouse for six months?"

"—safe*houses*, plural. Even longer than that. Before coming here we were kept on Gibraltar. Then on a retired Army colonel's *finca* in Spain."

"Why didn't you just get the hell out?"

"—because, for a while, it was too good a story."

"—but it sounds like George Smiley in gridlock in Swindon . . ."

"—but the main reason was it was stupid to leave without docs. Without docs it made it all worthless."

"—were there any?"

"—somewhere, yes. Tons of them. He had built his security

network on blackmail, on docs. And I knew he still had all that documentation. I knew he had gotten all his Bucharest papers out of Romania. And he had some place—maybe here, maybe in London—where he had hidden the rest."

"—and you think he would have told you where they are?"

"—worth the wait, don't you think? To expose a network of illegal trade in unfiltered blood—in *Europe* for christsake? And he was starting to crack under the pressure. Really crack. He was slowly but surely going berserk."

"—so who killed him?" I say.

She watches me finish wrapping her right hand.

"The mirror," she answers.

She tries to pull back her hand but I hold it.

"What the hell does that mean?" I ask.

"The mirror killed him," she says.

"Was it in this hand?" I ask her, holding up her right hand. "Or in this one?" I ask, holding the left.

"No I swear," she maintains.

She starts to tremble, shaking her head.

"We had a fight—they had just moved us again, a new place. It was a horrible place, the worst yet. In Golders Green, if you can believe it. The kitchen was downstairs and we had to share it with the agents. There was a flat in the basement, where they were living—our quarters were upstairs. But there was no privacy, really, for any of us. They were playing their music in the basement flat while Adam and I were having our dinner in the kitchen and Adam went downstairs to ask them to turn down the volume—his way of asking—to bully, to order. The men assigned to us—I think they hated him, really, hated his tactics, his manner. They were all team men, trained to be part of a team, and he was an autocrat, a man used to his own absolute power. So the volume goes down and five minutes later one of them—not Kevin—is back up in the kitchen saying a conference call has come through for Adam on the radio phone from the chief op. Adam takes the call in the flat in the basement and the next thing all hell is loose. The chief has called to say that they've had a security meeting on his case and they've decided to stop moving him around and he tells Adam they're going to move us—permanently—to a military base."

She blinks a couple of times, shifts her weight.

"Did he think the two things were related—his yelling at loud music followed by a new sort of quarantine?"

"Absolutely. So he went—he went crazy. Came upstairs. Threw our dinner around—threw me up the stairs. Understand—I didn't know what was going on at that point . . . We get upstairs."

She takes a breath.

"—he's shouting how he was a hero for this nation. How this nation promised him a certain kind of living. How he thought he'd be taken care of—a stately guarded house in the country somewhere. And he's charging around through this tirade waving his arms and—you saw him—he was a big man, and there was this mirror in the bathroom. Big goddamn mirror, that plate kind, a wall. This was a new place, remember, new house—you can't go around and say oh by the way, take down all the mirrors—I mean, what a joke. So somehow the scene moves from the bedroom into the bathroom and—well, glass everywhere."

She looks around.

"—glass *everywhere*, mirror pieces . . ."

Her shoulders shake.

"—and we're in the bathroom and I'm picking up pieces of mirror, big chunks from the floor, and one of the guys comes upstairs and says What's going on? and Adam tells him to get the fuck out and slams the door. What happened next was all glass. Glass—and then, slowly, blood. Breaking glass—it kept breaking, hitting it, breaking under his feet. And I had some pieces of it in my hands, not a lot, a few pieces, and while he was yelling at me, he made my hands into fists around the glass and held them like that while he was shouting—then he pushed me back and he started to . . . pick up the pieces and . . ."

She moves her hands.

She moves her hands up to her chest.

"—he tried to stab you?"

"—*no* . . . *him* . . . he started stabbing at himself with pieces of the glass, his chest, he started beating on his chest with glass, jabbing at himself all up and down his arms—"

She lets out a wordless noise like someone moaning in a dream and looks back at her newly bandaged hands.

"I got out of there real fast, out of the room."

She narrows her eyes.

"I had to open this hand—" She raises the left one. "—I had to open this hand to get the door open. I'll never forget it. There was no pain 'til I opened my hand—no blood at all . . ."

I take her hands again.

"—then I got downstairs and told them to go up, that I was scared he'd do something to himself, and one of them went and Kevin fixed my hands. And I heard Adam shouting at the one who went to go the hell away—and then he came back down and things got quiet. Things got very quiet . . . and then some music started coming from upstairs, from the radio, some violins on something classical—and Kevin fixed us both some tea and I said you better go up and see if he's okay, if he needs help—and he came back down and said the Boss is fine, he's resting, all tucked up in bed. I guess this was about, I don't know, seven, eight o'clock, maybe later—living like that you lose all sense of time. There was a sitting room —a small front room—on the same floor as the kitchen, where the TV was, and I went in there and sat a long time. I could hear them downstairs, and I could hear the radio upstairs and I sat there, between them, and stared at the door. They had wired the door. It was a loose wire, a trip one, with no delay. But it would take one of them maybe ten seconds —maybe more—to get up the stairs from the basement. Ten seconds was not a great lead, but it was something, at least, it was *time*, and I used to be fast, as fast as the fastest of them, even if I didn't know where I was going. I could just go—start to go. Just head off. I sat there a really long time talking to the door. Have you ever talked to a door—?"

I nod my head.

"After a while I hear them go to bed in the basement. Maybe midnight, by then. I lose my courage. One of those moments when you realize that you've lost your strength, you've lost your momentum. I go upstairs. He's in bed."

She looks at me.

". . . we hadn't been sleeping with each other for months. I don't remember when it stopped, only how. We slept in the same bed if we had to, but we didn't touch. A lamp was on, on the bureau, next to the radio—I turn them both off. And I notice he isn't snoring. My winter coat's on top of a suitcase in the corner and I take it and lie down on the bed, on top of the covers, and put my coat over me."

She stops.

There's a noise at the front of the house, the sound of the gate to my stairs being opened, and she reaches for me.

"—it's okay," I say, rubbing her arm, "it's okay . . ."

There's the slap of the mail slot and the sound of receding footsteps outside.

"*—mailman*," I say.

She closes her eyes.

She calms her breathing.

"—sometime around daybreak, it must have been five—I wake up feeling cold. Not just cold—cold, and . . . The whole mattress, all the sheets, the bedspread, everything, was soaked through with blood . . ."

"—*shit*," I say.

"—there was a smell—you know that blood smell, have you ever smelled that much blood—?"

She stares at me.

". . . but he didn't look dead. He didn't look dead . . ." she repeats, her voice trailing off.

"—and you left?"

She nods.

"—you didn't wake anyone up, tell anyone?"

"I put a jacket on and walked down the stairs and walked out of the door."

Her voice breaks.

"—that was . . . yesterday morning."

"Lilith, no one is going to believe that you killed him," I tell her, "not with those men there, those Kevins, as witnesses—"

"I let him . . . *bleed to death* . . ."

"—*they* let him bleed to death—"

A loud buzz—the doorbell—shocks us both.

"—*oh my god*," she whispers.

I put my arms around her.

Another jolting buzz, long, insistent, followed by two short ones, a pause, the sound of steps, again.

"—let's get out of here," I say.

She clutches me.

We stand and move apart.

In the bedroom she makes a gesture with her arms and

says, "—I should have gotten dressed before you wrapped my hands—"

I look at her.

"—you have any clothes?"

She shakes her head.

I go to my bureau, find some sweatpants and a long-sleeved polo.

So this is it I'm thinking.

"Noah?" she says.

I turn around.

The bed we used to sleep in is between us.

"Do you have a camera?"

I nod, wanting so much, right now, to snap a photo, fix the way she looks in time and stop the moment.

"Can we take it with us?" she requests.

"—sure," I answer.

I watch her fumble with the sash of the kimono—see how I've bandaged up her fingers like she's going ten full rounds.

"—let me," I say.

My hands shake something awful as I do it.

A second passes as we stand together, then I slip the whole thing off her shoulders.

You think you know this, but you never do, you never learn how Love will move.

She says, "—isn't this the way we started?" as she lifts her arms out to her sides like she is going to fly and I fold myself, my life, around her, saying, don't stop, don't stop now, don't ever stop, we were born to do this.